SCOOBY-DOO!™ TEAM-UP

VOLUME 5

Sholly Fisch Writer **Dario Brizuela** **Scott Jeralds** **Dave Alvarez** Artists
Franco Riesco **Silvana Brys** **Dave Alvarez** Colorists **Saida Temofonte** Letterer
Dario Brizuela and **Franco Riesco** Collection Cover Artists

PLASTIC MAN created by **JACK COLE**

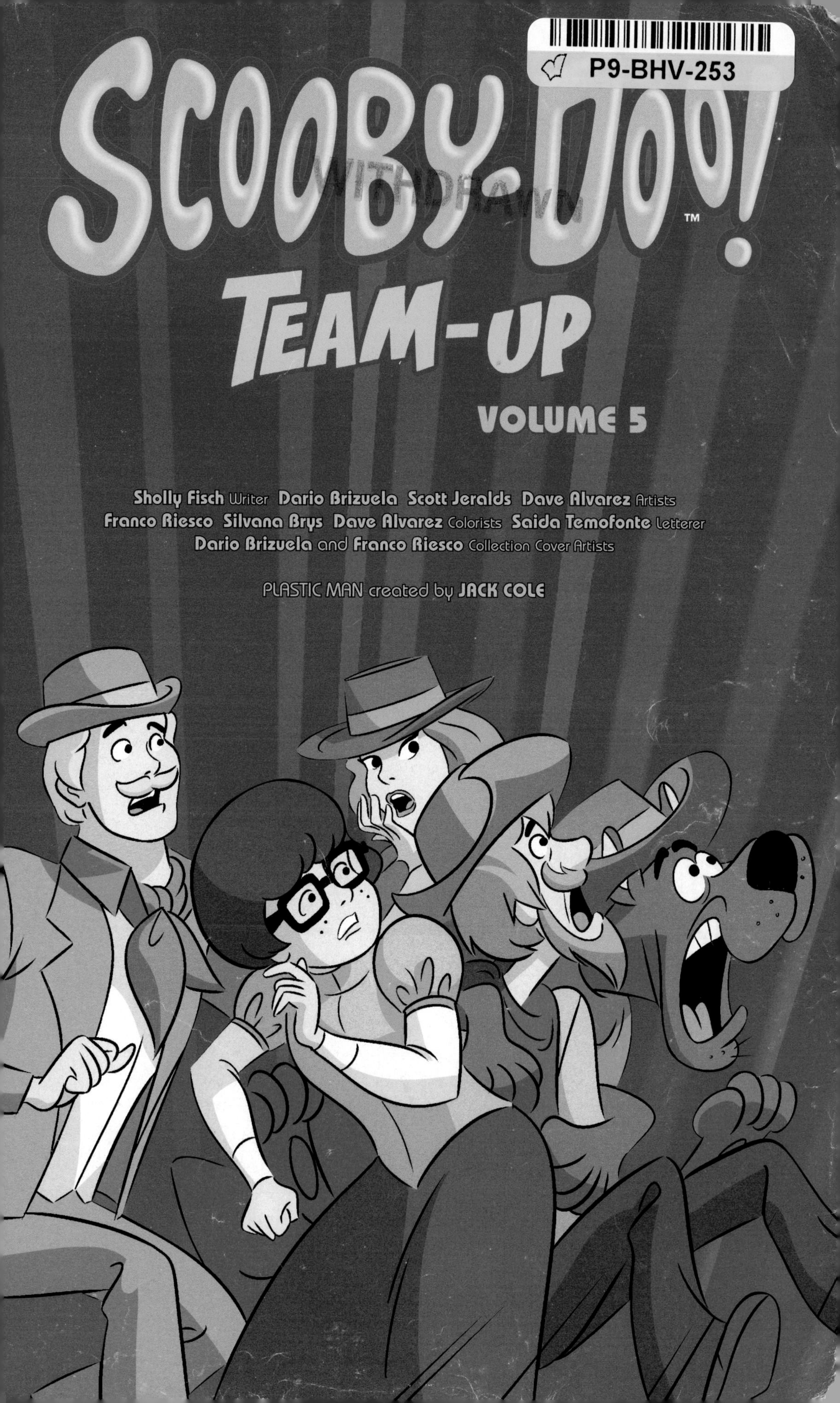

SCOOBY-DOO TEAM-UP VOLUME 5

Published by DC Comics.
Compilation and all new material Copyright © 2018
Hanna-Barbera and DC Comics. All Rights Reserved.

Originally published in single magazine form in SCOOBY-DOO TEAM-UP 25-30 and online as Digital Chapters 49-60. Copyright © 2017 Hanna-Barbera and DC Comics. All
Rights Reserved. All DC characters, their distinctive likenesses and related elements featured in this publication are trademarks of DC Comics. The stories, characters and
incidents featured in this publication are entirely fictional. DC Comics does not read or accept unsolicited submissions of ideas, stories or artwork.

DC Comics, 2900 West Alameda Ave., Burbank, CA 91505
Printed by LSC Communications, Kendallville, IN, USA. 4/27/18. First Printing.
ISBN: 978-1-4012-8419-0

Library of Congress Cataloging-in-Publication Data is available.

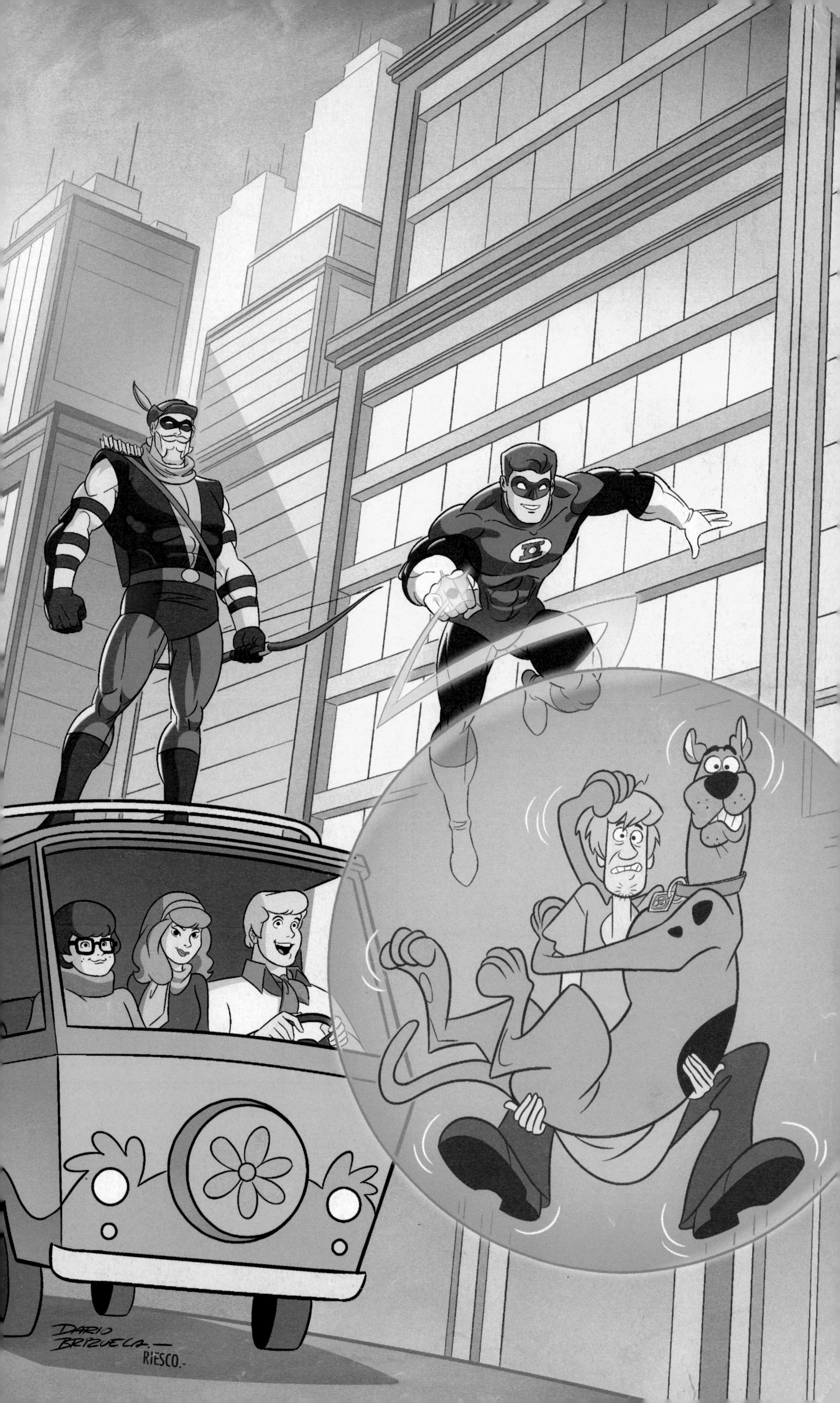
DARIO
BRIZUELA
RIESCO.-

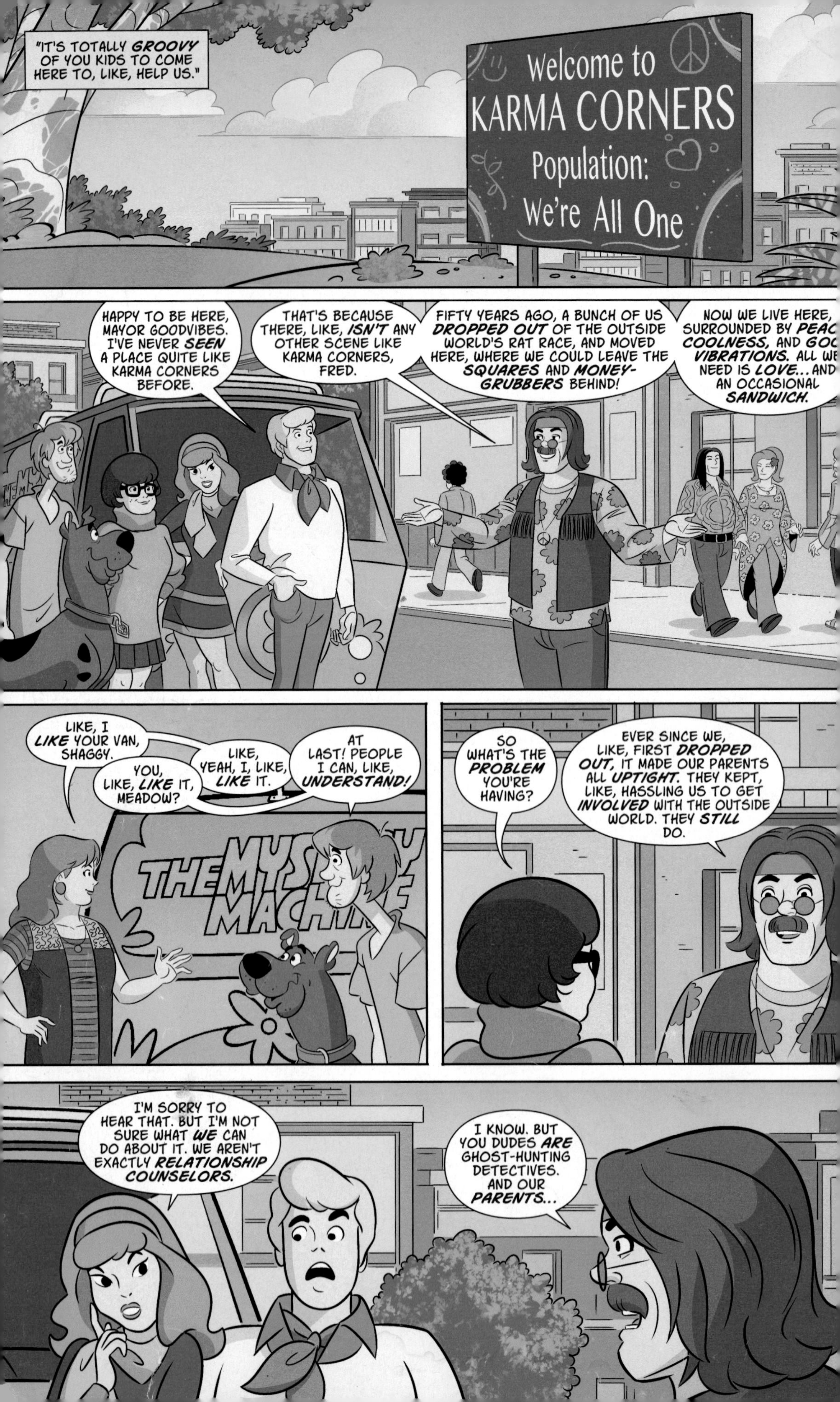
"IT'S TOTALLY GROOVY OF YOU KIDS TO COME HERE TO, LIKE, HELP US."
Welcome to KARMA CORNERS Population: We're All One
HAPPY TO BE HERE, MAYOR GOODVIBES. I'VE NEVER SEEN A PLACE QUITE LIKE KARMA CORNERS BEFORE.
THAT'S BECAUSE THERE, LIKE, ISN'T ANY OTHER SCENE LIKE KARMA CORNERS, FRED.
FIFTY YEARS AGO, A BUNCH OF US DROPPED OUT OF THE OUTSIDE WORLD'S RAT RACE, AND MOVED HERE, WHERE WE COULD LEAVE THE SQUARES AND MONEY-GRUBBERS BEHIND!
NOW WE LIVE HERE, SURROUNDED BY PEAC COOLNESS, AND GOO VIBRATIONS. ALL WE NEED IS LOVE... AND AN OCCASIONAL SANDWICH.
LIKE, I LIKE YOUR VAN, SHAGGY.
YOU, LIKE, LIKE IT, MEADOW?
LIKE, YEAH, I, LIKE, LIKE IT.
AT LAST! PEOPLE I CAN, LIKE, UNDERSTAND!
THE MYS MACHI
SO WHAT'S THE PROBLEM YOU'RE HAVING?
EVER SINCE WE, LIKE, FIRST DROPPED OUT, IT MADE OUR PARENTS ALL UPTIGHT. THEY KEPT, LIKE, HASSLING US TO GET INVOLVED WITH THE OUTSIDE WORLD. THEY STILL DO.
I'M SORRY TO HEAR THAT. BUT I'M NOT SURE WHAT WE CAN DO ABOUT IT. WE AREN'T EXACTLY RELATIONSHIP COUNSELORS.
I KNOW. BUT YOU DUDES ARE GHOST-HUNTING DETECTIVES. AND OUR PARENTS...

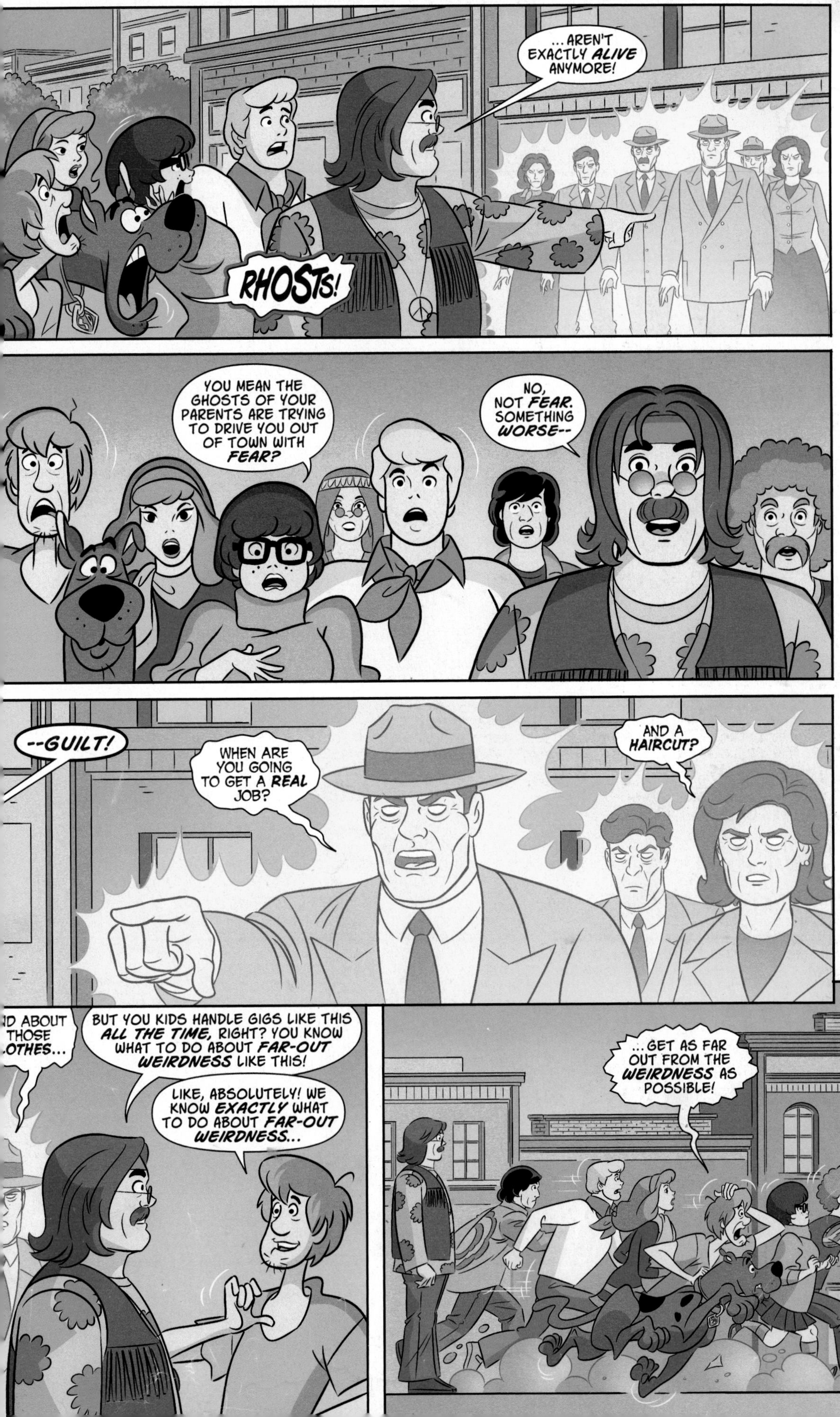
...AREN'T EXACTLY ALIVE ANYMORE!
RHOSTS!
YOU MEAN THE GHOSTS OF YOUR PARENTS ARE TRYING TO DRIVE YOU OUT OF TOWN WITH FEAR?
NO, NOT FEAR. SOMETHING WORSE--
--GUILT!
WHEN ARE YOU GOING TO GET A REAL JOB?
AND A HAIRCUT?
ND ABOUT THOSE LOTHES...
BUT YOU KIDS HANDLE GIGS LIKE THIS ALL THE TIME, RIGHT? YOU KNOW WHAT TO DO ABOUT FAR-OUT WEIRDNESS LIKE THIS!
LIKE, ABSOLUTELY! WE KNOW EXACTLY WHAT TO DO ABOUT FAR-OUT WEIRDNESS...
...GET AS FAR OUT FROM THE WEIRDNESS AS POSSIBLE!

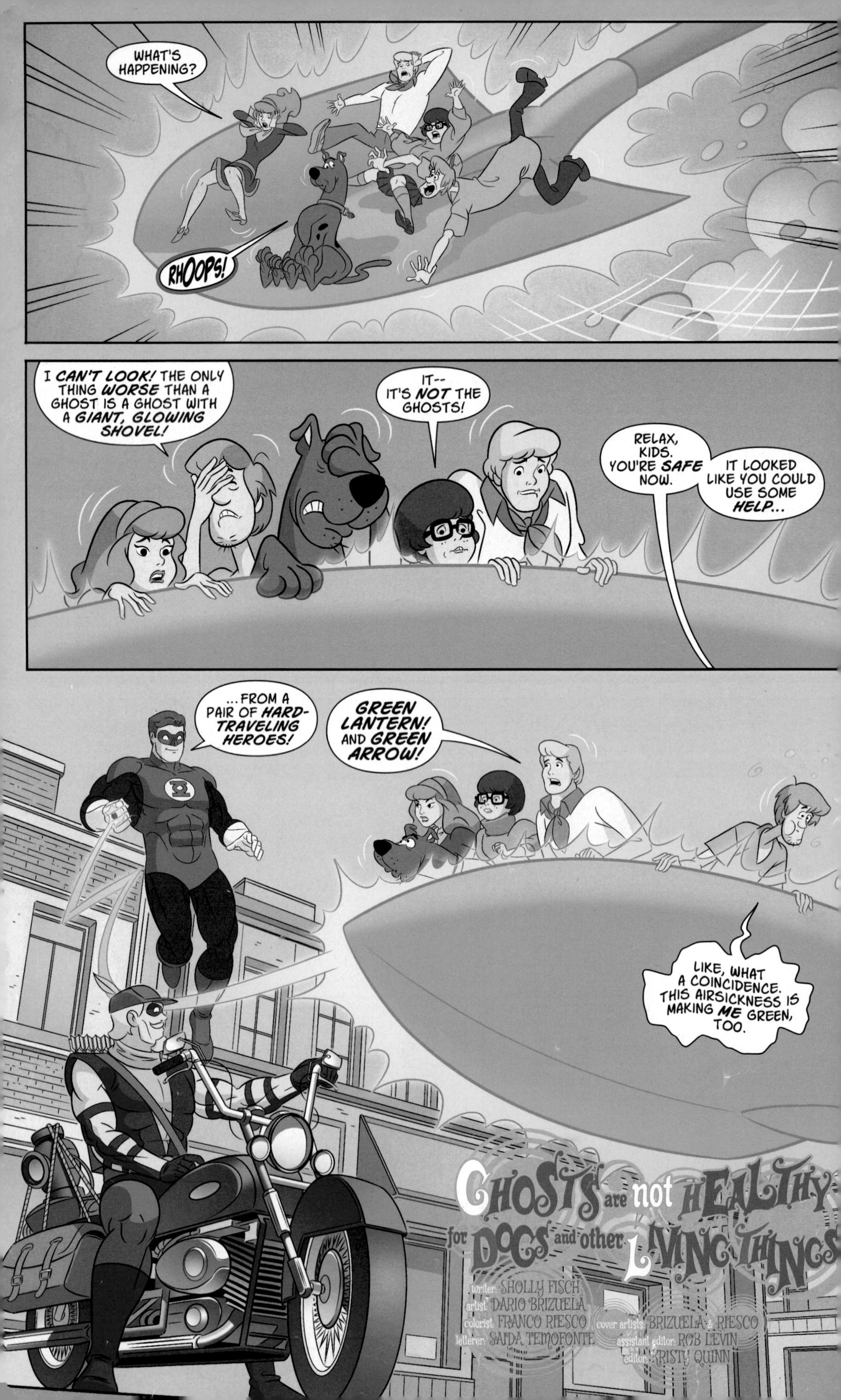
WHAT'S HAPPENING?
RHOOPS!
I CAN'T LOOK! THE ONLY THING WORSE THAN A GHOST IS A GHOST WITH A GIANT, GLOWING SHOVEL!
IT-- IT'S NOT THE GHOSTS!
RELAX, KIDS. YOU'RE SAFE NOW.
IT LOOKED LIKE YOU COULD USE SOME HELP...
...FROM A PAIR OF HARD-TRAVELING HEROES!
GREEN LANTERN! AND GREEN ARROW!
LIKE, WHAT A COINCIDENCE. THIS AIRSICKNESS IS MAKING ME GREEN, TOO.
GHOSTS are not HEALTHY for DOGS and other LIVING THINGS
writer: SHOLLY FISCH
artist: DARIO BRIZUELA
colorist: FRANCO RIESCO
letterer: SAIDA TEMOFONTE
cover artists: BRIZUELA & RIESCO
assistant editor: ROB LEVIN
editor: KRISTY QUINN

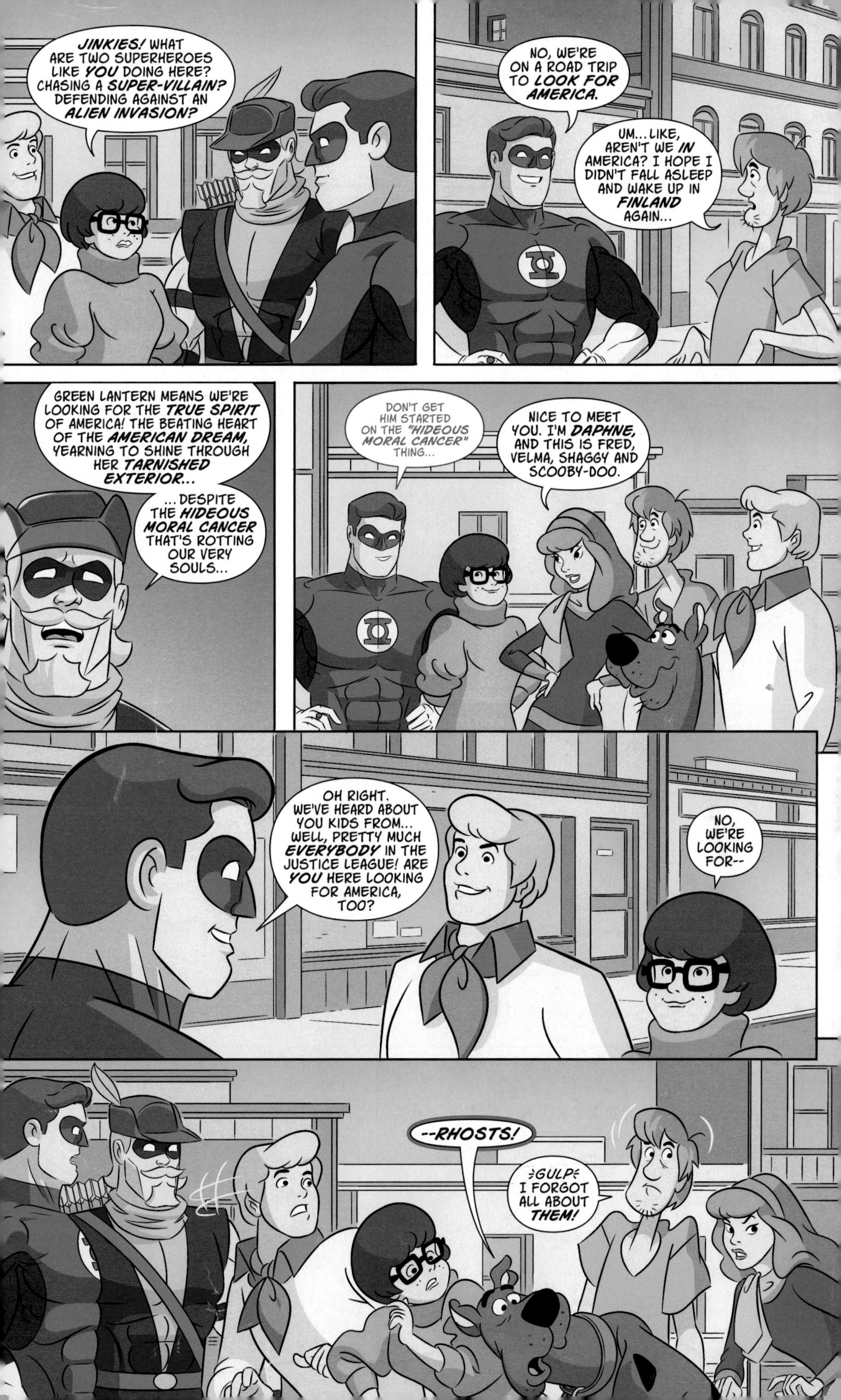
JINKIES! WHAT ARE TWO SUPERHEROES LIKE YOU DOING HERE? CHASING A SUPER-VILLAIN? DEFENDING AGAINST AN ALIEN INVASION?
NO, WE'RE ON A ROAD TRIP TO LOOK FOR AMERICA.
UM... LIKE, AREN'T WE IN AMERICA? I HOPE I DIDN'T FALL ASLEEP AND WAKE UP IN FINLAND AGAIN...
GREEN LANTERN MEANS WE'RE LOOKING FOR THE TRUE SPIRIT OF AMERICA! THE BEATING HEART OF THE AMERICAN DREAM, YEARNING TO SHINE THROUGH HER TARNISHED EXTERIOR...
... DESPITE THE HIDEOUS MORAL CANCER THAT'S ROTTING OUR VERY SOULS...
DON'T GET HIM STARTED ON THE "HIDEOUS MORAL CANCER" THING...
NICE TO MEET YOU. I'M DAPHNE, AND THIS IS FRED, VELMA, SHAGGY AND SCOOBY-DOO.
OH RIGHT. WE'VE HEARD ABOUT YOU KIDS FROM... WELL, PRETTY MUCH EVERYBODY IN THE JUSTICE LEAGUE! ARE YOU HERE LOOKING FOR AMERICA, TOO?
NO, WE'RE LOOKING FOR--
--RHOSTS!
GULP I FORGOT ALL ABOUT THEM!

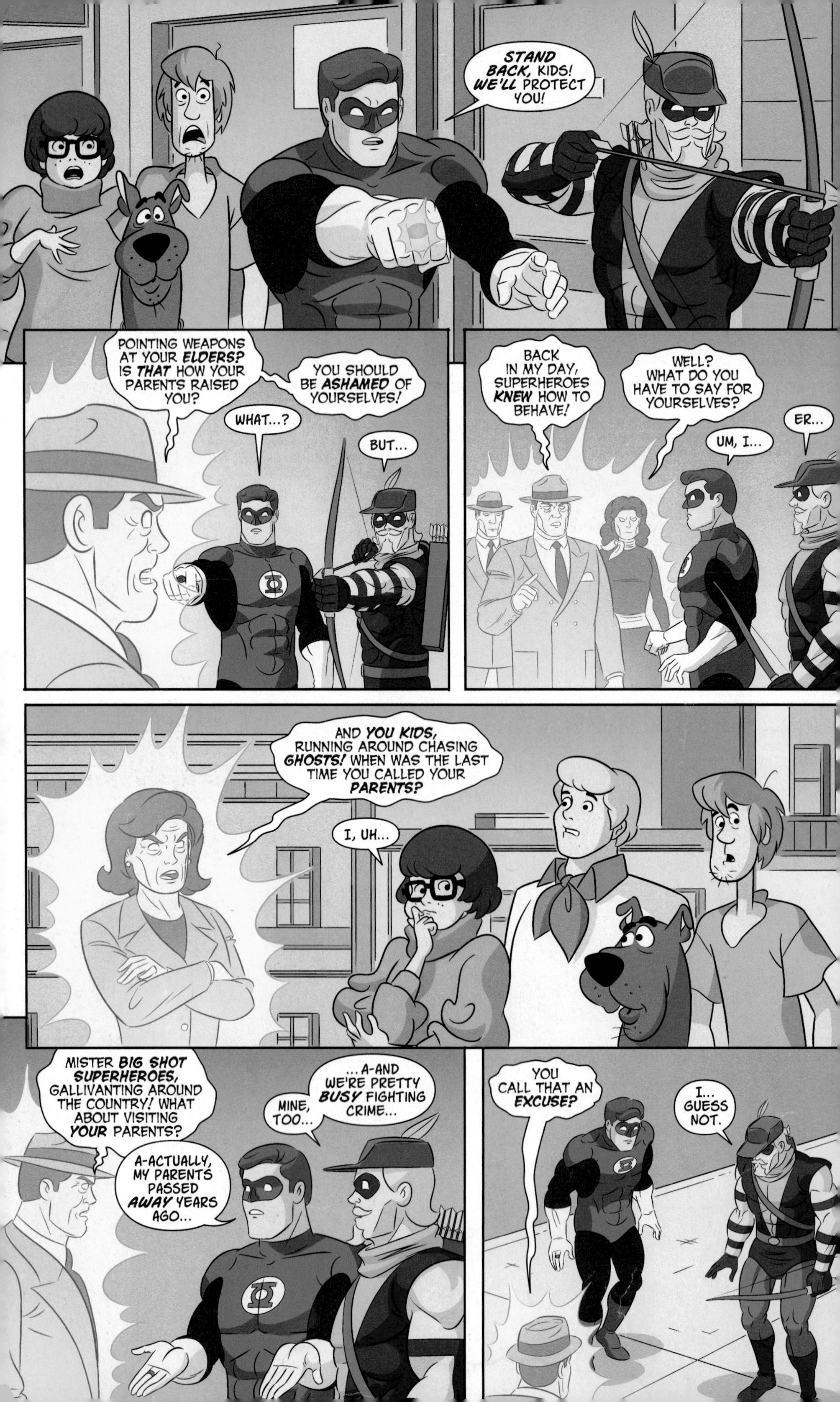

STAND BACK, KIDS! WE'LL PROTECT YOU!
POINTING WEAPONS AT YOUR ELDERS? IS THAT HOW YOUR PARENTS RAISED YOU?
YOU SHOULD BE ASHAMED OF YOURSELVES!
WHAT...?
BUT...
BACK IN MY DAY, SUPERHEROES KNEW HOW TO BEHAVE!
WELL? WHAT DO YOU HAVE TO SAY FOR YOURSELVES?
UM, I...
ER...
AND YOU KIDS, RUNNING AROUND CHASING GHOSTS! WHEN WAS THE LAST TIME YOU CALLED YOUR PARENTS?
I, UH...
MISTER BIG SHOT SUPERHEROES, GALLIVANTING AROUND THE COUNTRY! WHAT ABOUT VISITING YOUR PARENTS?
A-ACTUALLY, MY PARENTS PASSED AWAY YEARS AGO...
MINE, TOO...
...A-AND WE'RE PRETTY BUSY FIGHTING CRIME...
YOU CALL THAT AN EXCUSE?
I... GUESS NOT.

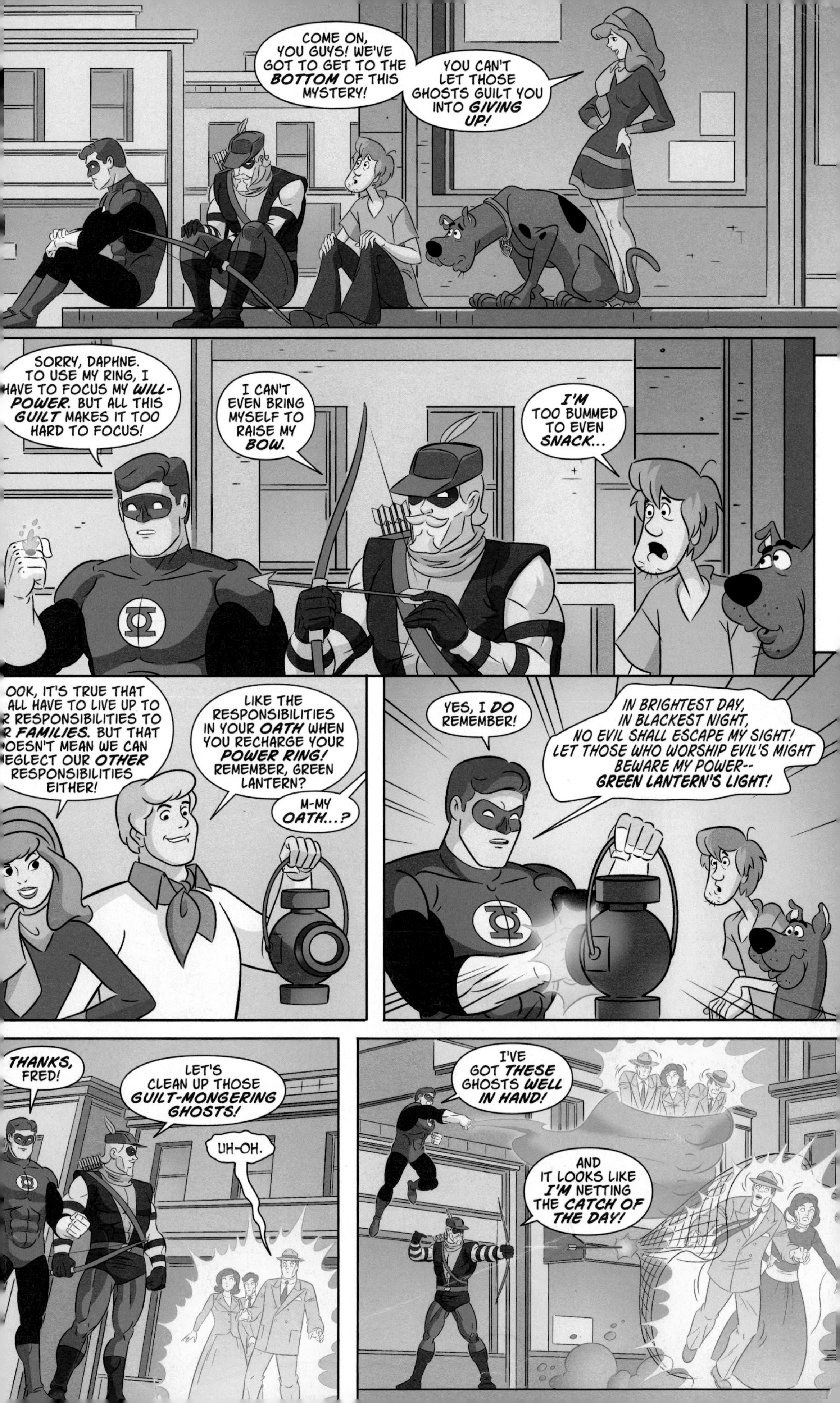

COME ON, YOU GUYS! WE'VE GOT TO GET TO THE BOTTOM OF THIS MYSTERY!
YOU CAN'T LET THOSE GHOSTS GUILT YOU INTO GIVING UP!
SORRY, DAPHNE. TO USE MY RING, I HAVE TO FOCUS MY WILL-POWER. BUT ALL THIS GUILT MAKES IT TOO HARD TO FOCUS!
I CAN'T EVEN BRING MYSELF TO RAISE MY BOW.
I'M TOO BUMMED TO EVEN SNACK...
OOK, IT'S TRUE THAT ALL HAVE TO LIVE UP TO R RESPONSIBILITIES TO R FAMILIES. BUT THAT OESN'T MEAN WE CAN EGLECT OUR OTHER RESPONSIBILITIES EITHER!
LIKE THE RESPONSIBILITIES IN YOUR OATH WHEN YOU RECHARGE YOUR POWER RING! REMEMBER, GREEN LANTERN?
M-MY OATH...?
YES, I DO REMEMBER!
IN BRIGHTEST DAY, IN BLACKEST NIGHT, NO EVIL SHALL ESCAPE MY SIGHT! LET THOSE WHO WORSHIP EVIL'S MIGHT BEWARE MY POWER-- GREEN LANTERN'S LIGHT!
THANKS, FRED!
LET'S CLEAN UP THOSE GUILT-MONGERING GHOSTS!
UH-OH.
I'VE GOT THESE GHOSTS WELL IN HAND!
AND IT LOOKS LIKE I'M NETTING THE CATCH OF THE DAY!

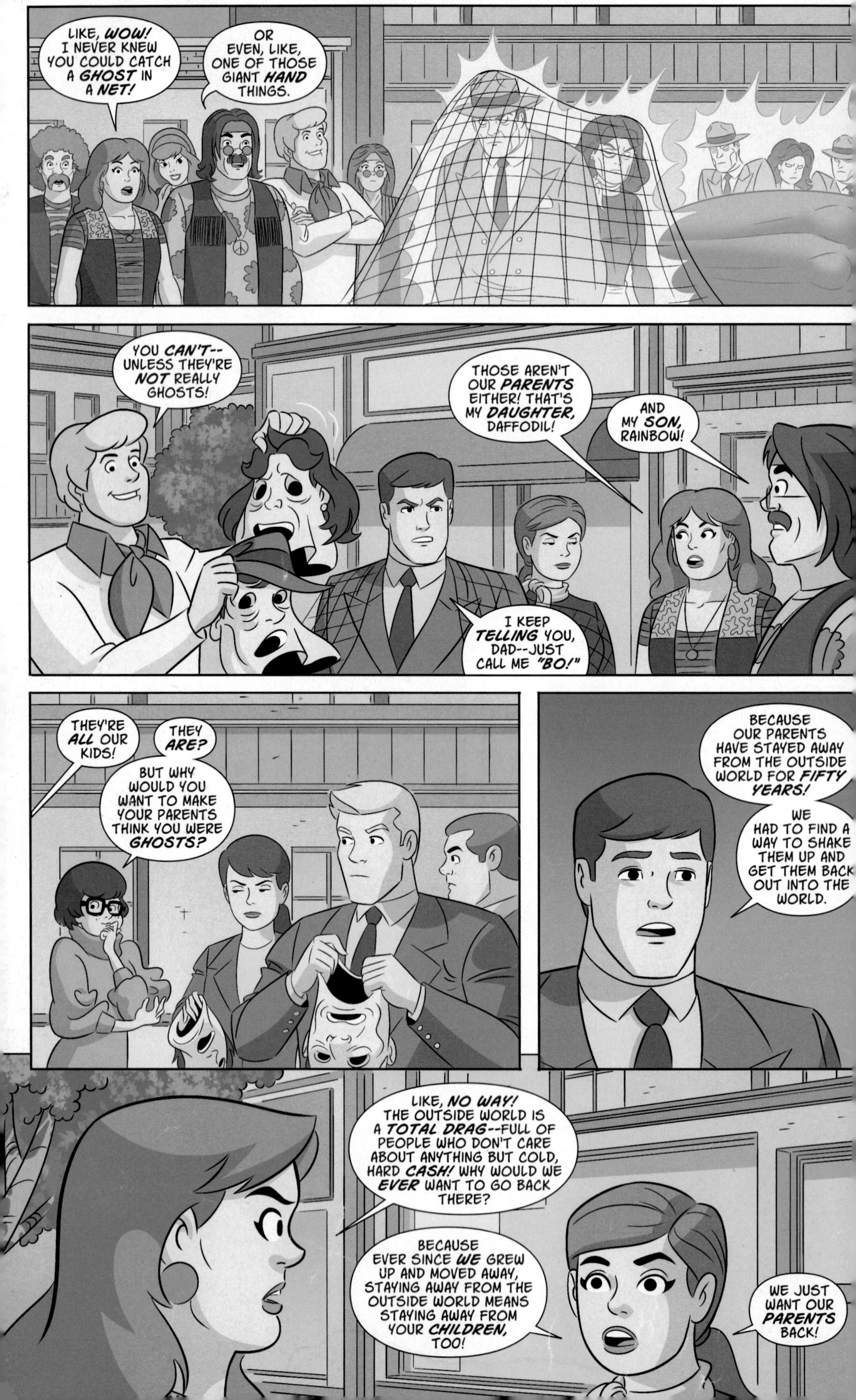

LIKE, WOW! I NEVER KNEW YOU COULD CATCH A GHOST IN A NET!
OR EVEN, LIKE, ONE OF THOSE GIANT HAND THINGS.
YOU CAN'T-- UNLESS THEY'RE NOT REALLY GHOSTS!
THOSE AREN'T OUR PARENTS EITHER! THAT'S MY DAUGHTER, DAFFODIL!
AND MY SON, RAINBOW!
I KEEP TELLING YOU, DAD--JUST CALL ME "BO!"
THEY'RE ALL OUR KIDS!
THEY ARE?
BUT WHY WOULD YOU WANT TO MAKE YOUR PARENTS THINK YOU WERE GHOSTS?
BECAUSE OUR PARENTS HAVE STAYED AWAY FROM THE OUTSIDE WORLD FOR FIFTY YEARS!
WE HAD TO FIND A WAY TO SHAKE THEM UP AND GET THEM BACK OUT INTO THE WORLD.
LIKE, NO WAY! THE OUTSIDE WORLD IS A TOTAL DRAG--FULL OF PEOPLE WHO DON'T CARE ABOUT ANYTHING BUT COLD, HARD CASH! WHY WOULD WE EVER WANT TO GO BACK THERE?
BECAUSE EVER SINCE WE GREW UP AND MOVED AWAY, STAYING AWAY FROM THE OUTSIDE WORLD MEANS STAYING AWAY FROM YOUR CHILDREN, TOO!
WE JUST WANT OUR PARENTS BACK!

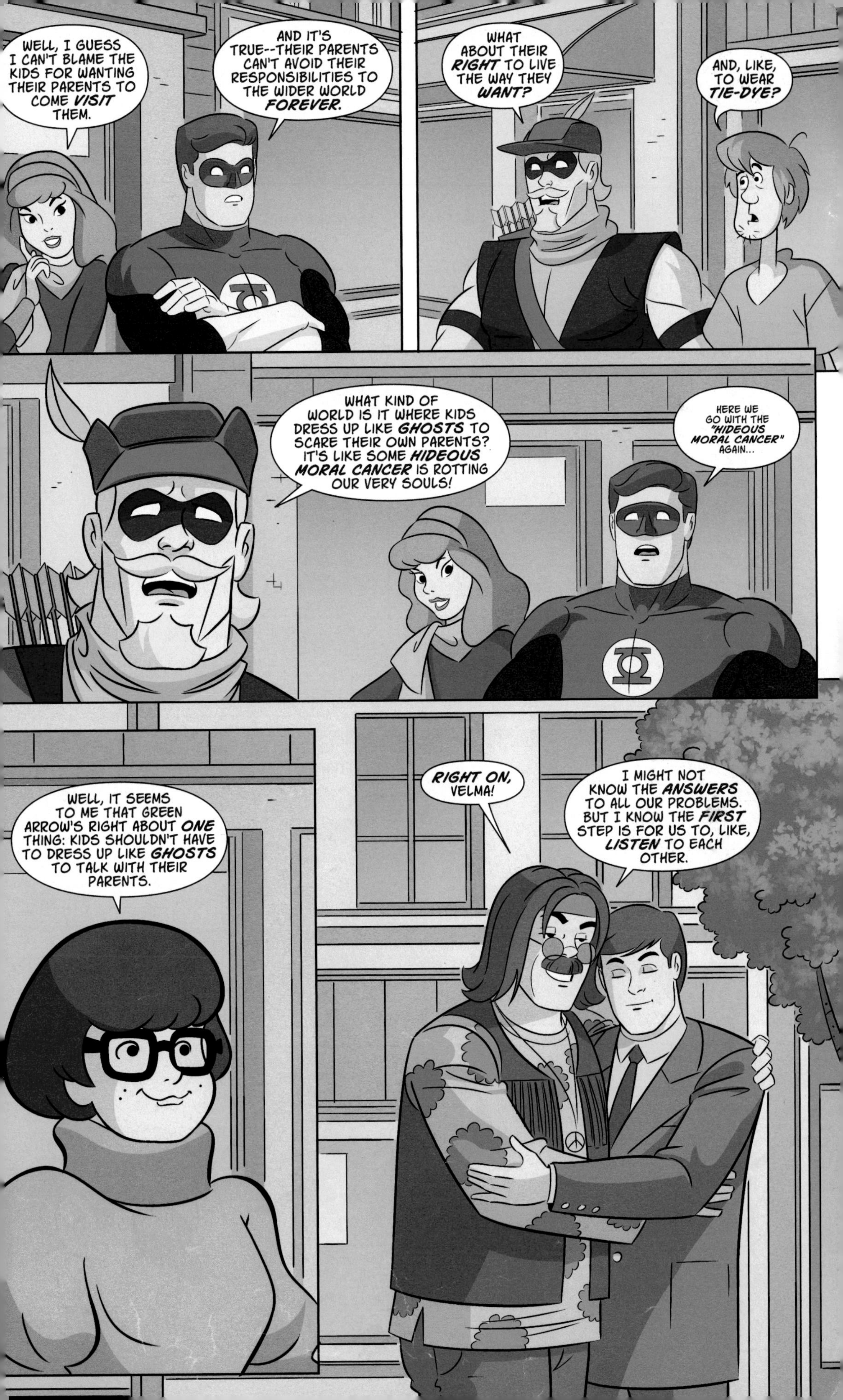
WELL, I GUESS I CAN'T BLAME THE KIDS FOR WANTING THEIR PARENTS TO COME ***VISIT*** THEM.
AND IT'S TRUE--THEIR PARENTS CAN'T AVOID THEIR RESPONSIBILITIES TO THE WIDER WORLD ***FOREVER.***
WHAT ABOUT THEIR ***RIGHT*** TO LIVE THE WAY THEY ***WANT?***
AND, LIKE, TO WEAR ***TIE-DYE?***
WHAT KIND OF WORLD IS IT WHERE KIDS DRESS UP LIKE ***GHOSTS*** TO SCARE THEIR OWN PARENTS? IT'S LIKE SOME ***HIDEOUS MORAL CANCER*** IS ROTTING OUR VERY SOULS!
HERE WE GO WITH THE ***"HIDEOUS MORAL CANCER"*** AGAIN...
WELL, IT SEEMS TO ME THAT GREEN ARROW'S RIGHT ABOUT ***ONE*** THING: KIDS SHOULDN'T HAVE TO DRESS UP LIKE ***GHOSTS*** TO TALK WITH THEIR PARENTS.
RIGHT ON, VELMA!
I MIGHT NOT KNOW THE ***ANSWERS*** TO ALL OUR PROBLEMS. BUT I KNOW THE ***FIRST*** STEP IS FOR US TO, LIKE, ***LISTEN*** TO EACH OTHER.

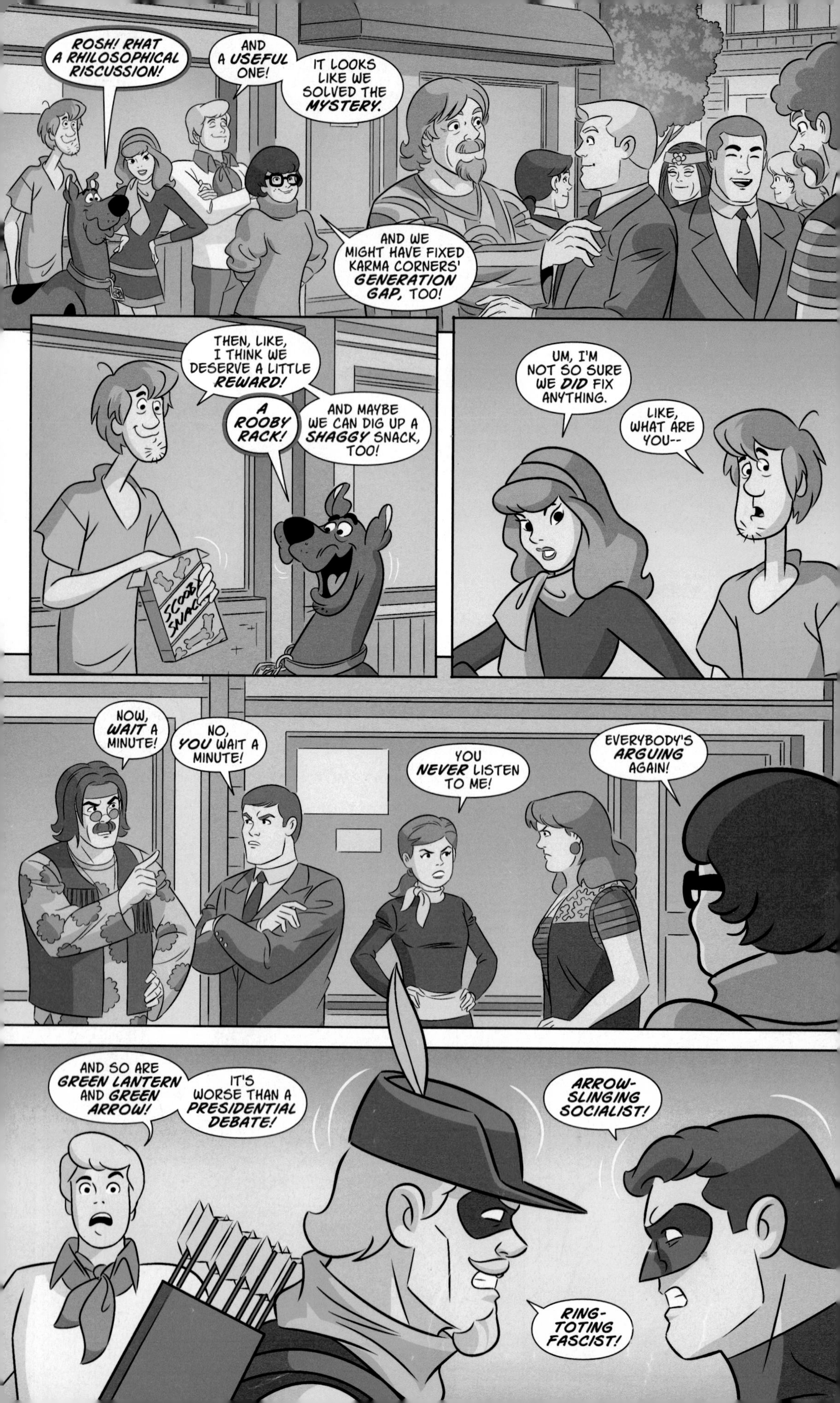
ROSH! RHAT A RHILOSOPHICAL RISCUSSION!
AND A USEFUL ONE!
IT LOOKS LIKE WE SOLVED THE MYSTERY.
AND WE MIGHT HAVE FIXED KARMA CORNERS' GENERATION GAP, TOO!
THEN, LIKE, I THINK WE DESERVE A LITTLE REWARD!
A ROOBY RACK!
AND MAYBE WE CAN DIG UP A SHAGGY SNACK, TOO!
UM, I'M NOT SO SURE WE DID FIX ANYTHING.
LIKE, WHAT ARE YOU--
NOW, WAIT A MINUTE!
NO, YOU WAIT A MINUTE!
YOU NEVER LISTEN TO ME!
EVERYBODY'S ARGUING AGAIN!
AND SO ARE GREEN LANTERN AND GREEN ARROW!
IT'S WORSE THAN A PRESIDENTIAL DEBATE!
ARROW-SLINGING SOCIALIST!
RING-TOTING FASCIST!

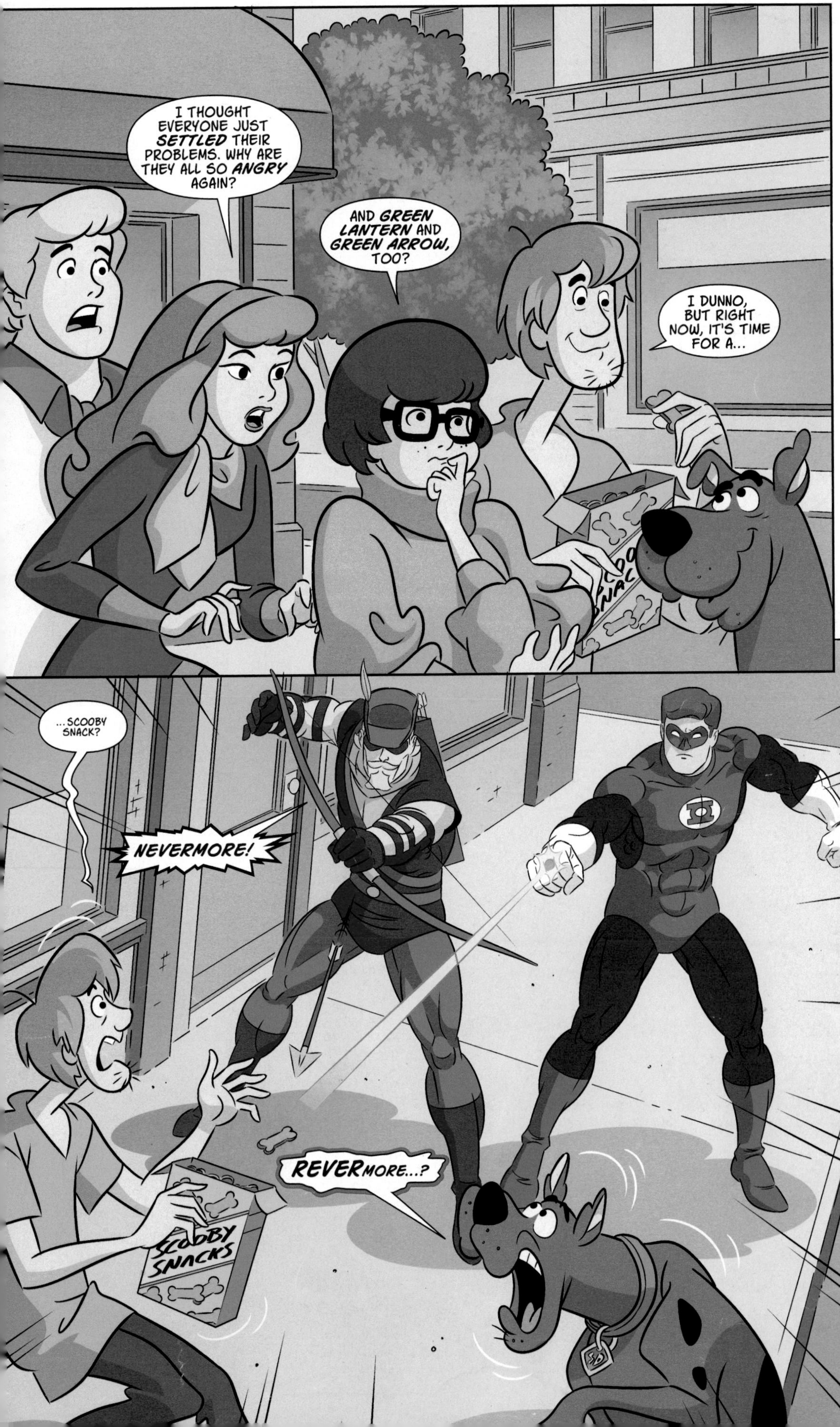

I THOUGHT EVERYONE JUST SETTLED THEIR PROBLEMS. WHY ARE THEY ALL SO ANGRY AGAIN?
AND GREEN LANTERN AND GREEN ARROW, TOO?
I DUNNO, BUT RIGHT NOW, IT'S TIME FOR A...
...SCOOBY SNACK?
NEVERMORE!
REVERMORE...?
SCOOBY SNACKS

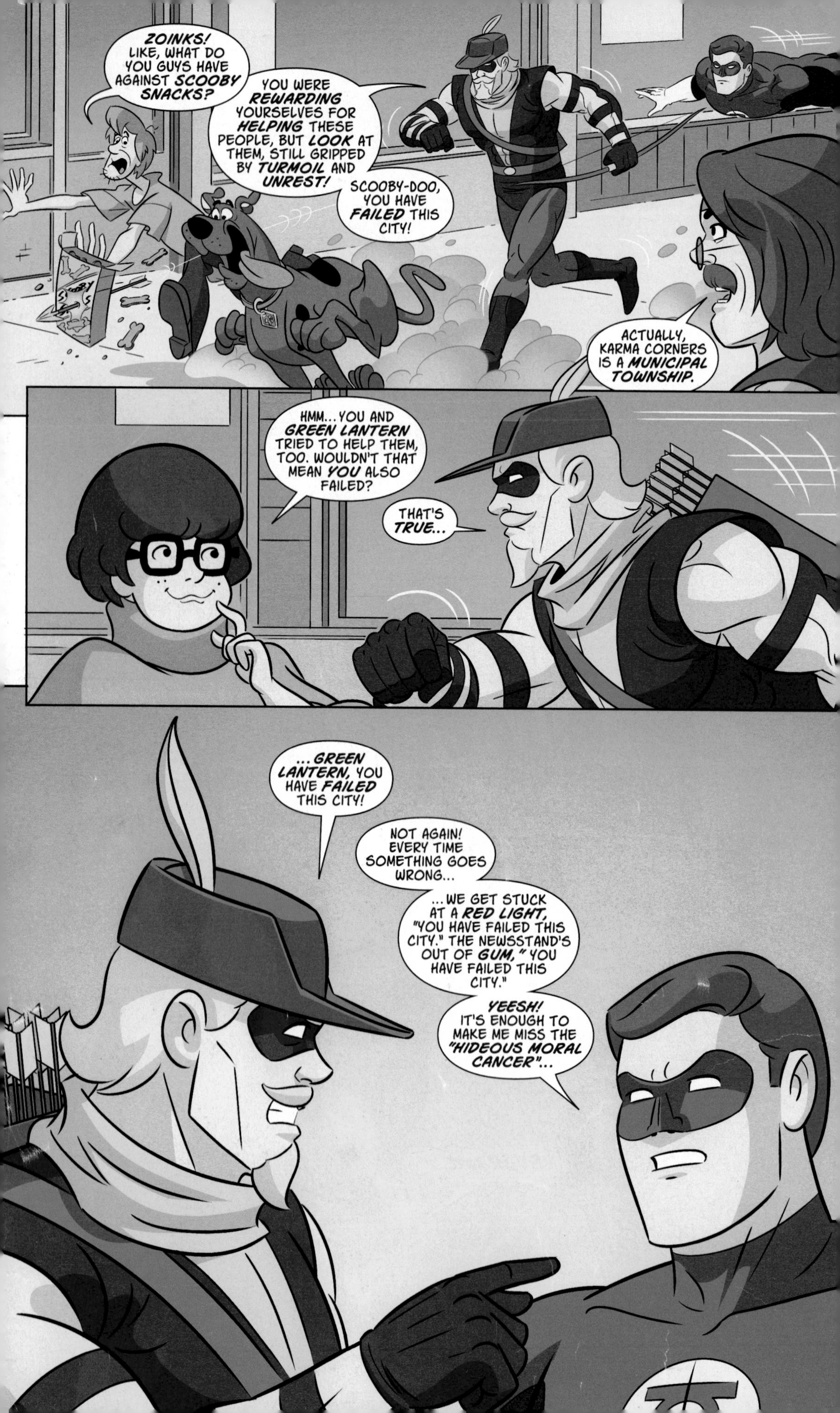
ZOINKS! LIKE, WHAT DO YOU GUYS HAVE AGAINST SCOOBY SNACKS?
YOU WERE REWARDING YOURSELVES FOR HELPING THESE PEOPLE, BUT LOOK AT THEM, STILL GRIPPED BY TURMOIL AND UNREST!
SCOOBY-DOO, YOU HAVE FAILED THIS CITY!
ACTUALLY, KARMA CORNERS IS A MUNICIPAL TOWNSHIP.
HMM... YOU AND GREEN LANTERN TRIED TO HELP THEM, TOO. WOULDN'T THAT MEAN YOU ALSO FAILED?
THAT'S TRUE...
...GREEN LANTERN, YOU HAVE FAILED THIS CITY!
NOT AGAIN! EVERY TIME SOMETHING GOES WRONG...
...WE GET STUCK AT A RED LIGHT, "YOU HAVE FAILED THIS CITY." THE NEWSSTAND'S OUT OF GUM, "YOU HAVE FAILED THIS CITY."
YEESH! IT'S ENOUGH TO MAKE ME MISS THE "HIDEOUS MORAL CANCER"...

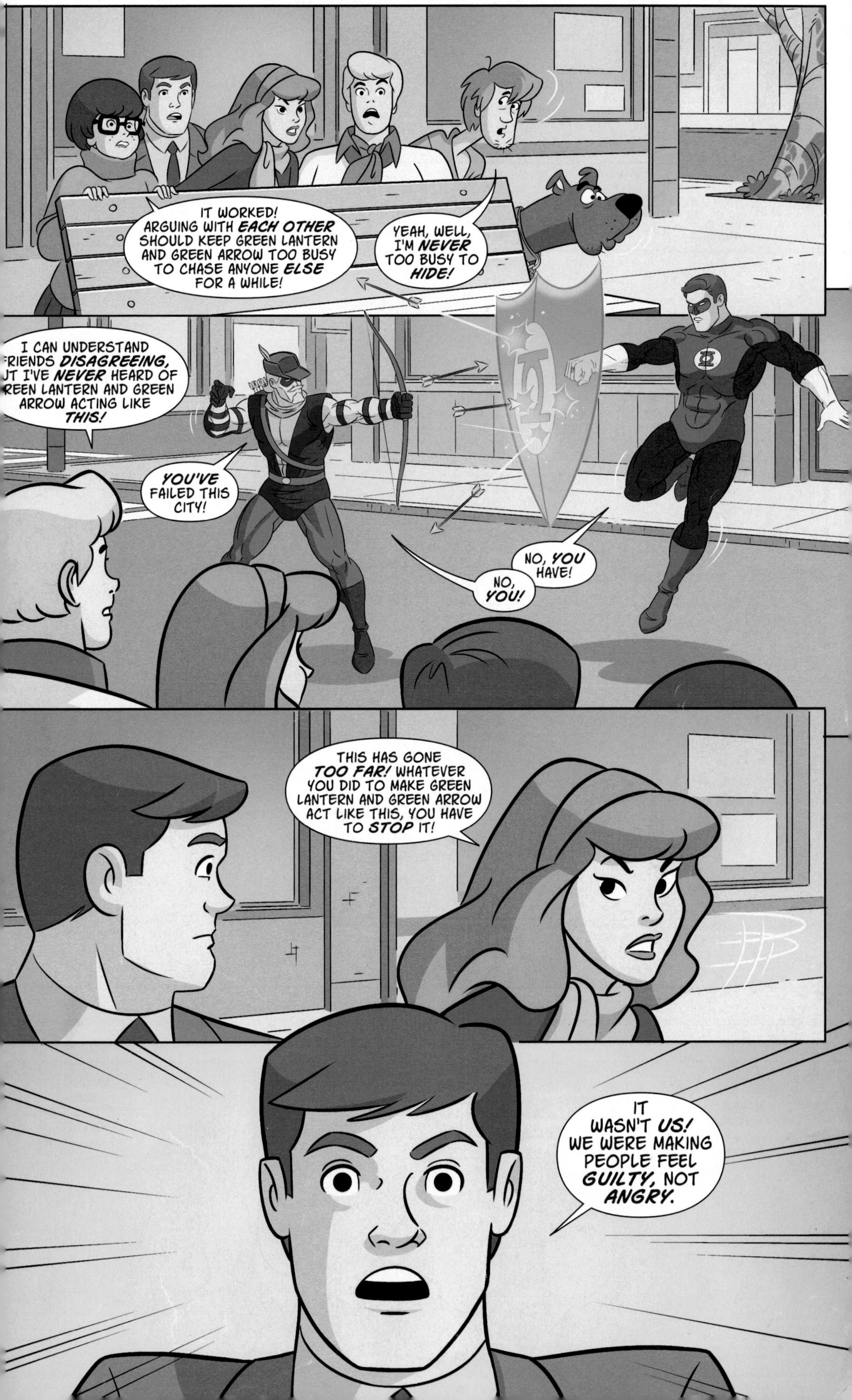
IT WORKED! ARGUING WITH EACH OTHER SHOULD KEEP GREEN LANTERN AND GREEN ARROW TOO BUSY TO CHASE ANYONE ELSE FOR A WHILE!
YEAH, WELL, I'M NEVER TOO BUSY TO HIDE!
I CAN UNDERSTAND FRIENDS DISAGREEING, UT I'VE NEVER HEARD OF REEN LANTERN AND GREEN ARROW ACTING LIKE THIS!
YOU'VE FAILED THIS CITY!
NO, YOU HAVE!
NO, YOU!
THIS HAS GONE TOO FAR! WHATEVER YOU DID TO MAKE GREEN LANTERN AND GREEN ARROW ACT LIKE THIS, YOU HAVE TO STOP IT!
IT WASN'T US! WE WERE MAKING PEOPLE FEEL GUILTY, NOT ANGRY.

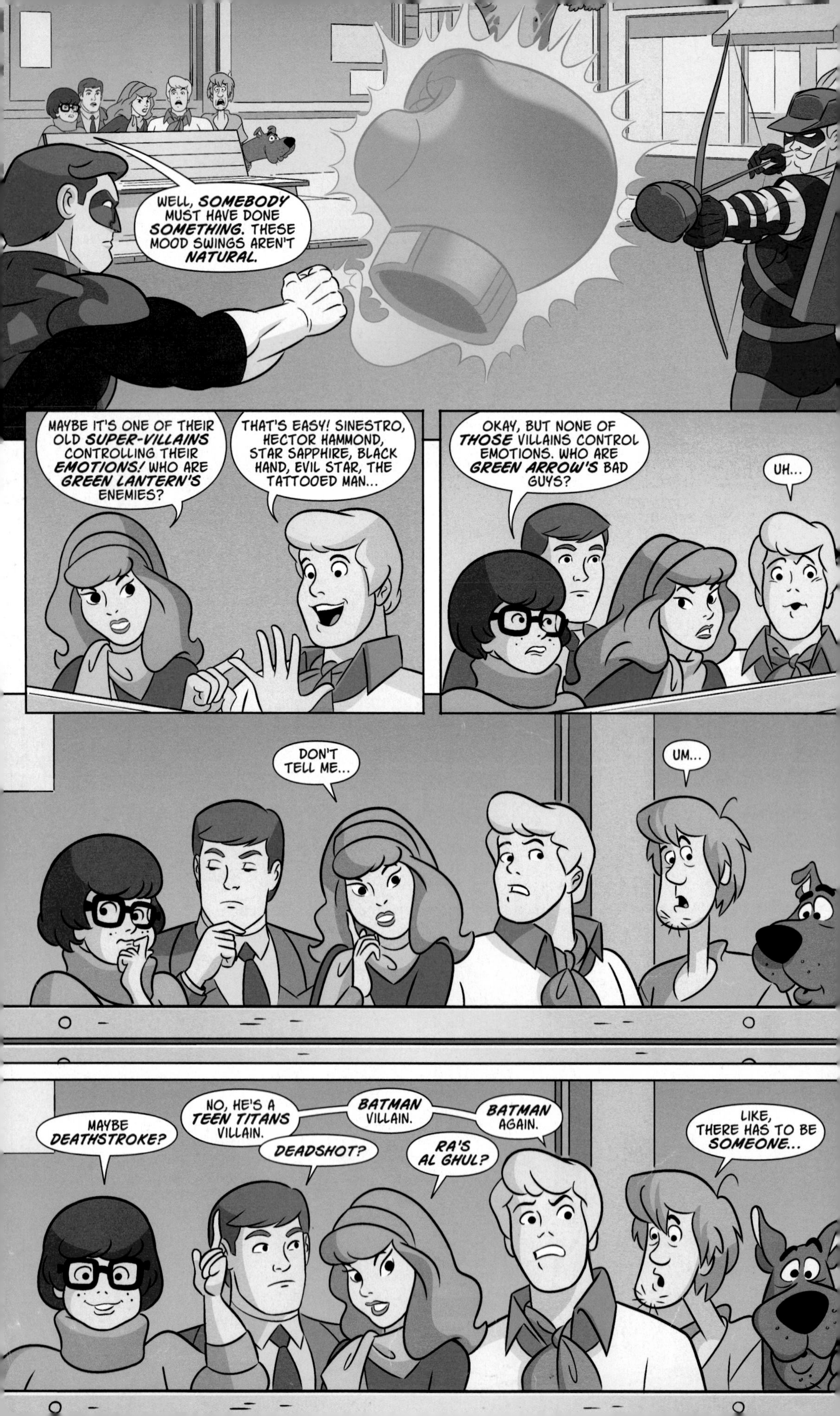
WELL, *SOMEBODY* MUST HAVE DONE *SOMETHING*. THESE MOOD SWINGS AREN'T *NATURAL*.
MAYBE IT'S ONE OF THEIR OLD *SUPER-VILLAINS* CONTROLLING THEIR *EMOTIONS!* WHO ARE *GREEN LANTERN'S* ENEMIES?
THAT'S EASY! SINESTRO, HECTOR HAMMOND, STAR SAPPHIRE, BLACK HAND, EVIL STAR, THE TATTOOED MAN...
OKAY, BUT NONE OF *THOSE* VILLAINS CONTROL EMOTIONS. WHO ARE *GREEN ARROW'S* BAD GUYS?
UH...
DON'T TELL ME...
UM...
MAYBE *DEATHSTROKE?*
NO, HE'S A *TEEN TITANS* VILLAIN.
DEADSHOT?
BATMAN VILLAIN.
RA'S AL GHUL?
BATMAN AGAIN.
LIKE, THERE HAS TO BE *SOMEONE...*

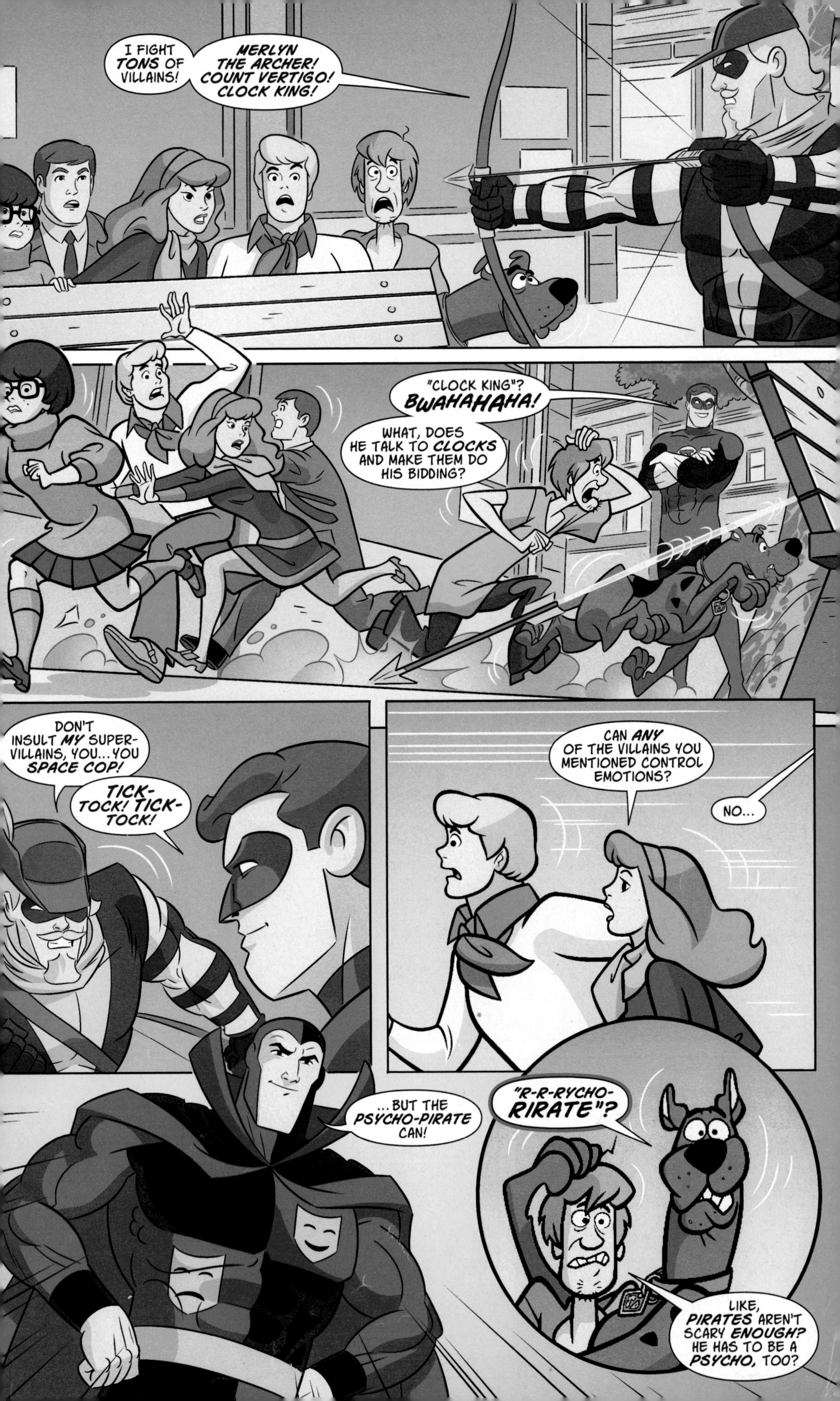

I FIGHT TONS OF VILLAINS!
MERLYN THE ARCHER! COUNT VERTIGO! CLOCK KING!
"CLOCK KING"? BWAHAHAHA!
WHAT, DOES HE TALK TO CLOCKS AND MAKE THEM DO HIS BIDDING?
DON'T INSULT MY SUPER-VILLAINS, YOU...YOU SPACE COP!
TICK-TOCK! TICK-TOCK!
CAN ANY OF THE VILLAINS YOU MENTIONED CONTROL EMOTIONS?
NO...
...BUT THE PSYCHO-PIRATE CAN!
"R-R-RYCHO-RIRATE"?
LIKE, PIRATES AREN'T SCARY ENOUGH? HE HAS TO BE A PSYCHO, TOO?

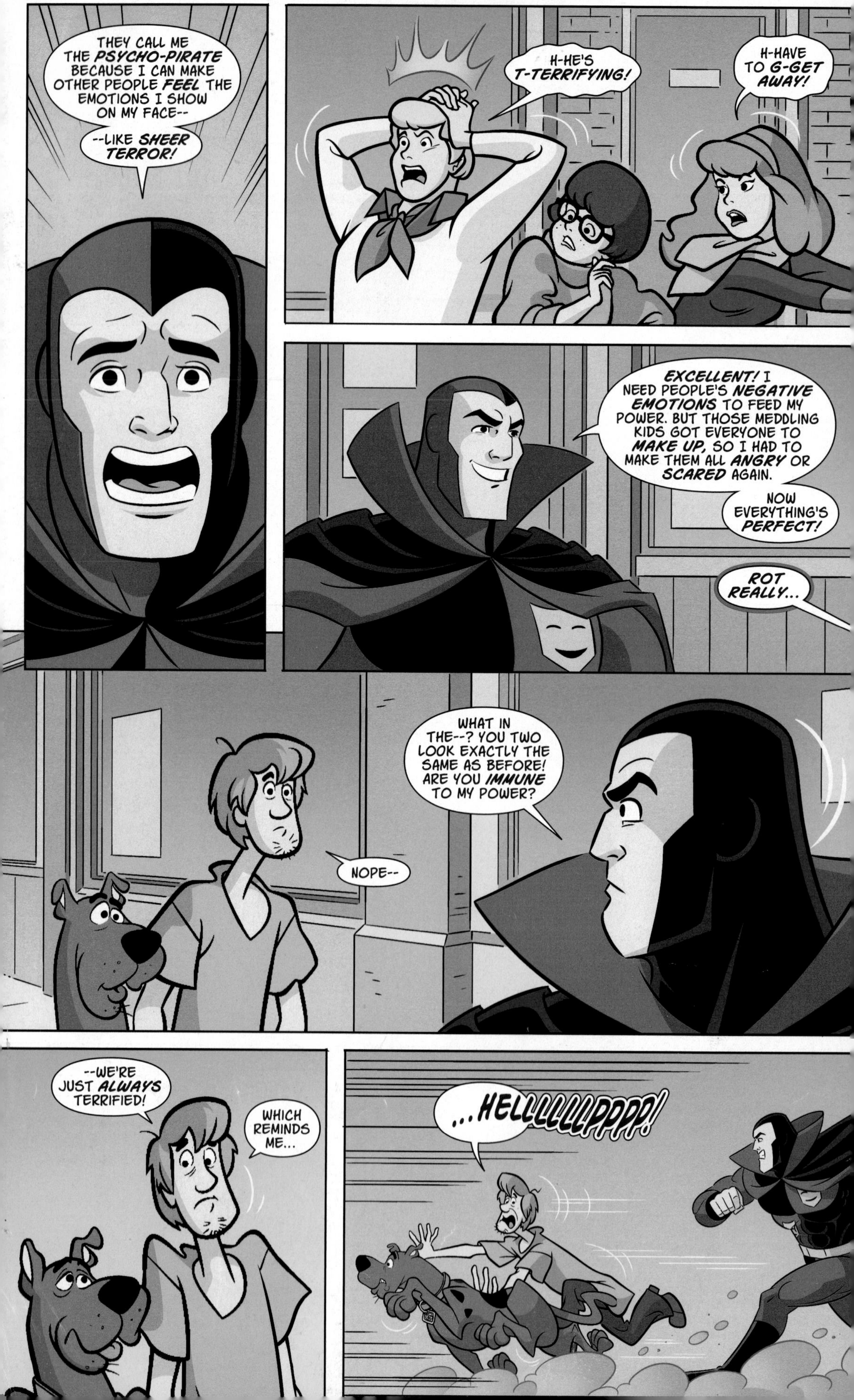

THEY CALL ME THE PSYCHO-PIRATE BECAUSE I CAN MAKE OTHER PEOPLE FEEL THE EMOTIONS I SHOW ON MY FACE--
--LIKE SHEER TERROR!
H-HE'S T-TERRIFYING!
H-HAVE TO G-GET AWAY!
EXCELLENT! I NEED PEOPLE'S NEGATIVE EMOTIONS TO FEED MY POWER. BUT THOSE MEDDLING KIDS GOT EVERYONE TO MAKE UP, SO I HAD TO MAKE THEM ALL ANGRY OR SCARED AGAIN.
NOW EVERYTHING'S PERFECT!
ROT REALLY...
WHAT IN THE--? YOU TWO LOOK EXACTLY THE SAME AS BEFORE! ARE YOU IMMUNE TO MY POWER?
NOPE--
--WE'RE JUST ALWAYS TERRIFIED!
WHICH REMINDS ME...
...HELLLLLLLPPPP!

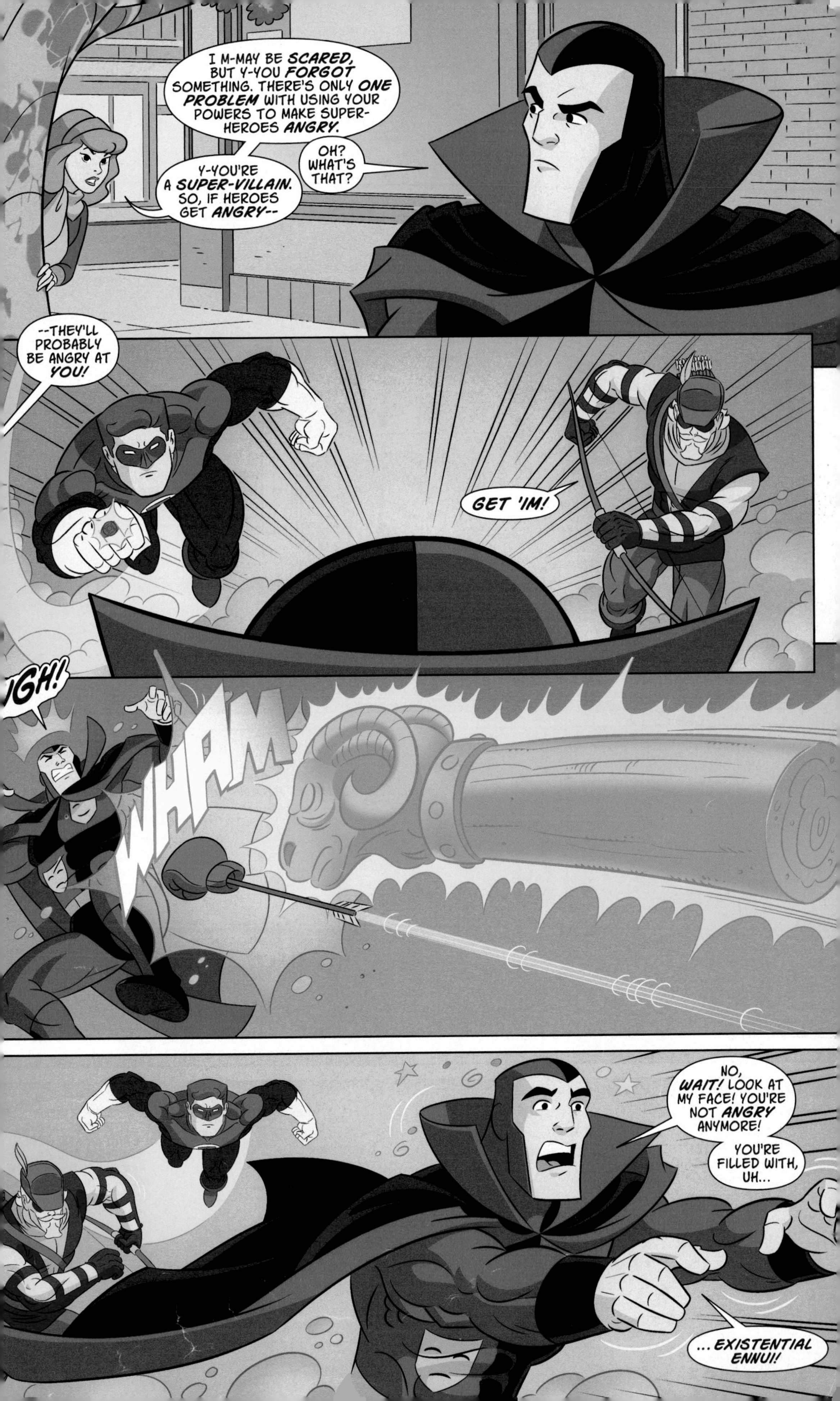
I M-MAY BE SCARED, BUT Y-YOU FORGOT SOMETHING. THERE'S ONLY ONE PROBLEM WITH USING YOUR POWERS TO MAKE SUPER-HEROES ANGRY.
OH? WHAT'S THAT?
Y-YOU'RE A SUPER-VILLAIN. SO, IF HEROES GET ANGRY--
--THEY'LL PROBABLY BE ANGRY AT YOU!
GET 'IM!
GH!
WHAM
NO, WAIT! LOOK AT MY FACE! YOU'RE NOT ANGRY ANYMORE!
YOU'RE FILLED WITH, UH...
... EXISTENTIAL ENNUI!!

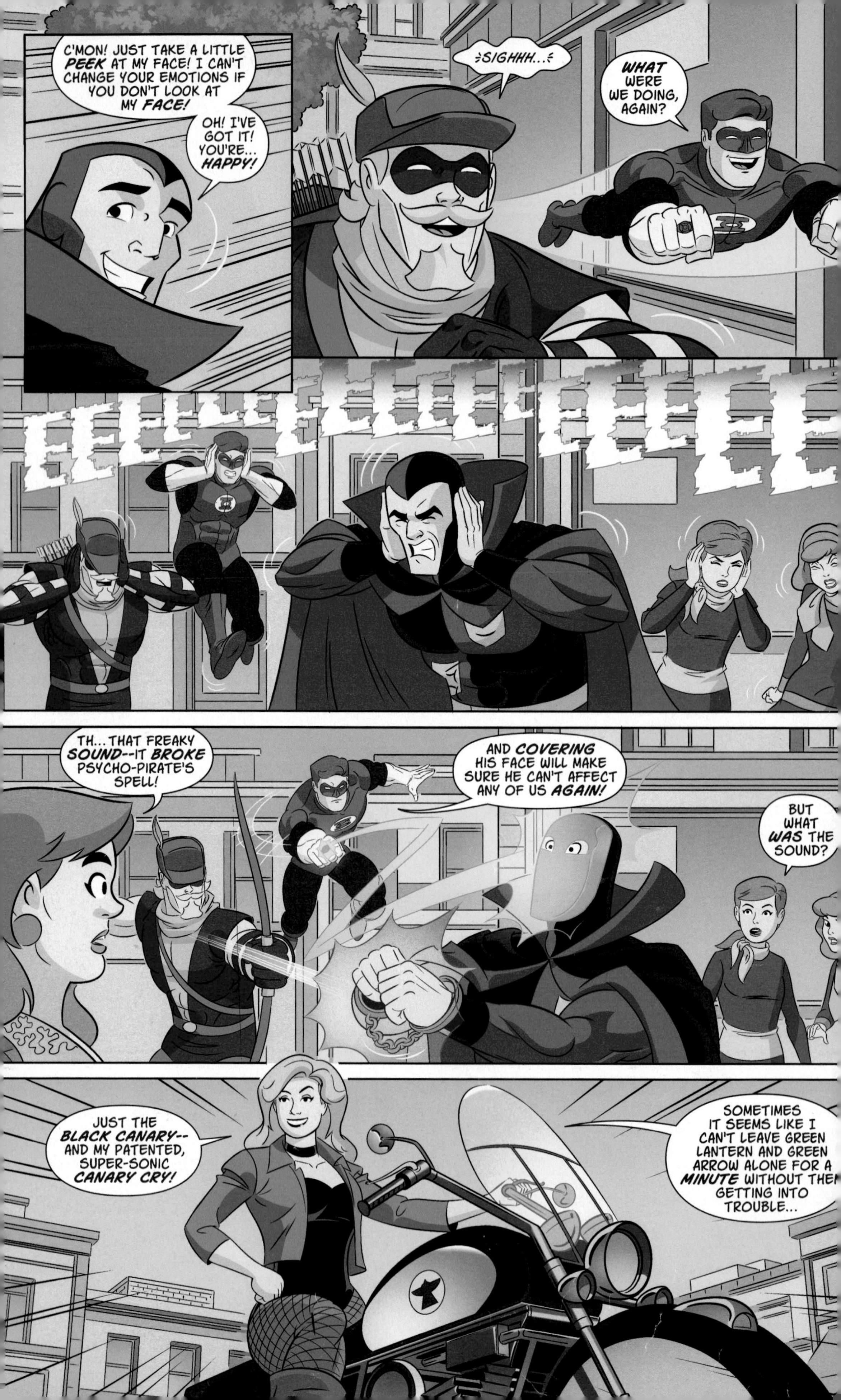
C'MON! JUST TAKE A LITTLE PEEK AT MY FACE! I CAN'T CHANGE YOUR EMOTIONS IF YOU DON'T LOOK AT MY FACE!
OH! I'VE GOT IT! YOU'RE... HAPPY!
SIGHHH...
WHAT WERE WE DOING, AGAIN?
EEEEEEEEEEEEEEEEEE
TH... THAT FREAKY SOUND--IT BROKE PSYCHO-PIRATE'S SPELL!
AND COVERING HIS FACE WILL MAKE SURE HE CAN'T AFFECT ANY OF US AGAIN!
BUT WHAT WAS THE SOUND?
JUST THE BLACK CANARY-- AND MY PATENTED, SUPER-SONIC CANARY CRY!
SOMETIMES IT SEEMS LIKE I CAN'T LEAVE GREEN LANTERN AND GREEN ARROW ALONE FOR A MINUTE WITHOUT THEM GETTING INTO TROUBLE...

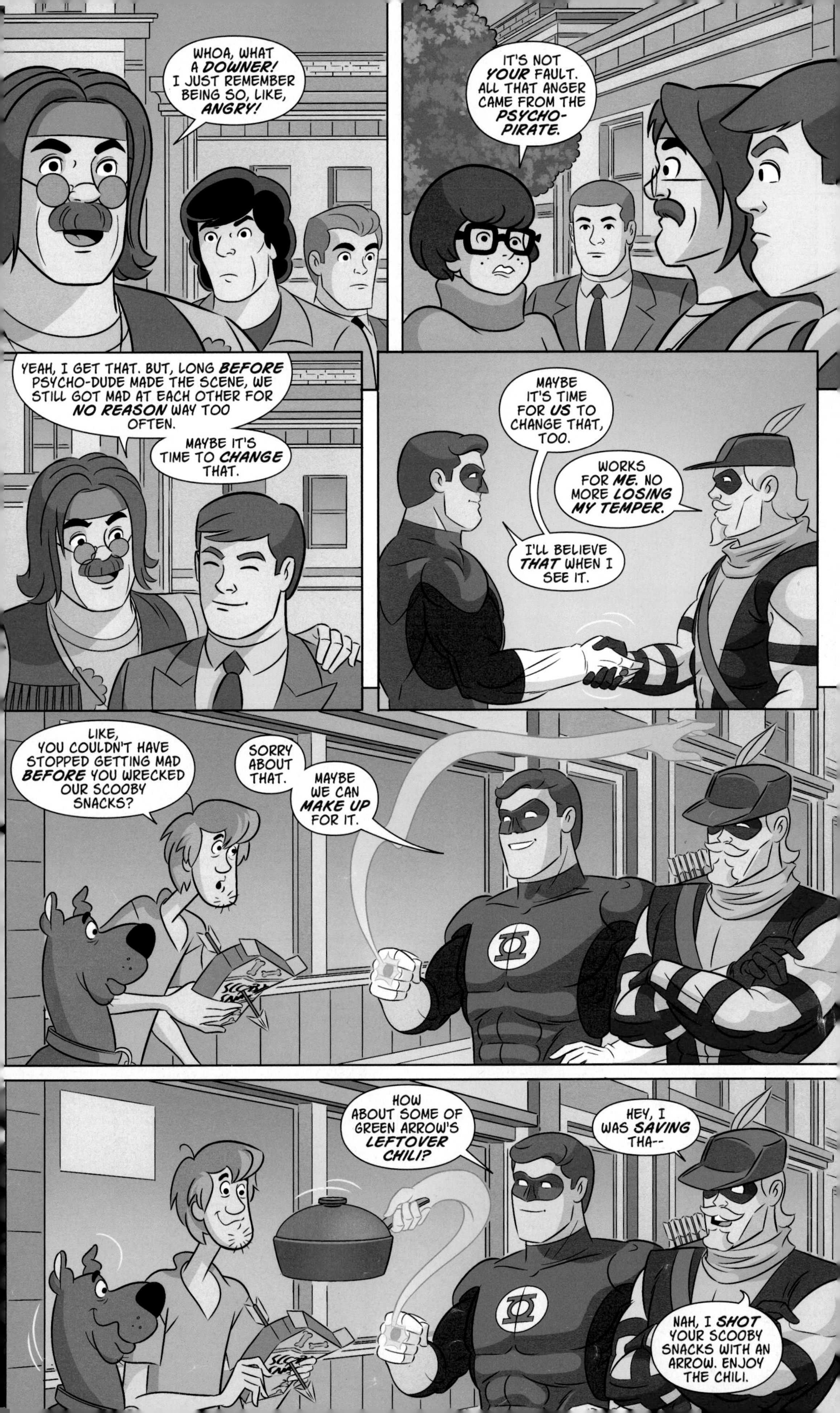
WHOA, WHAT A DOWNER! I JUST REMEMBER BEING SO, LIKE, ANGRY!
IT'S NOT YOUR FAULT. ALL THAT ANGER CAME FROM THE PSYCHO-PIRATE.
YEAH, I GET THAT. BUT, LONG BEFORE PSYCHO-DUDE MADE THE SCENE, WE STILL GOT MAD AT EACH OTHER FOR NO REASON WAY TOO OFTEN.
MAYBE IT'S TIME TO CHANGE THAT.
MAYBE IT'S TIME FOR US TO CHANGE THAT, TOO.
WORKS FOR ME. NO MORE LOSING MY TEMPER.
I'LL BELIEVE THAT WHEN I SEE IT.
LIKE, YOU COULDN'T HAVE STOPPED GETTING MAD BEFORE YOU WRECKED OUR SCOOBY SNACKS?
SORRY ABOUT THAT.
MAYBE WE CAN MAKE UP FOR IT.
HOW ABOUT SOME OF GREEN ARROW'S LEFTOVER CHILI?
HEY, I WAS SAVING THA--
NAH, I SHOT YOUR SCOOBY SNACKS WITH AN ARROW. ENJOY THE CHILI.

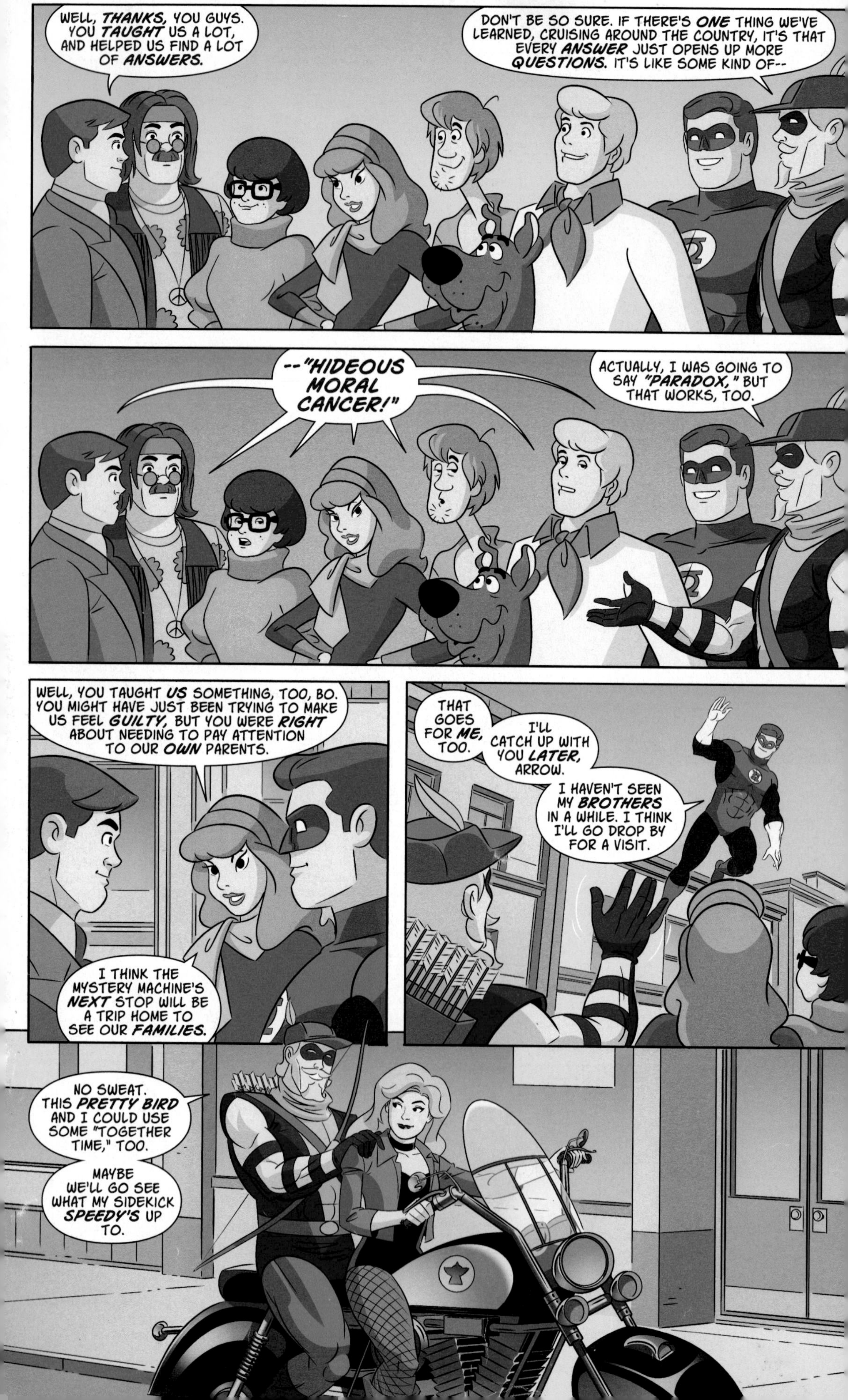
WELL, THANKS, YOU GUYS. YOU TAUGHT US A LOT, AND HELPED US FIND A LOT OF ANSWERS.
DON'T BE SO SURE. IF THERE'S ONE THING WE'VE LEARNED, CRUISING AROUND THE COUNTRY, IT'S THAT EVERY ANSWER JUST OPENS UP MORE QUESTIONS. IT'S LIKE SOME KIND OF--
--"HIDEOUS MORAL CANCER!"
ACTUALLY, I WAS GOING TO SAY "PARADOX," BUT THAT WORKS, TOO.
WELL, YOU TAUGHT US SOMETHING, TOO, BO. YOU MIGHT HAVE JUST BEEN TRYING TO MAKE US FEEL GUILTY, BUT YOU WERE RIGHT ABOUT NEEDING TO PAY ATTENTION TO OUR OWN PARENTS.
I THINK THE MYSTERY MACHINE'S NEXT STOP WILL BE A TRIP HOME TO SEE OUR FAMILIES.
THAT GOES FOR ME, TOO.
I'LL CATCH UP WITH YOU LATER, ARROW.
I HAVEN'T SEEN MY BROTHERS IN A WHILE. I THINK I'LL GO DROP BY FOR A VISIT.
NO SWEAT. THIS PRETTY BIRD AND I COULD USE SOME "TOGETHER TIME," TOO.
MAYBE WE'LL GO SEE WHAT MY SIDEKICK SPEEDY'S UP TO.

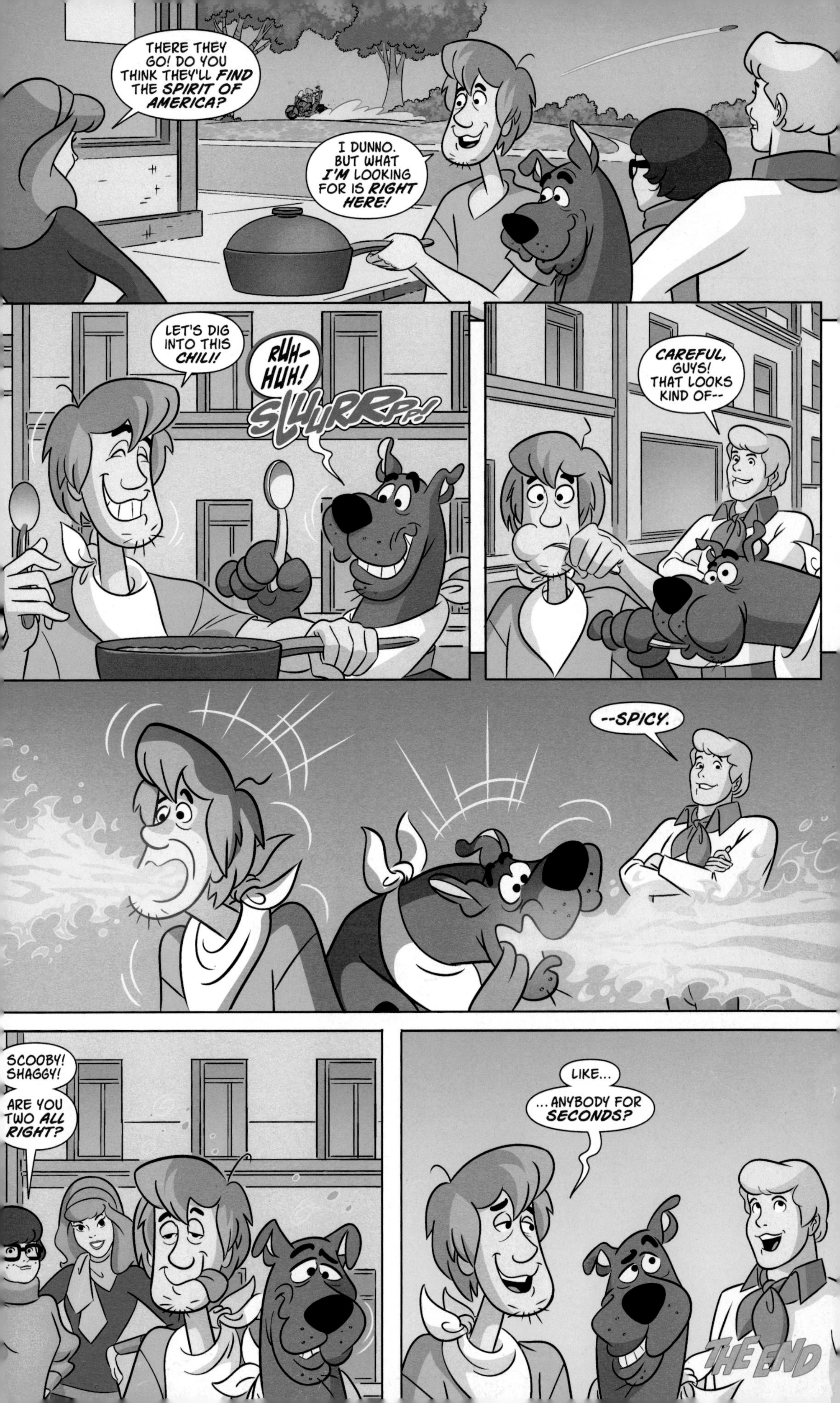
THERE THEY GO! DO YOU THINK THEY'LL FIND THE SPIRIT OF AMERICA?
I DUNNO. BUT WHAT I'M LOOKING FOR IS RIGHT HERE!
LET'S DIG INTO THIS CHILI!
RUH-HUH!
SLUURRPP!
CAREFUL, GUYS! THAT LOOKS KIND OF--
--SPICY.
SCOOBY! SHAGGY!
ARE YOU TWO ALL RIGHT?
LIKE...
...ANYBODY FOR SECONDS?
THE END

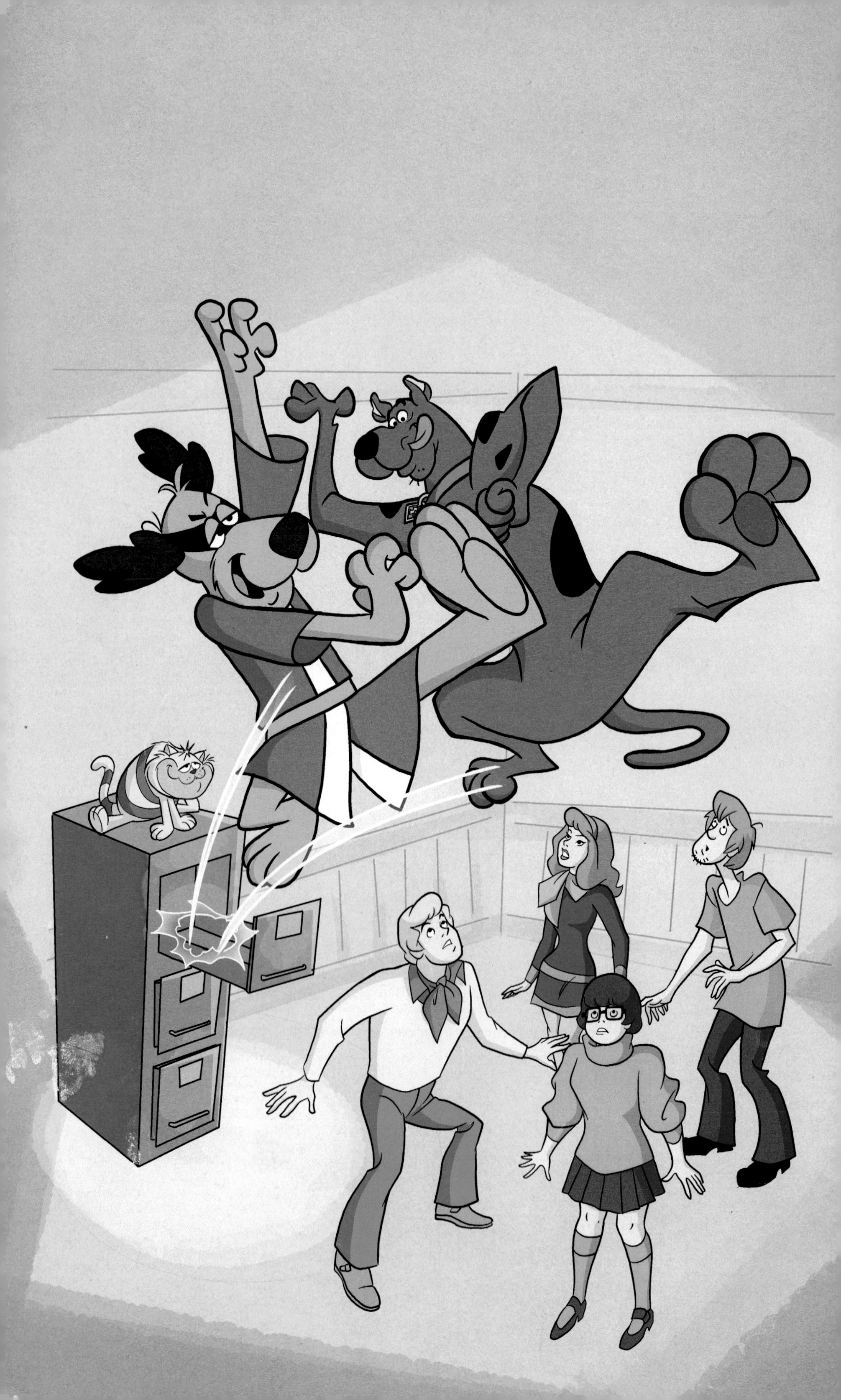

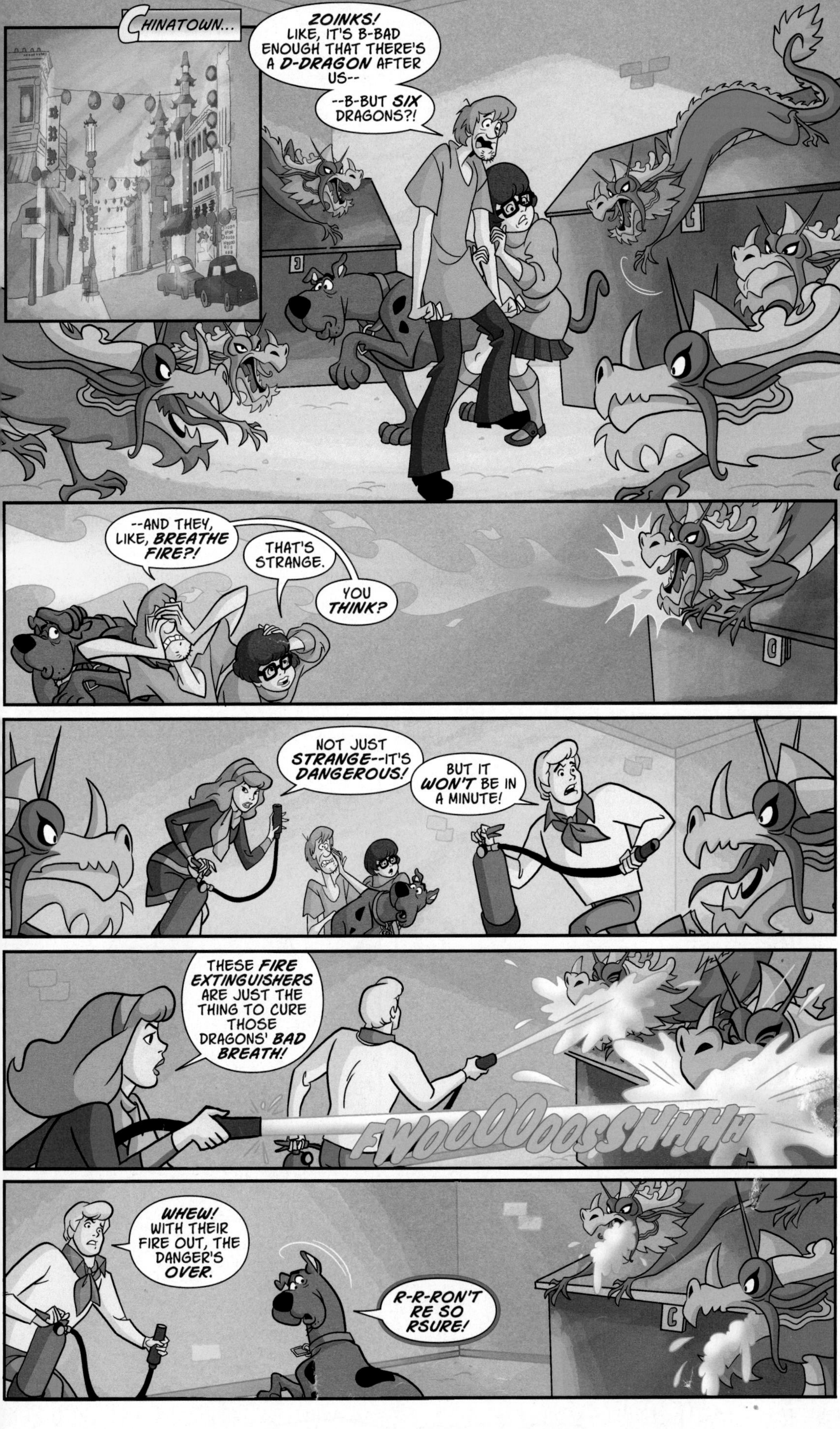

CHINATOWN...
ZOINKS! LIKE, IT'S B-BAD ENOUGH THAT THERE'S A D-DRAGON AFTER US--
--B-BUT SIX DRAGONS?!
--AND THEY, LIKE, BREATHE FIRE?!
THAT'S STRANGE.
YOU THINK?
NOT JUST STRANGE--IT'S DANGEROUS!
BUT IT WON'T BE IN A MINUTE!
THESE FIRE EXTINGUISHERS ARE JUST THE THING TO CURE THOSE DRAGONS' BAD BREATH!
FWOOOOOOOSHHHH
WHEW! WITH THEIR FIRE OUT, THE DANGER'S OVER.
R-R-RON'T RE SO RSURE!

enter the DRAGON, exit SCOOBY-DOO

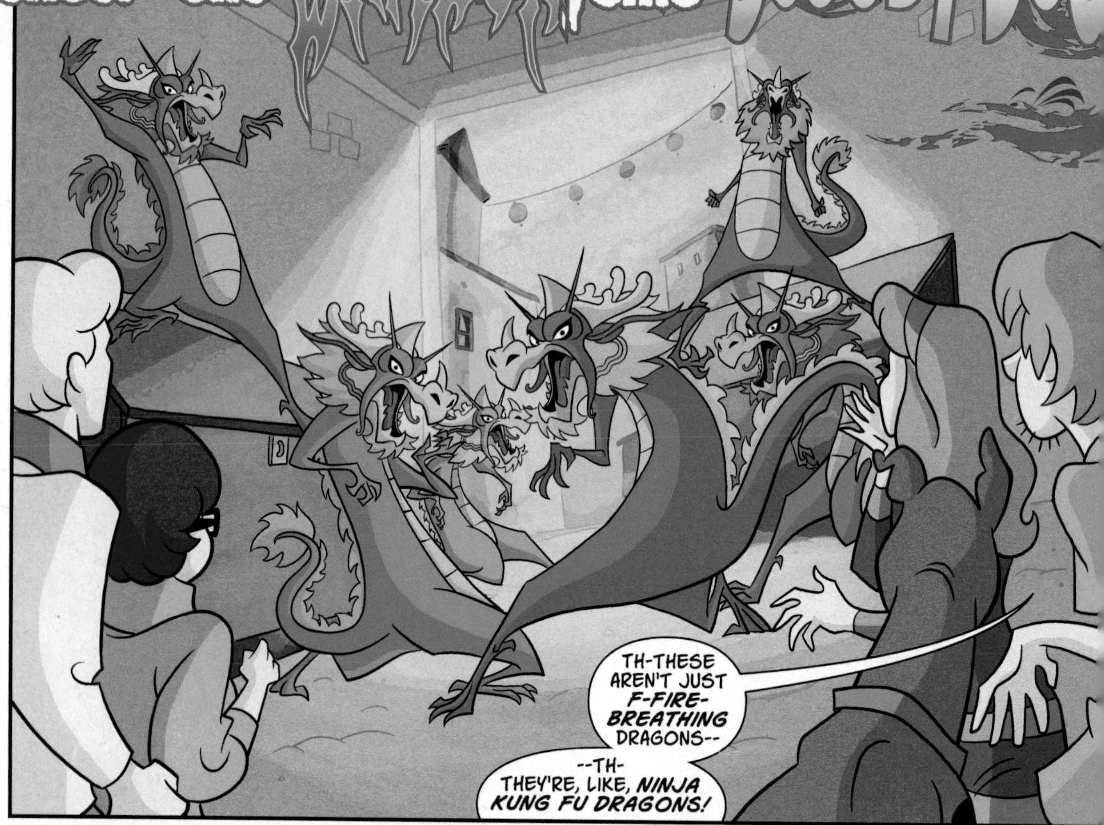

TH-THESE AREN'T JUST F-FIRE-BREATHING DRAGONS--
--TH-THEY'RE, LIKE, NINJA KUNG FU DRAGONS!

writer: SHOLLY FISCH artist: SCOTT JERALDS colorist: SILVANA BRYS letterer: SAIDA TEMOFONTE

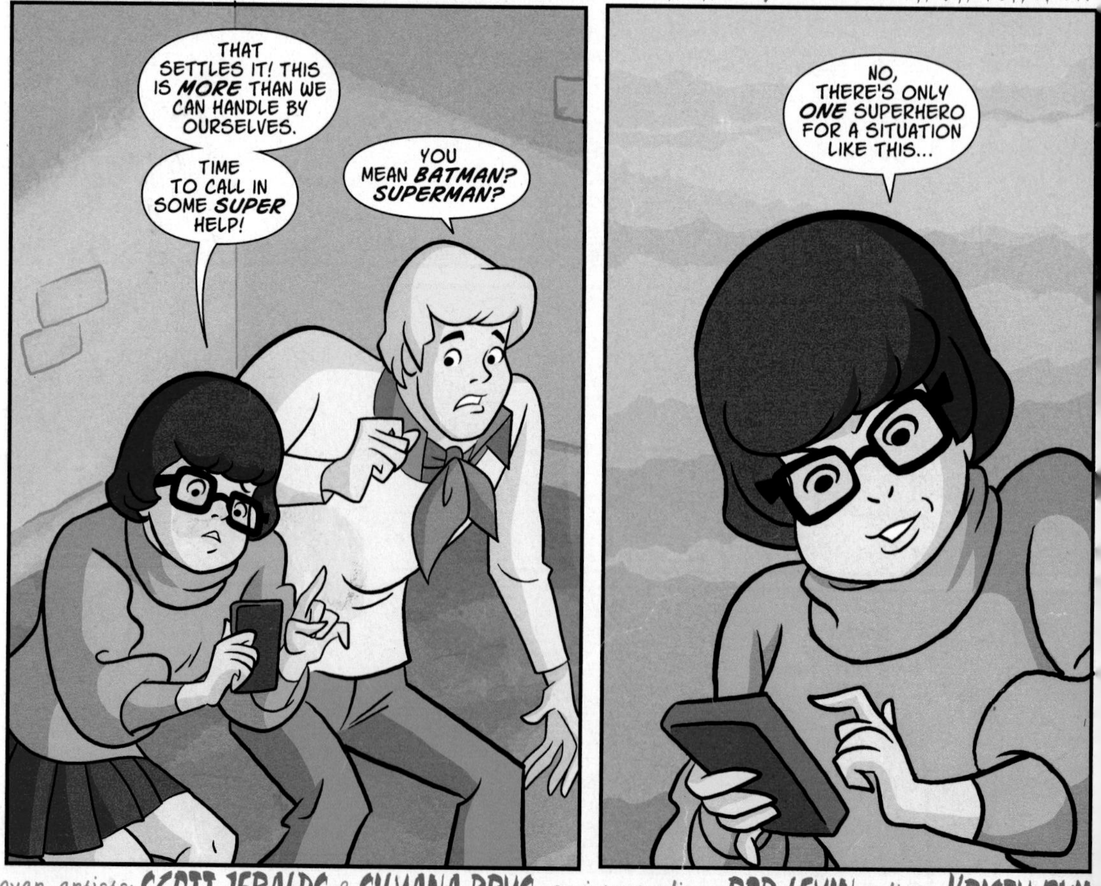

THAT SETTLES IT! THIS IS MORE THAN WE CAN HANDLE BY OURSELVES.
TIME TO CALL IN SOME SUPER HELP!
YOU MEAN BATMAN? SUPERMAN?
NO, THERE'S ONLY ONE SUPERHERO FOR A SITUATION LIKE THIS...

cover artists: SCOTT JERALDS & SILVANA BRYS assistant editor: ROB LEVIN editor: KRISTY QUINN

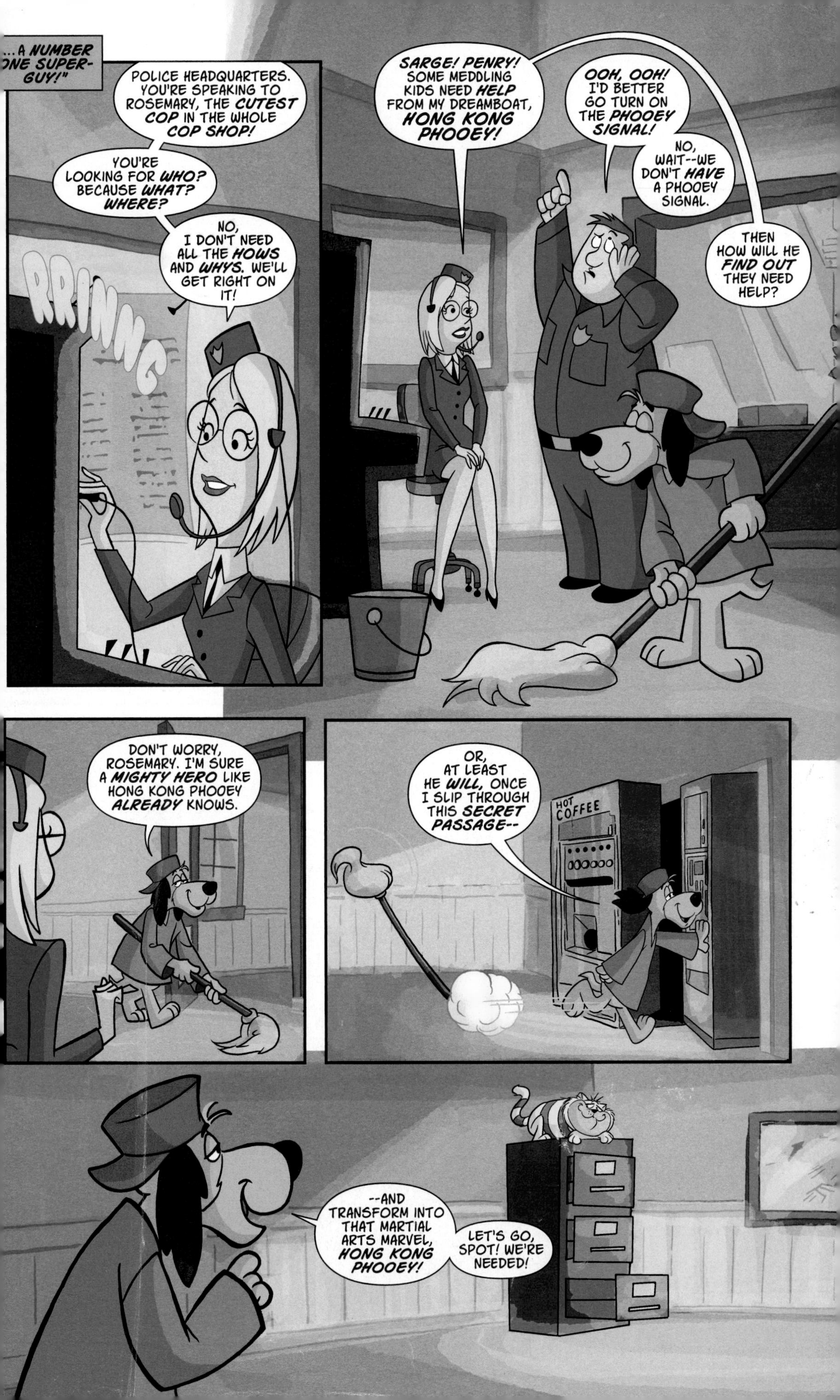

...A NUMBER ONE SUPER-GUY!"
POLICE HEADQUARTERS. YOU'RE SPEAKING TO ROSEMARY, THE CUTEST COP IN THE WHOLE COP SHOP!
YOU'RE LOOKING FOR WHO? BECAUSE WHAT? WHERE?
NO, I DON'T NEED ALL THE HOWS AND WHYS. WE'LL GET RIGHT ON IT!
RRINNG
SARGE! PENRY! SOME MEDDLING KIDS NEED HELP FROM MY DREAMBOAT, HONG KONG PHOOEY!
OOH, OOH! I'D BETTER GO TURN ON THE PHOOEY SIGNAL!
NO, WAIT--WE DON'T HAVE A PHOOEY SIGNAL.
THEN HOW WILL HE FIND OUT THEY NEED HELP?
DON'T WORRY, ROSEMARY. I'M SURE A MIGHTY HERO LIKE HONG KONG PHOOEY ALREADY KNOWS.
OR, AT LEAST HE WILL, ONCE I SLIP THROUGH THIS SECRET PASSAGE--
HOT COFFEE
--AND TRANSFORM INTO THAT MARTIAL ARTS MARVEL, HONG KONG PHOOEY!
LET'S GO, SPOT! WE'RE NEEDED!

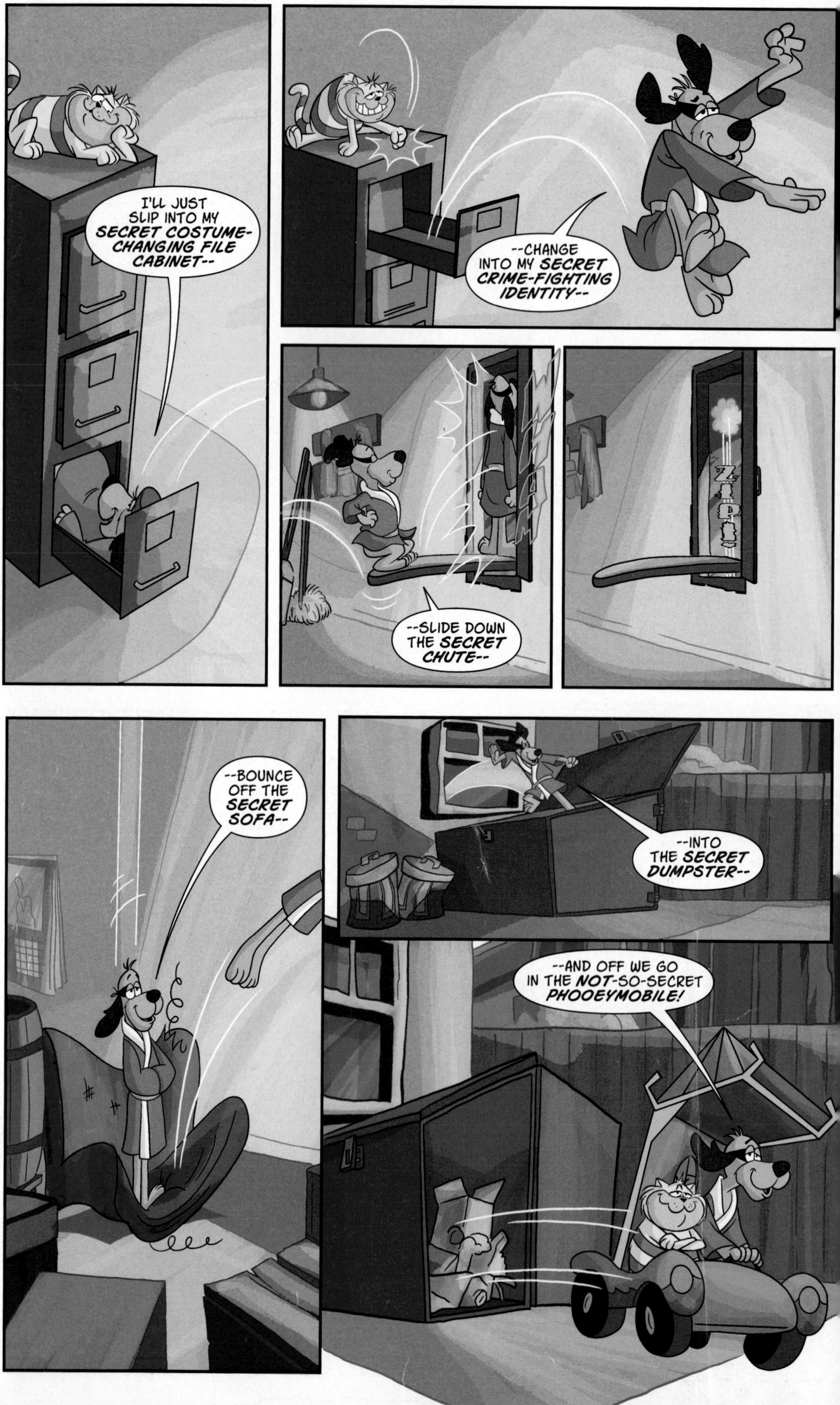
I'LL JUST SLIP INTO MY SECRET COSTUME-CHANGING FILE CABINET--
--CHANGE INTO MY SECRET CRIME-FIGHTING IDENTITY--
--SLIDE DOWN THE SECRET CHUTE--
ZIP!
--BOUNCE OFF THE SECRET SOFA--
--INTO THE SECRET DUMPSTER--
--AND OFF WE GO IN THE NOT-SO-SECRET PHOOEYMOBILE!

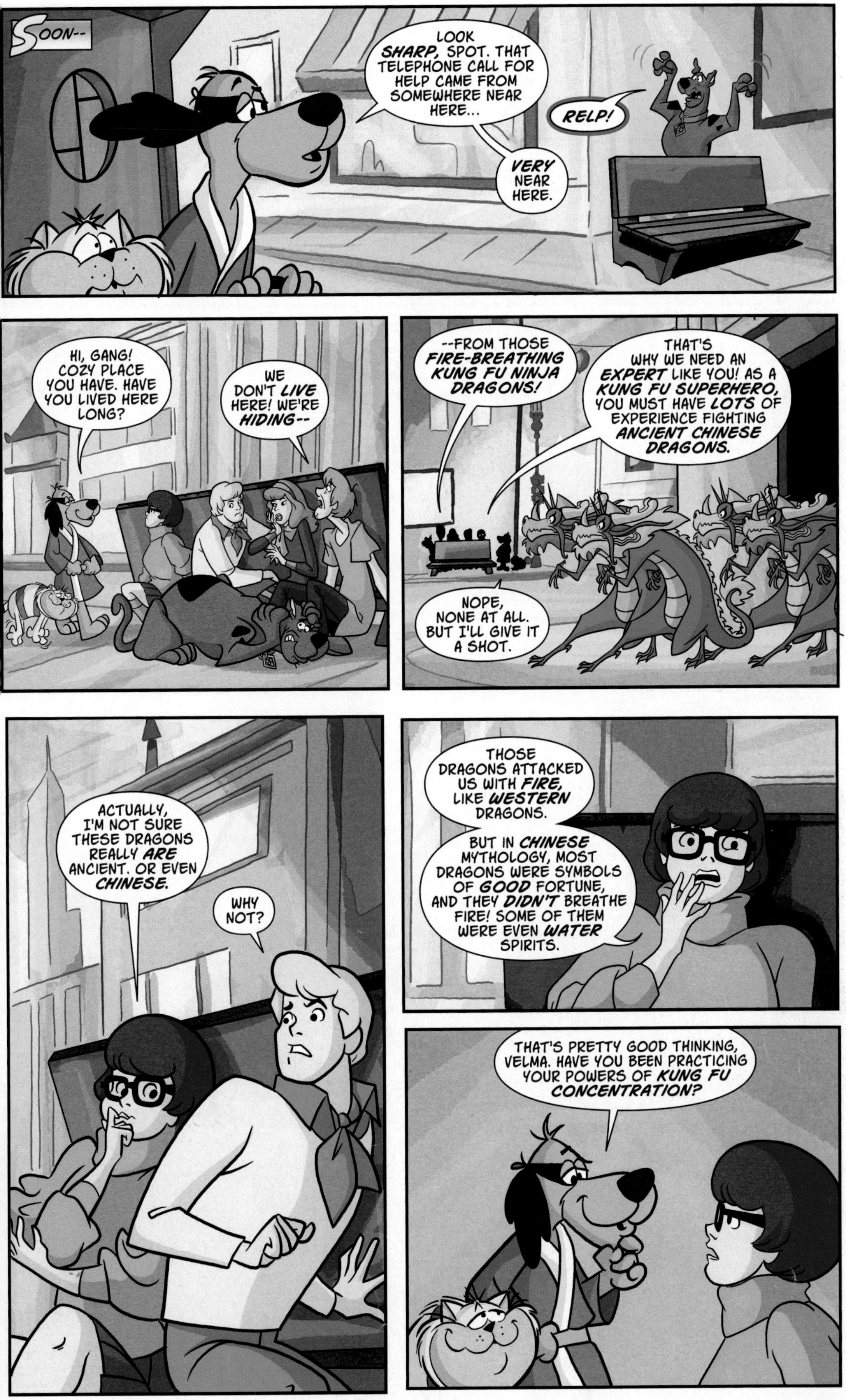
SOON--
LOOK SHARP, SPOT. THAT TELEPHONE CALL FOR HELP CAME FROM SOMEWHERE NEAR HERE...
VERY NEAR HERE.
RELP!
HI, GANG! COZY PLACE YOU HAVE. HAVE YOU LIVED HERE LONG?
WE DON'T LIVE HERE! WE'RE HIDING--
--FROM THOSE FIRE-BREATHING KUNG FU NINJA DRAGONS!
THAT'S WHY WE NEED AN EXPERT LIKE YOU! AS A KUNG FU SUPERHERO, YOU MUST HAVE LOTS OF EXPERIENCE FIGHTING ANCIENT CHINESE DRAGONS.
NOPE, NONE AT ALL. BUT I'LL GIVE IT A SHOT.
ACTUALLY, I'M NOT SURE THESE DRAGONS REALLY ARE ANCIENT. OR EVEN CHINESE.
WHY NOT?
THOSE DRAGONS ATTACKED US WITH FIRE, LIKE WESTERN DRAGONS.
BUT IN CHINESE MYTHOLOGY, MOST DRAGONS WERE SYMBOLS OF GOOD FORTUNE, AND THEY DIDN'T BREATHE FIRE! SOME OF THEM WERE EVEN WATER SPIRITS.
THAT'S PRETTY GOOD THINKING, VELMA. HAVE YOU BEEN PRACTICING YOUR POWERS OF KUNG FU CONCENTRATION?

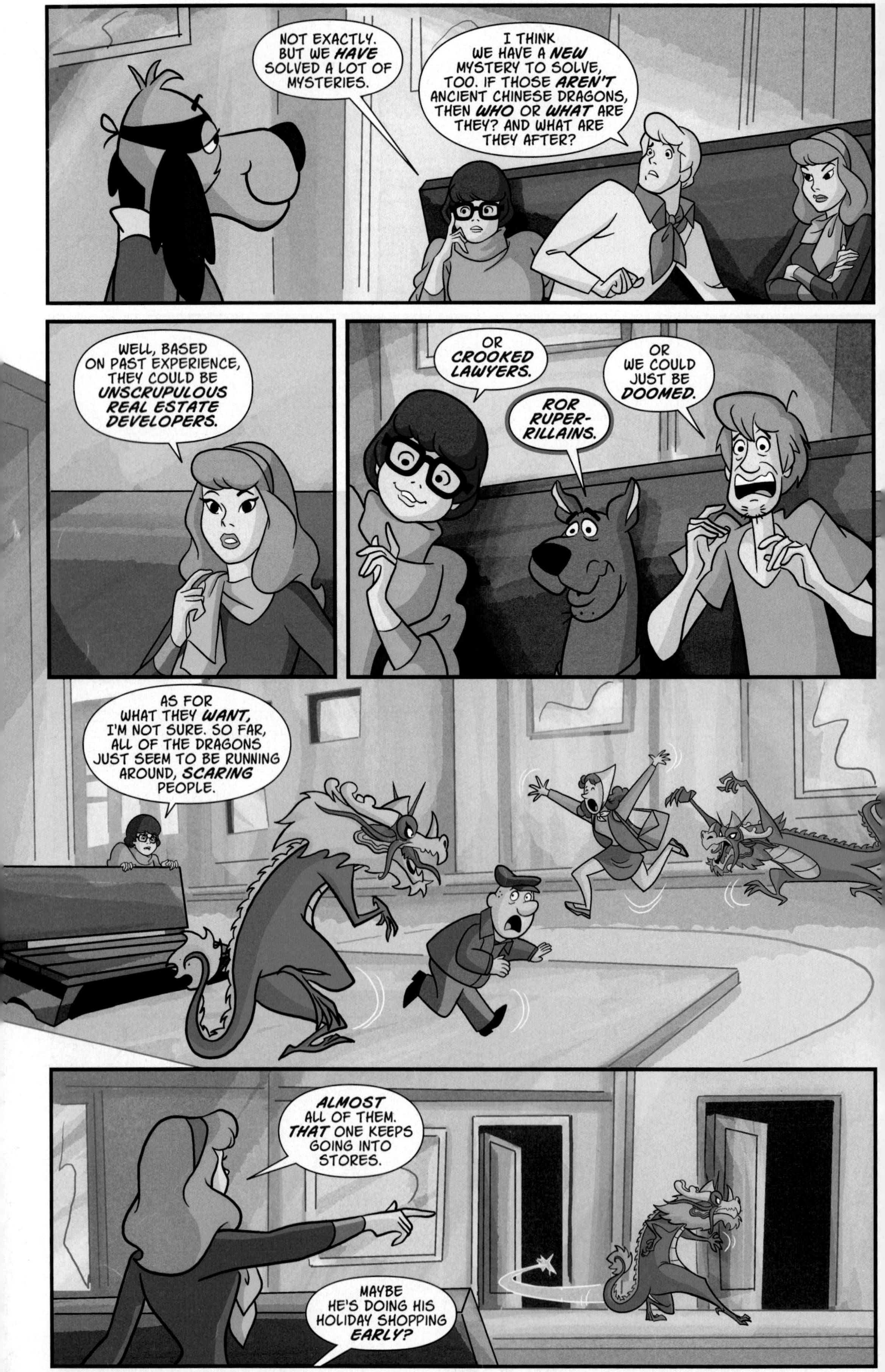

NOT EXACTLY. BUT WE *HAVE* SOLVED A LOT OF MYSTERIES.
I THINK WE HAVE A *NEW* MYSTERY TO SOLVE, TOO. IF THOSE *AREN'T* ANCIENT CHINESE DRAGONS, THEN *WHO* OR *WHAT* ARE THEY? AND WHAT ARE THEY AFTER?
WELL, BASED ON PAST EXPERIENCE, THEY COULD BE *UNSCRUPULOUS REAL ESTATE DEVELOPERS.*
OR *CROOKED LAWYERS.*
ROR RUPER-RILLAINS.
OR WE COULD JUST BE *DOOMED.*
AS FOR WHAT THEY *WANT,* I'M NOT SURE. SO FAR, ALL OF THE DRAGONS JUST SEEM TO BE RUNNING AROUND, *SCARING* PEOPLE.
ALMOST ALL OF THEM. *THAT* ONE KEEPS GOING INTO STORES.
MAYBE HE'S DOING HIS HOLIDAY SHOPPING *EARLY?*

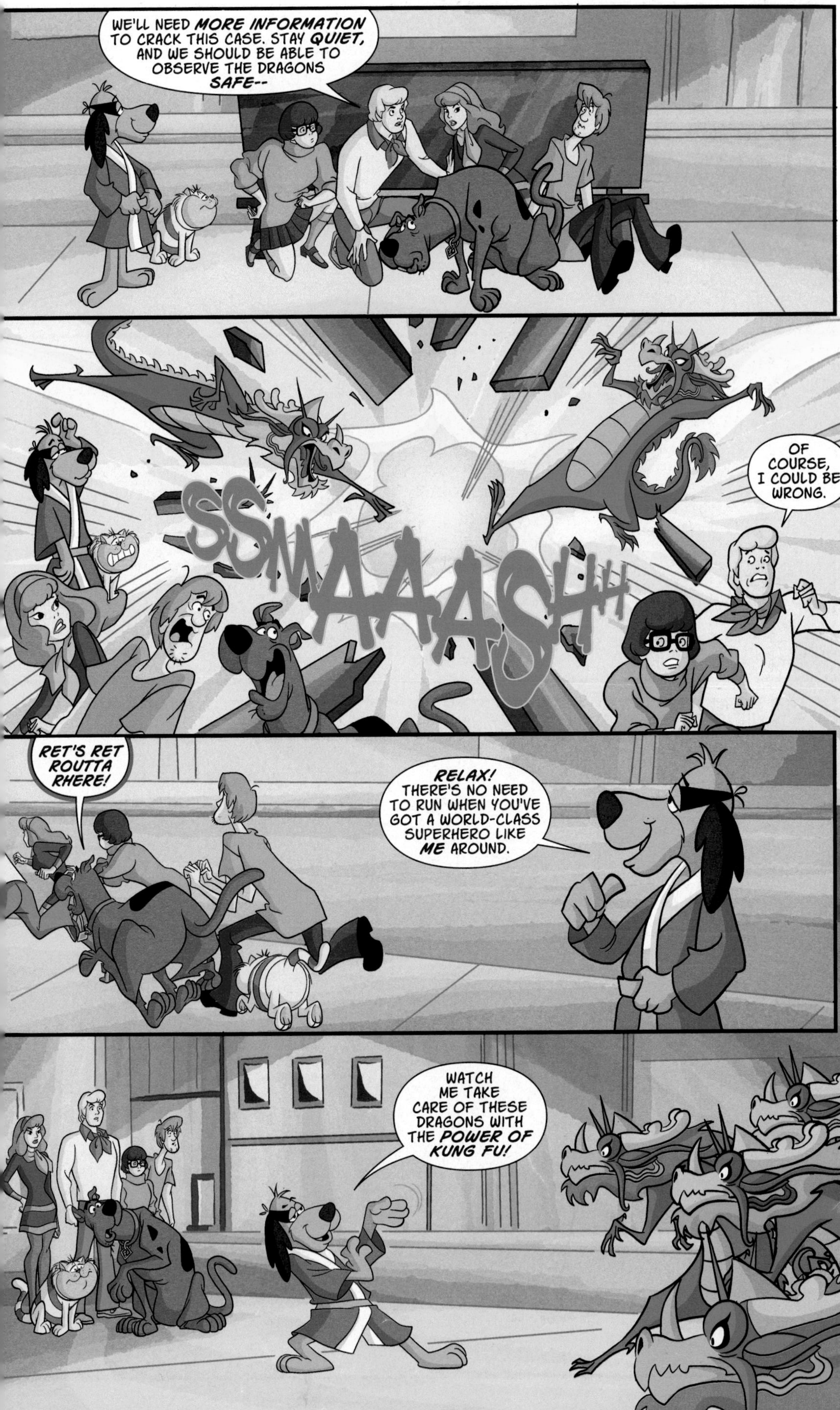
WE'LL NEED MORE INFORMATION TO CRACK THIS CASE. STAY QUIET, AND WE SHOULD BE ABLE TO OBSERVE THE DRAGONS SAFE--
SSMAAASHHH
OF COURSE, I COULD BE WRONG.
RET'S RET ROUTTA RHERE!
RELAX! THERE'S NO NEED TO RUN WHEN YOU'VE GOT A WORLD-CLASS SUPERHERO LIKE ME AROUND.
WATCH ME TAKE CARE OF THESE DRAGONS WITH THE POWER OF KUNG FU!

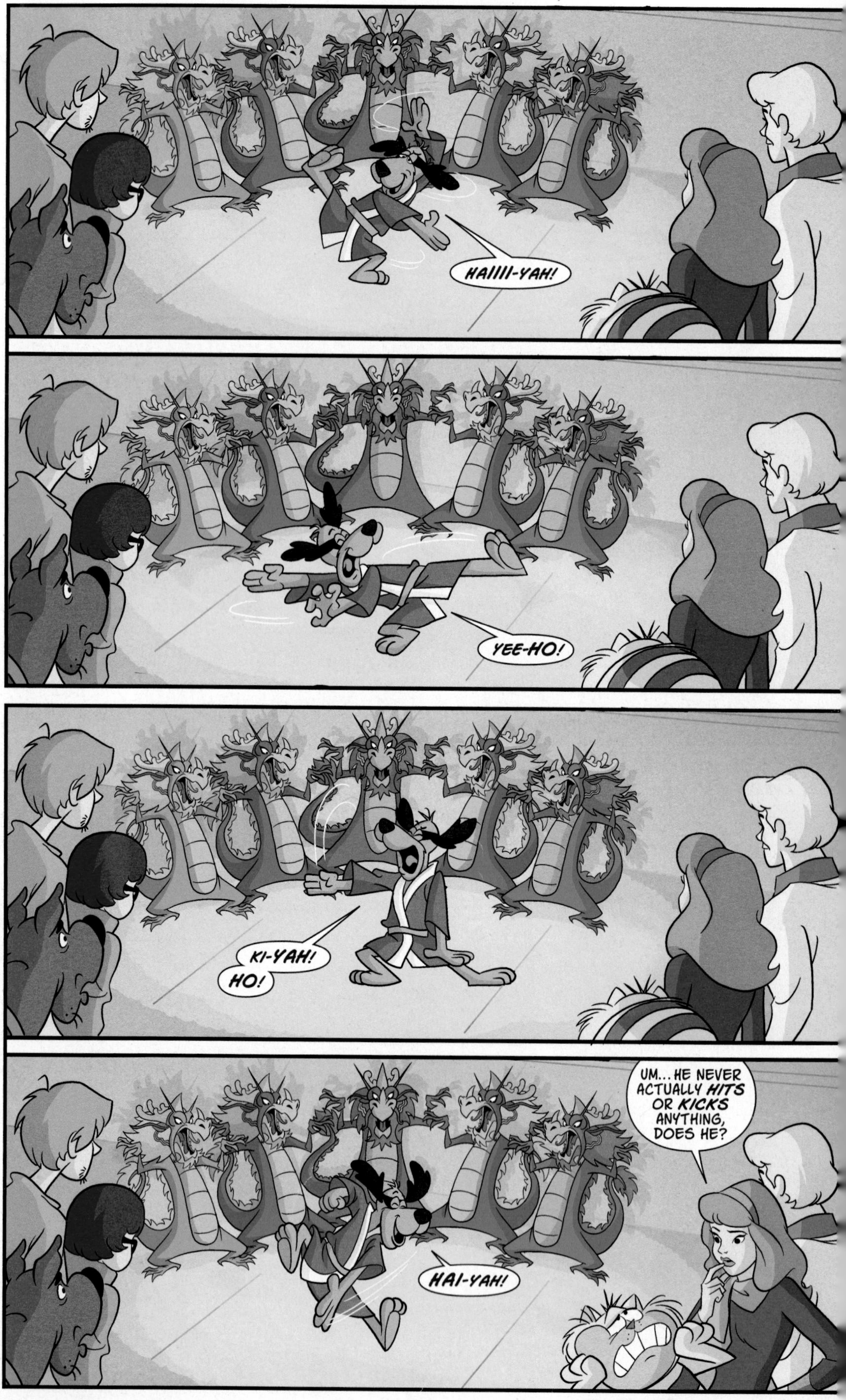
HAIIII-YAH!
YEE-HO!
KI-YAH!
HO!
UM... HE NEVER ACTUALLY HITS OR KICKS ANYTHING, DOES HE?
HAI-YAH!

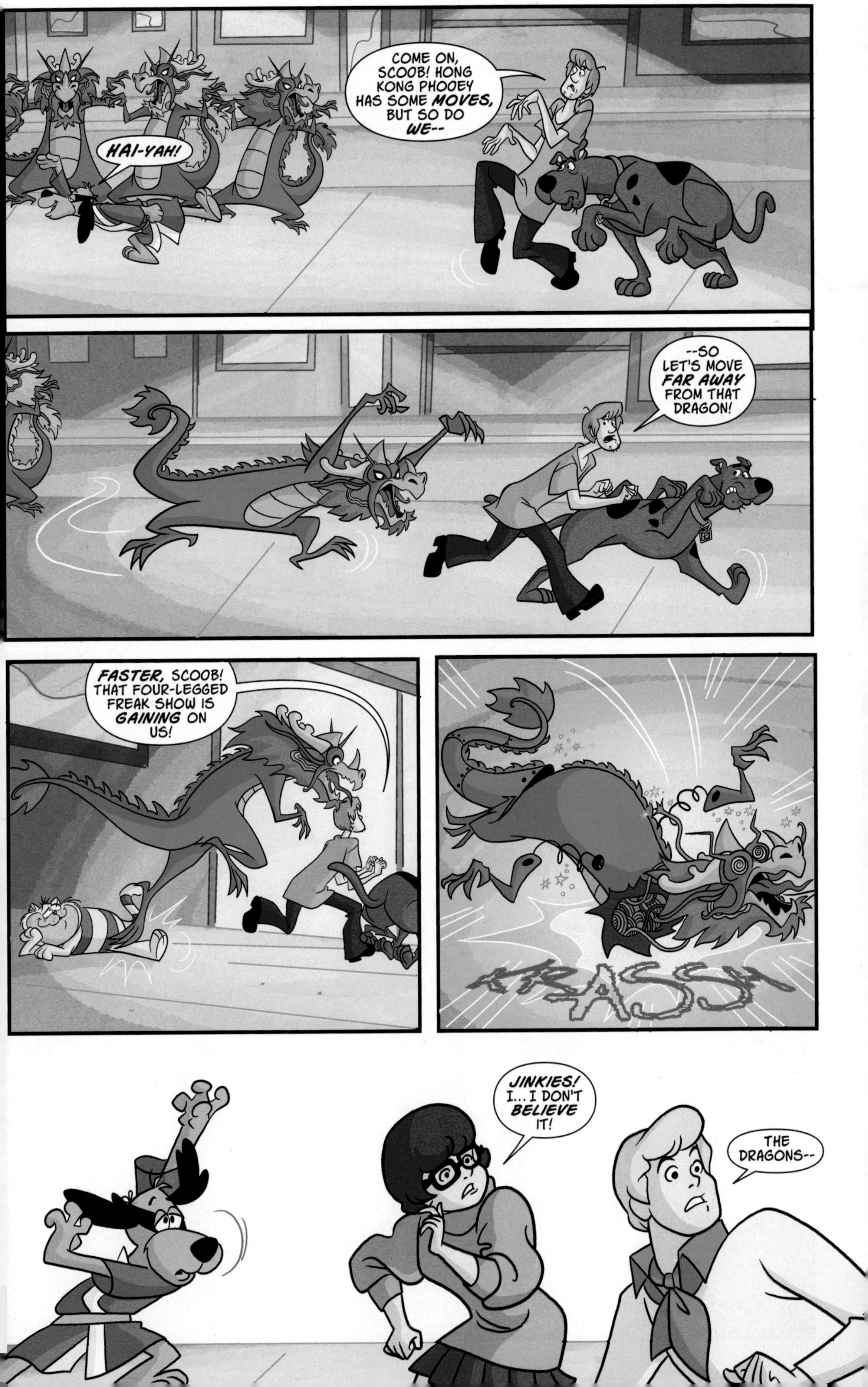
COME ON, SCOOB! HONG KONG PHOOEY HAS SOME MOVES, BUT SO DO WE--
HAI-YAH!
--SO LET'S MOVE FAR AWAY FROM THAT DRAGON!
FASTER, SCOOB! THAT FOUR-LEGGED FREAK SHOW IS GAINING ON US!
KRASSH
JINKIES! I... I DON'T BELIEVE IT!
THE DRAGONS--

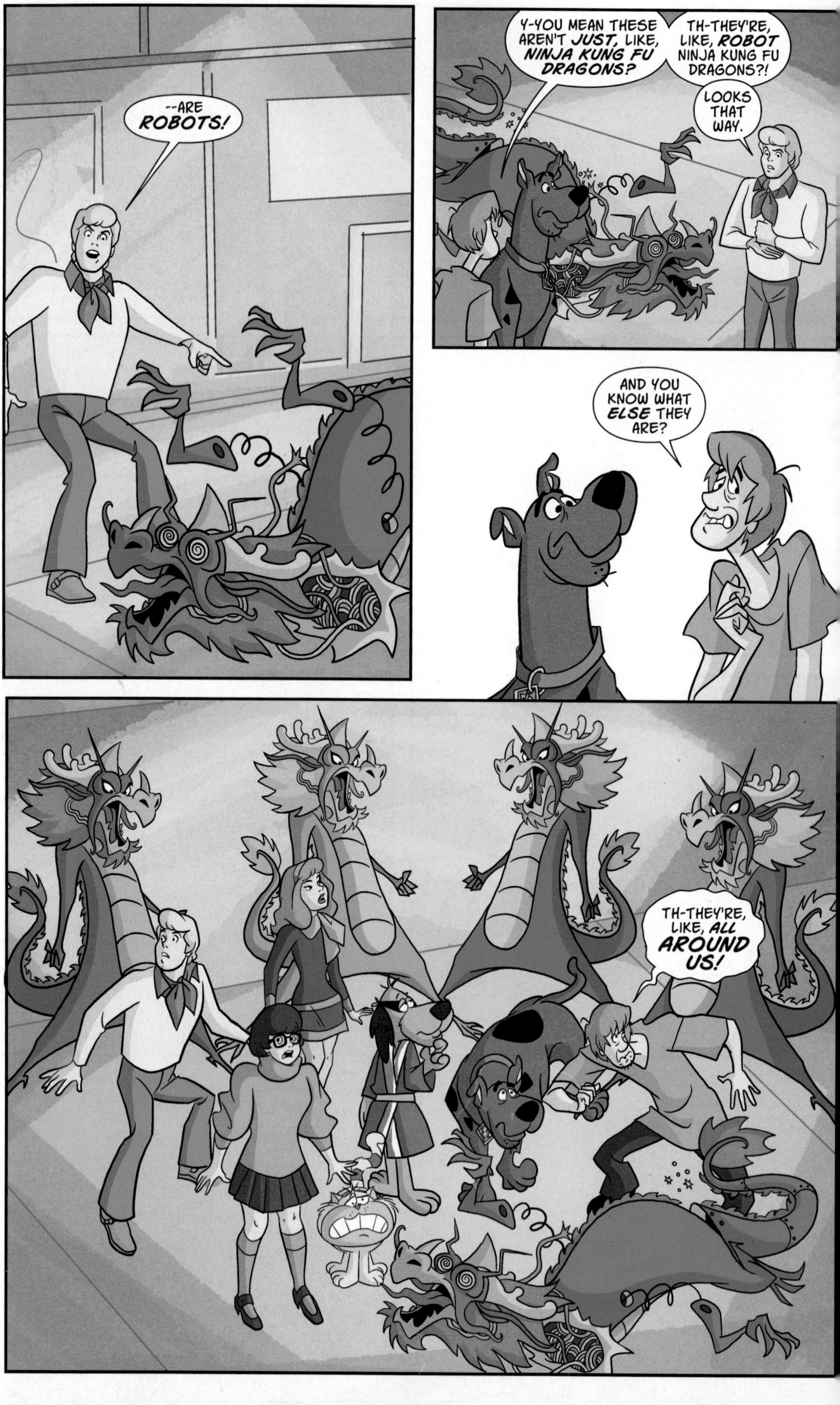
--ARE *ROBOTS!*
Y-YOU MEAN THESE AREN'T *JUST,* LIKE, *NINJA KUNG FU DRAGONS?*
TH-THEY'RE, LIKE, *ROBOT* NINJA KUNG FU DRAGONS?!
LOOKS THAT WAY.
AND YOU KNOW WHAT *ELSE* THEY ARE?
TH-THEY'RE, LIKE, *ALL AROUND US!*

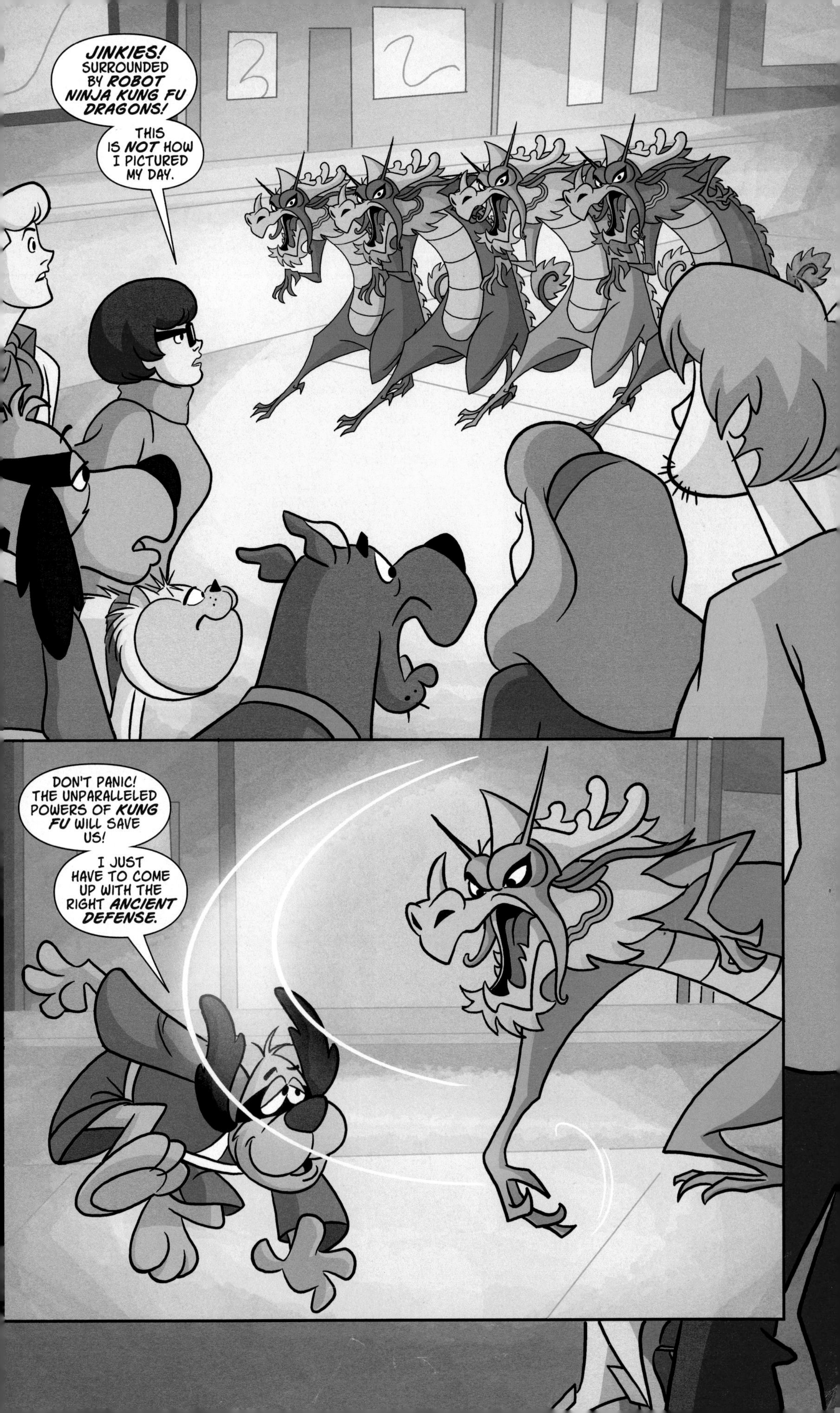
JINKIES! SURROUNDED BY ROBOT NINJA KUNG FU DRAGONS!
THIS IS NOT HOW I PICTURED MY DAY.
DON'T PANIC! THE UNPARALLELED POWERS OF KUNG FU WILL SAVE US!
I JUST HAVE TO COME UP WITH THE RIGHT ANCIENT DEFENSE.

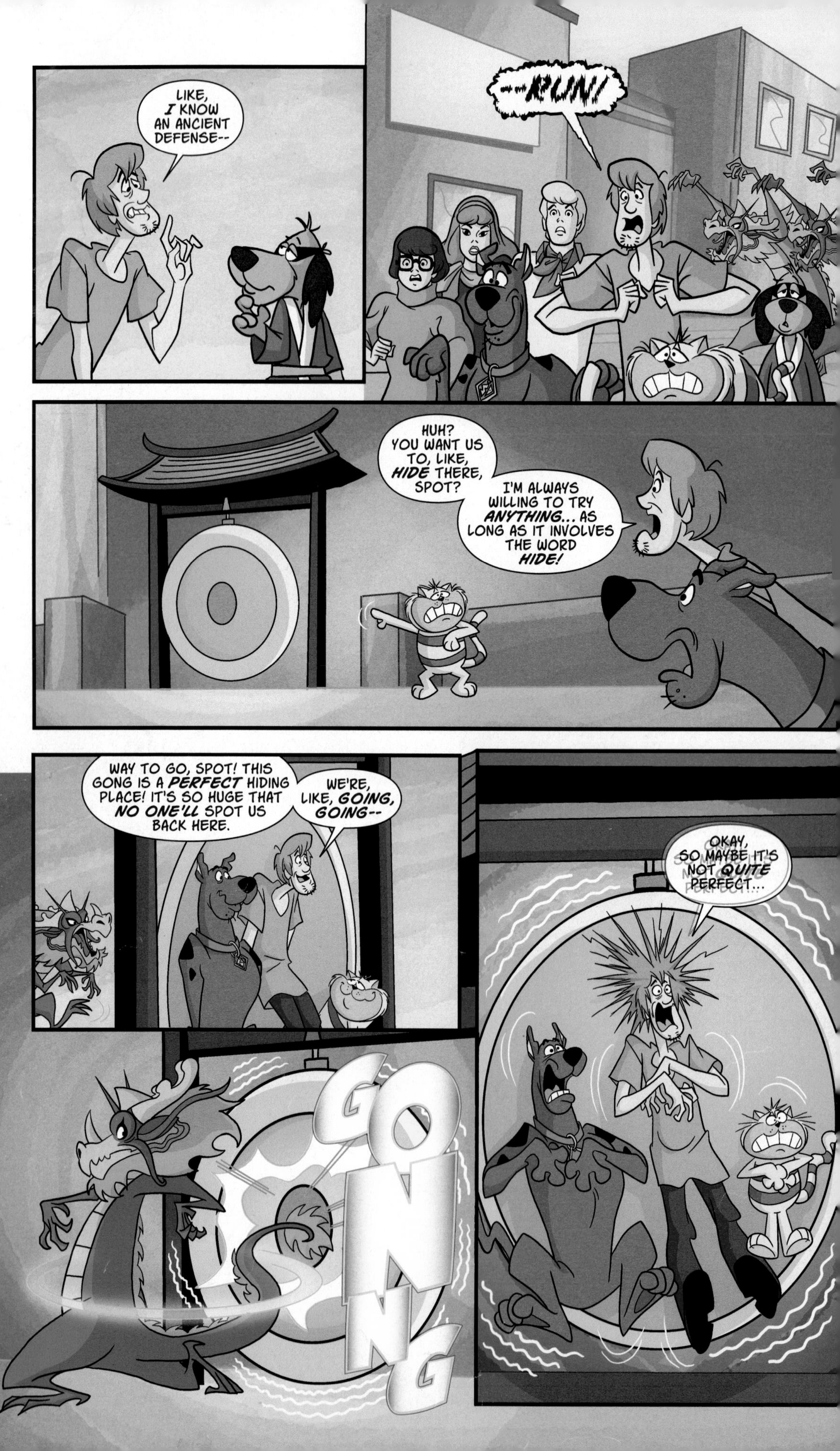

LIKE, *I* KNOW AN ANCIENT DEFENSE--
--RUN!
HUH? YOU WANT US TO, LIKE, *HIDE* THERE, SPOT?
I'M ALWAYS WILLING TO TRY *ANYTHING*... AS LONG AS IT INVOLVES THE WORD *HIDE!*
WAY TO GO, SPOT! THIS GONG IS A *PERFECT* HIDING PLACE! IT'S SO HUGE THAT *NO ONE'LL* SPOT US BACK HERE.
WE'RE, LIKE, *GOING, GOING*--
GONNNG
OKAY, SO MAYBE IT'S NOT *QUITE* PERFECT...

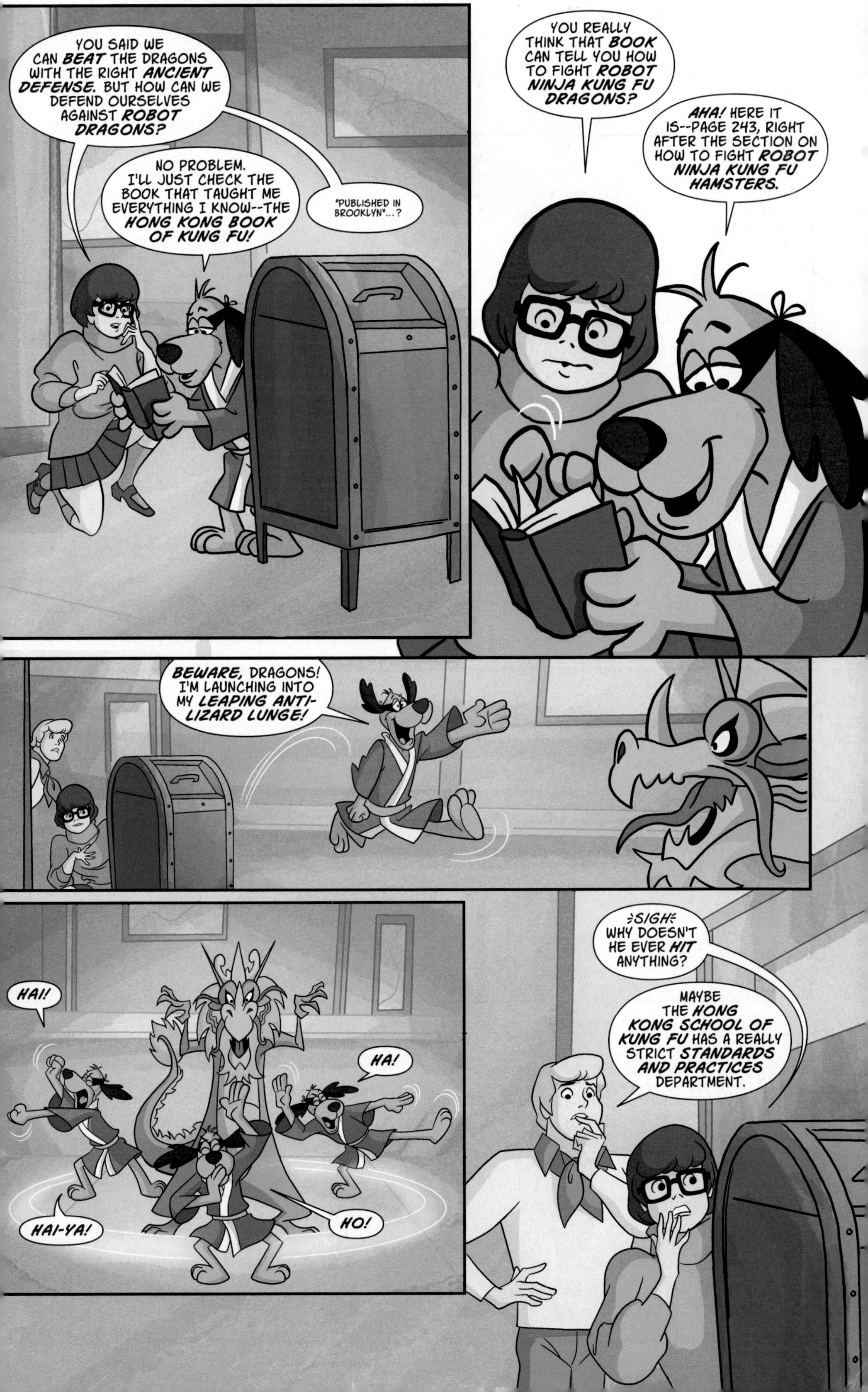

YOU SAID WE CAN BEAT THE DRAGONS WITH THE RIGHT ANCIENT DEFENSE. BUT HOW CAN WE DEFEND OURSELVES AGAINST ROBOT DRAGONS?
NO PROBLEM. I'LL JUST CHECK THE BOOK THAT TAUGHT ME EVERYTHING I KNOW--THE HONG KONG BOOK OF KUNG FU!
"PUBLISHED IN BROOKLYN"...?
YOU REALLY THINK THAT BOOK CAN TELL YOU HOW TO FIGHT ROBOT NINJA KUNG FU DRAGONS?
AHA! HERE IT IS--PAGE 243, RIGHT AFTER THE SECTION ON HOW TO FIGHT ROBOT NINJA KUNG FU HAMSTERS.
BEWARE, DRAGONS! I'M LAUNCHING INTO MY LEAPING ANTI-LIZARD LUNGE!
HAI!
HA!
HAI-YA!
HO!
SIGH WHY DOESN'T HE EVER HIT ANYTHING?
MAYBE THE HONG KONG SCHOOL OF KUNG FU HAS A REALLY STRICT STANDARDS AND PRACTICES DEPARTMENT.

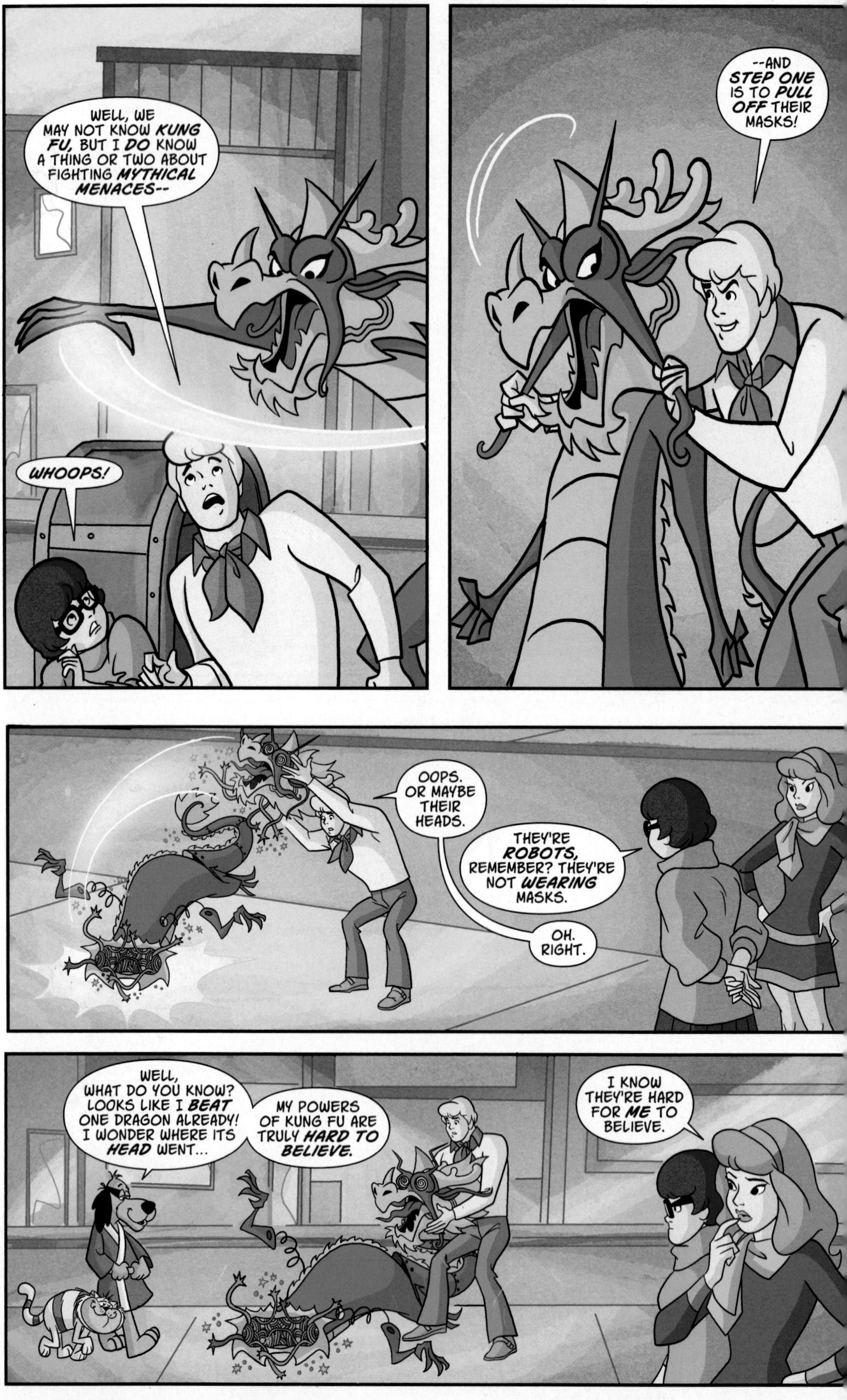

WELL, WE MAY NOT KNOW KUNG FU, BUT I DO KNOW A THING OR TWO ABOUT FIGHTING MYTHICAL MENACES--
WHOOPS!
--AND STEP ONE IS TO PULL OFF THEIR MASKS!
OOPS. OR MAYBE THEIR HEADS.
THEY'RE ROBOTS, REMEMBER? THEY'RE NOT WEARING MASKS.
OH. RIGHT.
WELL, WHAT DO YOU KNOW? LOOKS LIKE I BEAT ONE DRAGON ALREADY! I WONDER WHERE ITS HEAD WENT...
MY POWERS OF KUNG FU ARE TRULY HARD TO BELIEVE.
I KNOW THEY'RE HARD FOR ME TO BELIEVE.

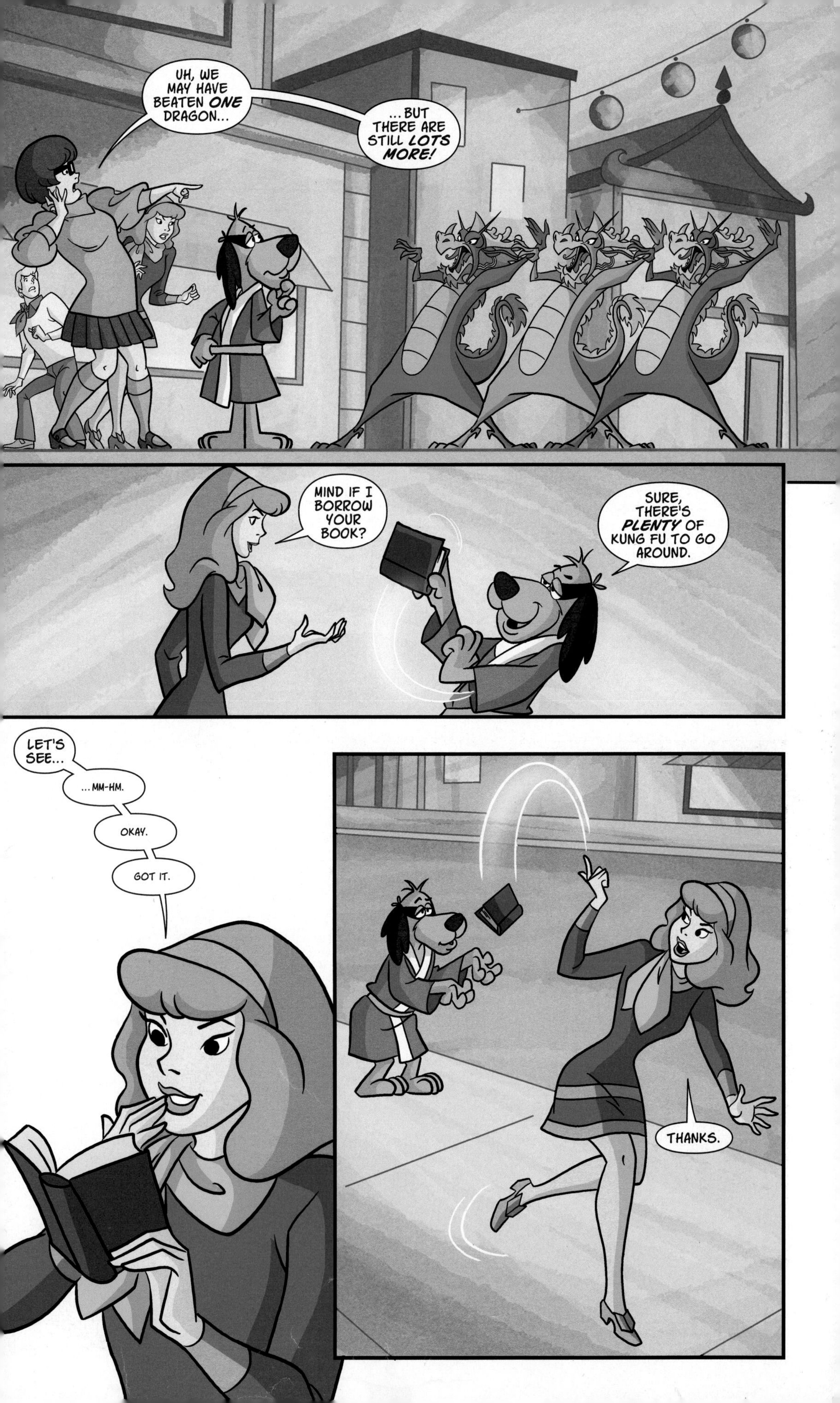
UH, WE MAY HAVE BEATEN *ONE* DRAGON...
...BUT THERE ARE STILL *LOTS MORE!*
MIND IF I BORROW YOUR BOOK?
SURE, THERE'S *PLENTY* OF KUNG FU TO GO AROUND.
LET'S SEE...
...MM-HM.
OKAY.
GOT IT.
THANKS.

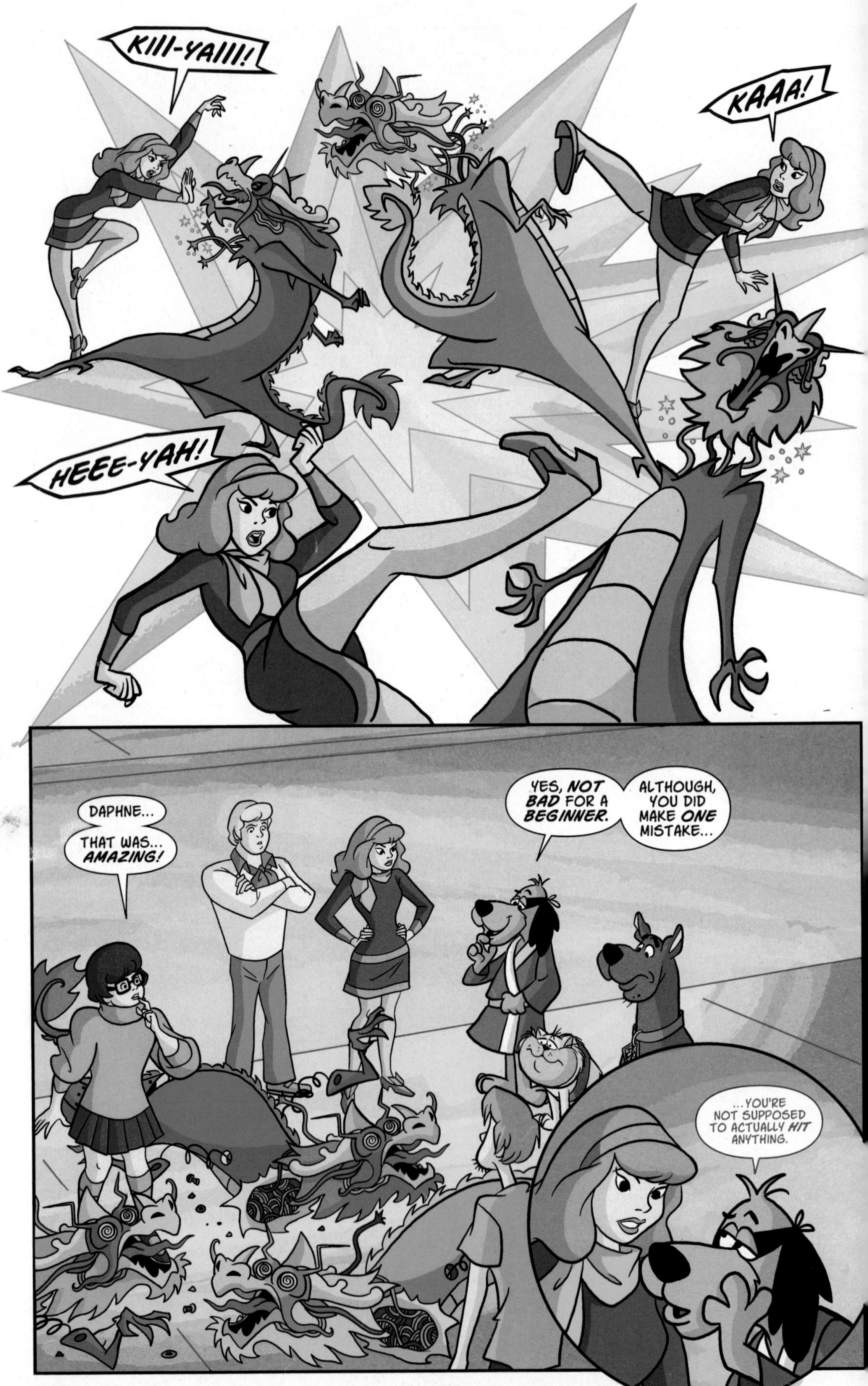
KIII-YAIII!
KAAA!
HEEE-YAH!
DAPHNE...
THAT WAS... AMAZING!
YES, NOT BAD FOR A BEGINNER.
ALTHOUGH, YOU DID MAKE ONE MISTAKE...
...YOU'RE NOT SUPPOSED TO ACTUALLY HIT ANYTHING.

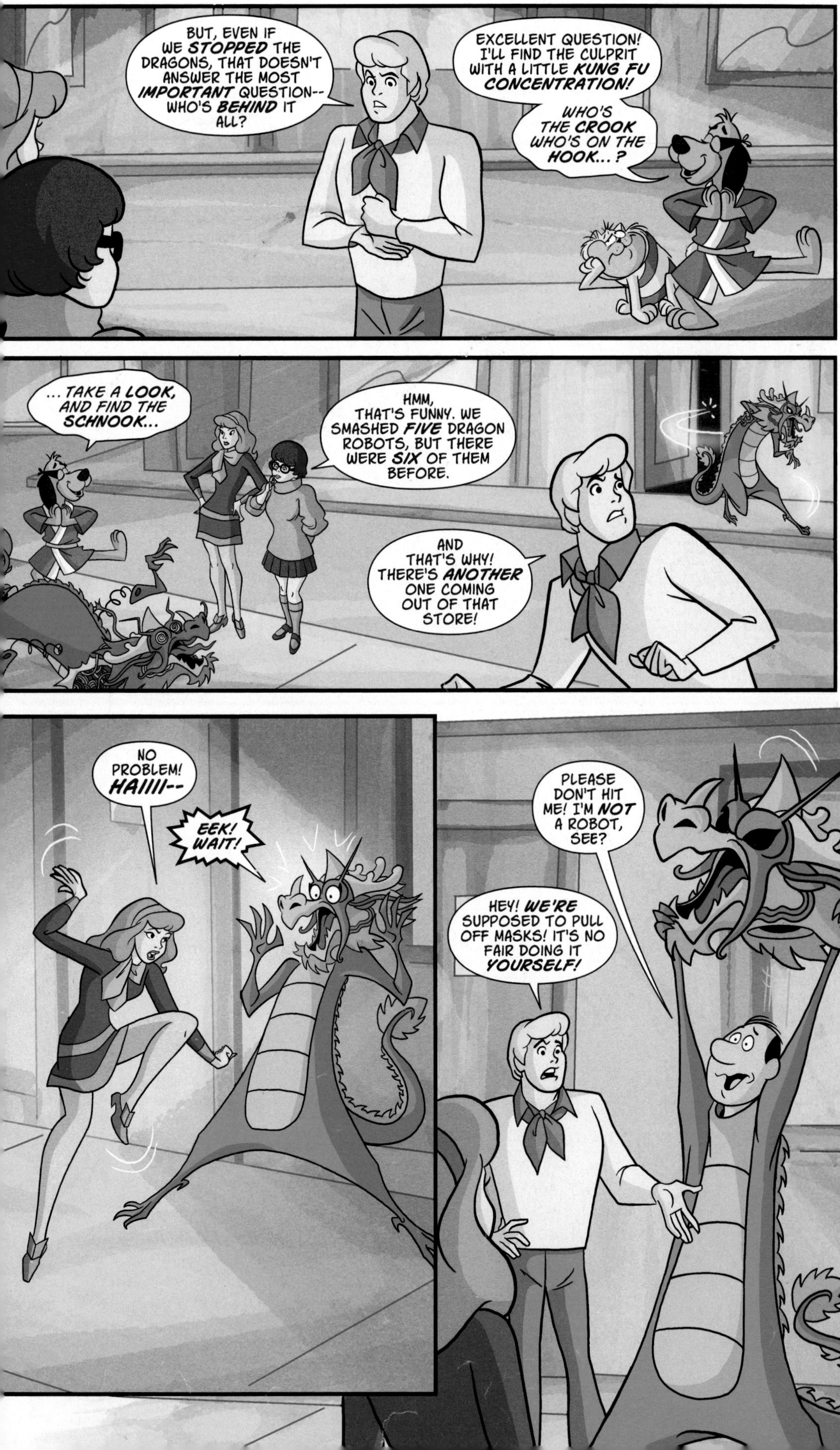

BUT, EVEN IF WE STOPPED THE DRAGONS, THAT DOESN'T ANSWER THE MOST IMPORTANT QUESTION-- WHO'S BEHIND IT ALL?
EXCELLENT QUESTION! I'LL FIND THE CULPRIT WITH A LITTLE KUNG FU CONCENTRATION!
WHO'S THE CROOK WHO'S ON THE HOOK...?
...TAKE A LOOK, AND FIND THE SCHNOOK...
HMM, THAT'S FUNNY. WE SMASHED FIVE DRAGON ROBOTS, BUT THERE WERE SIX OF THEM BEFORE.
AND THAT'S WHY! THERE'S ANOTHER ONE COMING OUT OF THAT STORE!
NO PROBLEM! HAIIII--
EEK! WAIT!
PLEASE DON'T HIT ME! I'M NOT A ROBOT, SEE?
HEY! WE'RE SUPPOSED TO PULL OFF MASKS! IT'S NO FAIR DOING IT YOURSELF!

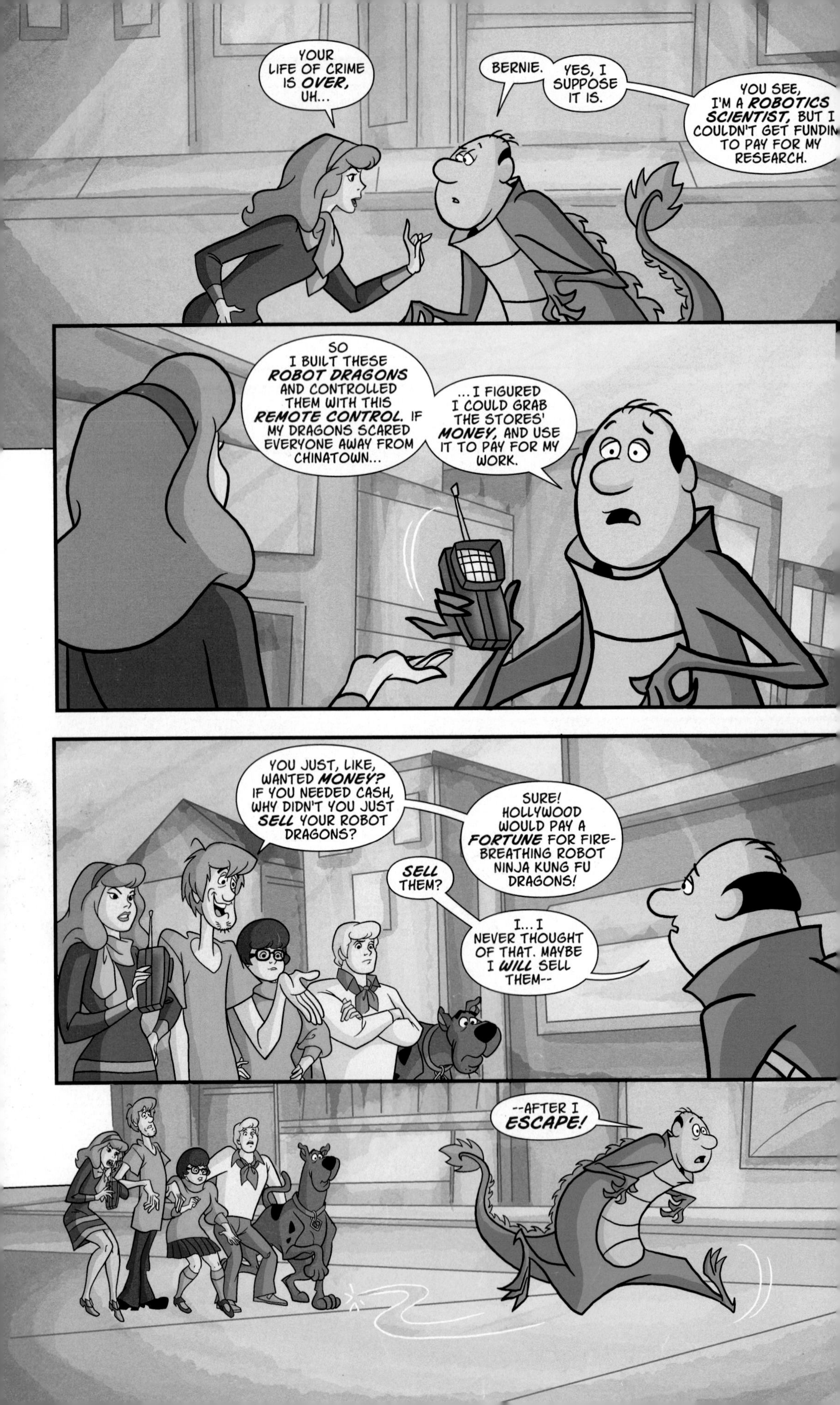

YOUR LIFE OF CRIME IS OVER, UH...
BERNIE.
YES, I SUPPOSE IT IS.
YOU SEE, I'M A ROBOTICS SCIENTIST, BUT I COULDN'T GET FUNDIN TO PAY FOR MY RESEARCH.
SO I BUILT THESE ROBOT DRAGONS AND CONTROLLED THEM WITH THIS REMOTE CONTROL. IF MY DRAGONS SCARED EVERYONE AWAY FROM CHINATOWN...
...I FIGURED I COULD GRAB THE STORES' MONEY, AND USE IT TO PAY FOR MY WORK.
YOU JUST, LIKE, WANTED MONEY? IF YOU NEEDED CASH, WHY DIDN'T YOU JUST SELL YOUR ROBOT DRAGONS?
SURE! HOLLYWOOD WOULD PAY A FORTUNE FOR FIRE-BREATHING ROBOT NINJA KUNG FU DRAGONS!
SELL THEM?
I... I NEVER THOUGHT OF THAT. MAYBE I WILL SELL THEM--
--AFTER I ESCAPE!

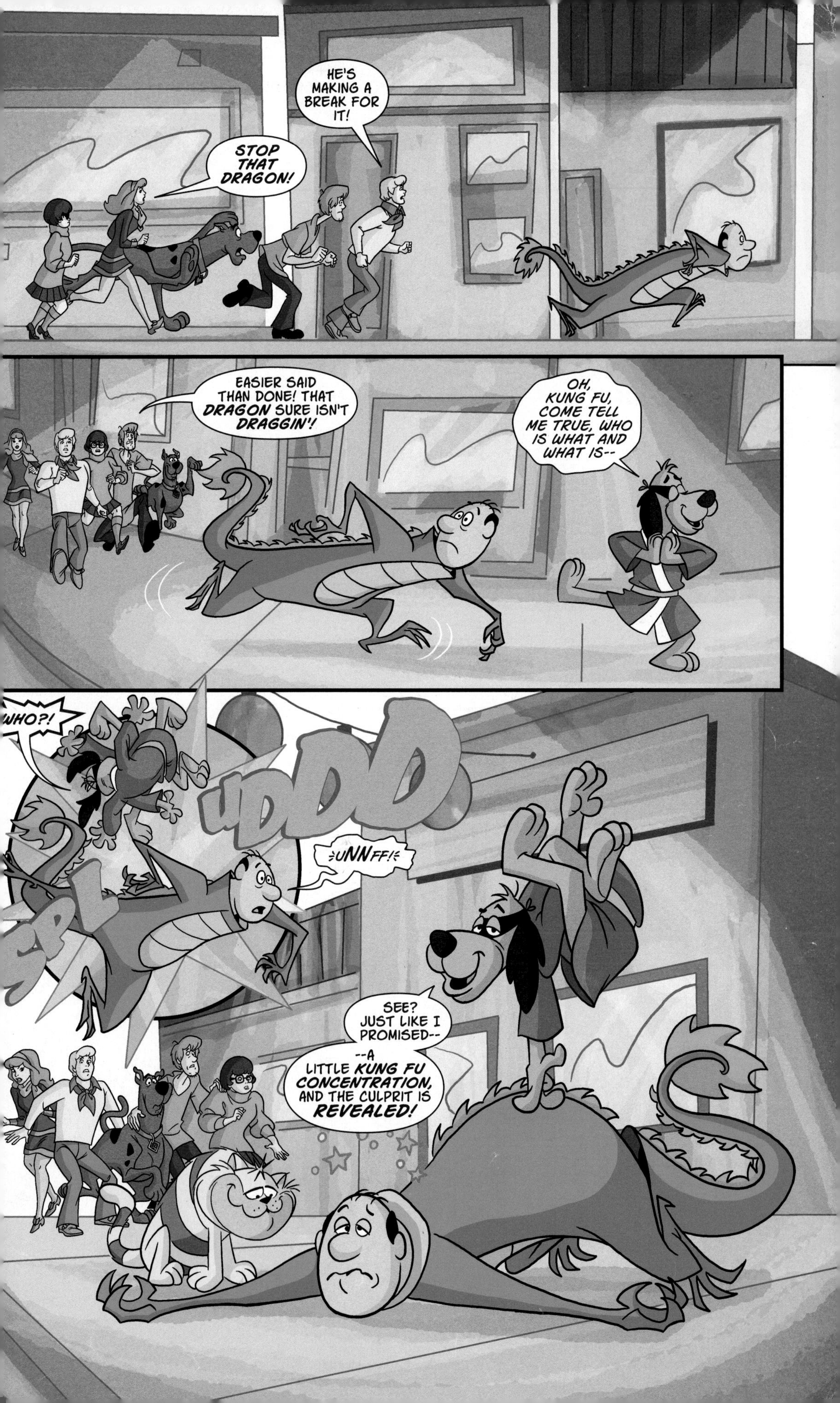

STOP THAT DRAGON!
HE'S MAKING A BREAK FOR IT!
EASIER SAID THAN DONE! THAT DRAGON SURE ISN'T DRAGGIN'!
OH, KUNG FU, COME TELL ME TRUE, WHO IS WHAT AND WHAT IS--
WHO?!
UDDD
SPL
UNNFF!
SEE? JUST LIKE I PROMISED--
--A LITTLE KUNG FU CONCENTRATION, AND THE CULPRIT IS REVEALED!

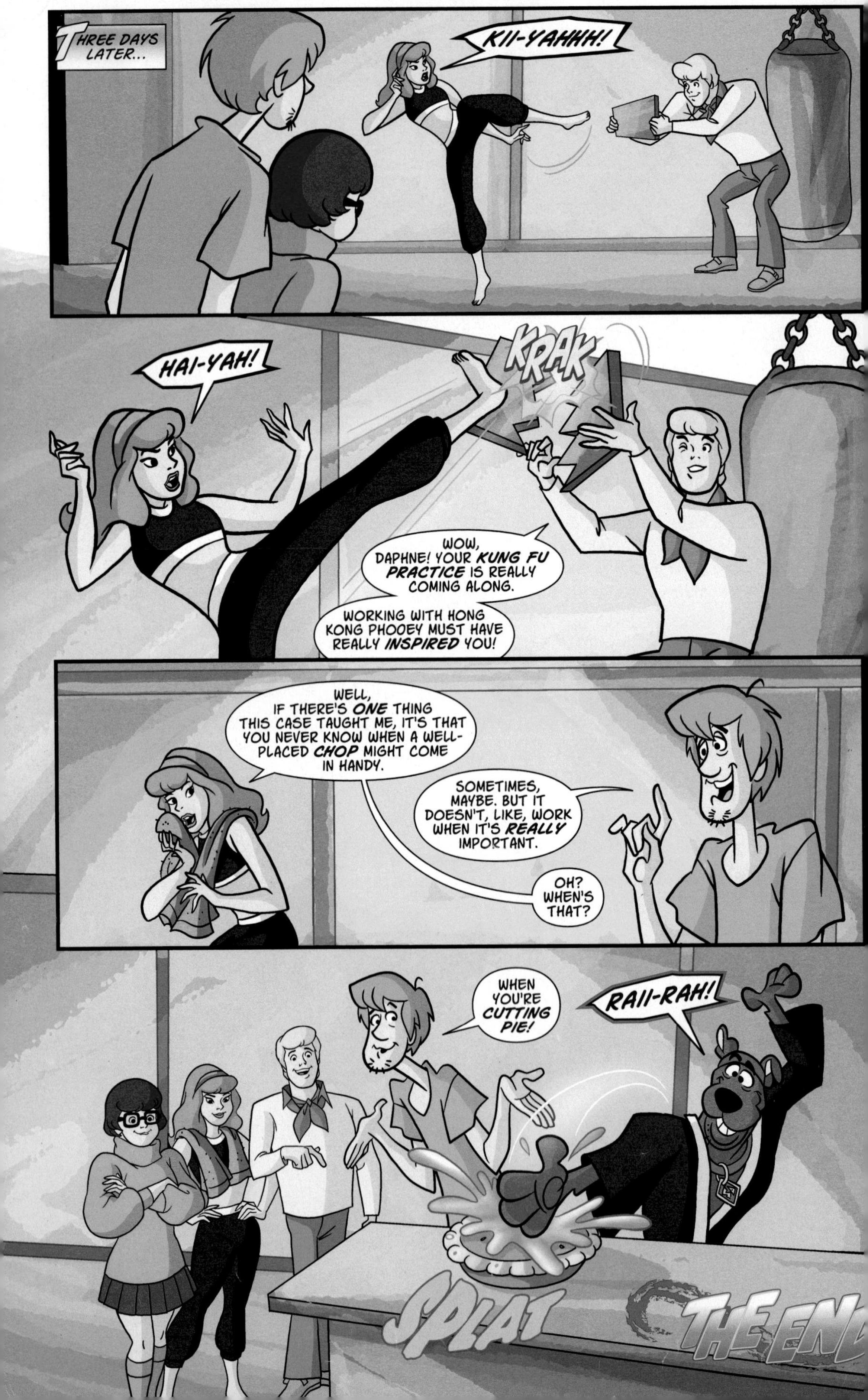
THREE DAYS LATER...
KII-YAHHH!
HAI-YAH!
KRAK
WOW, DAPHNE! YOUR KUNG FU PRACTICE IS REALLY COMING ALONG.
WORKING WITH HONG KONG PHOOEY MUST HAVE REALLY INSPIRED YOU!
WELL, IF THERE'S ONE THING THIS CASE TAUGHT ME, IT'S THAT YOU NEVER KNOW WHEN A WELL-PLACED CHOP MIGHT COME IN HANDY.
SOMETIMES, MAYBE. BUT IT DOESN'T, LIKE, WORK WHEN IT'S REALLY IMPORTANT.
OH? WHEN'S THAT?
WHEN YOU'RE CUTTING PIE!
RAII-RAH!
SPLAT
THE END

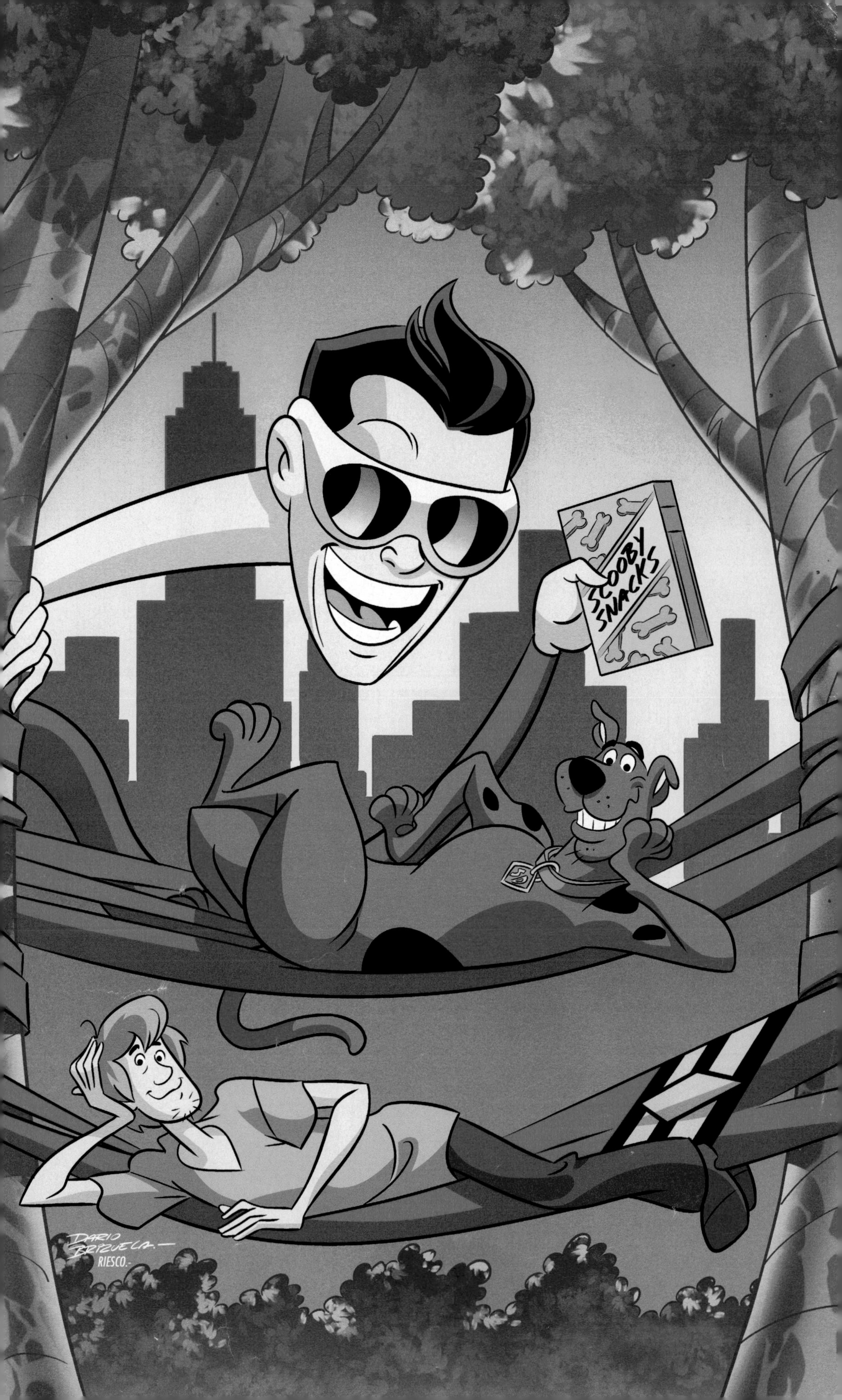
SCOOBY SNACKS
DARIO BRIZUELA
RIESCO.

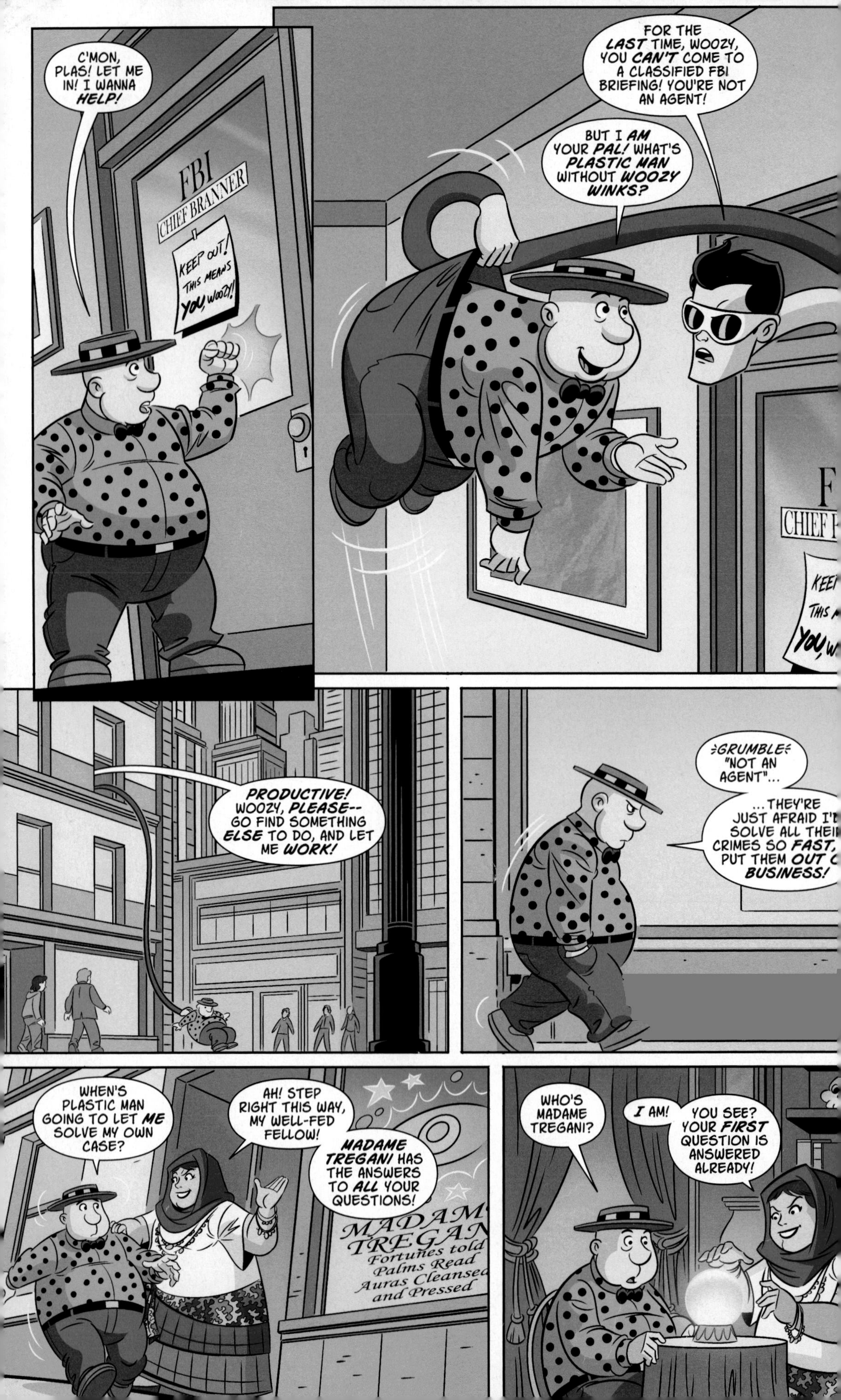
C'MON, PLAS! LET ME IN! I WANNA HELP!
FBI
CHIEF BRANNER
KEEP OUT! THIS MEANS YOU, WOOZY!
FOR THE LAST TIME, WOOZY, YOU CAN'T COME TO A CLASSIFIED FBI BRIEFING! YOU'RE NOT AN AGENT!
BUT I AM YOUR PAL! WHAT'S PLASTIC MAN WITHOUT WOOZY WINKS?
PRODUCTIVE! WOOZY, PLEASE-- GO FIND SOMETHING ELSE TO DO, AND LET ME WORK!
GRUMBLE "NOT AN AGENT"...
WHEN'S PLASTIC MAN GOING TO LET ME SOLVE MY OWN CASE?
AH! STEP RIGHT THIS WAY, MY WELL-FED FELLOW!
MADAME TREGANI HAS THE ANSWERS TO ALL YOUR QUESTIONS!
Fortunes told
Palms Read
and Pressed
WHO'S MADAME TREGANI?
I AM!
YOU SEE? YOUR FIRST QUESTION IS ANSWERED ALREADY!

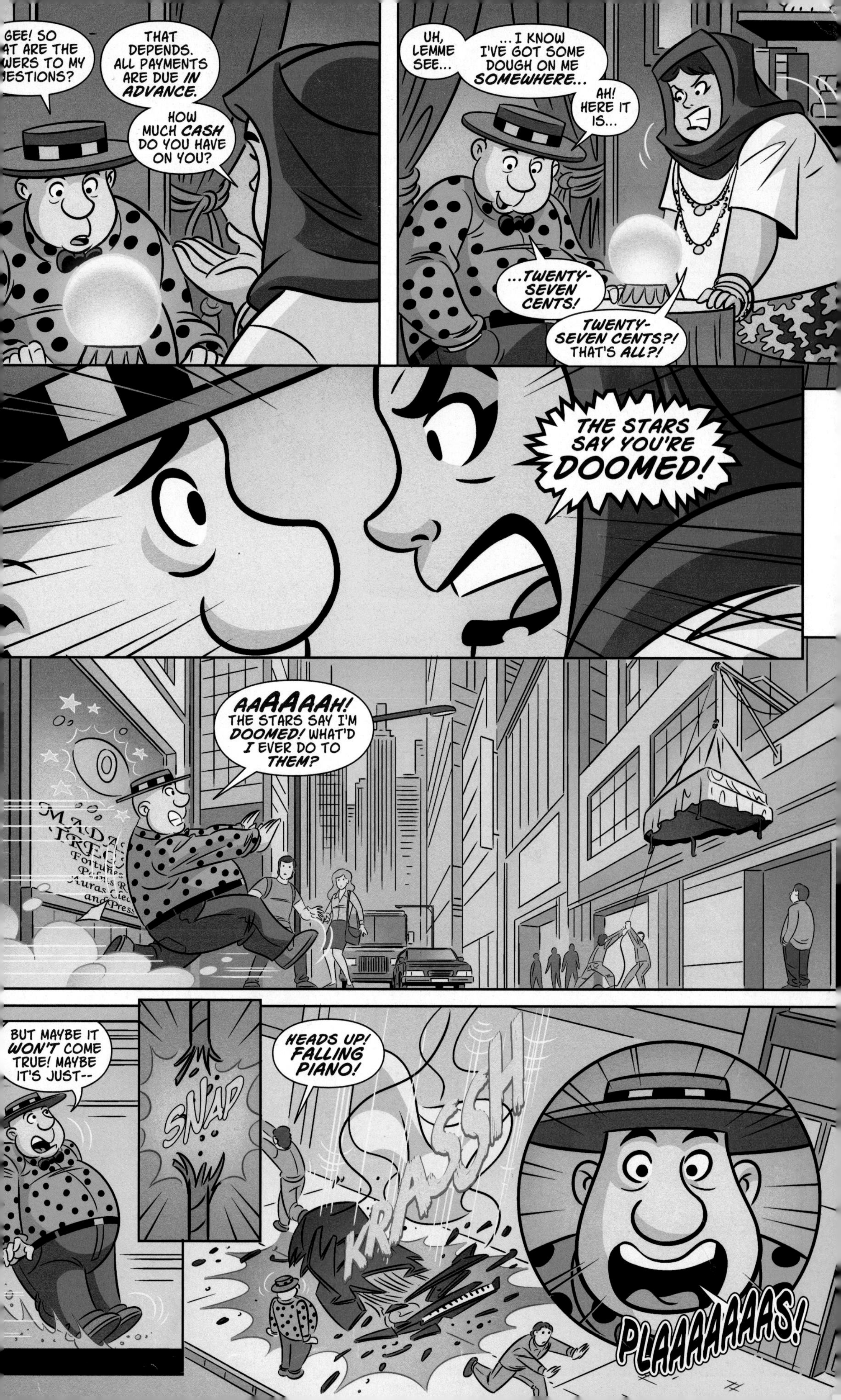

GEE! SO
AT ARE THE
WERS TO MY
ESTIONS?
THAT DEPENDS. ALL PAYMENTS ARE DUE *IN ADVANCE.*
HOW MUCH *CASH* DO YOU HAVE ON YOU?
UH, LEMME SEE...
...I KNOW I'VE GOT SOME DOUGH ON ME *SOMEWHERE...*
AH! HERE IT IS...
...TWENTY-SEVEN CENTS!
TWENTY-SEVEN CENTS?! THAT'S *ALL?!*
THE STARS SAY YOU'RE *DOOMED!*
AAAAAAH! THE STARS SAY I'M *DOOMED!* WHAT'D *I* EVER DO TO *THEM?*
BUT MAYBE IT *WON'T* COME TRUE! MAYBE IT'S JUST--
SNAP
HEADS UP! FALLING PIANO!
KRASSSH
PLAAAAAAAS!

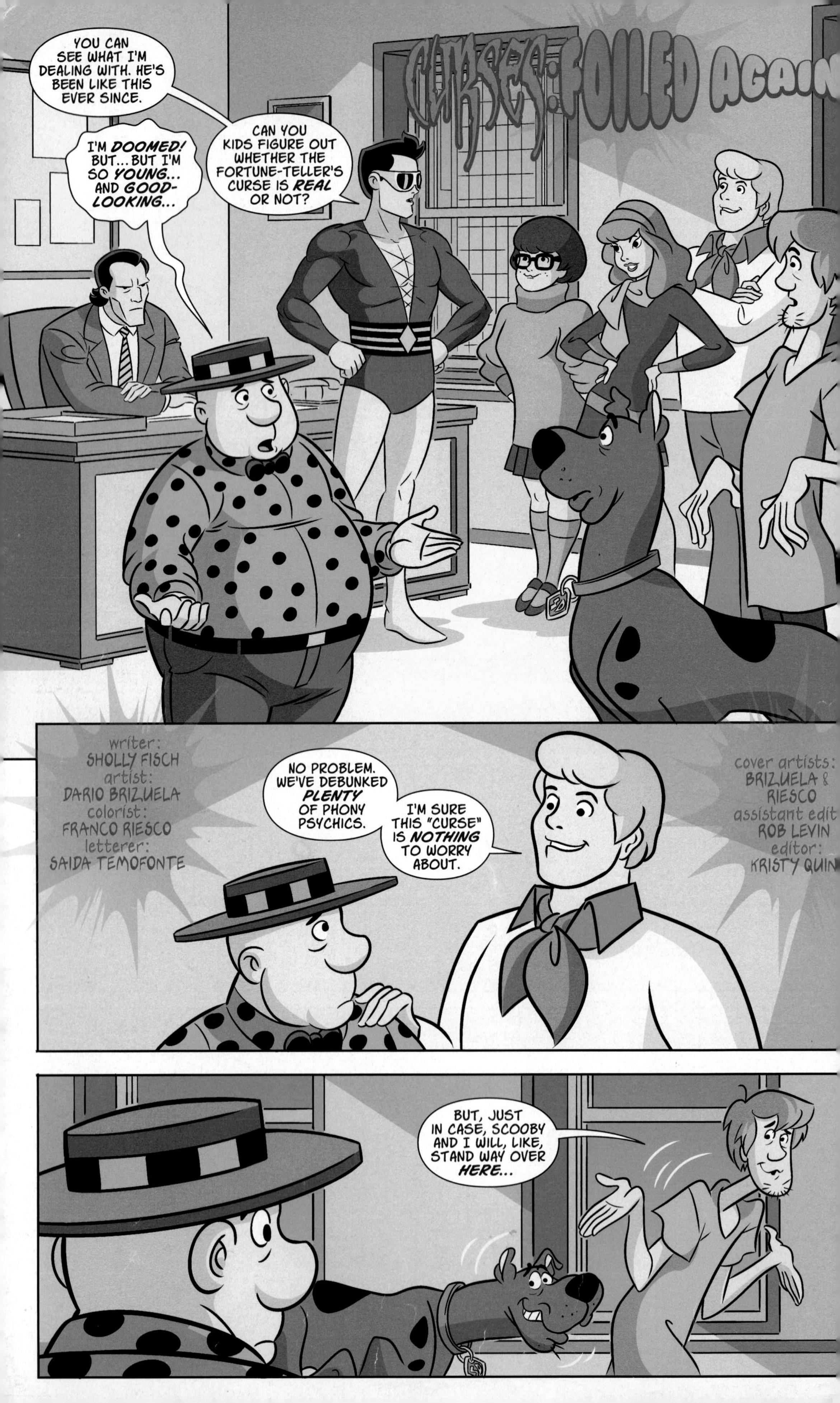

CURSES: FOILED AGAIN
YOU CAN SEE WHAT I'M DEALING WITH. HE'S BEEN LIKE THIS EVER SINCE.
I'M DOOMED! BUT... BUT I'M SO YOUNG... AND GOOD-LOOKING...
CAN YOU KIDS FIGURE OUT WHETHER THE FORTUNE-TELLER'S CURSE IS REAL OR NOT?
writer: SHOLLY FISCH
artist: DARIO BRIZUELA
colorist: FRANCO RIESCO
letterer: SAIDA TEMOFONTE
NO PROBLEM. WE'VE DEBUNKED PLENTY OF PHONY PSYCHICS.
I'M SURE THIS "CURSE" IS NOTHING TO WORRY ABOUT.
cover artists: BRIZUELA & RIESCO
assistant edit ROB LEVIN
editor: KRISTY QUIN
BUT, JUST IN CASE, SCOOBY AND I WILL, LIKE, STAND WAY OVER HERE...

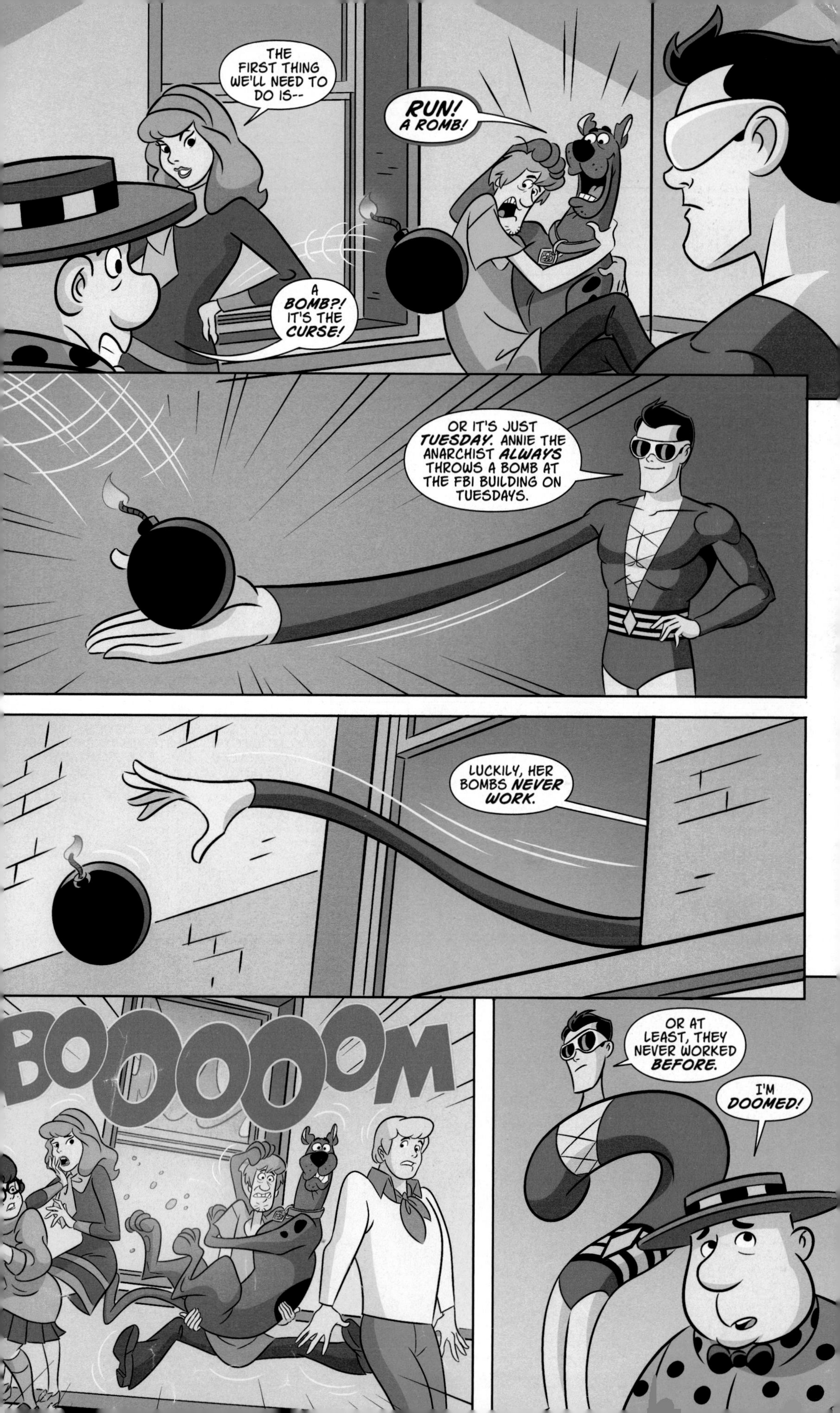

THE FIRST THING WE'LL NEED TO DO IS--
RUN! A ROMB!
A BOMB?! IT'S THE CURSE!
OR IT'S JUST TUESDAY. ANNIE THE ANARCHIST ALWAYS THROWS A BOMB AT THE FBI BUILDING ON TUESDAYS.
LUCKILY, HER BOMBS NEVER WORK.
BOOOOOM
OR AT LEAST, THEY NEVER WORKED BEFORE.
I'M DOOMED!

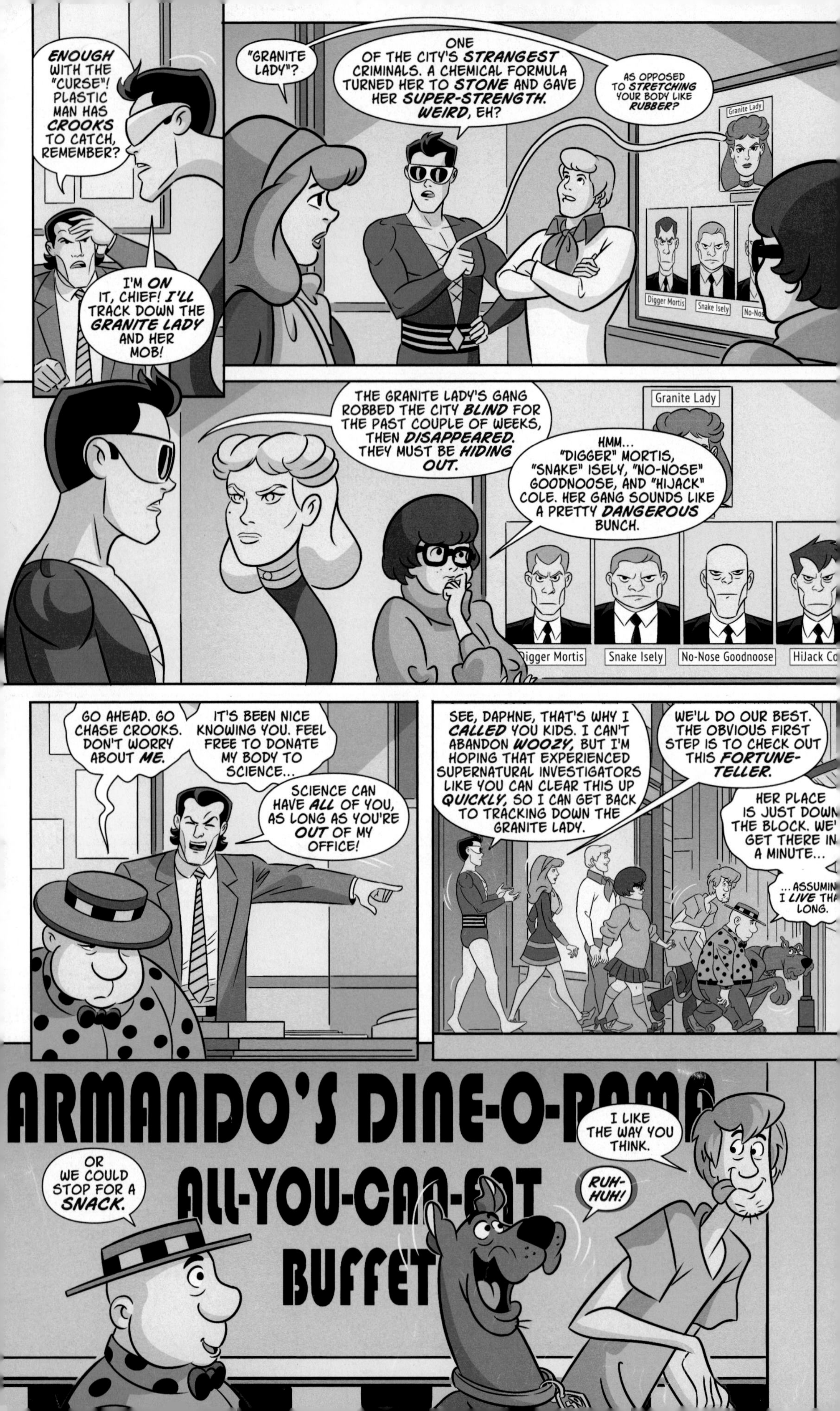
ENOUGH WITH THE "CURSE"! PLASTIC MAN HAS CROOKS TO CATCH, REMEMBER?
I'M ON IT, CHIEF! I'LL TRACK DOWN THE GRANITE LADY AND HER MOB!
"GRANITE LADY"?
ONE OF THE CITY'S STRANGEST CRIMINALS. A CHEMICAL FORMULA TURNED HER TO STONE AND GAVE HER SUPER-STRENGTH. WEIRD, EH?
AS OPPOSED TO STRETCHING YOUR BODY LIKE RUBBER?
Granite Lady
Digger Mortis
Snake Isely
THE GRANITE LADY'S GANG ROBBED THE CITY BLIND FOR THE PAST COUPLE OF WEEKS, THEN DISAPPEARED. THEY MUST BE HIDING OUT.
HMM... "DIGGER" MORTIS, "SNAKE" ISELY, "NO-NOSE" GOODNOOSE, AND "HIJACK" COLE. HER GANG SOUNDS LIKE A PRETTY DANGEROUS BUNCH.
Granite Lady
Snake Isely
No-Nose Goodnoose
GO AHEAD. GO CHASE CROOKS. DON'T WORRY ABOUT ME.
IT'S BEEN NICE KNOWING YOU. FEEL FREE TO DONATE MY BODY TO SCIENCE...
SCIENCE CAN HAVE ALL OF YOU, AS LONG AS YOU'RE OUT OF MY OFFICE!
SEE, DAPHNE, THAT'S WHY I CALLED YOU KIDS. I CAN'T ABANDON WOOZY, BUT I'M HOPING THAT EXPERIENCED SUPERNATURAL INVESTIGATORS LIKE YOU CAN CLEAR THIS UP QUICKLY, SO I CAN GET BACK TO TRACKING DOWN THE GRANITE LADY.
WE'LL DO OUR BEST. THE OBVIOUS FIRST STEP IS TO CHECK OUT THIS FORTUNE-TELLER.
BUFFET
OR WE COULD STOP FOR A SNACK.
I LIKE THE WAY YOU THINK.
RUH-HUH!

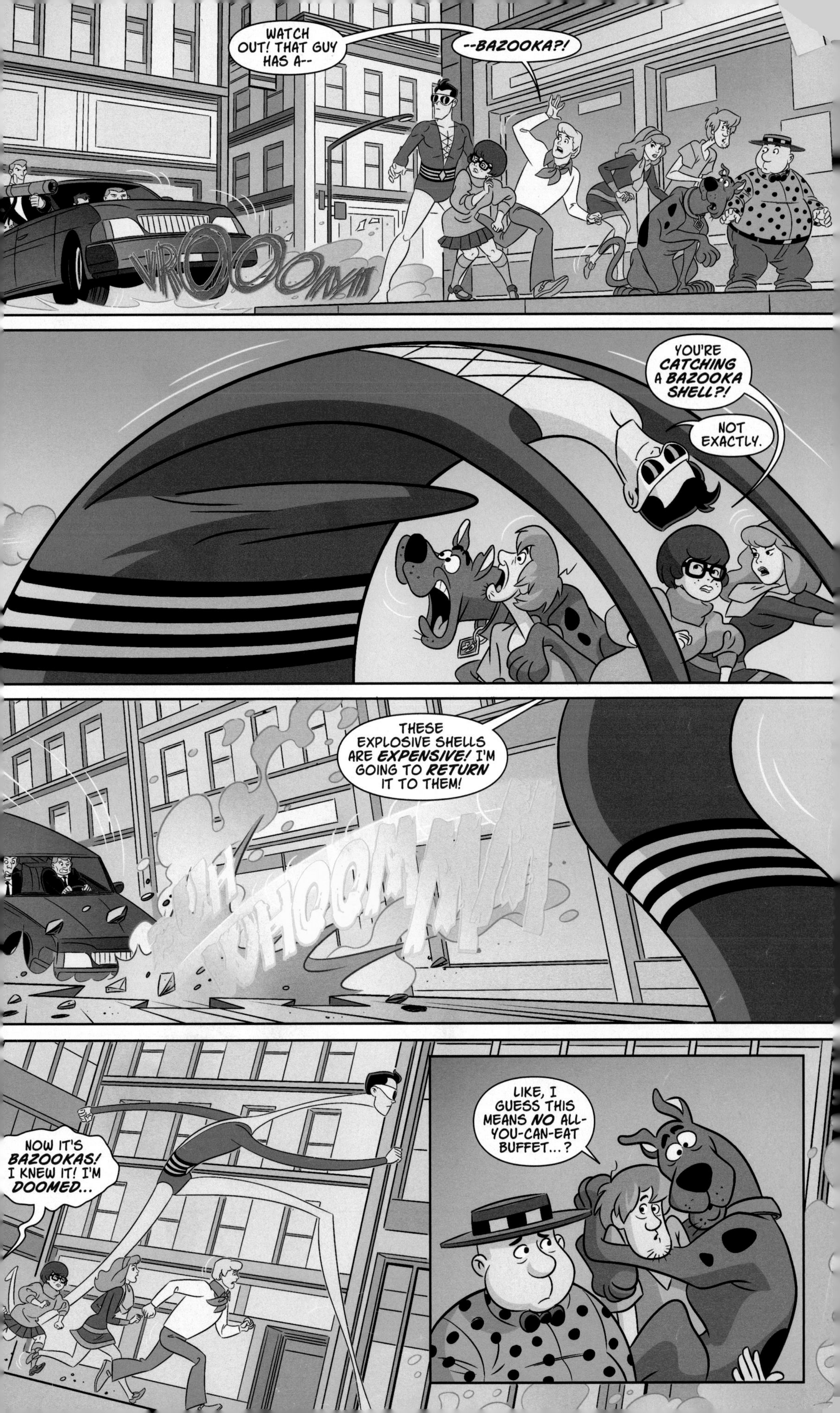
WATCH OUT! THAT GUY HAS A--
--BAZOOKA?!
VROOOOM!!!
YOU'RE CATCHING A BAZOOKA SHELL?!
NOT EXACTLY.
THESE EXPLOSIVE SHELLS ARE EXPENSIVE! I'M GOING TO RETURN IT TO THEM!
NOW IT'S BAZOOKAS! I KNEW IT! I'M DOOMED...
LIKE, I GUESS THIS MEANS NO ALL-YOU-CAN-EAT BUFFET...?

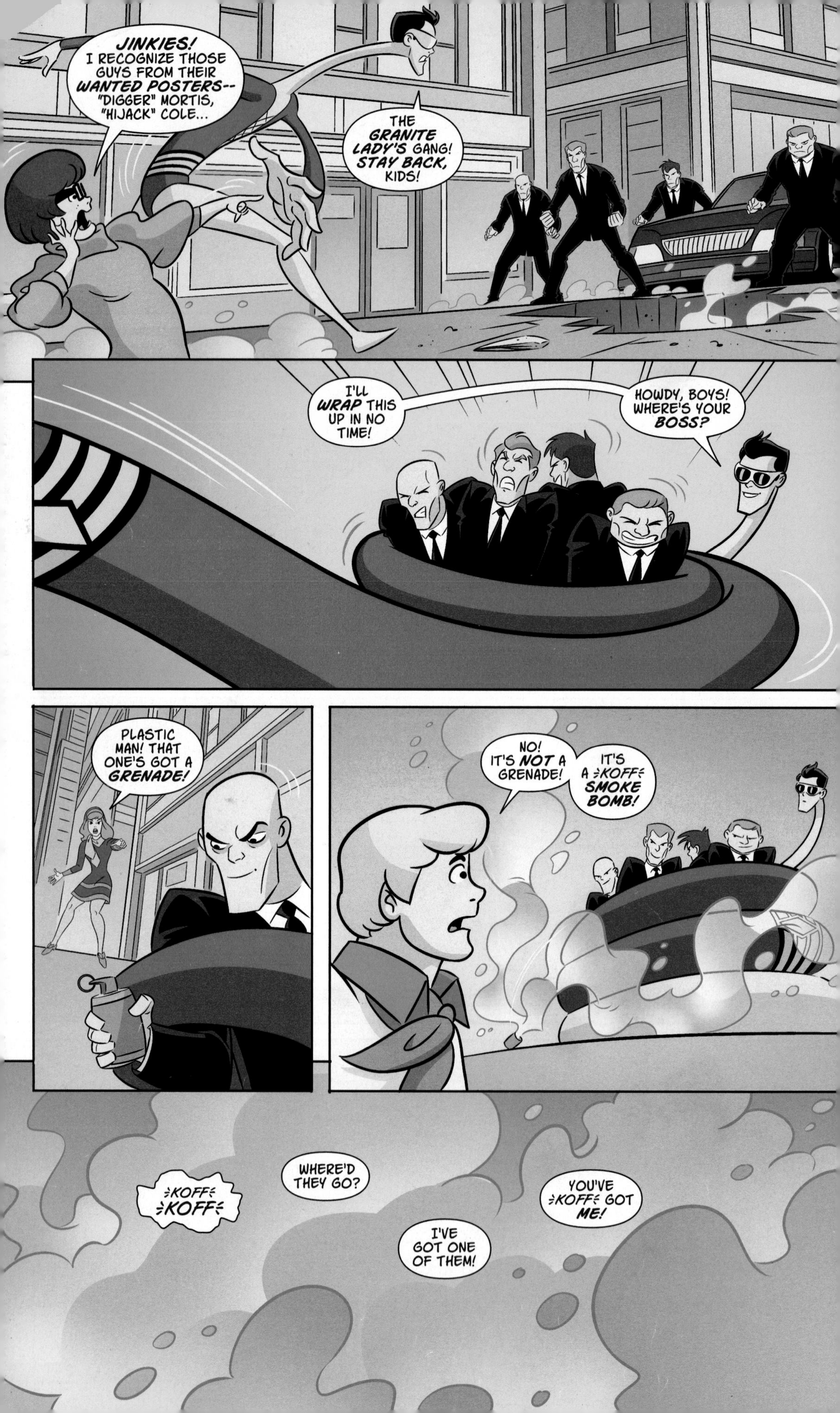

JINKIES! I RECOGNIZE THOSE GUYS FROM THEIR WANTED POSTERS-- "DIGGER" MORTIS, "HIJACK" COLE...
THE GRANITE LADY'S GANG! STAY BACK, KIDS!
I'LL WRAP THIS UP IN NO TIME!
HOWDY, BOYS! WHERE'S YOUR BOSS?
PLASTIC MAN! THAT ONE'S GOT A GRENADE!
NO! IT'S NOT A GRENADE!
IT'S A ⁅KOFF⁆ SMOKE BOMB!
⁅KOFF⁆ ⁅KOFF⁆
WHERE'D THEY GO?
I'VE GOT ONE OF THEM!
YOU'VE ⁅KOFF⁆ GOT ME!

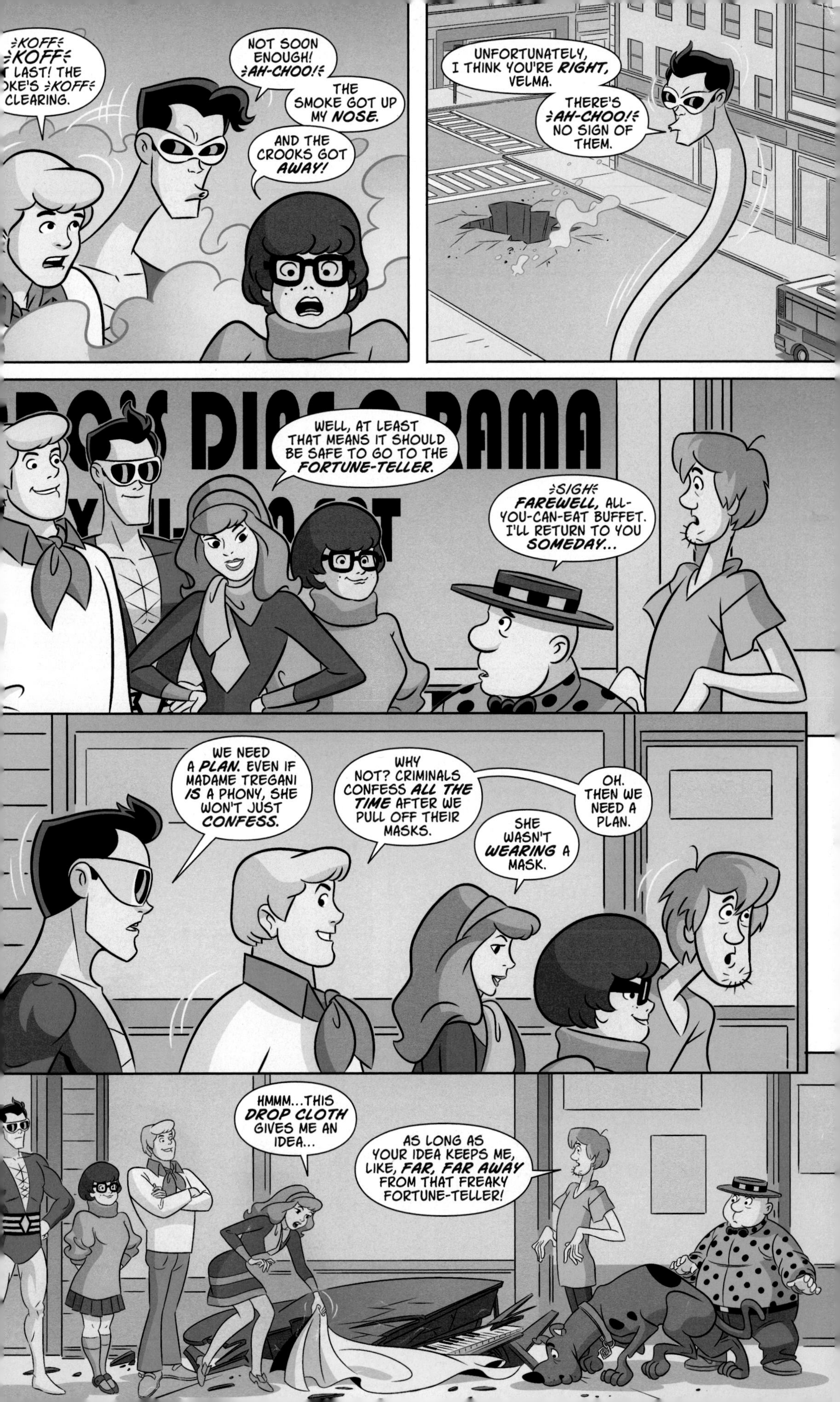

≷KOFF≶ ≷KOFF≶ T LAST! THE OKE'S ≷KOFF≶ CLEARING.
NOT SOON ENOUGH! ≷AH-CHOO!≶
THE SMOKE GOT UP MY NOSE.
AND THE CROOKS GOT AWAY!
UNFORTUNATELY, I THINK YOU'RE RIGHT, VELMA.
THERE'S ≷AH-CHOO!≶ NO SIGN OF THEM.
WELL, AT LEAST THAT MEANS IT SHOULD BE SAFE TO GO TO THE FORTUNE-TELLER.
≷SIGH≶ FAREWELL, ALL-YOU-CAN-EAT BUFFET. I'LL RETURN TO YOU SOMEDAY...
WE NEED A PLAN. EVEN IF MADAME TREGANI IS A PHONY, SHE WON'T JUST CONFESS.
WHY NOT? CRIMINALS CONFESS ALL THE TIME AFTER WE PULL OFF THEIR MASKS.
SHE WASN'T WEARING A MASK.
OH. THEN WE NEED A PLAN.
HMMM...THIS DROP CLOTH GIVES ME AN IDEA...
AS LONG AS YOUR IDEA KEEPS ME, LIKE, FAR, FAR AWAY FROM THAT FREAKY FORTUNE-TELLER!

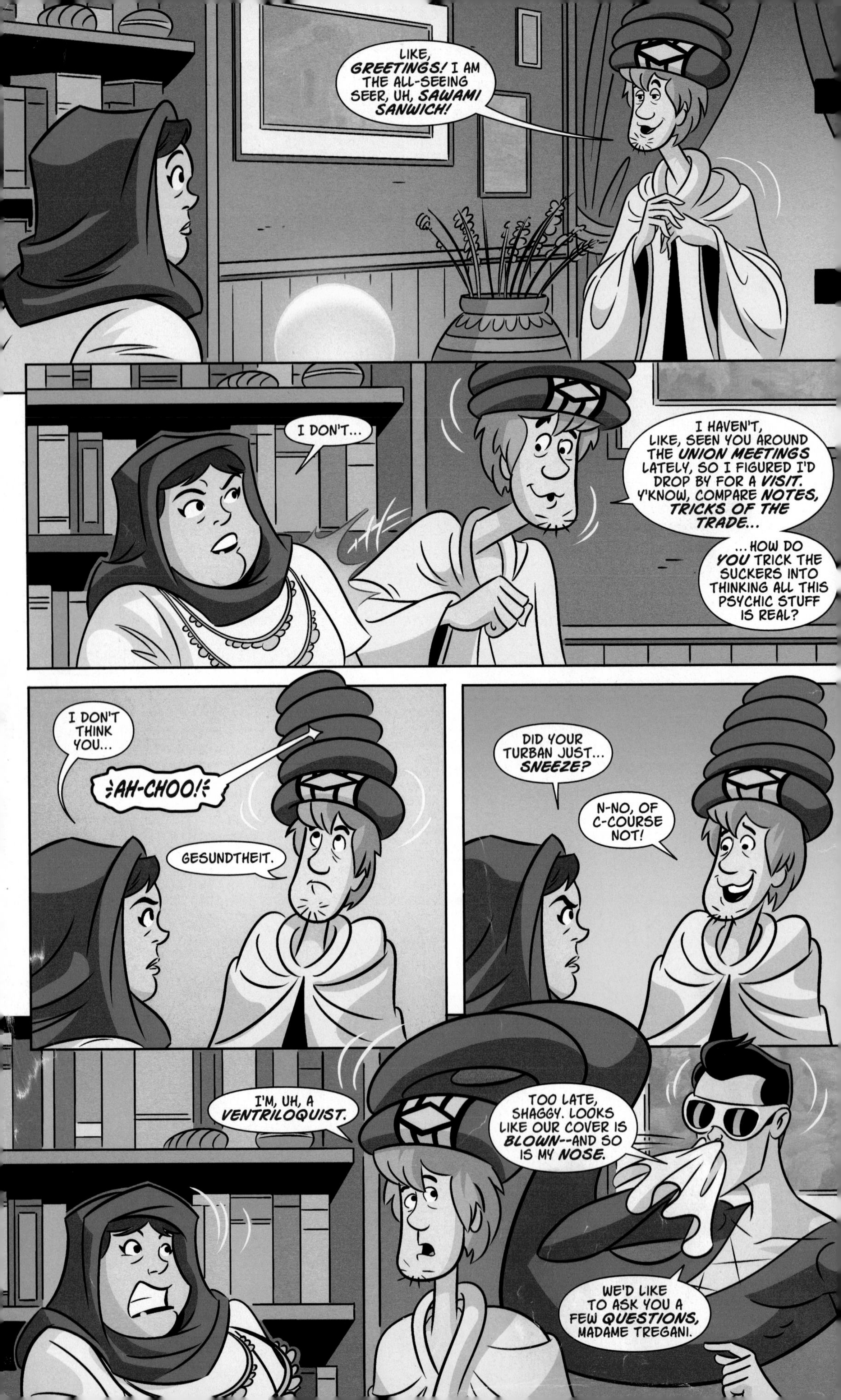
LIKE, GREETINGS! I AM THE ALL-SEEING SEER, UH, SAWAMI SANWICH!
I DON'T...
I HAVEN'T, LIKE, SEEN YOU AROUND THE UNION MEETINGS LATELY, SO I FIGURED I'D DROP BY FOR A VISIT. Y'KNOW, COMPARE NOTES, TRICKS OF THE TRADE...
...HOW DO YOU TRICK THE SUCKERS INTO THINKING ALL THIS PSYCHIC STUFF IS REAL?
I DON'T THINK YOU...
AH-CHOO!
GESUNDTHEIT.
DID YOUR TURBAN JUST... SNEEZE?
N-NO, OF C-COURSE NOT!
I'M, UH, A VENTRILOQUIST.
TOO LATE, SHAGGY. LOOKS LIKE OUR COVER IS BLOWN--AND SO IS MY NOSE.
WE'D LIKE TO ASK YOU A FEW QUESTIONS, MADAME TREGANI.

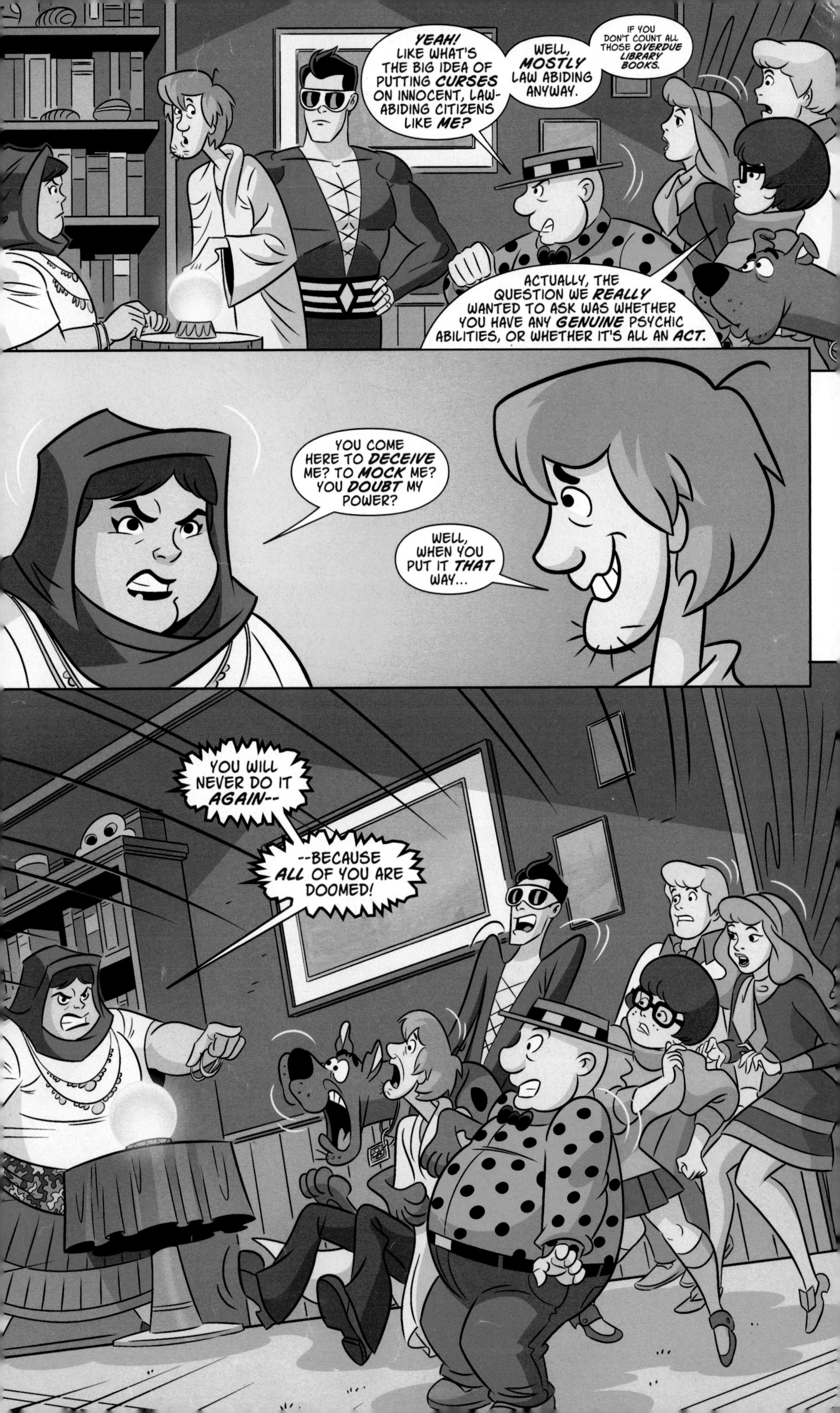
YEAH! LIKE WHAT'S THE BIG IDEA OF PUTTING CURSES ON INNOCENT, LAW-ABIDING CITIZENS LIKE ME?
WELL, MOSTLY LAW ABIDING ANYWAY.
IF YOU DON'T COUNT ALL THOSE OVERDUE LIBRARY BOOKS.
ACTUALLY, THE QUESTION WE REALLY WANTED TO ASK WAS WHETHER YOU HAVE ANY GENUINE PSYCHIC ABILITIES, OR WHETHER IT'S ALL AN ACT.
YOU COME HERE TO DECEIVE ME? TO MOCK ME? YOU DOUBT MY POWER?
WELL, WHEN YOU PUT IT THAT WAY...
YOU WILL NEVER DO IT AGAIN--
--BECAUSE ALL OF YOU ARE DOOMED!

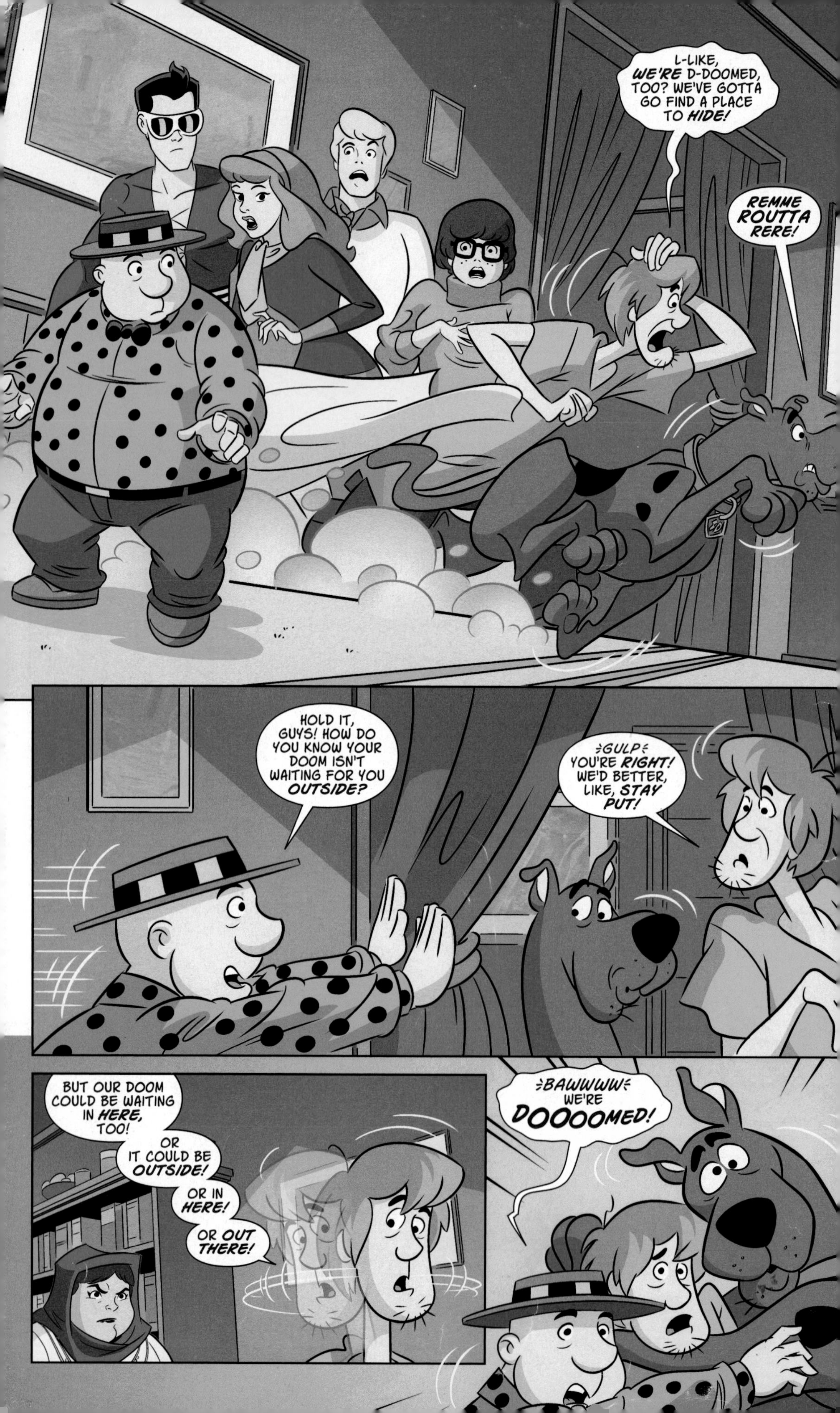
L-LIKE, WE'RE D-DOOMED, TOO? WE'VE GOTTA GO FIND A PLACE TO HIDE!
REMME ROUTTA RERE!
HOLD IT, GUYS! HOW DO YOU KNOW YOUR DOOM ISN'T WAITING FOR YOU OUTSIDE?
GULP YOU'RE RIGHT! WE'D BETTER, LIKE, STAY PUT!
BUT OUR DOOM COULD BE WAITING IN HERE, TOO!
OR IT COULD BE OUTSIDE!
OR IN HERE!
OR OUT THERE!
BAWWWW WE'RE DOOOOMED!

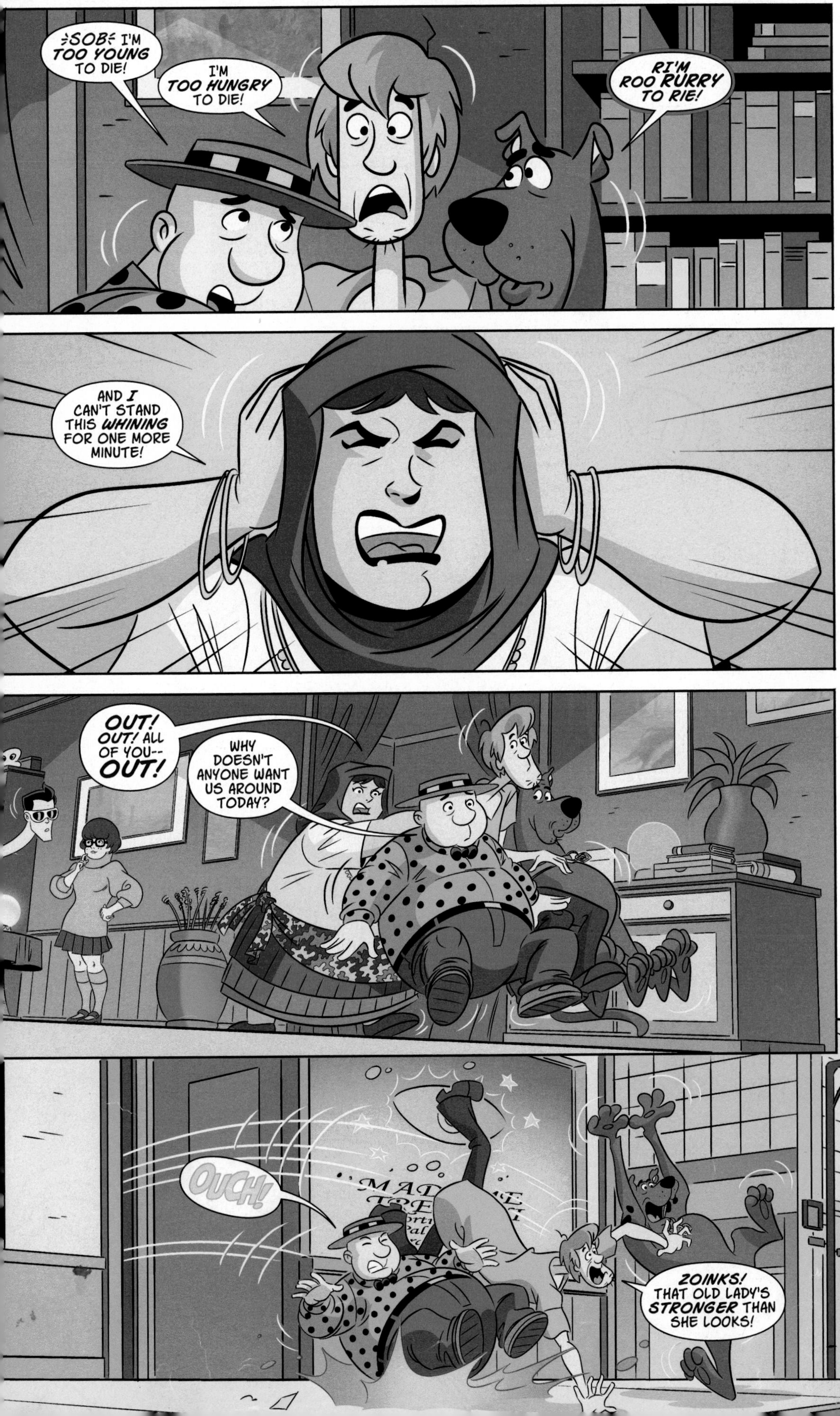
SOB I'M TOO YOUNG TO DIE!
I'M TOO HUNGRY TO DIE!
RI'M ROO RURRY TO RIE!
AND I CAN'T STAND THIS WHINING FOR ONE MORE MINUTE!
OUT! OUT! ALL OF YOU-- OUT!
WHY DOESN'T ANYONE WANT US AROUND TODAY?
OUCH!
ZOINKS! THAT OLD LADY'S STRONGER THAN SHE LOOKS!

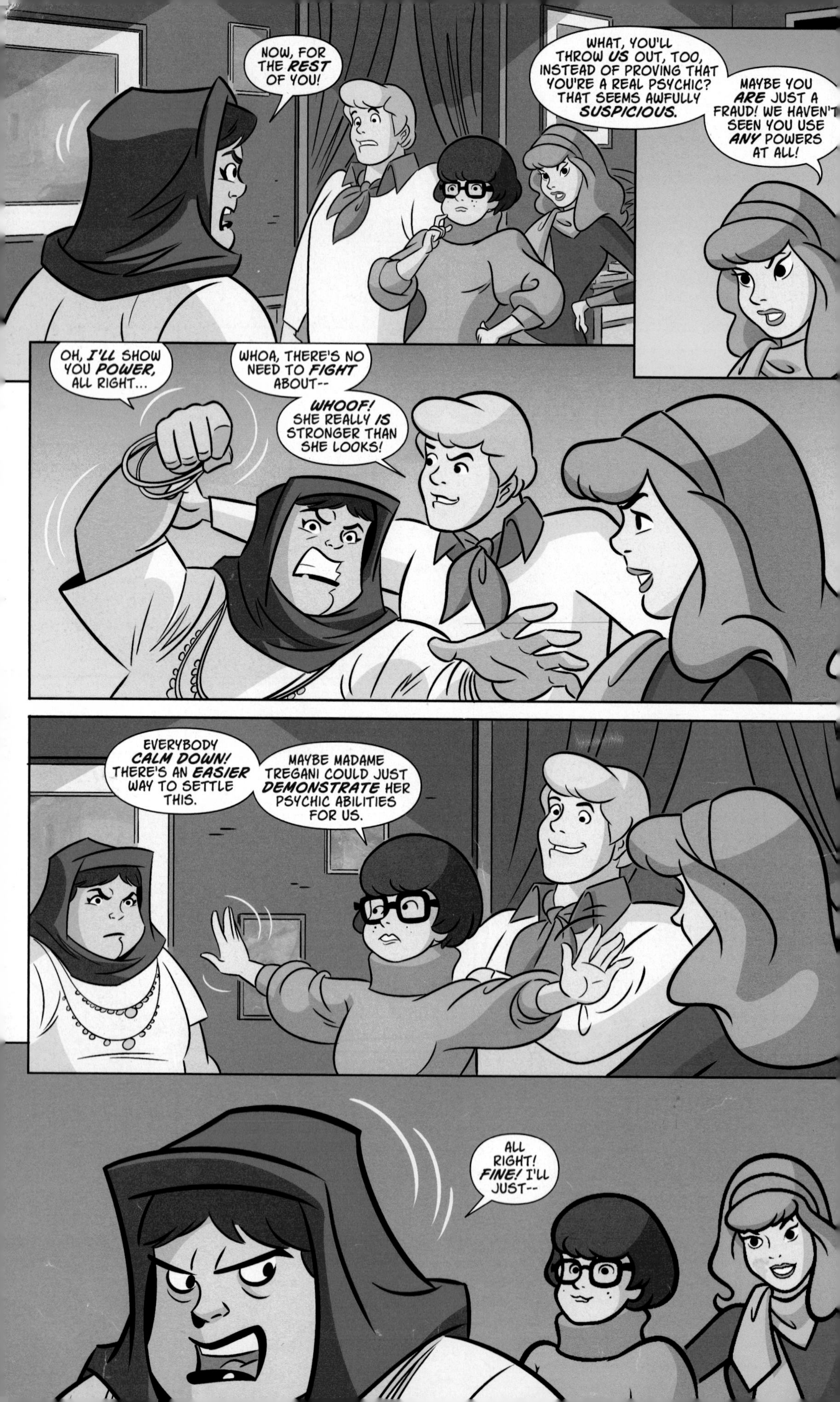
NOW, FOR THE REST OF YOU!
WHAT, YOU'LL THROW US OUT, TOO, INSTEAD OF PROVING THAT YOU'RE A REAL PSYCHIC? THAT SEEMS AWFULLY SUSPICIOUS.
MAYBE YOU ARE JUST A FRAUD! WE HAVEN'T SEEN YOU USE ANY POWERS AT ALL!
OH, I'LL SHOW YOU POWER, ALL RIGHT...
WHOA, THERE'S NO NEED TO FIGHT ABOUT--
WHOOF! SHE REALLY IS STRONGER THAN SHE LOOKS!
EVERYBODY CALM DOWN! THERE'S AN EASIER WAY TO SETTLE THIS.
MAYBE MADAME TREGANI COULD JUST DEMONSTRATE HER PSYCHIC ABILITIES FOR US.
ALL RIGHT! FINE! I'LL JUST--

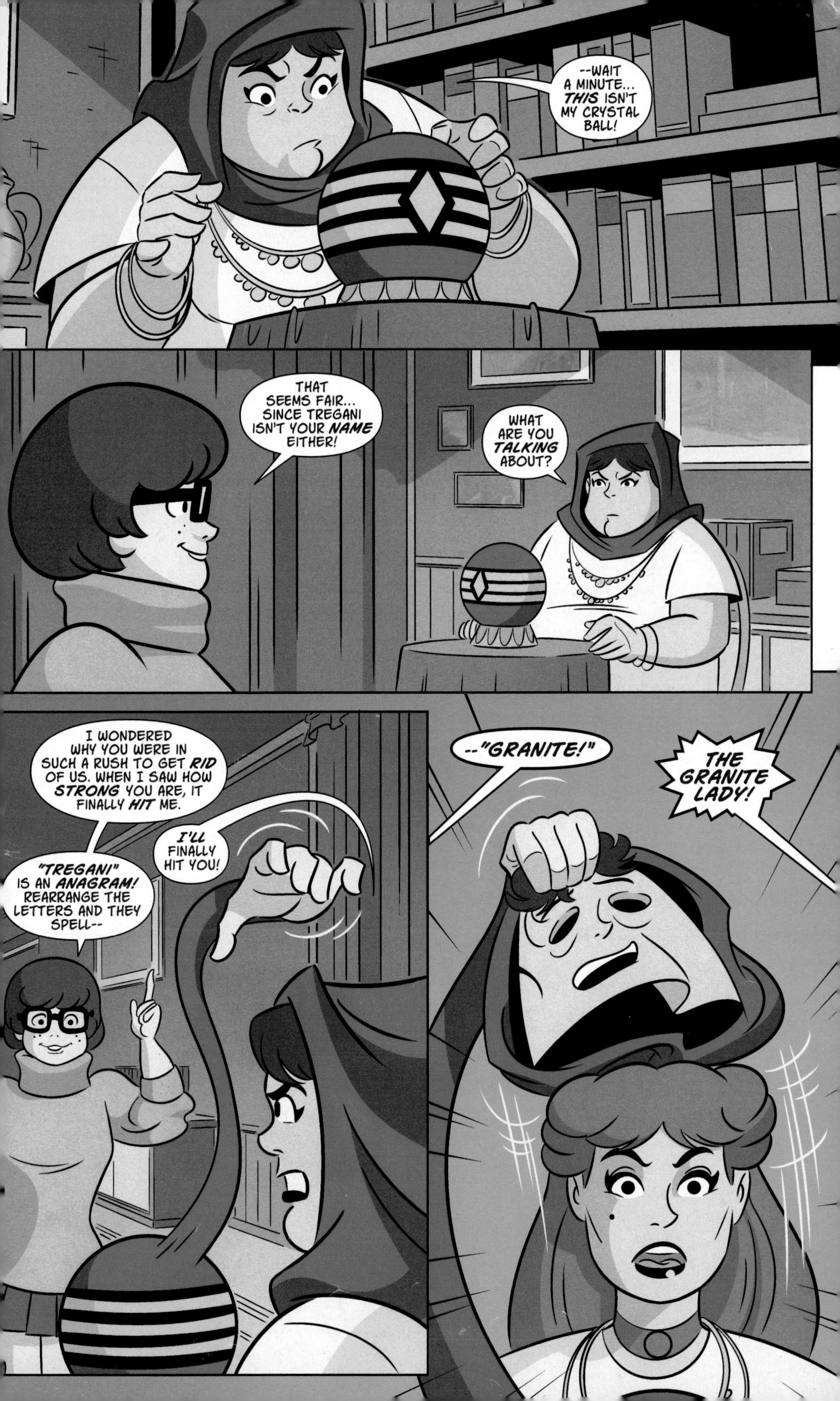
--WAIT A MINUTE... THIS ISN'T MY CRYSTAL BALL!
THAT SEEMS FAIR... SINCE TREGANI ISN'T YOUR NAME EITHER!
WHAT ARE YOU TALKING ABOUT?
I WONDERED WHY YOU WERE IN SUCH A RUSH TO GET RID OF US. WHEN I SAW HOW STRONG YOU ARE, IT FINALLY HIT ME.
"TREGANI" IS AN ANAGRAM! REARRANGE THE LETTERS AND THEY SPELL--
I'LL FINALLY HIT YOU!
--"GRANITE!"
THE GRANITE LADY!

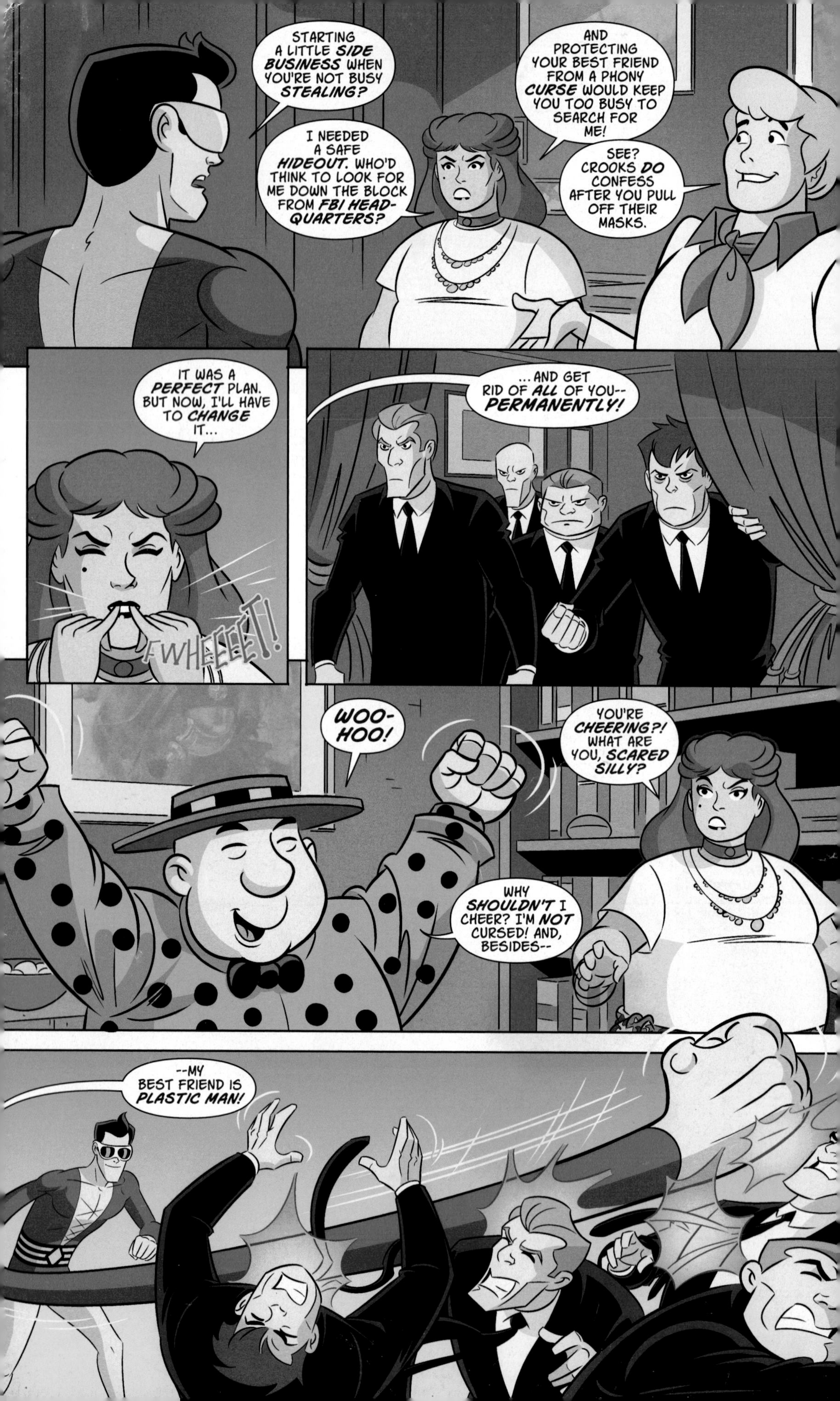
STARTING A LITTLE SIDE BUSINESS WHEN YOU'RE NOT BUSY STEALING?
I NEEDED A SAFE HIDEOUT. WHO'D THINK TO LOOK FOR ME DOWN THE BLOCK FROM FBI HEAD-QUARTERS?
AND PROTECTING YOUR BEST FRIEND FROM A PHONY CURSE WOULD KEEP YOU TOO BUSY TO SEARCH FOR ME!
SEE? CROOKS DO CONFESS AFTER YOU PULL OFF THEIR MASKS.
IT WAS A PERFECT PLAN. BUT NOW, I'LL HAVE TO CHANGE IT...
FWHEEEET!
...AND GET RID OF ALL OF YOU-- PERMANENTLY!
WOO-HOO!
YOU'RE CHEERING?! WHAT ARE YOU, SCARED SILLY?
WHY SHOULDN'T I CHEER? I'M NOT CURSED! AND, BESIDES--
--MY BEST FRIEND IS PLASTIC MAN!

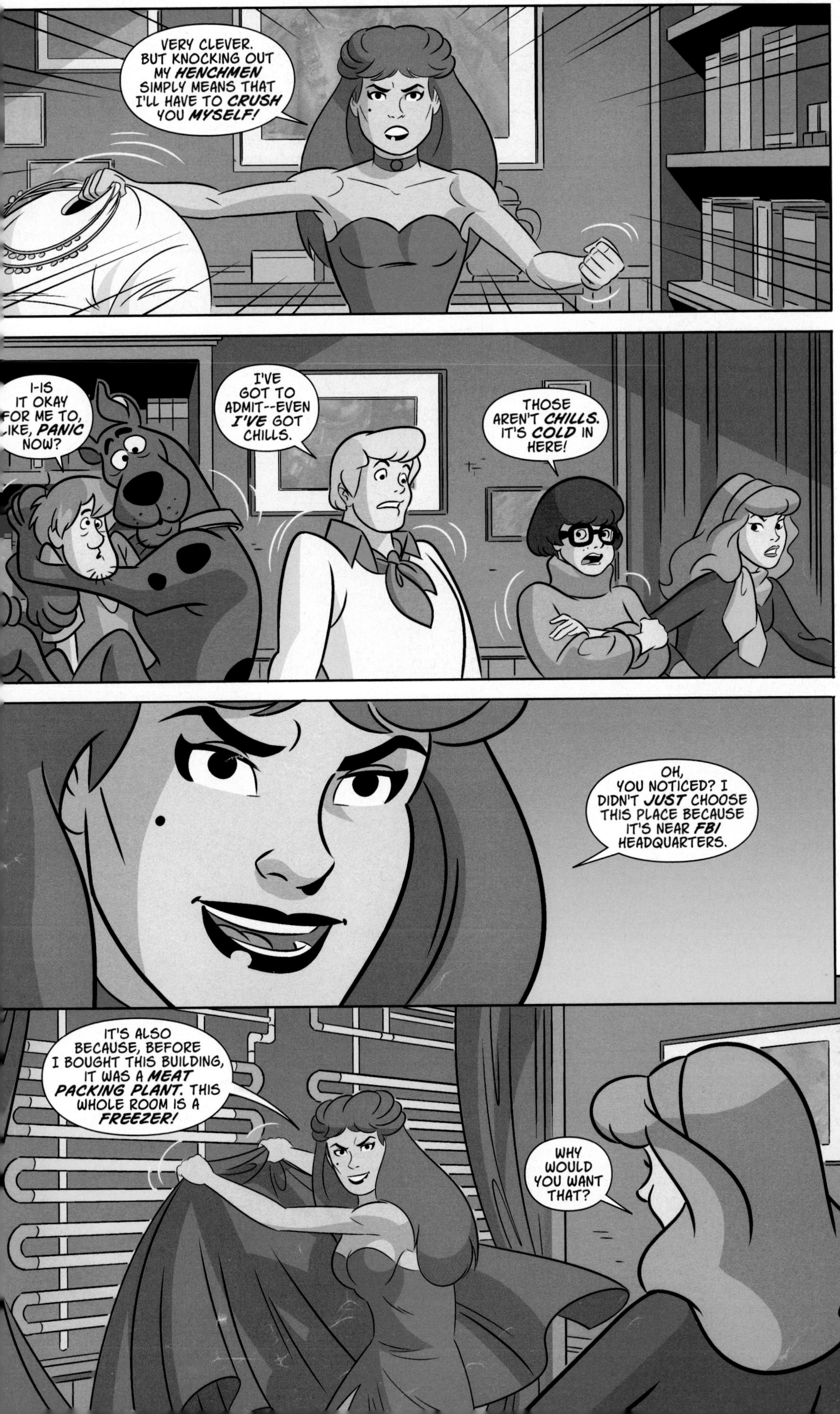
VERY CLEVER. BUT KNOCKING OUT MY HENCHMEN SIMPLY MEANS THAT I'LL HAVE TO CRUSH YOU MYSELF!
I-IS IT OKAY FOR ME TO, LIKE, PANIC NOW?
I'VE GOT TO ADMIT--EVEN I'VE GOT CHILLS.
THOSE AREN'T CHILLS. IT'S COLD IN HERE!
OH, YOU NOTICED? I DIDN'T JUST CHOOSE THIS PLACE BECAUSE IT'S NEAR FBI HEADQUARTERS.
IT'S ALSO BECAUSE, BEFORE I BOUGHT THIS BUILDING, IT WAS A MEAT PACKING PLANT. THIS WHOLE ROOM IS A FREEZER!
WHY WOULD YOU WANT THAT?

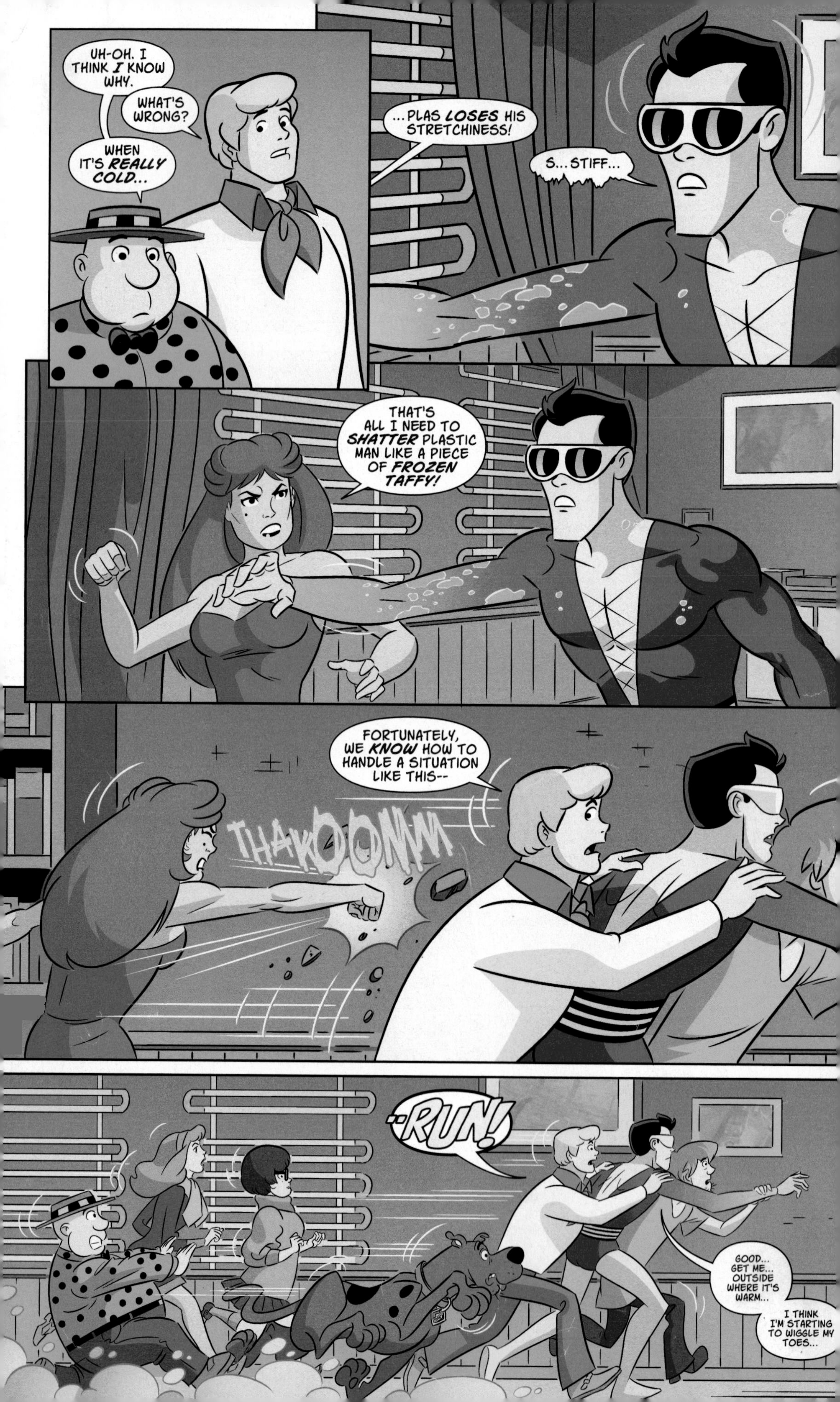

UH-OH. I THINK I KNOW WHY.
WHAT'S WRONG?
WHEN IT'S REALLY COLD...
...PLAS LOSES HIS STRETCHINESS!
S... STIFF...
THAT'S ALL I NEED TO SHATTER PLASTIC MAN LIKE A PIECE OF FROZEN TAFFY!
FORTUNATELY, WE KNOW HOW TO HANDLE A SITUATION LIKE THIS--
THAKOOMM
--RUN!
GOOD... GET ME... OUTSIDE WHERE IT'S WARM...
I THINK I'M STARTING TO WIGGLE MY TOES...

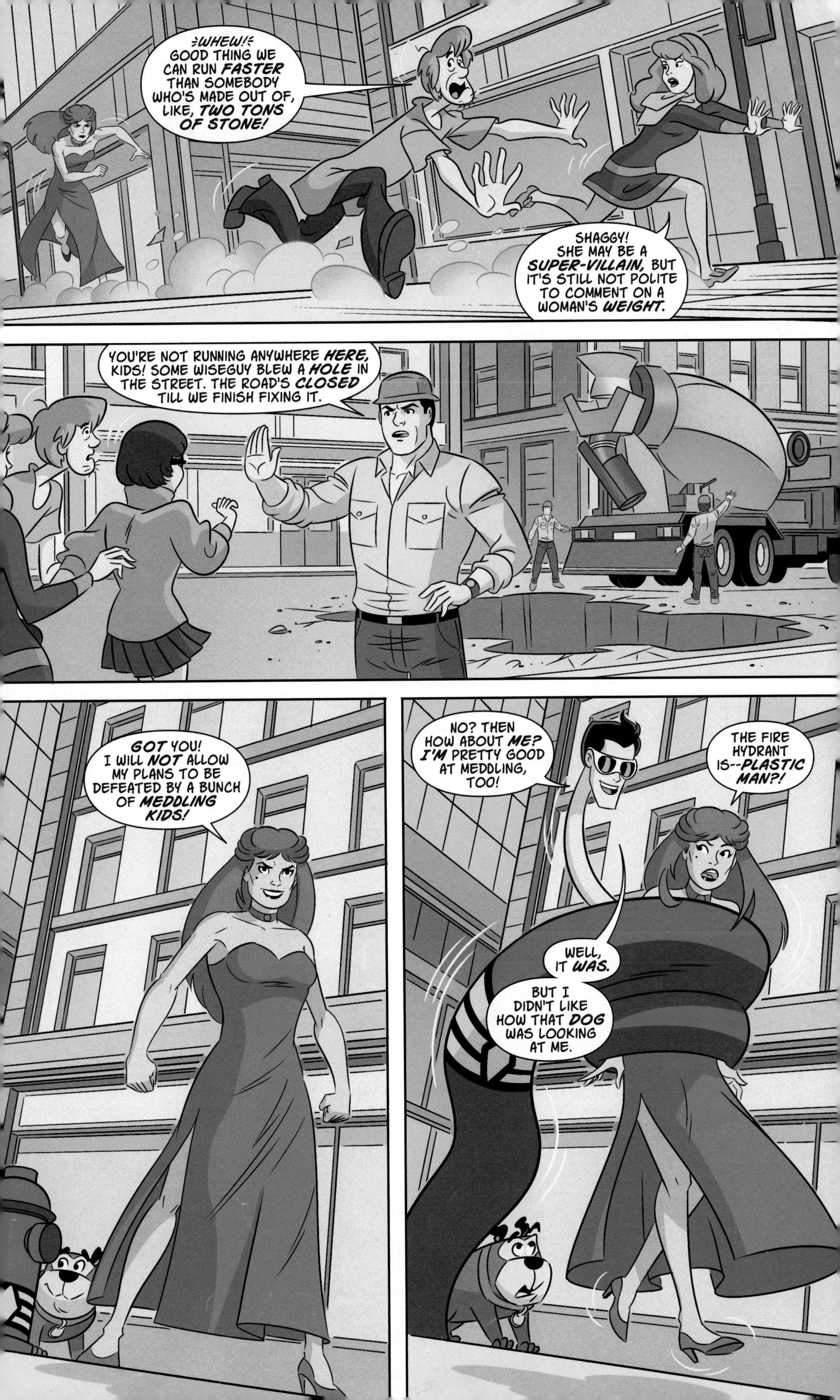
WHEW! GOOD THING WE CAN RUN FASTER THAN SOMEBODY WHO'S MADE OUT OF, LIKE, TWO TONS OF STONE!
SHAGGY! SHE MAY BE A SUPER-VILLAIN, BUT IT'S STILL NOT POLITE TO COMMENT ON A WOMAN'S WEIGHT.
YOU'RE NOT RUNNING ANYWHERE HERE, KIDS! SOME WISEGUY BLEW A HOLE IN THE STREET. THE ROAD'S CLOSED TILL WE FINISH FIXING IT.
GOT YOU! I WILL NOT ALLOW MY PLANS TO BE DEFEATED BY A BUNCH OF MEDDLING KIDS!
NO? THEN HOW ABOUT ME? I'M PRETTY GOOD AT MEDDLING, TOO!
THE FIRE HYDRANT IS--PLASTIC MAN?!
WELL, IT WAS.
BUT I DIDN'T LIKE HOW THAT DOG WAS LOOKING AT ME.

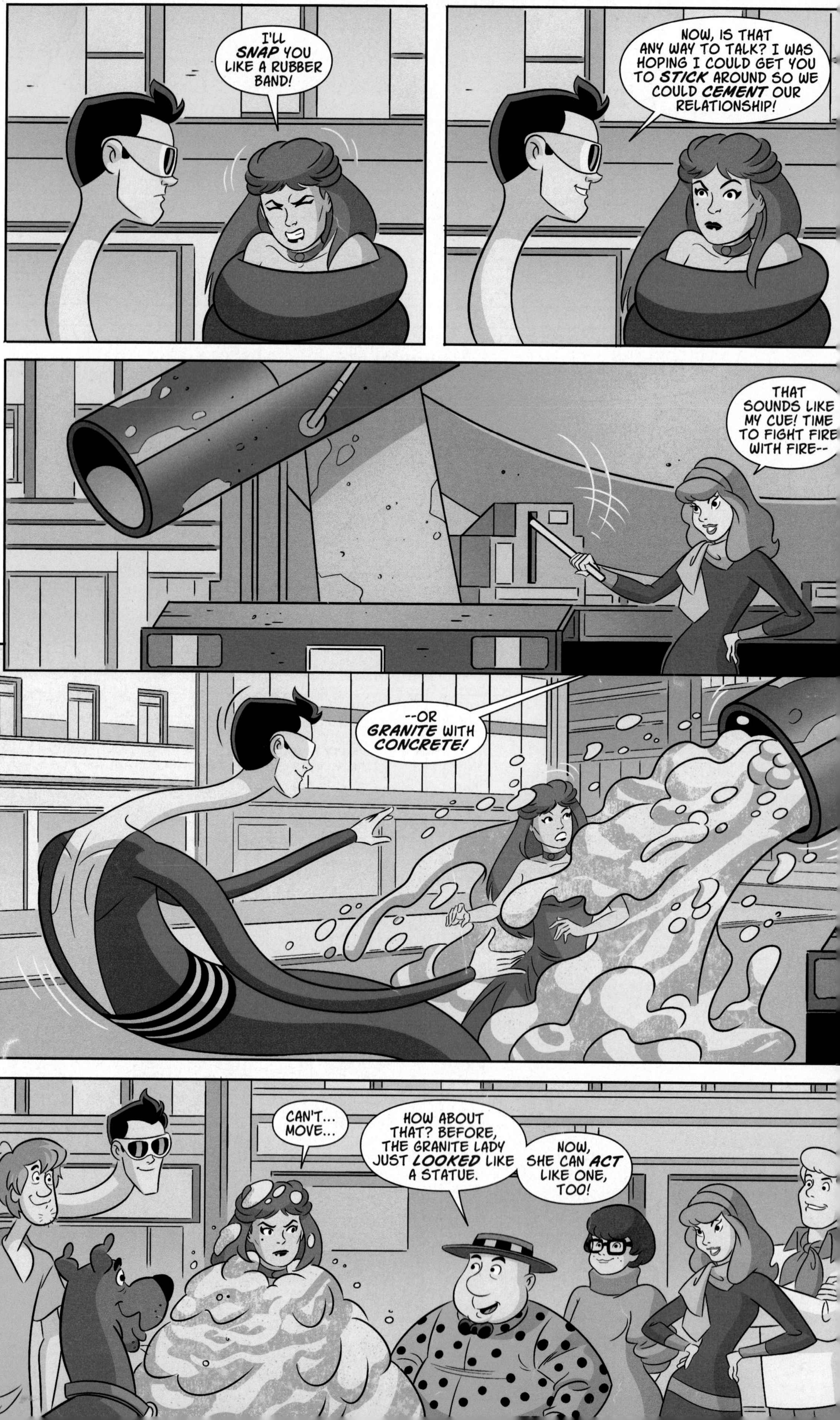
I'LL *SNAP* YOU LIKE A RUBBER BAND!
NOW, IS THAT ANY WAY TO TALK? I WAS HOPING I COULD GET YOU TO *STICK* AROUND SO WE COULD *CEMENT* OUR RELATIONSHIP!
THAT SOUNDS LIKE MY CUE! TIME TO FIGHT FIRE WITH FIRE--
--OR *GRANITE* WITH *CONCRETE!*
CAN'T... MOVE...
HOW ABOUT THAT? BEFORE, THE GRANITE LADY JUST *LOOKED* LIKE A STATUE.
NOW, SHE CAN *ACT* LIKE ONE, TOO!

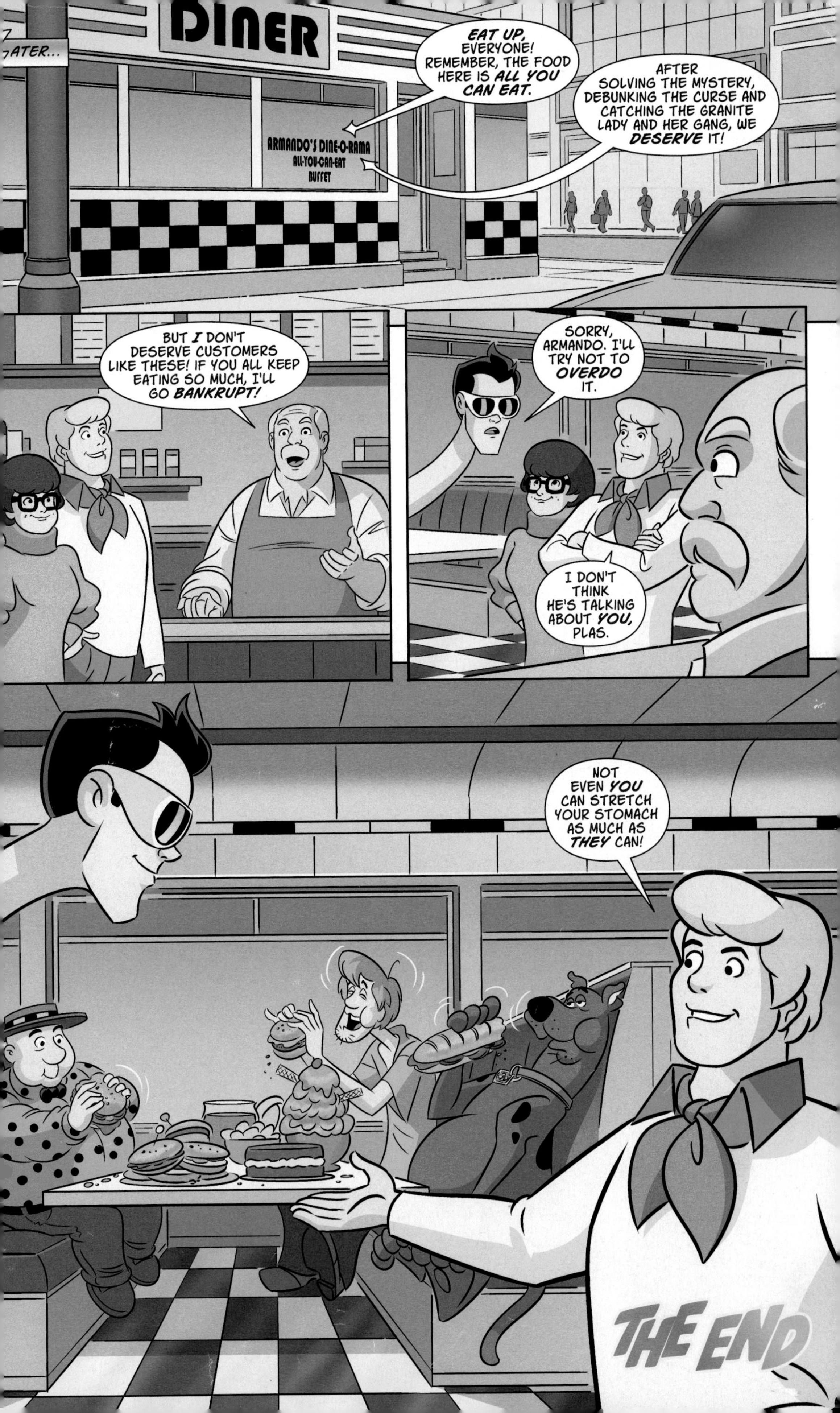

DINER
LATER...
ARMANDO'S DINE-O-RAMA
ALL-YOU-CAN-EAT
BUFFET
EAT UP, EVERYONE! REMEMBER, THE FOOD HERE IS ALL YOU CAN EAT.
AFTER SOLVING THE MYSTERY, DEBUNKING THE CURSE AND CATCHING THE GRANITE LADY AND HER GANG, WE DESERVE IT!
BUT I DON'T DESERVE CUSTOMERS LIKE THESE! IF YOU ALL KEEP EATING SO MUCH, I'LL GO BANKRUPT!
SORRY, ARMANDO. I'LL TRY NOT TO OVERDO IT.
I DON'T THINK HE'S TALKING ABOUT YOU, PLAS.
NOT EVEN YOU CAN STRETCH YOUR STOMACH AS MUCH AS THEY CAN!
THE END

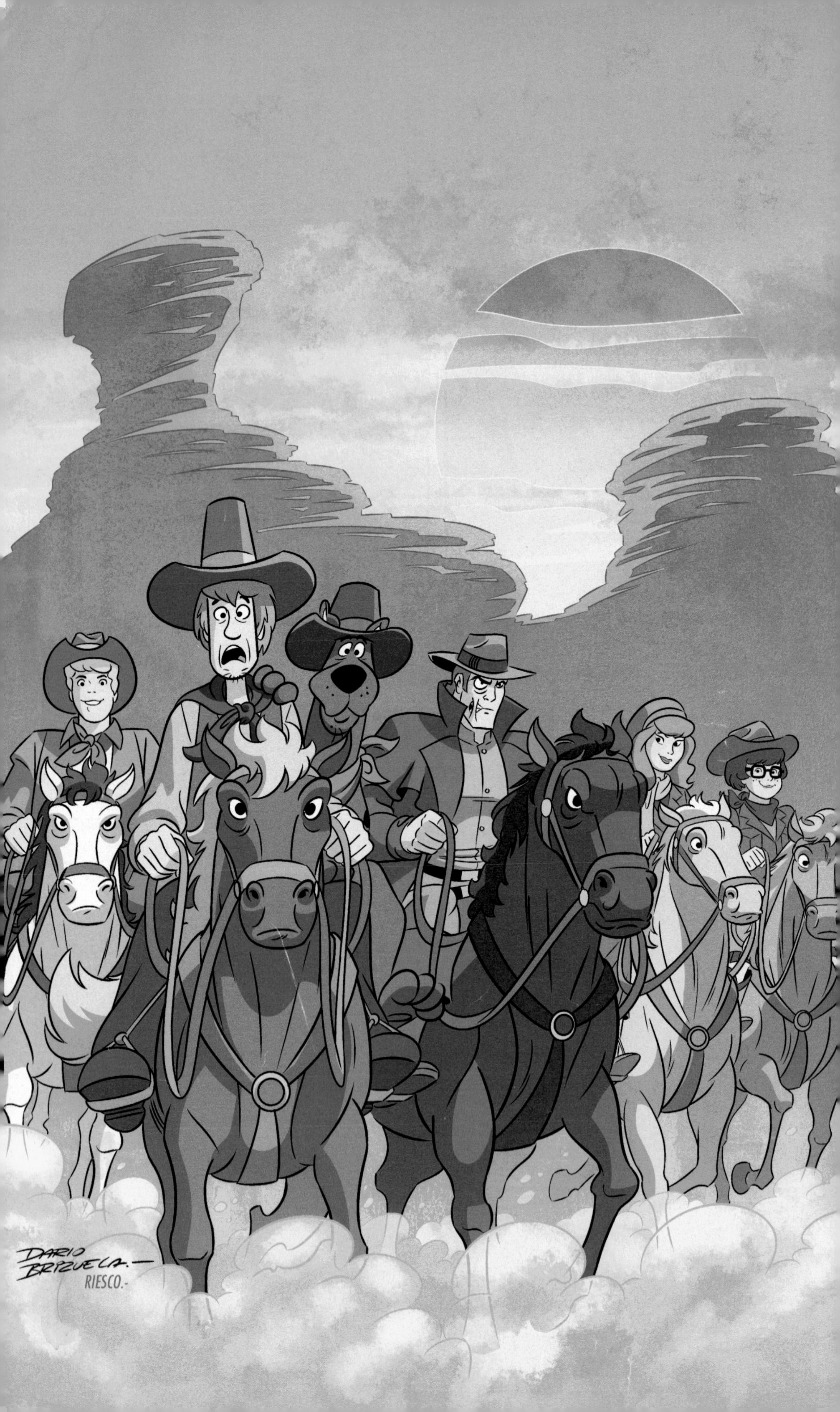
DARIO BRIZUELA
RIESCO.-

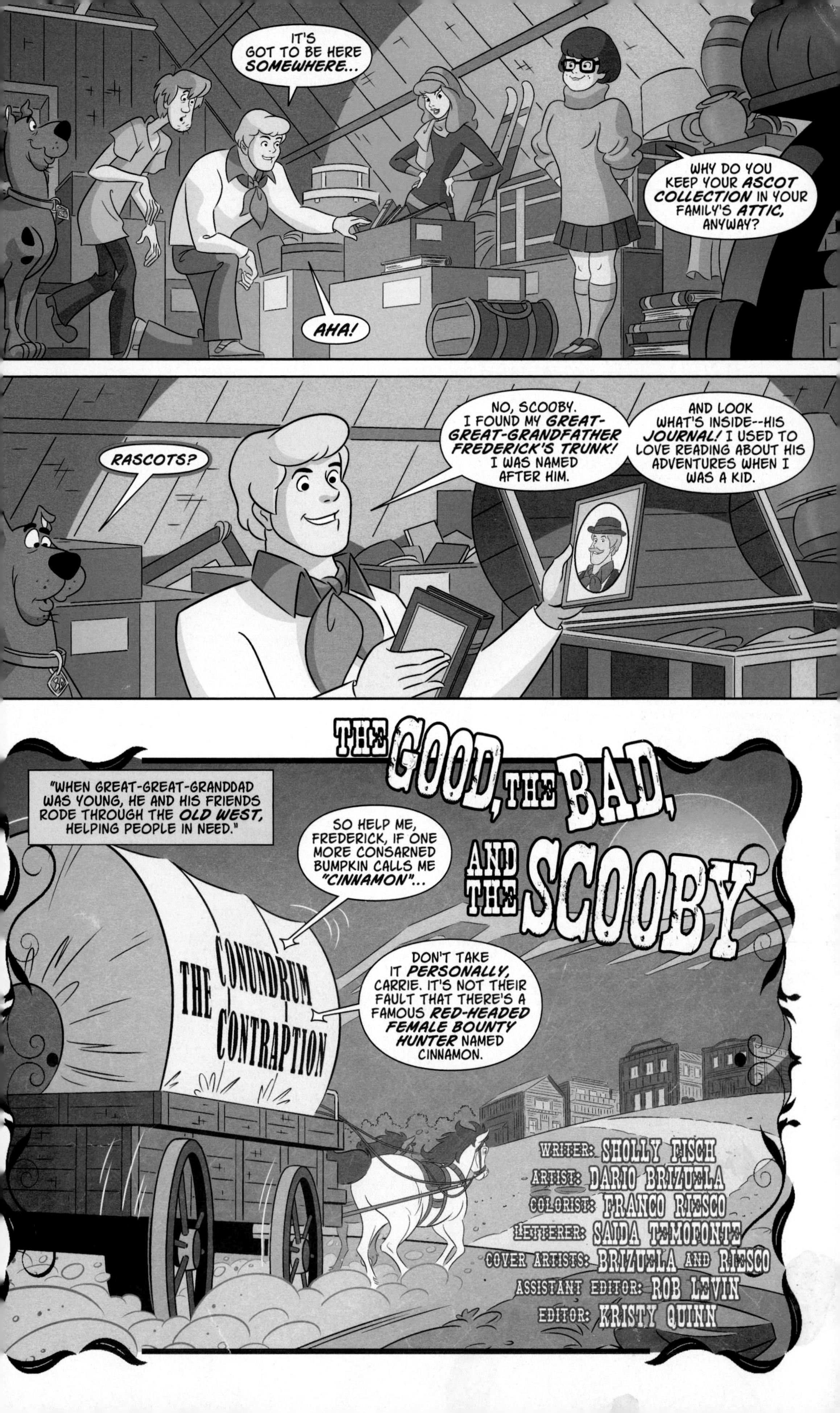

IT'S GOT TO BE HERE SOMEWHERE...
AHA!
WHY DO YOU KEEP YOUR ASCOT COLLECTION IN YOUR FAMILY'S ATTIC, ANYWAY?
RASCOTS?
NO, SCOOBY. I FOUND MY GREAT-GREAT-GRANDFATHER FREDERICK'S TRUNK! I WAS NAMED AFTER HIM.
AND LOOK WHAT'S INSIDE--HIS JOURNAL! I USED TO LOVE READING ABOUT HIS ADVENTURES WHEN I WAS A KID.
THE GOOD, THE BAD, AND THE SCOOBY
"WHEN GREAT-GREAT-GRANDDAD WAS YOUNG, HE AND HIS FRIENDS RODE THROUGH THE OLD WEST, HELPING PEOPLE IN NEED."
SO HELP ME, FREDERICK, IF ONE MORE CONSARNED BUMPKIN CALLS ME "CINNAMON"...
THE CONUNDRUM CONTRAPTION
DON'T TAKE IT PERSONALLY, CARRIE. IT'S NOT THEIR FAULT THAT THERE'S A FAMOUS RED-HEADED FEMALE BOUNTY HUNTER NAMED CINNAMON.
WRITER: SHOLLY FISCH
ARTIST: DARIO BRIZUELA
COLORIST: FRANCO RIESCO
LETTERER: SAIDA TEMOFONTE
COVER ARTISTS: BRIZUELA AND RIESCO
ASSISTANT EDITOR: ROB LEVIN
EDITOR: KRISTY QUINN

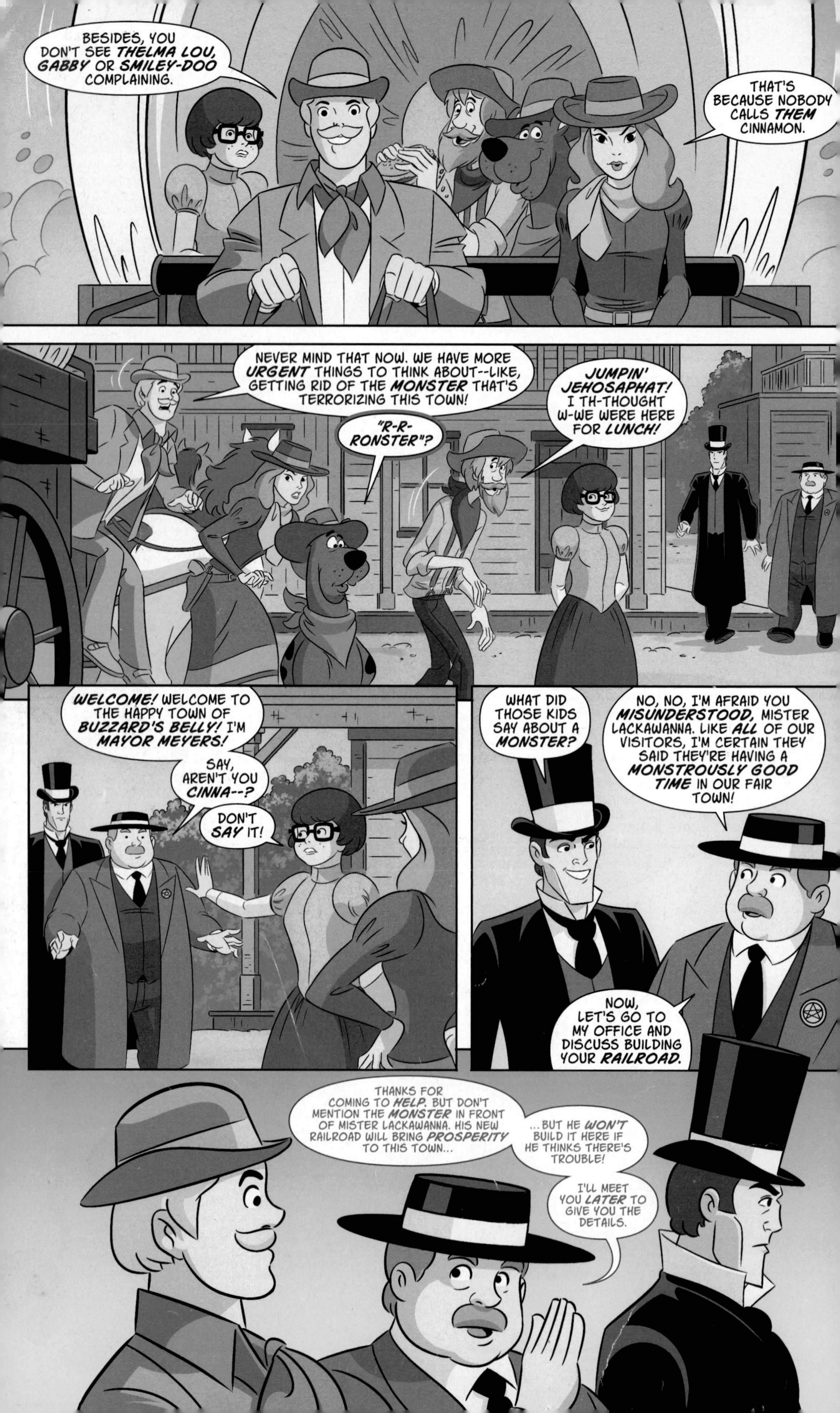

BESIDES, YOU DON'T SEE THELMA LOU, GABBY OR SMILEY-DOO COMPLAINING.
THAT'S BECAUSE NOBODY CALLS THEM CINNAMON.
NEVER MIND THAT NOW. WE HAVE MORE URGENT THINGS TO THINK ABOUT--LIKE, GETTING RID OF THE MONSTER THAT'S TERRORIZING THIS TOWN!
"R-R-RONSTER"?
JUMPIN' JEHOSAPHAT! I TH-THOUGHT W-WE WERE HERE FOR LUNCH!
WELCOME! WELCOME TO THE HAPPY TOWN OF BUZZARD'S BELLY! I'M MAYOR MEYERS!
SAY, AREN'T YOU CINNA--?
DON'T SAY IT!
WHAT DID THOSE KIDS SAY ABOUT A MONSTER?
NO, NO, I'M AFRAID YOU MISUNDERSTOOD, MISTER LACKAWANNA. LIKE ALL OF OUR VISITORS, I'M CERTAIN THEY SAID THEY'RE HAVING A MONSTROUSLY GOOD TIME IN OUR FAIR TOWN!
NOW, LET'S GO TO MY OFFICE AND DISCUSS BUILDING YOUR RAILROAD.
THANKS FOR COMING TO HELP. BUT DON'T MENTION THE MONSTER IN FRONT OF MISTER LACKAWANNA. HIS NEW RAILROAD WILL BRING PROSPERITY TO THIS TOWN...
...BUT HE WON'T BUILD IT HERE IF HE THINKS THERE'S TROUBLE!
I'LL MEET YOU LATER TO GIVE YOU THE DETAILS.

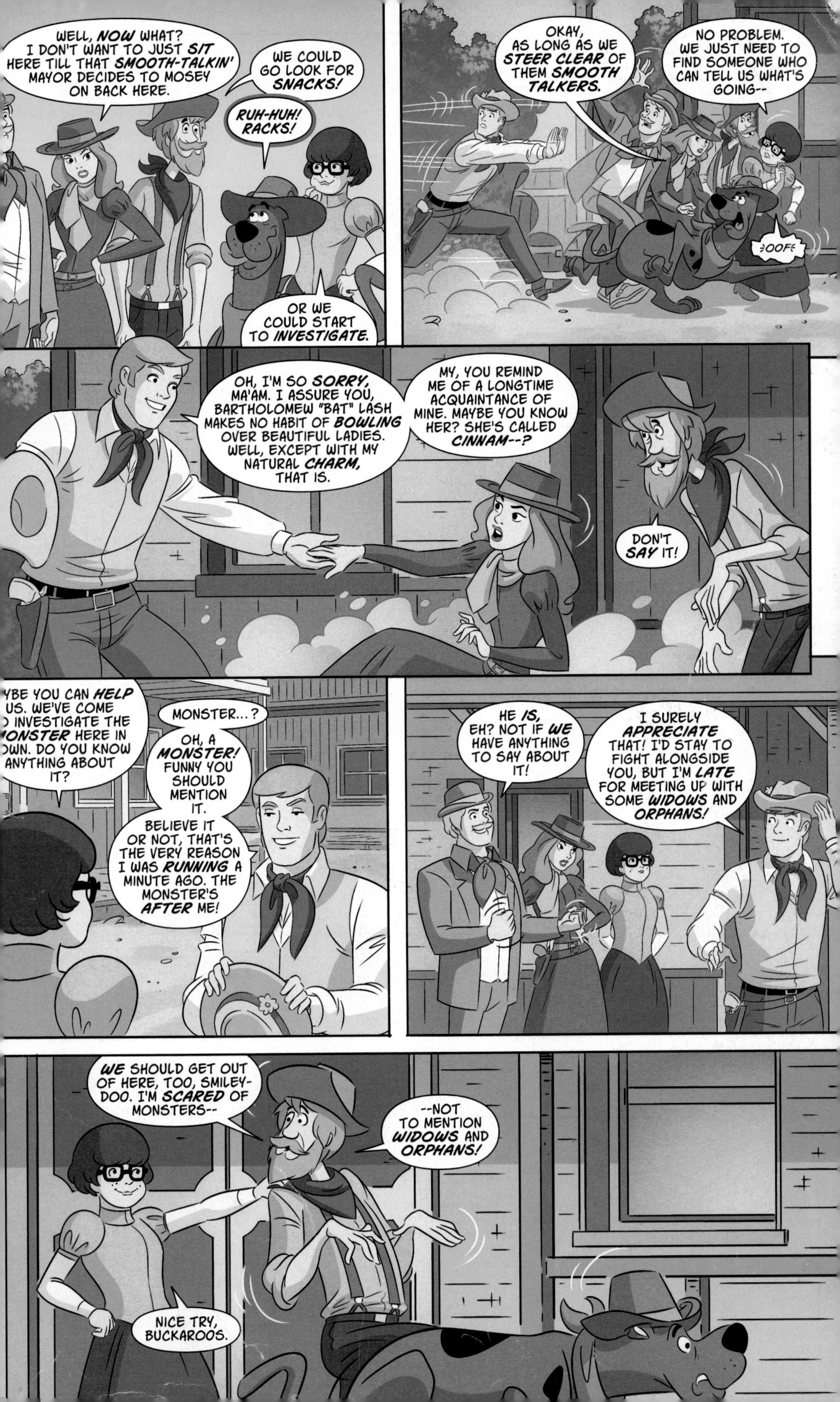

WELL, NOW WHAT? I DON'T WANT TO JUST SIT HERE TILL THAT SMOOTH-TALKIN' MAYOR DECIDES TO MOSEY ON BACK HERE.
WE COULD GO LOOK FOR SNACKS!
RUH-HUH! RACKS!
OR WE COULD START TO INVESTIGATE.
OKAY, AS LONG AS WE STEER CLEAR OF THEM SMOOTH TALKERS.
NO PROBLEM. WE JUST NEED TO FIND SOMEONE WHO CAN TELL US WHAT'S GOING--
OOF
OH, I'M SO SORRY, MA'AM. I ASSURE YOU, BARTHOLOMEW "BAT" LASH MAKES NO HABIT OF BOWLING OVER BEAUTIFUL LADIES. WELL, EXCEPT WITH MY NATURAL CHARM, THAT IS.
MY, YOU REMIND ME OF A LONGTIME ACQUAINTANCE OF MINE. MAYBE YOU KNOW HER? SHE'S CALLED CINNAM--?
DON'T SAY IT!
YBE YOU CAN HELP US. WE'VE COME INVESTIGATE THE ONSTER HERE IN WN. DO YOU KNOW ANYTHING ABOUT IT?
MONSTER...?
OH, A MONSTER! FUNNY YOU SHOULD MENTION IT.
BELIEVE IT OR NOT, THAT'S THE VERY REASON I WAS RUNNING A MINUTE AGO. THE MONSTER'S AFTER ME!
HE IS, EH? NOT IF WE HAVE ANYTHING TO SAY ABOUT IT!
I SURELY APPRECIATE THAT! I'D STAY TO FIGHT ALONGSIDE YOU, BUT I'M LATE FOR MEETING UP WITH SOME WIDOWS AND ORPHANS!
WE SHOULD GET OUT OF HERE, TOO, SMILEY-DOO. I'M SCARED OF MONSTERS--
--NOT TO MENTION WIDOWS AND ORPHANS!
NICE TRY, BUCKAROOS.

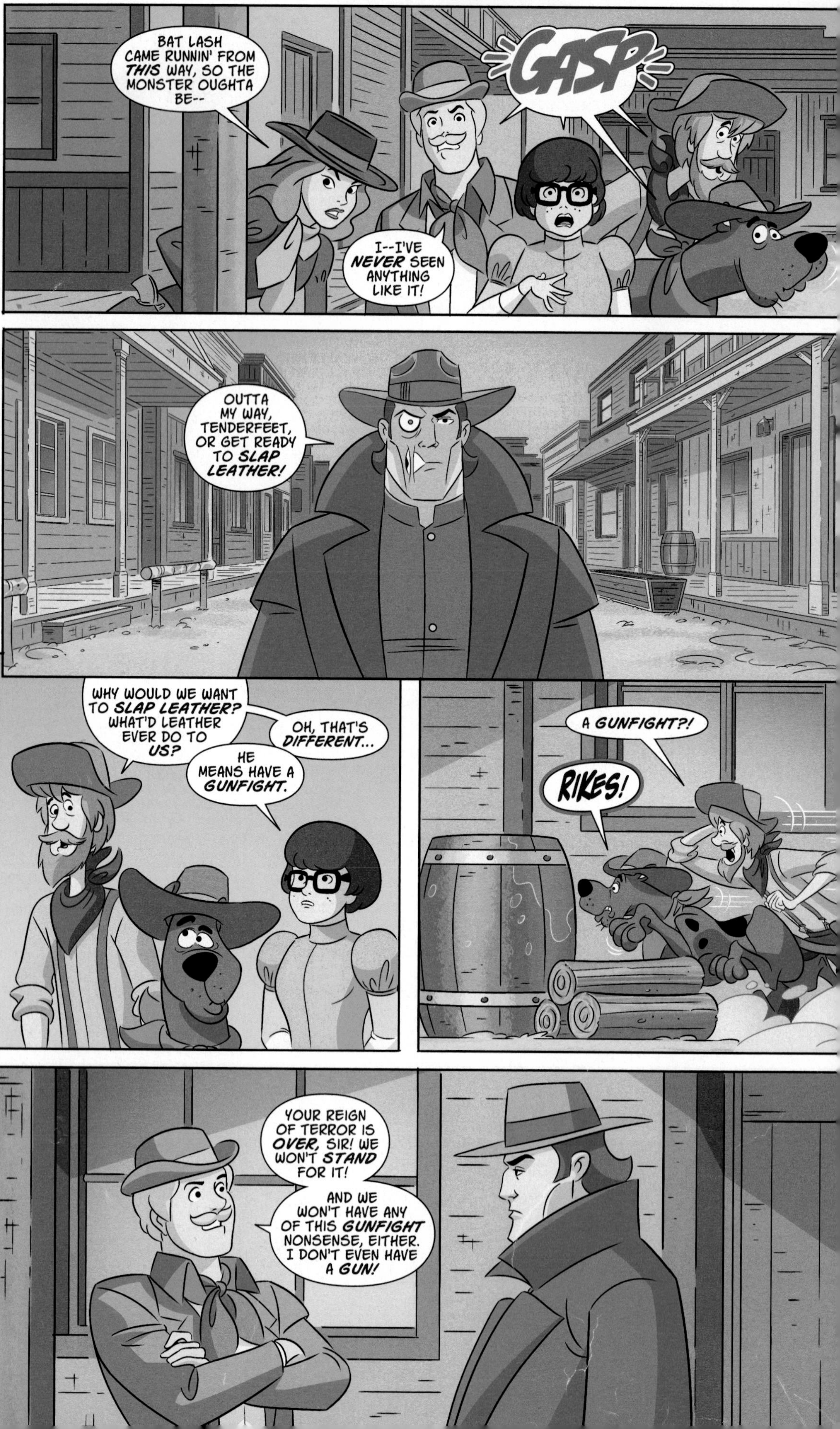
BAT LASH CAME RUNNIN' FROM THIS WAY, SO THE MONSTER OUGHTA BE--
GASP
I--I'VE NEVER SEEN ANYTHING LIKE IT!
OUTTA MY WAY, TENDERFEET, OR GET READY TO SLAP LEATHER!
WHY WOULD WE WANT TO SLAP LEATHER? WHAT'D LEATHER EVER DO TO US?
HE MEANS HAVE A GUNFIGHT.
OH, THAT'S DIFFERENT...
A GUNFIGHT?!
RIKES!
YOUR REIGN OF TERROR IS OVER, SIR! WE WON'T STAND FOR IT!
AND WE WON'T HAVE ANY OF THIS GUNFIGHT NONSENSE, EITHER. I DON'T EVEN HAVE A GUN!

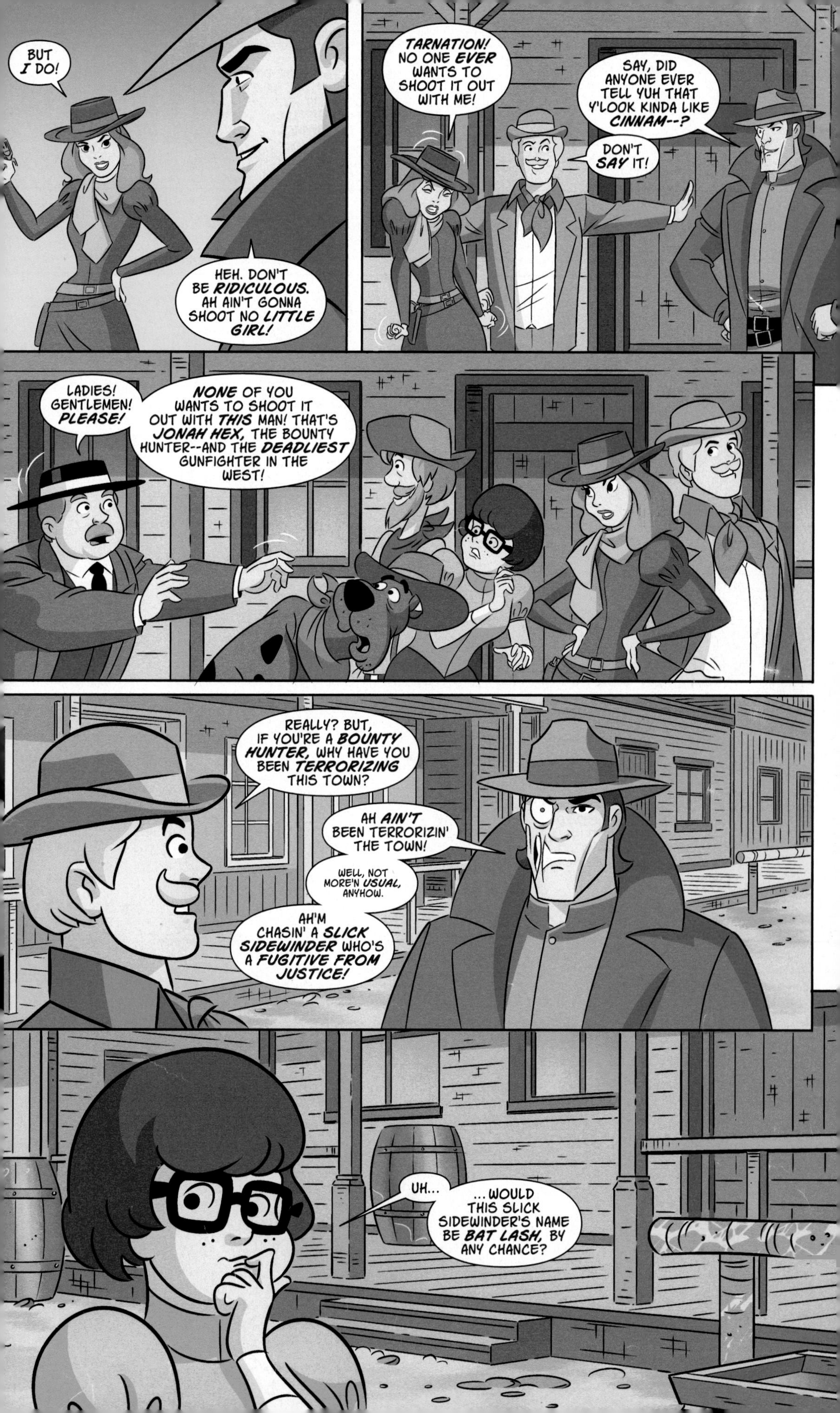

BUT I DO!
HEH. DON'T BE RIDICULOUS. AH AIN'T GONNA SHOOT NO LITTLE GIRL!
TARNATION! NO ONE EVER WANTS TO SHOOT IT OUT WITH ME!
SAY, DID ANYONE EVER TELL YUH THAT Y'LOOK KINDA LIKE CINNAM--?
DON'T SAY IT!
LADIES! GENTLEMEN! PLEASE!
NONE OF YOU WANTS TO SHOOT IT OUT WITH THIS MAN! THAT'S JONAH HEX, THE BOUNTY HUNTER--AND THE DEADLIEST GUNFIGHTER IN THE WEST!
REALLY? BUT, IF YOU'RE A BOUNTY HUNTER, WHY HAVE YOU BEEN TERRORIZING THIS TOWN?
AH AIN'T BEEN TERRORIZIN' THE TOWN!
WELL, NOT MORE'N USUAL, ANYHOW.
AH'M CHASIN' A SLICK SIDEWINDER WHO'S A FUGITIVE FROM JUSTICE!
UH...
...WOULD THIS SLICK SIDEWINDER'S NAME BE BAT LASH, BY ANY CHANCE?

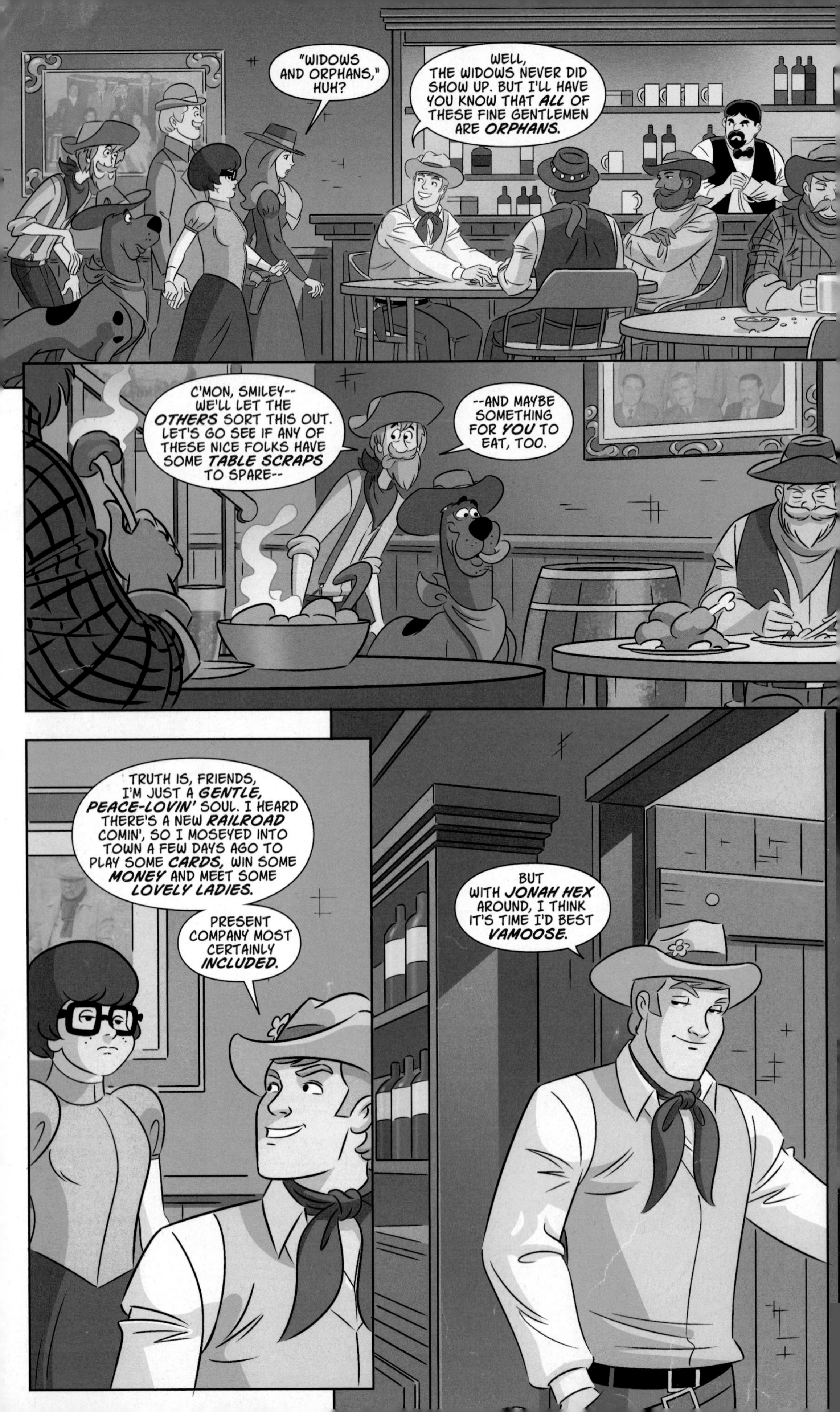
"WIDOWS AND ORPHANS," HUH?
WELL, THE WIDOWS NEVER DID SHOW UP. BUT I'LL HAVE YOU KNOW THAT ALL OF THESE FINE GENTLEMEN ARE ORPHANS.
C'MON, SMILEY-- WE'LL LET THE OTHERS SORT THIS OUT. LET'S GO SEE IF ANY OF THESE NICE FOLKS HAVE SOME TABLE SCRAPS TO SPARE--
--AND MAYBE SOMETHING FOR YOU TO EAT, TOO.
TRUTH IS, FRIENDS, I'M JUST A GENTLE, PEACE-LOVIN' SOUL. I HEARD THERE'S A NEW RAILROAD COMIN', SO I MOSEYED INTO TOWN A FEW DAYS AGO TO PLAY SOME CARDS, WIN SOME MONEY AND MEET SOME LOVELY LADIES.
PRESENT COMPANY MOST CERTAINLY INCLUDED.
BUT WITH JONAH HEX AROUND, I THINK IT'S TIME I'D BEST VAMOOSE.

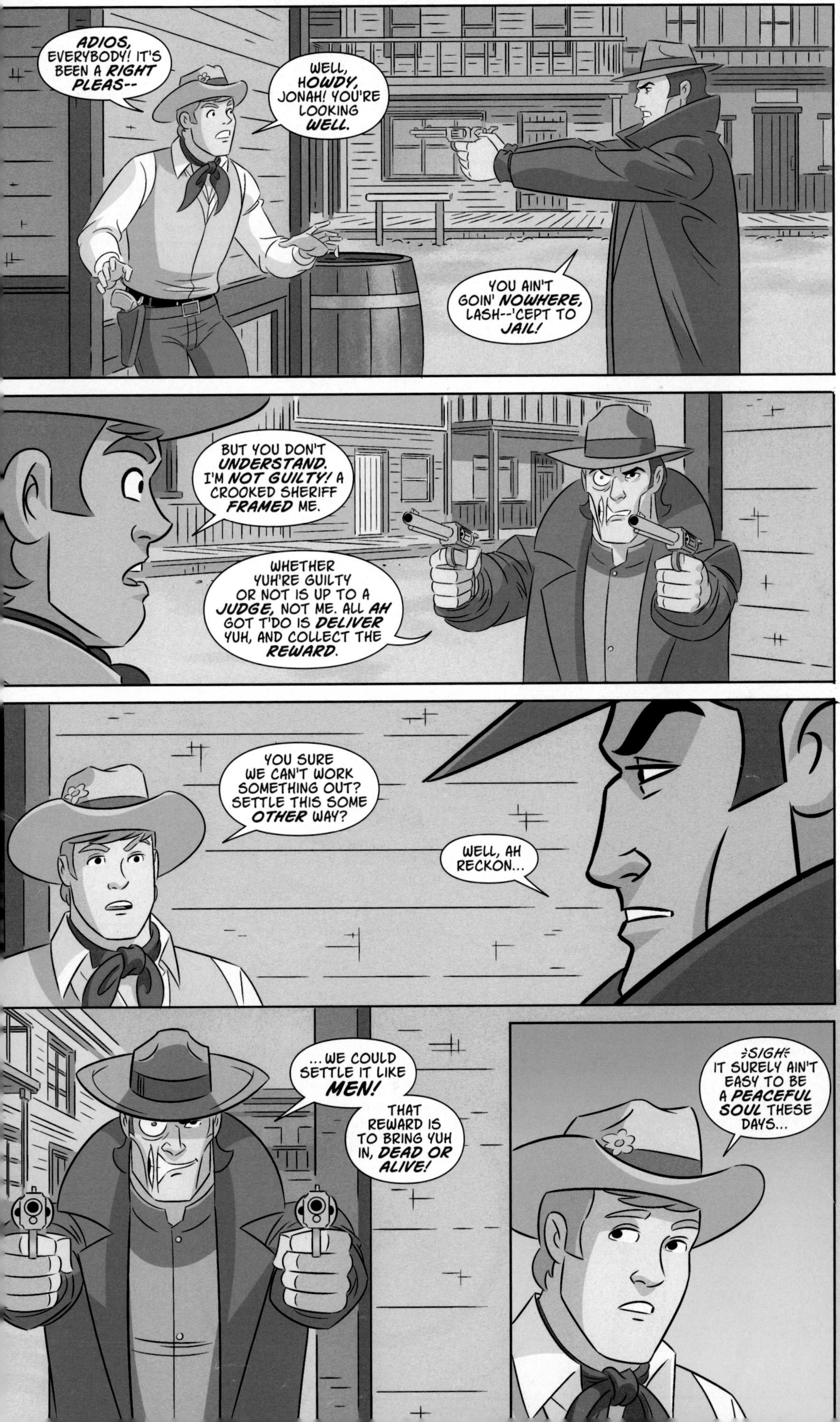
ADIOS, EVERYBODY! IT'S BEEN A RIGHT PLEAS--
WELL, HOWDY, JONAH! YOU'RE LOOKING WELL.
YOU AIN'T GOIN' NOWHERE, LASH--'CEPT TO JAIL!
BUT YOU DON'T UNDERSTAND. I'M NOT GUILTY! A CROOKED SHERIFF FRAMED ME.
WHETHER YUH'RE GUILTY OR NOT IS UP TO A JUDGE, NOT ME. ALL AH GOT T'DO IS DELIVER YUH, AND COLLECT THE REWARD.
YOU SURE WE CAN'T WORK SOMETHING OUT? SETTLE THIS SOME OTHER WAY?
WELL, AH RECKON...
...WE COULD SETTLE IT LIKE MEN!
THAT REWARD IS TO BRING YUH IN, DEAD OR ALIVE!
SIGH
IT SURELY AIN'T EASY TO BE A PEACEFUL SOUL THESE DAYS...

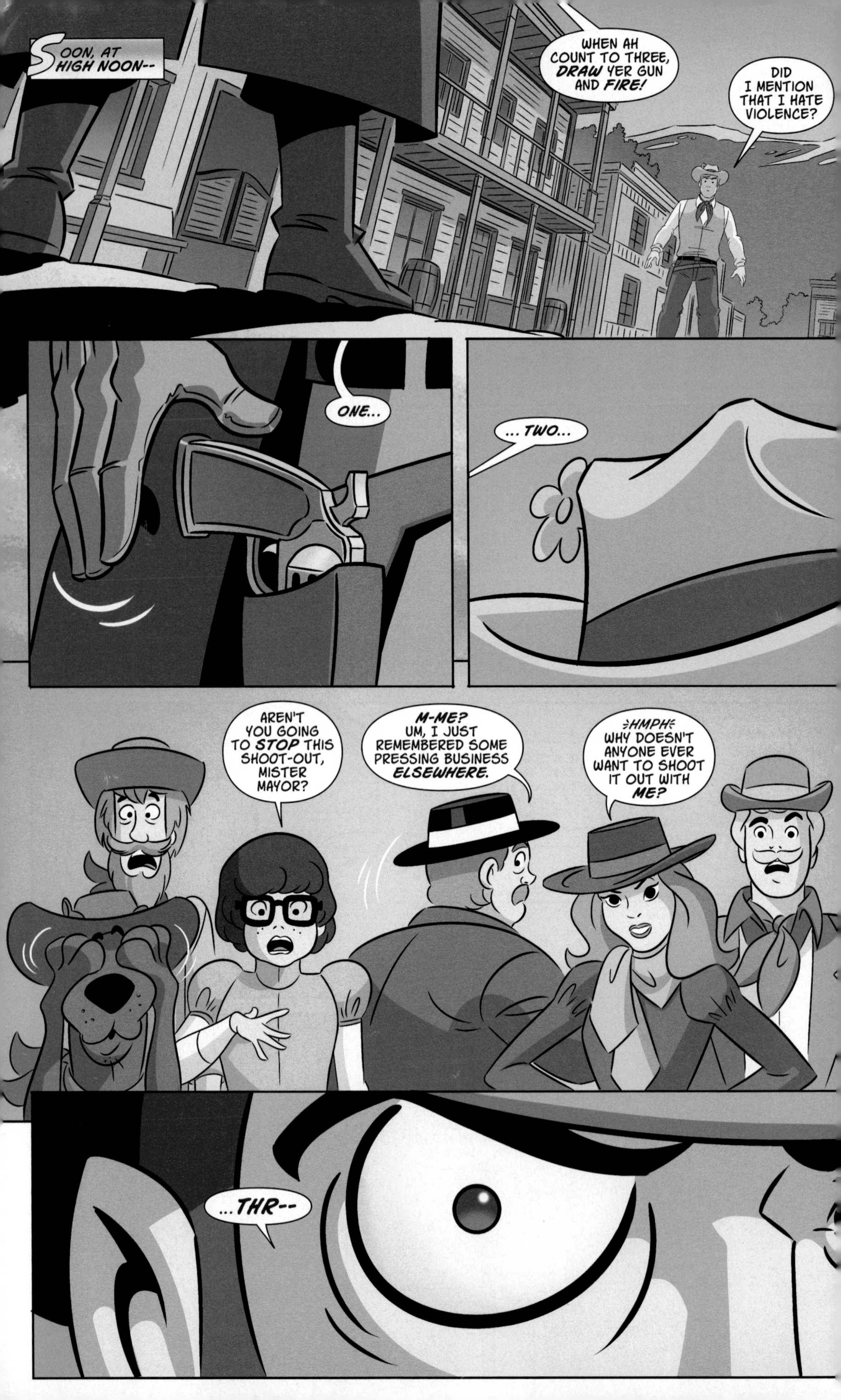

SOON, AT HIGH NOON--
WHEN AH COUNT TO THREE, DRAW YER GUN AND FIRE!
DID I MENTION THAT I HATE VIOLENCE?
ONE...
... TWO...
AREN'T YOU GOING TO STOP THIS SHOOT-OUT, MISTER MAYOR?
M-ME? UM, I JUST REMEMBERED SOME PRESSING BUSINESS ELSEWHERE.
HMPH WHY DOESN'T ANYONE EVER WANT TO SHOOT IT OUT WITH ME?
...THR--

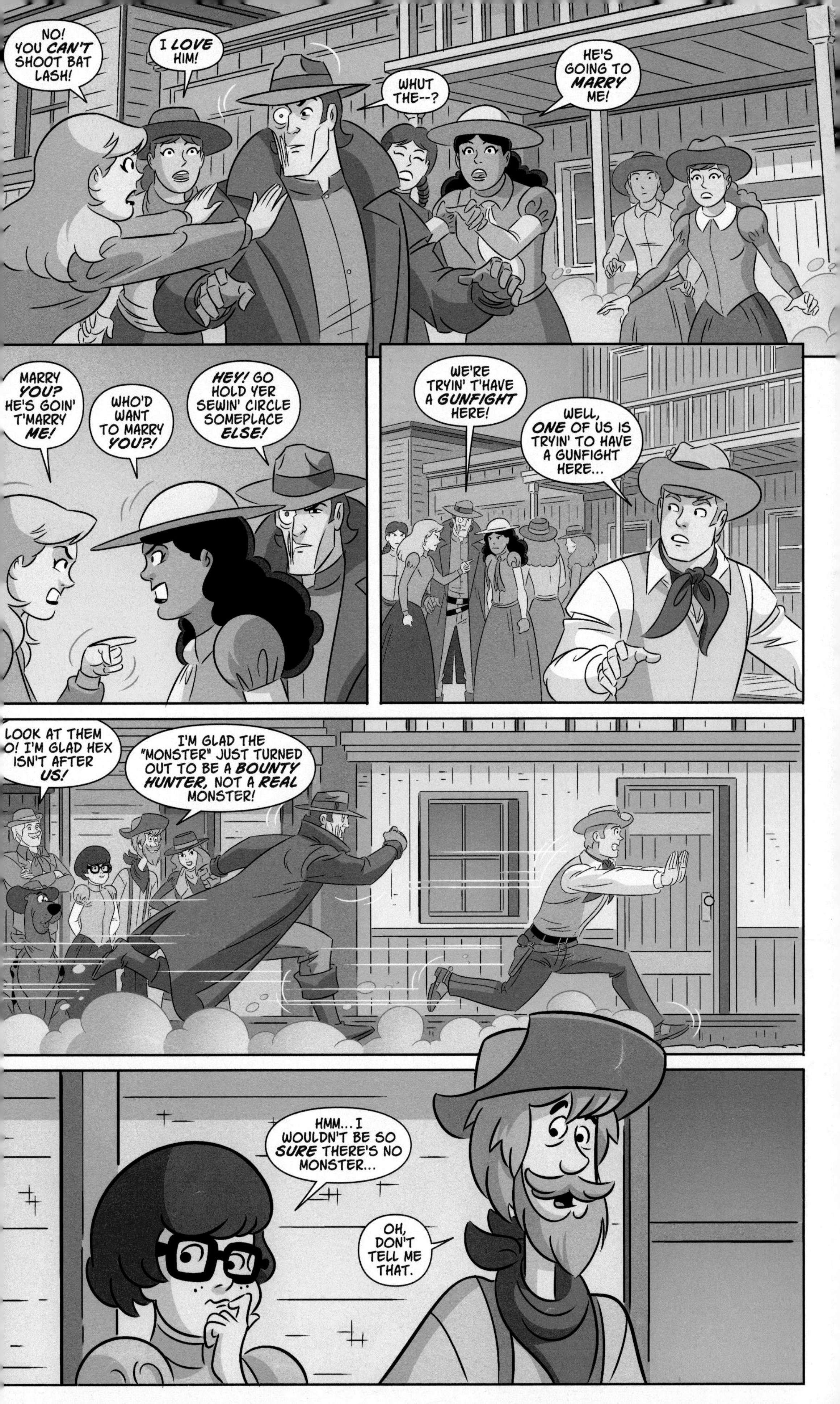
NO! YOU CAN'T SHOOT BAT LASH!
I LOVE HIM!
WHUT THE--?
HE'S GOING TO MARRY ME!
MARRY YOU? HE'S GOIN' T'MARRY ME!
WHO'D WANT TO MARRY YOU?!
HEY! GO HOLD YER SEWIN' CIRCLE SOMEPLACE ELSE!
WE'RE TRYIN' T'HAVE A GUNFIGHT HERE!
WELL, ONE OF US IS TRYIN' TO HAVE A GUNFIGHT HERE...
LOOK AT THEM GO! I'M GLAD HEX ISN'T AFTER US!
I'M GLAD THE "MONSTER" JUST TURNED OUT TO BE A BOUNTY HUNTER, NOT A REAL MONSTER!
HMM... I WOULDN'T BE SO SURE THERE'S NO MONSTER...
OH, DON'T TELL ME THAT.

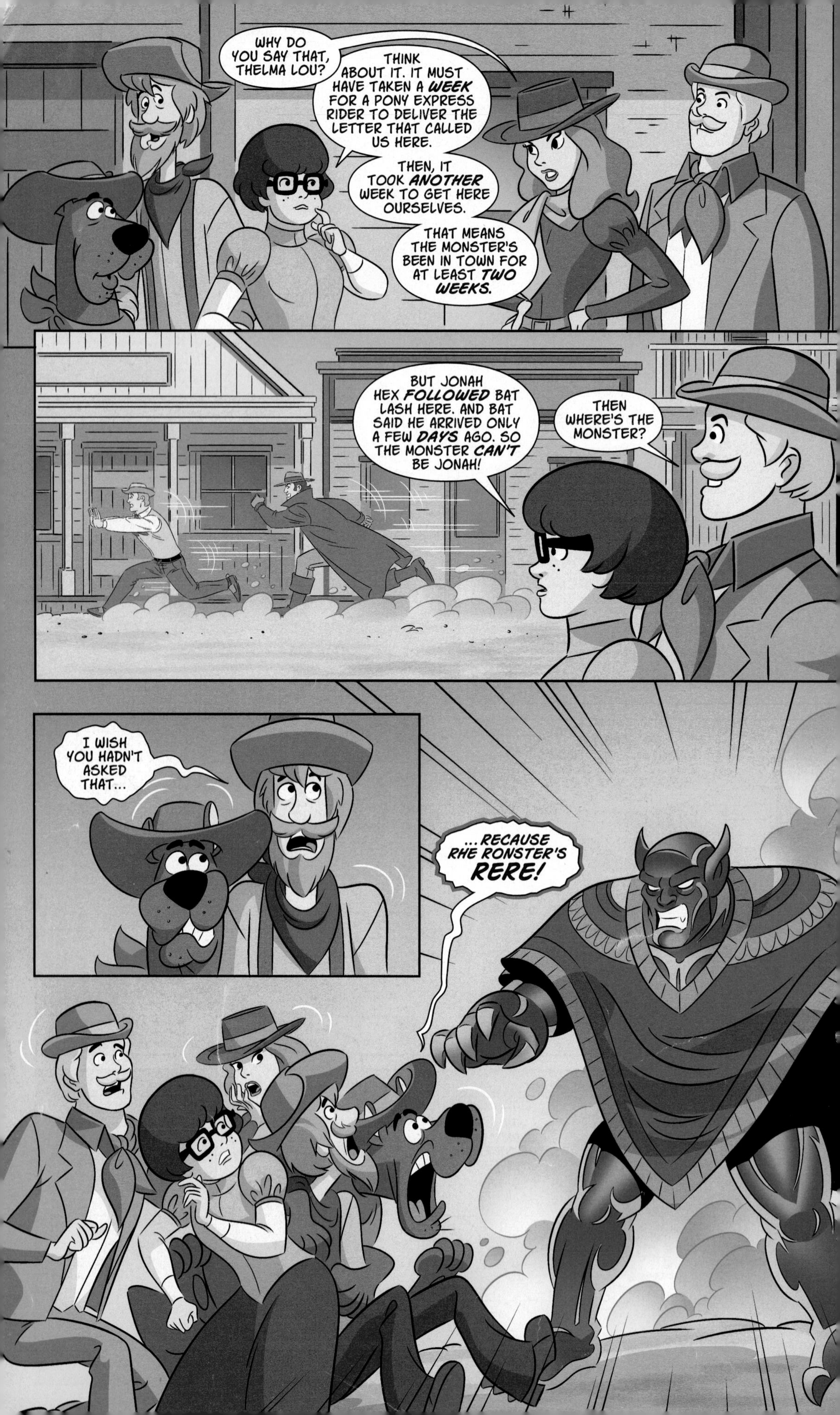

WHY DO YOU SAY THAT, THELMA LOU?
THINK ABOUT IT. IT MUST HAVE TAKEN A WEEK FOR A PONY EXPRESS RIDER TO DELIVER THE LETTER THAT CALLED US HERE.
THEN, IT TOOK ANOTHER WEEK TO GET HERE OURSELVES.
THAT MEANS THE MONSTER'S BEEN IN TOWN FOR AT LEAST TWO WEEKS.
BUT JONAH HEX FOLLOWED BAT LASH HERE. AND BAT SAID HE ARRIVED ONLY A FEW DAYS AGO. SO THE MONSTER CAN'T BE JONAH!
THEN WHERE'S THE MONSTER?
I WISH YOU HADN'T ASKED THAT...
...RECAUSE RHE RONSTER'S RERE!

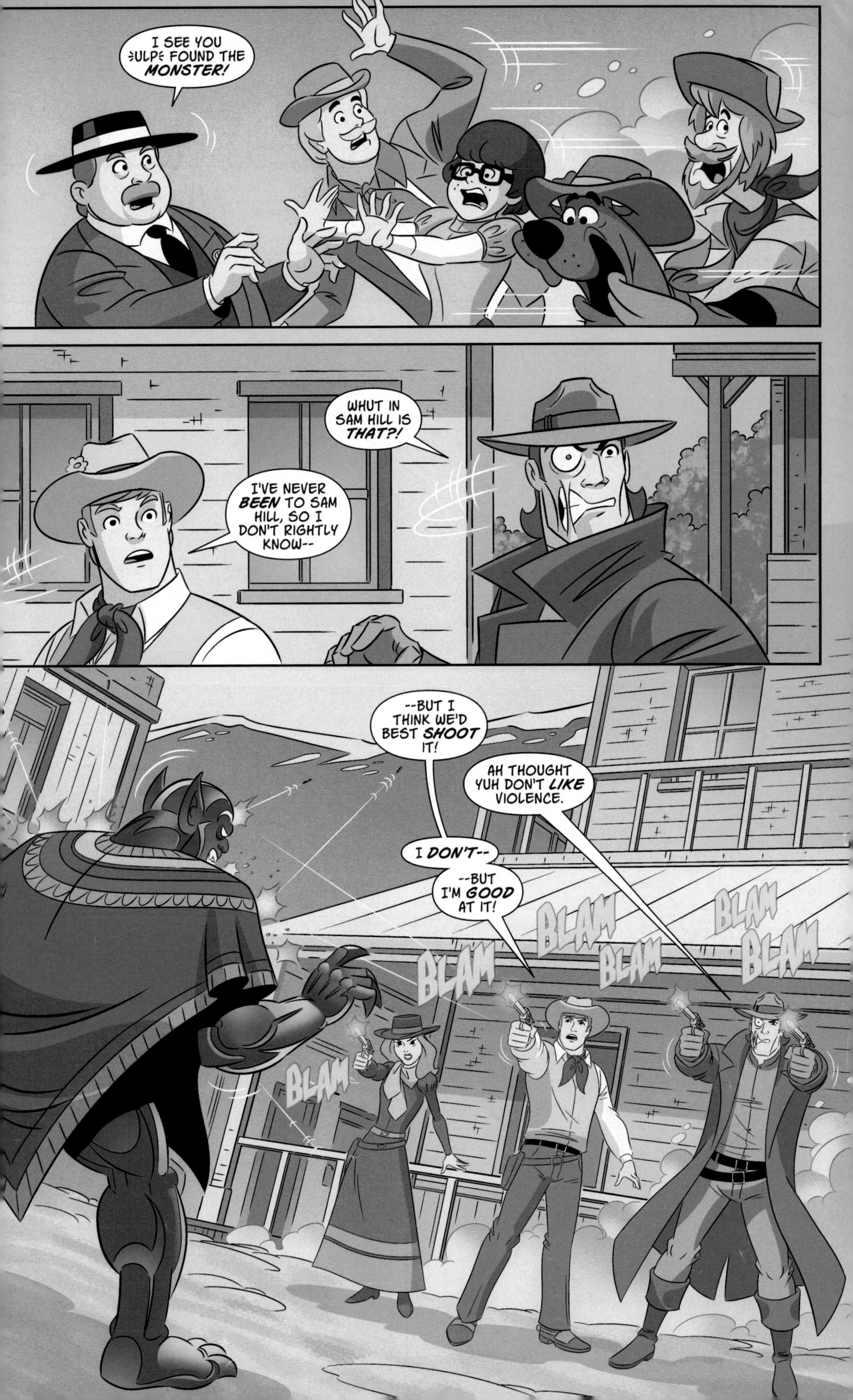
I SEE YOU ≷ULP≶ FOUND THE ***MONSTER!***
WHUT IN SAM HILL IS ***THAT?!***
I'VE NEVER ***BEEN*** TO SAM HILL, SO I DON'T RIGHTLY KNOW--
--BUT I THINK WE'D BEST ***SHOOT*** IT!
AH THOUGHT YUH DON'T ***LIKE*** VIOLENCE.
I ***DON'T***--
--BUT I'M ***GOOD*** AT IT!
BLAM
BLAM
BLAM
BLAM
BLAM
BLAM

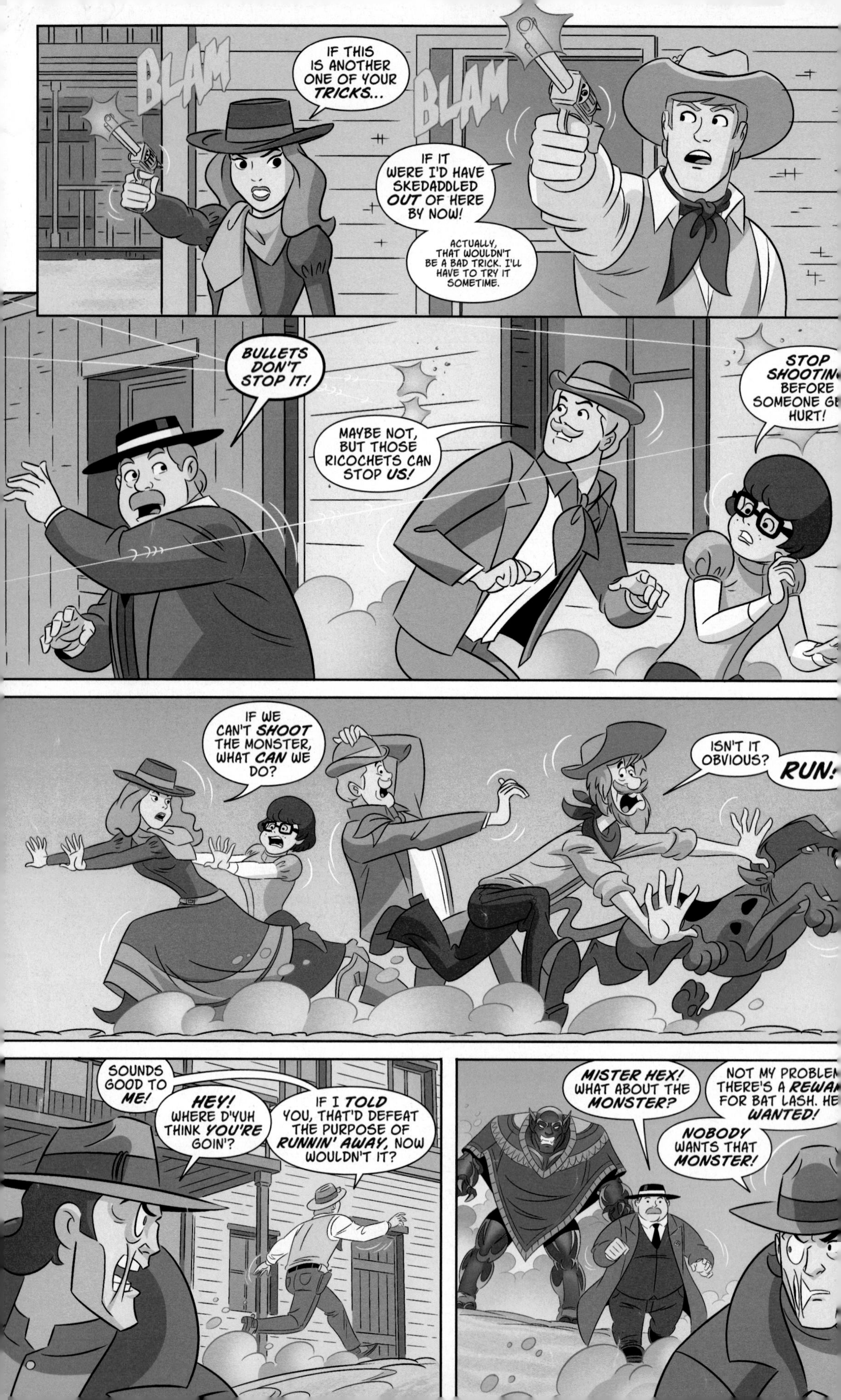
BLAM
IF THIS IS ANOTHER ONE OF YOUR TRICKS...
BLAM
IF IT WERE I'D HAVE SKEDADDLED OUT OF HERE BY NOW!
ACTUALLY, THAT WOULDN'T BE A BAD TRICK. I'LL HAVE TO TRY IT SOMETIME.
BULLETS DON'T STOP IT!
MAYBE NOT, BUT THOSE RICOCHETS CAN STOP US!
STOP SHOOTIN BEFORE SOMEONE G HURT!
IF WE CAN'T SHOOT THE MONSTER, WHAT CAN WE DO?
ISN'T IT OBVIOUS? RUN!
SOUNDS GOOD TO ME!
HEY! WHERE D'YUH THINK YOU'RE GOIN'?
IF I TOLD YOU, THAT'D DEFEAT THE PURPOSE OF RUNNIN' AWAY, NOW WOULDN'T IT?
MISTER HEX! WHAT ABOUT THE MONSTER?
NOT MY PROBLEM THERE'S A REWA FOR BAT LASH. HE WANTED!
NOBODY WANTS THAT MONSTER!

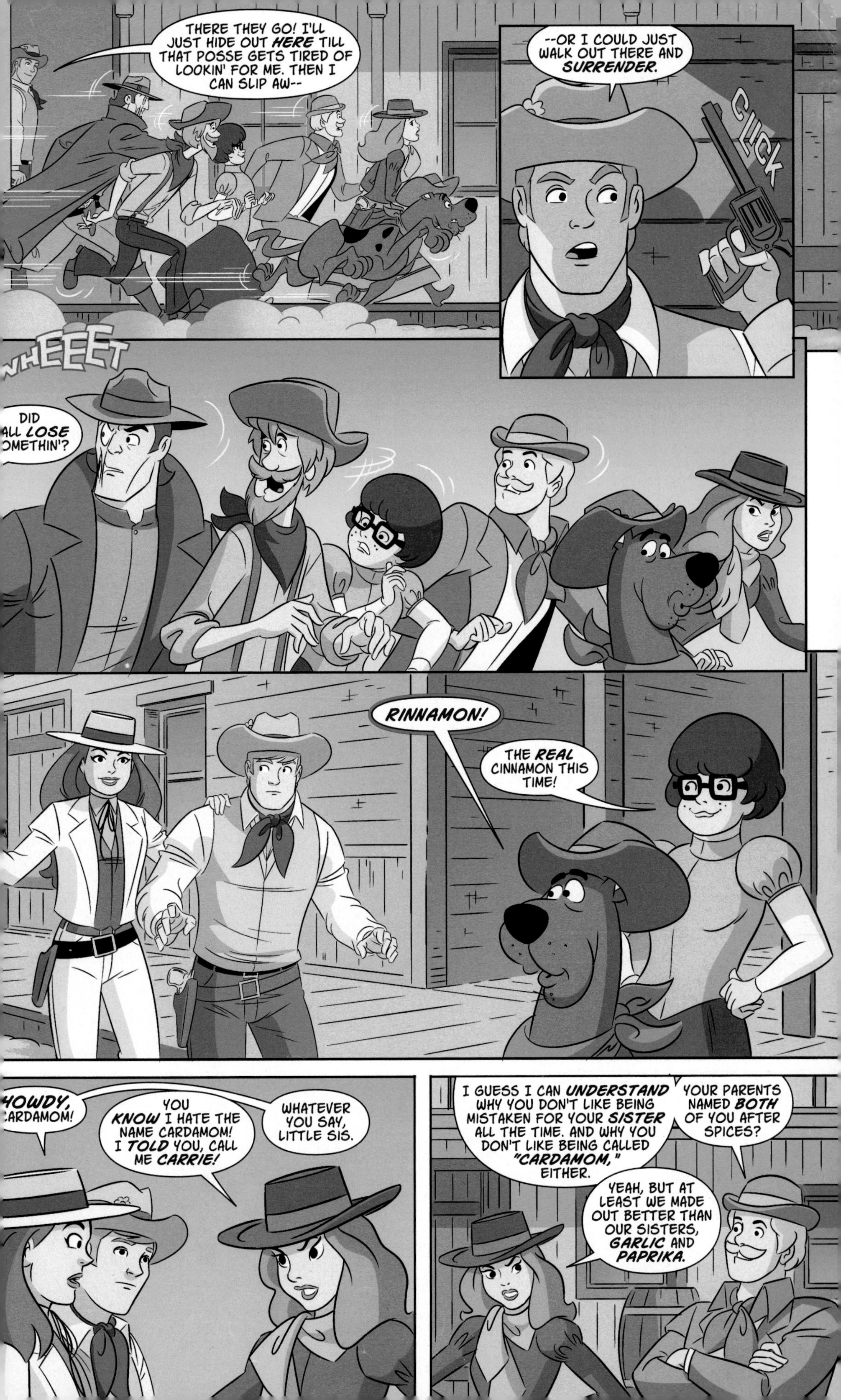
THERE THEY GO! I'LL JUST HIDE OUT HERE TILL THAT POSSE GETS TIRED OF LOOKIN' FOR ME. THEN I CAN SLIP AW--
--OR I COULD JUST WALK OUT THERE AND SURRENDER.
CLICK
WHEEET
DID ALL LOSE OMETHIN'?
RINNAMON!
THE REAL CINNAMON THIS TIME!
HOWDY, CARDAMOM!
YOU KNOW I HATE THE NAME CARDAMOM! I TOLD YOU, CALL ME CARRIE!
WHATEVER YOU SAY, LITTLE SIS.
I GUESS I CAN UNDERSTAND WHY YOU DON'T LIKE BEING MISTAKEN FOR YOUR SISTER ALL THE TIME. AND WHY YOU DON'T LIKE BEING CALLED "CARDAMOM," EITHER.
YOUR PARENTS NAMED BOTH OF YOU AFTER SPICES?
YEAH, BUT AT LEAST WE MADE OUT BETTER THAN OUR SISTERS, GARLIC AND PAPRIKA.

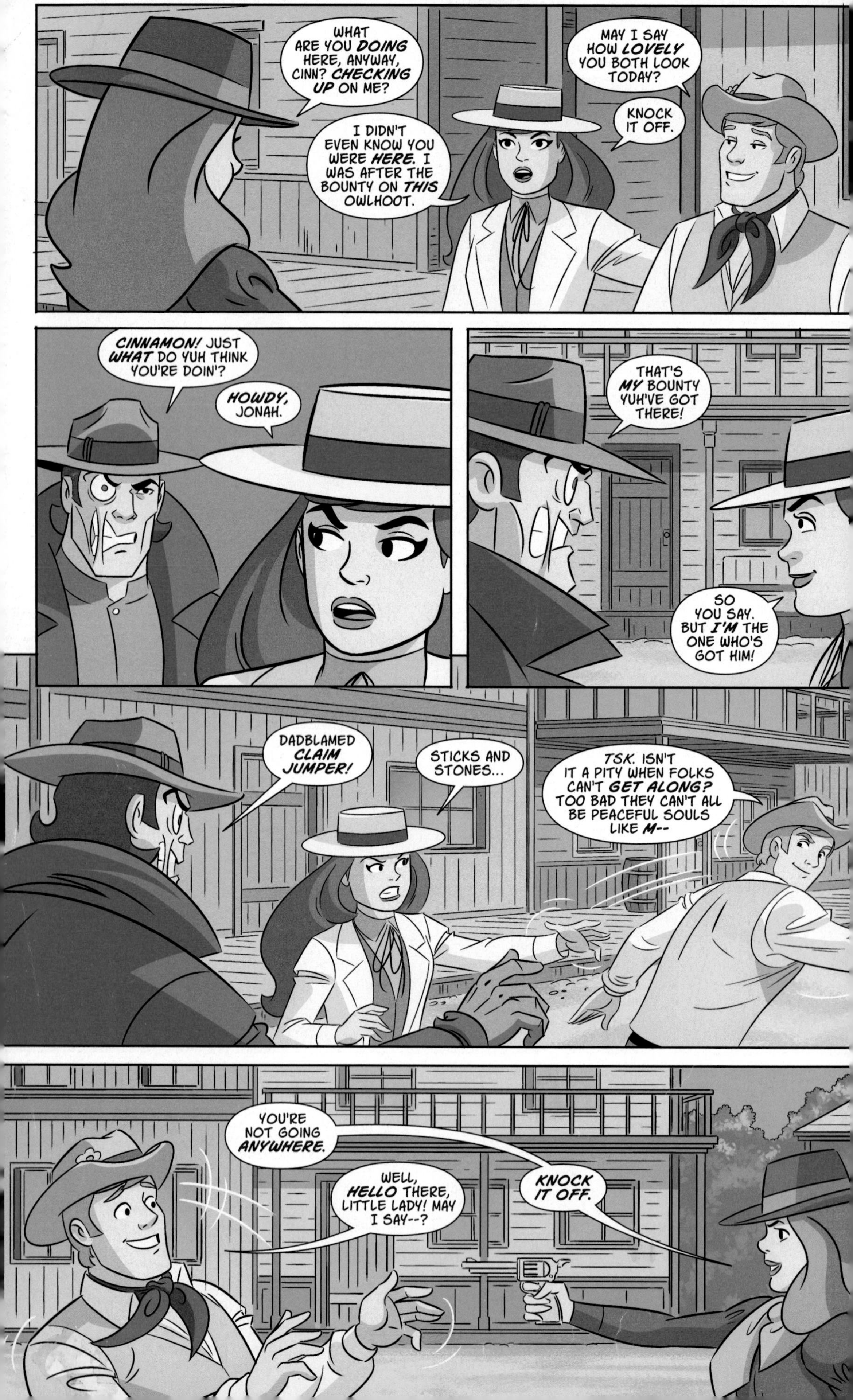
WHAT ARE YOU DOING HERE, ANYWAY, CINN? CHECKING UP ON ME?
I DIDN'T EVEN KNOW YOU WERE HERE. I WAS AFTER THE BOUNTY ON THIS OWLHOOT.
MAY I SAY HOW LOVELY YOU BOTH LOOK TODAY?
KNOCK IT OFF.
CINNAMON! JUST WHAT DO YUH THINK YOU'RE DOIN'?
HOWDY, JONAH.
THAT'S MY BOUNTY YUH'VE GOT THERE!
SO YOU SAY. BUT I'M THE ONE WHO'S GOT HIM!
DADBLAMED CLAIM JUMPER!
STICKS AND STONES...
TSK. ISN'T IT A PITY WHEN FOLKS CAN'T GET ALONG? TOO BAD THEY CAN'T ALL BE PEACEFUL SOULS LIKE M--
YOU'RE NOT GOING ANYWHERE.
WELL, HELLO THERE, LITTLE LADY! MAY I SAY--?
KNOCK IT OFF.

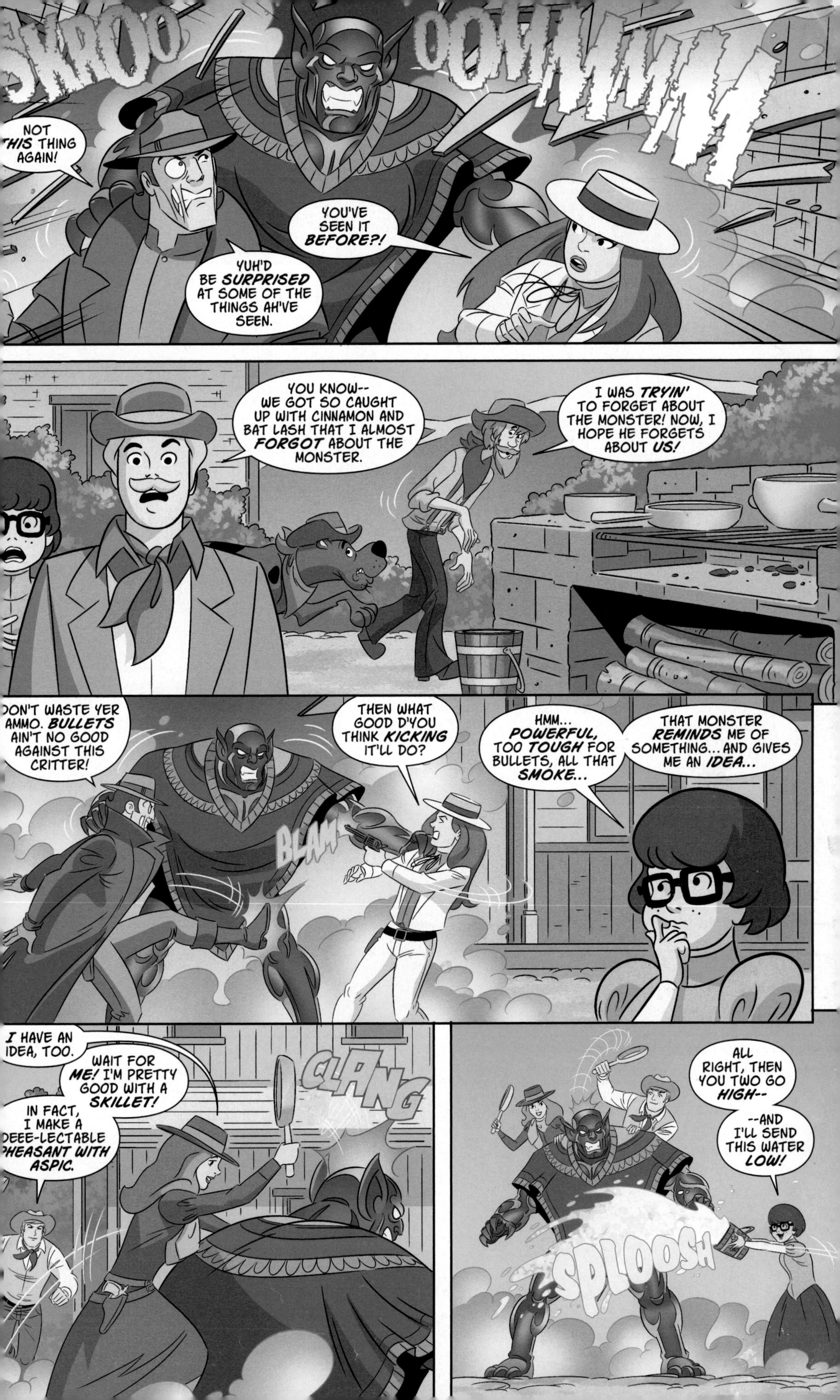
SKROOOOOWWMMM
NOT THIS THING AGAIN!
YOU'VE SEEN IT BEFORE?!
YUH'D BE SURPRISED AT SOME OF THE THINGS AH'VE SEEN.
YOU KNOW-- WE GOT SO CAUGHT UP WITH CINNAMON AND BAT LASH THAT I ALMOST FORGOT ABOUT THE MONSTER.
I WAS TRYIN' TO FORGET ABOUT THE MONSTER! NOW, I HOPE HE FORGETS ABOUT US!
DON'T WASTE YER AMMO. BULLETS AIN'T NO GOOD AGAINST THIS CRITTER!
THEN WHAT GOOD D'YOU THINK KICKING IT'LL DO?
BLAM
HMM... POWERFUL, TOO TOUGH FOR BULLETS, ALL THAT SMOKE...
THAT MONSTER REMINDS ME OF SOMETHING... AND GIVES ME AN IDEA...
I HAVE AN IDEA, TOO.
WAIT FOR ME! I'M PRETTY GOOD WITH A SKILLET!
IN FACT, I MAKE A DEEE-LECTABLE PHEASANT WITH ASPIC.
CLANG
ALL RIGHT, THEN YOU TWO GO HIGH--
--AND I'LL SEND THIS WATER LOW!
SPLOOSH

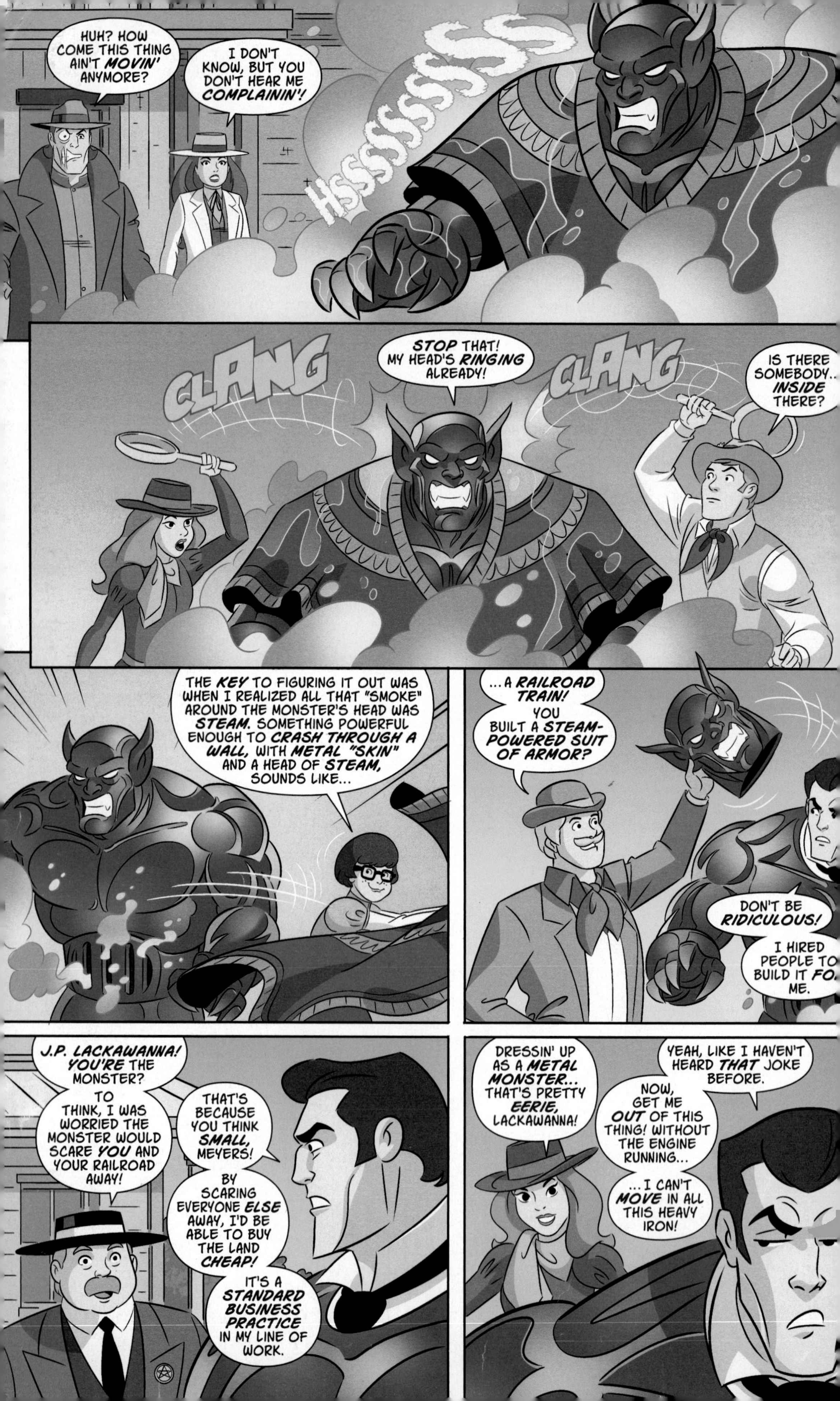

HUH? HOW COME THIS THING AIN'T MOVIN' ANYMORE?
I DON'T KNOW, BUT YOU DON'T HEAR ME COMPLAININ'!
HSSSSSSSSS
CLANG
STOP THAT! MY HEAD'S RINGING ALREADY!
CLANG
IS THERE SOMEBODY... INSIDE THERE?
THE KEY TO FIGURING IT OUT WAS WHEN I REALIZED ALL THAT "SMOKE" AROUND THE MONSTER'S HEAD WAS STEAM. SOMETHING POWERFUL ENOUGH TO CRASH THROUGH A WALL, WITH METAL "SKIN" AND A HEAD OF STEAM, SOUNDS LIKE...
...A RAILROAD TRAIN!
YOU BUILT A STEAM-POWERED SUIT OF ARMOR?
DON'T BE RIDICULOUS!
I HIRED PEOPLE TO BUILD IT FO ME.
J.P. LACKAWANNA! YOU'RE THE MONSTER?
TO THINK, I WAS WORRIED THE MONSTER WOULD SCARE YOU AND YOUR RAILROAD AWAY!
THAT'S BECAUSE YOU THINK SMALL, MEYERS!
BY SCARING EVERYONE ELSE AWAY, I'D BE ABLE TO BUY THE LAND CHEAP!
IT'S A STANDARD BUSINESS PRACTICE IN MY LINE OF WORK.
DRESSIN' UP AS A METAL MONSTER... THAT'S PRETTY EERIE, LACKAWANNA!
YEAH, LIKE I HAVEN'T HEARD THAT JOKE BEFORE.
NOW, GET ME OUT OF THIS THING! WITHOUT THE ENGINE RUNNING...
...I CAN'T MOVE IN ALL THIS HEAVY IRON!

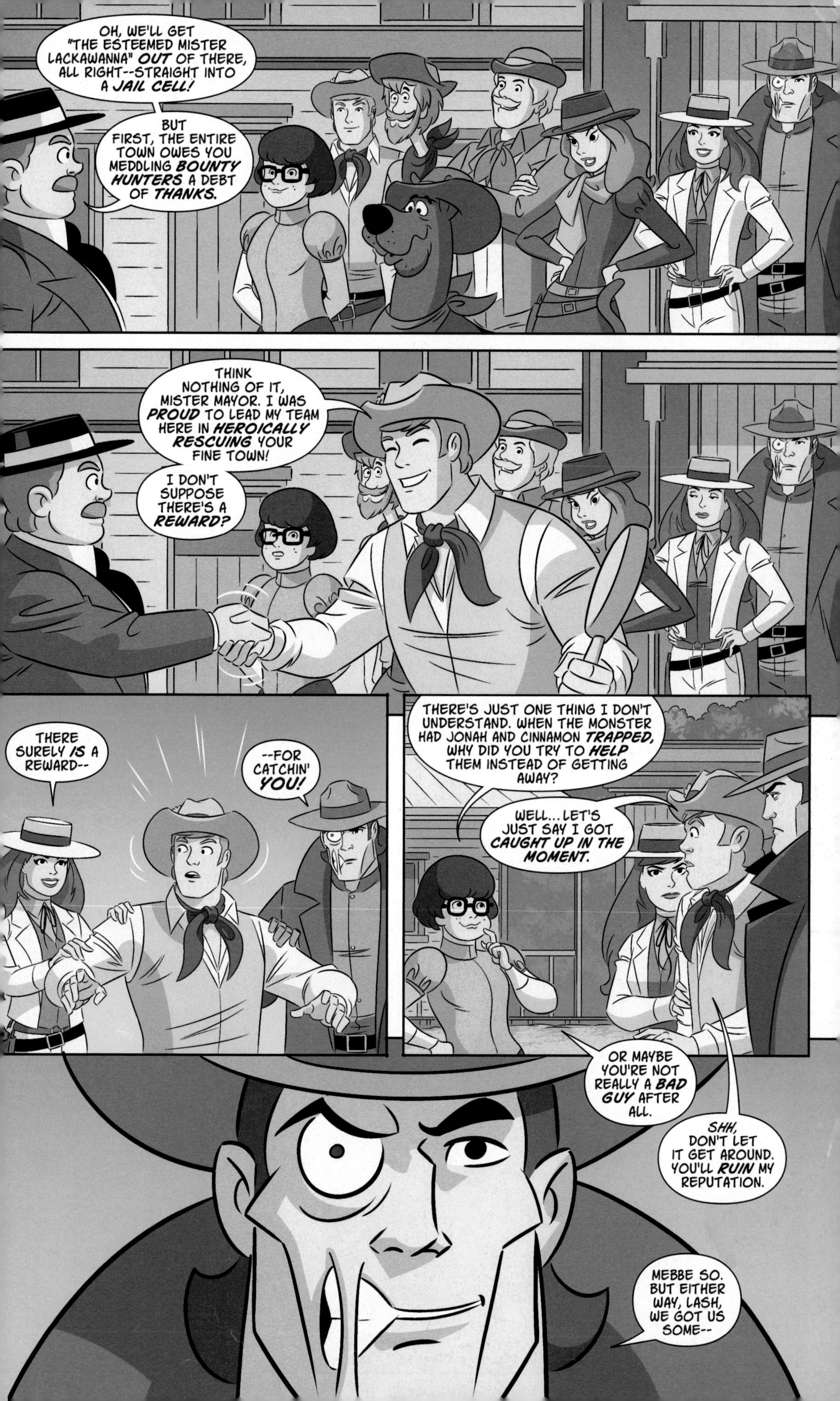

OH, WE'LL GET "THE ESTEEMED MISTER LACKAWANNA" OUT OF THERE, ALL RIGHT--STRAIGHT INTO A JAIL CELL!
BUT FIRST, THE ENTIRE TOWN OWES YOU MEDDLING BOUNTY HUNTERS A DEBT OF THANKS.
THINK NOTHING OF IT, MISTER MAYOR. I WAS PROUD TO LEAD MY TEAM HERE IN HEROICALLY RESCUING YOUR FINE TOWN!
I DON'T SUPPOSE THERE'S A REWARD?
THERE SURELY IS A REWARD--
--FOR CATCHIN' YOU!
THERE'S JUST ONE THING I DON'T UNDERSTAND. WHEN THE MONSTER HAD JONAH AND CINNAMON TRAPPED, WHY DID YOU TRY TO HELP THEM INSTEAD OF GETTING AWAY?
WELL... LET'S JUST SAY I GOT CAUGHT UP IN THE MOMENT.
OR MAYBE YOU'RE NOT REALLY A BAD GUY AFTER ALL.
SHH, DON'T LET IT GET AROUND. YOU'LL RUIN MY REPUTATION.
MEBBE SO. BUT EITHER WAY, LASH, WE GOT US SOME--

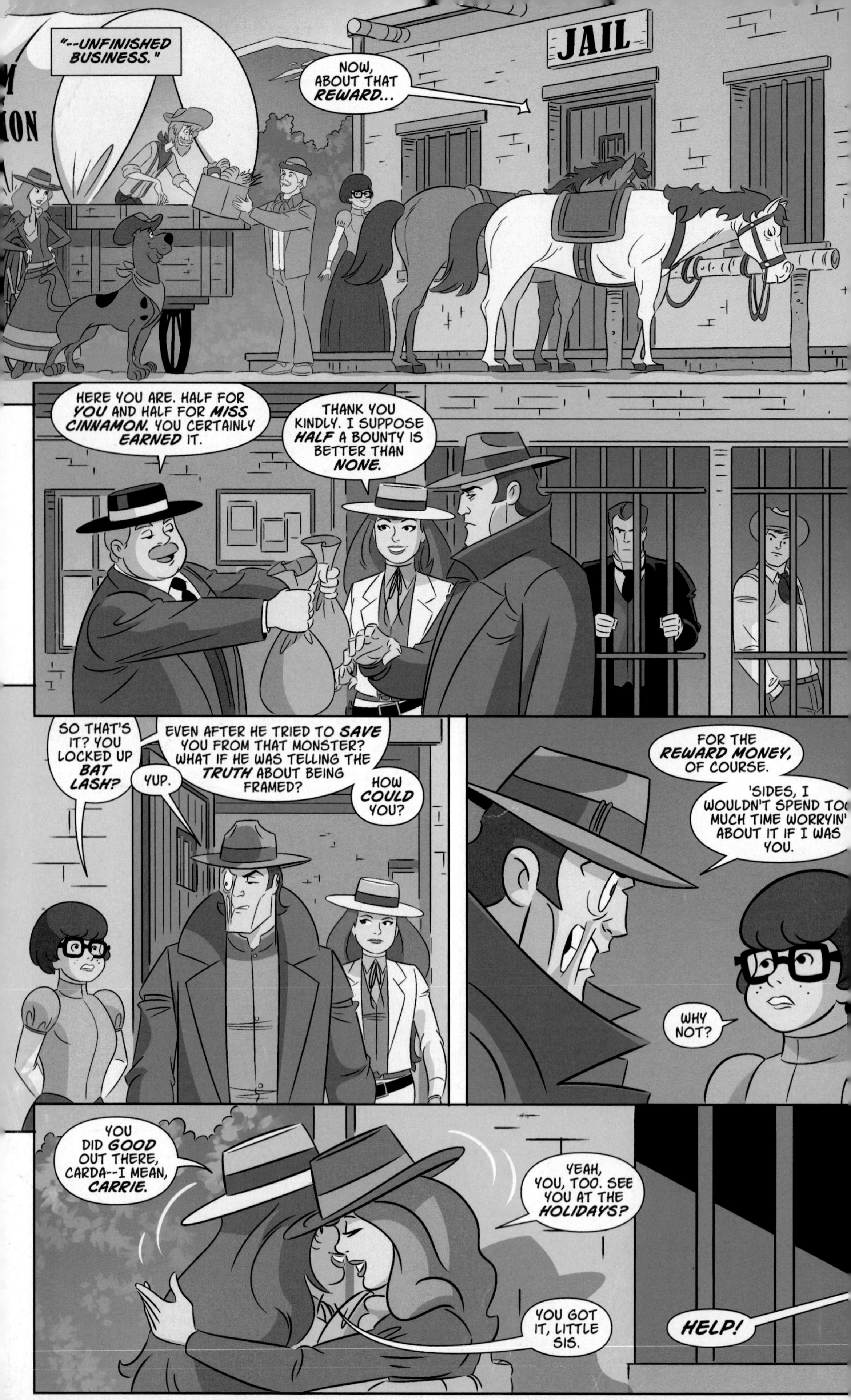
"--UNFINISHED BUSINESS."
NOW, ABOUT THAT REWARD...
JAIL
HERE YOU ARE. HALF FOR YOU AND HALF FOR MISS CINNAMON. YOU CERTAINLY EARNED IT.
THANK YOU KINDLY. I SUPPOSE HALF A BOUNTY IS BETTER THAN NONE.
SO THAT'S IT? YOU LOCKED UP BAT LASH?
YUP.
EVEN AFTER HE TRIED TO SAVE YOU FROM THAT MONSTER? WHAT IF HE WAS TELLING THE TRUTH ABOUT BEING FRAMED?
HOW COULD YOU?
FOR THE REWARD MONEY, OF COURSE.
'SIDES, I WOULDN'T SPEND TOO MUCH TIME WORRYIN' ABOUT IT IF I WAS YOU.
WHY NOT?
YOU DID GOOD OUT THERE, CARDA--I MEAN, CARRIE.
YEAH, YOU, TOO. SEE YOU AT THE HOLIDAYS?
YOU GOT IT, LITTLE SIS.
HELP!

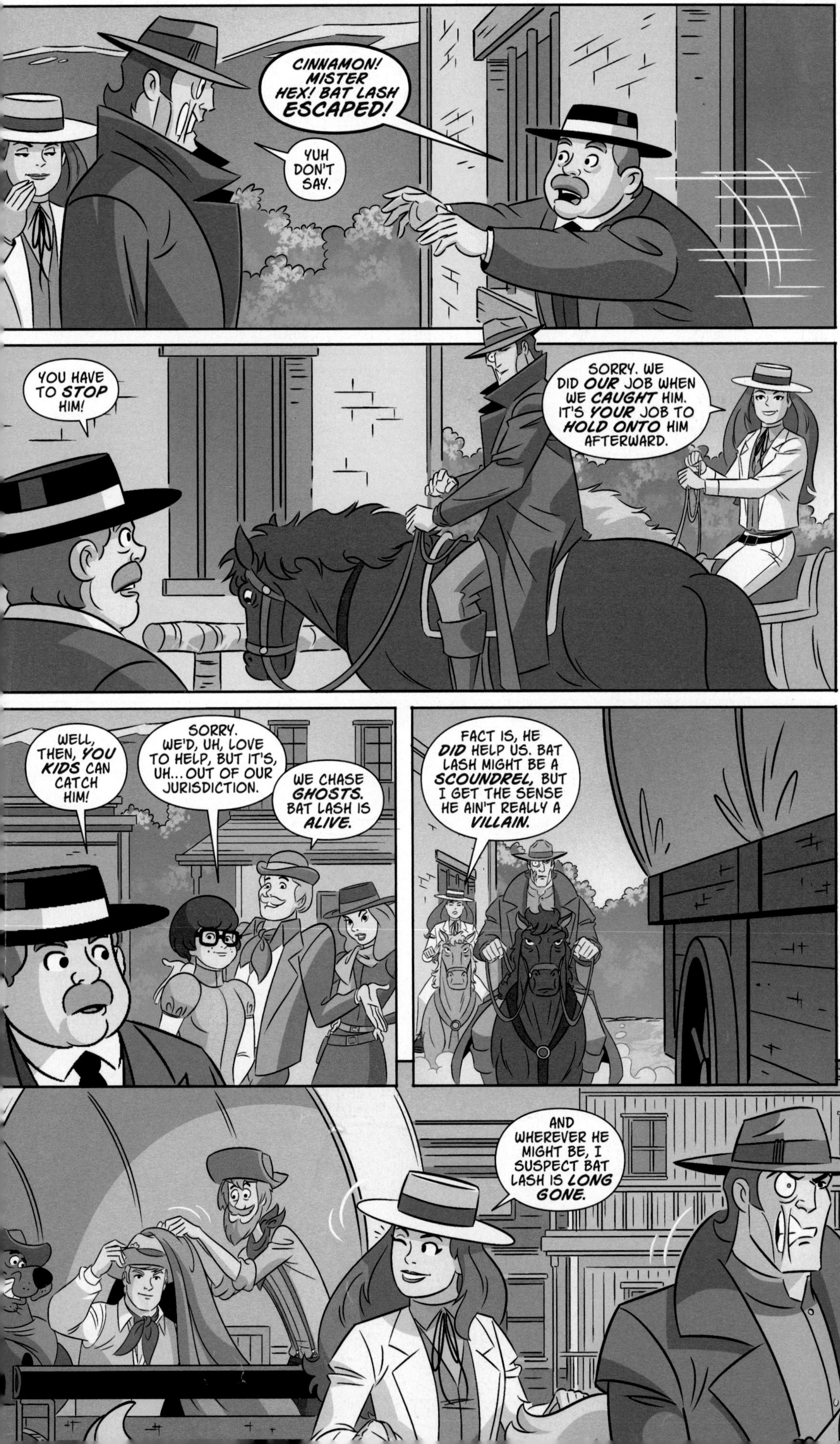
CINNAMON! MISTER HEX! BAT LASH ESCAPED!
YUH DON'T SAY.
YOU HAVE TO STOP HIM!
SORRY. WE DID OUR JOB WHEN WE CAUGHT HIM. IT'S YOUR JOB TO HOLD ONTO HIM AFTERWARD.
WELL, THEN, YOU KIDS CAN CATCH HIM!
SORRY. WE'D, UH, LOVE TO HELP, BUT IT'S, UH... OUT OF OUR JURISDICTION.
WE CHASE GHOSTS. BAT LASH IS ALIVE.
FACT IS, HE DID HELP US. BAT LASH MIGHT BE A SCOUNDREL, BUT I GET THE SENSE HE AIN'T REALLY A VILLAIN.
AND WHEREVER HE MIGHT BE, I SUSPECT BAT LASH IS LONG GONE.

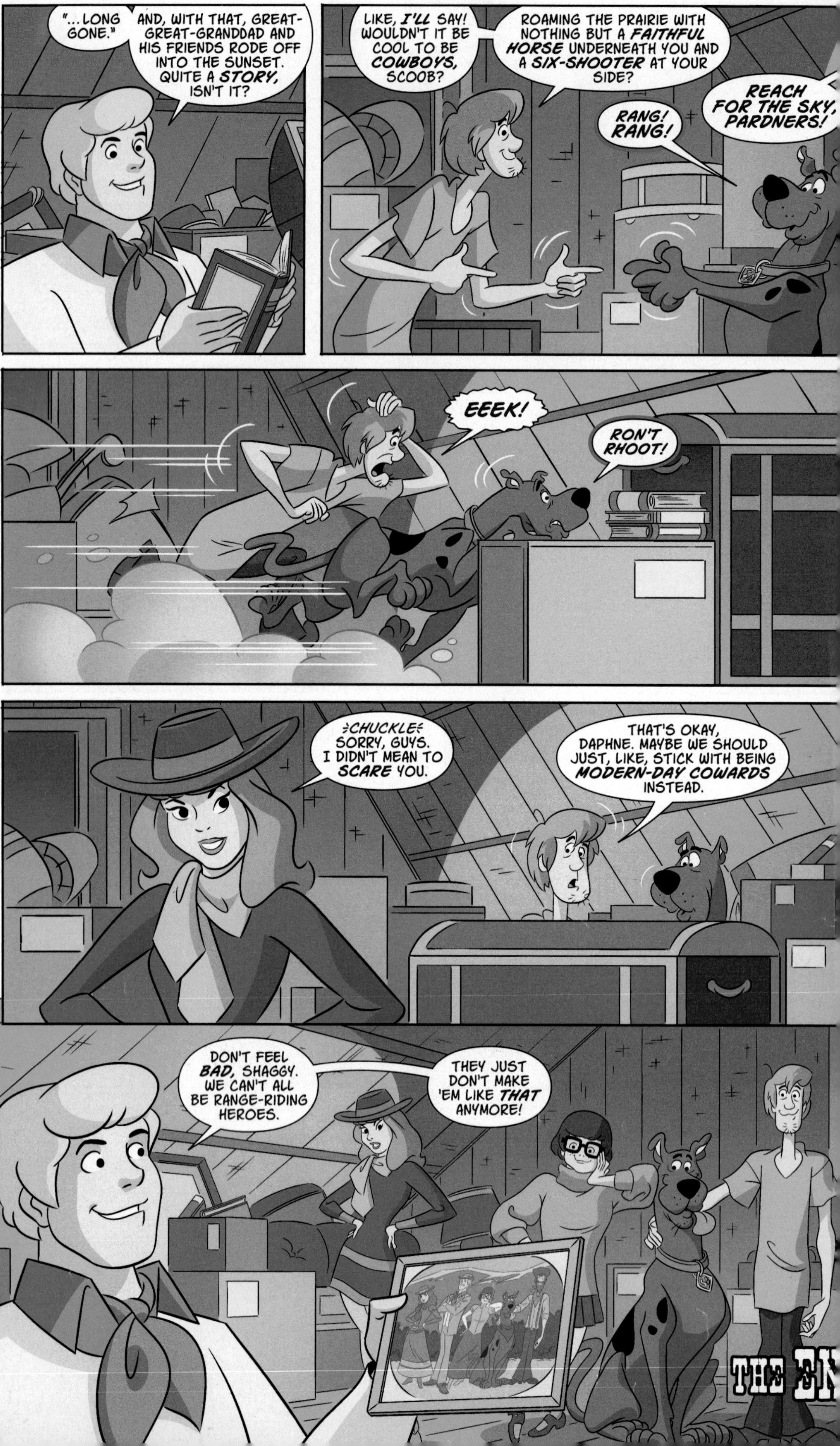
"...LONG GONE."
AND, WITH THAT, GREAT-GREAT-GRANDDAD AND HIS FRIENDS RODE OFF INTO THE SUNSET. QUITE A *STORY,* ISN'T IT?
LIKE, *I'LL* SAY! WOULDN'T IT BE COOL TO BE *COWBOYS,* SCOOB?
ROAMING THE PRAIRIE WITH NOTHING BUT A *FAITHFUL HORSE* UNDERNEATH YOU AND A *SIX-SHOOTER* AT YOUR SIDE?
RANG! RANG!
REACH FOR THE SKY, PARDNERS!
EEEK!
RON'T RHOOT!
CHUCKLE SORRY, GUYS. I DIDN'T MEAN TO *SCARE* YOU.
THAT'S OKAY, DAPHNE. MAYBE WE SHOULD JUST, LIKE, STICK WITH BEING *MODERN-DAY COWARDS* INSTEAD.
DON'T FEEL *BAD,* SHAGGY. WE CAN'T ALL BE RANGE-RIDING HEROES.
THEY JUST DON'T MAKE 'EM LIKE *THAT* ANYMORE!

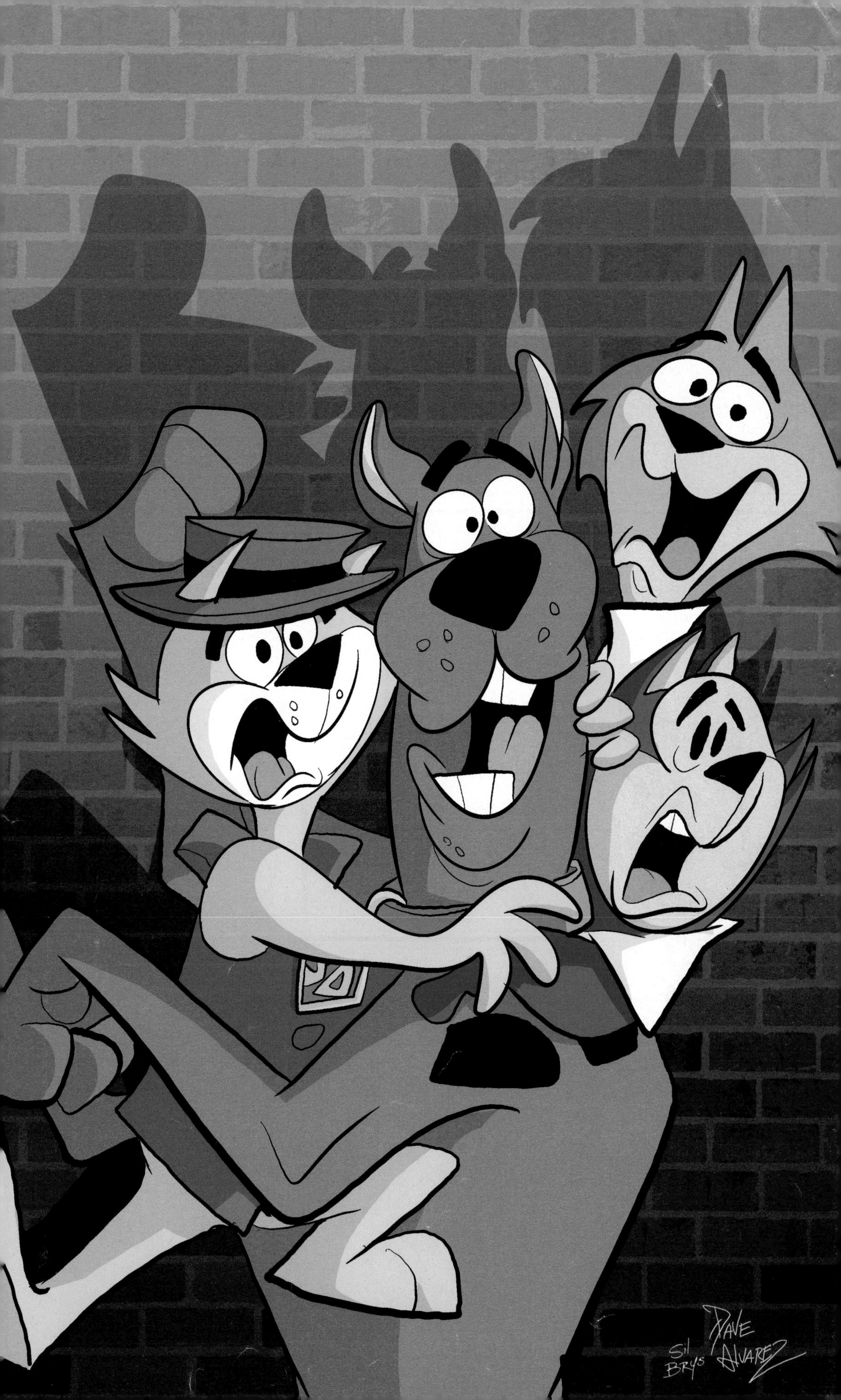
Dave Alvarez
Sil Brys

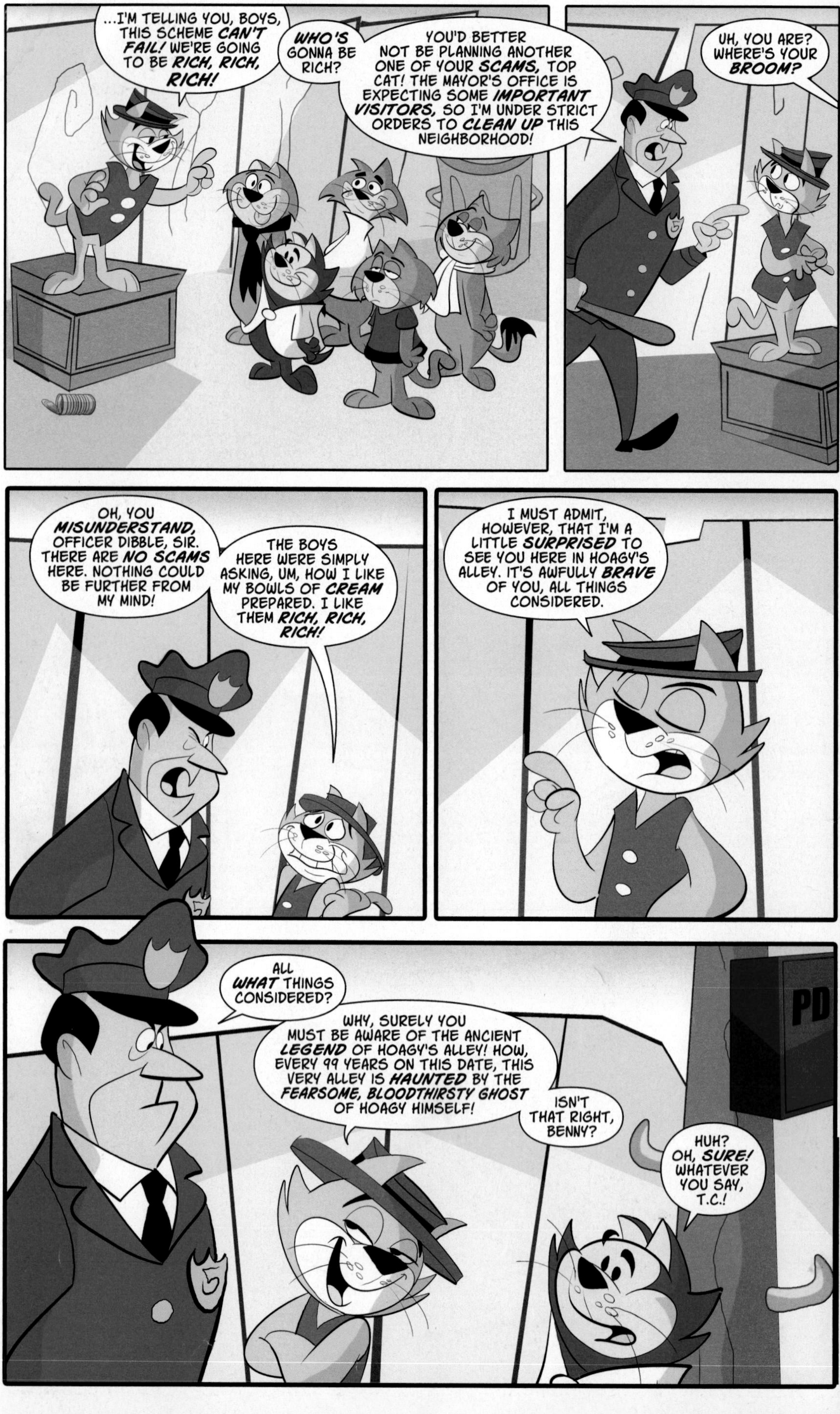
...I'M TELLING YOU, BOYS, THIS SCHEME CAN'T FAIL! WE'RE GOING TO BE RICH, RICH, RICH!
WHO'S GONNA BE RICH?
YOU'D BETTER NOT BE PLANNING ANOTHER ONE OF YOUR SCAMS, TOP CAT! THE MAYOR'S OFFICE IS EXPECTING SOME IMPORTANT VISITORS, SO I'M UNDER STRICT ORDERS TO CLEAN UP THIS NEIGHBORHOOD!
UH, YOU ARE? WHERE'S YOUR BROOM?
OH, YOU MISUNDERSTAND, OFFICER DIBBLE, SIR. THERE ARE NO SCAMS HERE. NOTHING COULD BE FURTHER FROM MY MIND!
THE BOYS HERE WERE SIMPLY ASKING, UM, HOW I LIKE MY BOWLS OF CREAM PREPARED. I LIKE THEM RICH, RICH, RICH!
I MUST ADMIT, HOWEVER, THAT I'M A LITTLE SURPRISED TO SEE YOU HERE IN HOAGY'S ALLEY. IT'S AWFULLY BRAVE OF YOU, ALL THINGS CONSIDERED.
ALL WHAT THINGS CONSIDERED?
WHY, SURELY YOU MUST BE AWARE OF THE ANCIENT LEGEND OF HOAGY'S ALLEY! HOW, EVERY 99 YEARS ON THIS DATE, THIS VERY ALLEY IS HAUNTED BY THE FEARSOME, BLOODTHIRSTY GHOST OF HOAGY HIMSELF!
ISN'T THAT RIGHT, BENNY?
HUH? OH, SURE! WHATEVER YOU SAY, T.C.!
PD

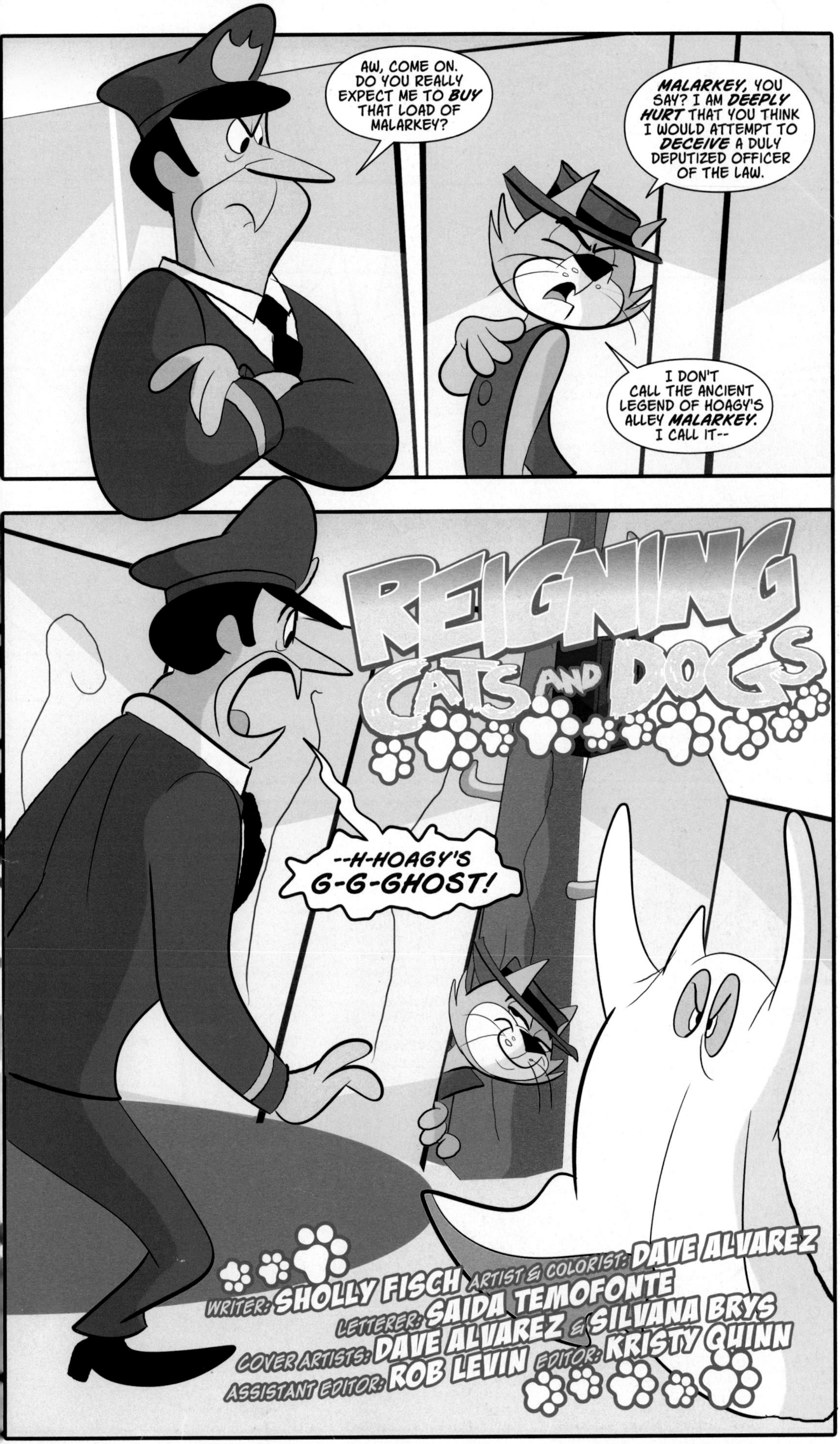
AW, COME ON. DO YOU REALLY EXPECT ME TO BUY THAT LOAD OF MALARKEY?
MALARKEY, YOU SAY? I AM DEEPLY HURT THAT YOU THINK I WOULD ATTEMPT TO DECEIVE A DULY DEPUTIZED OFFICER OF THE LAW.
I DON'T CALL THE ANCIENT LEGEND OF HOAGY'S ALLEY MALARKEY. I CALL IT--
REIGNING CATS AND DOGS
--H-HOAGY'S G-G-GHOST!
WRITER: SHOLLY FISCH ARTIST & COLORIST: DAVE ALVAREZ
LETTERER: SAIDA TEMOFONTE
COVER ARTISTS: DAVE ALVAREZ & SILVANA BRYS
ASSISTANT EDITOR: ROB LEVIN EDITOR: KRISTY QUINN

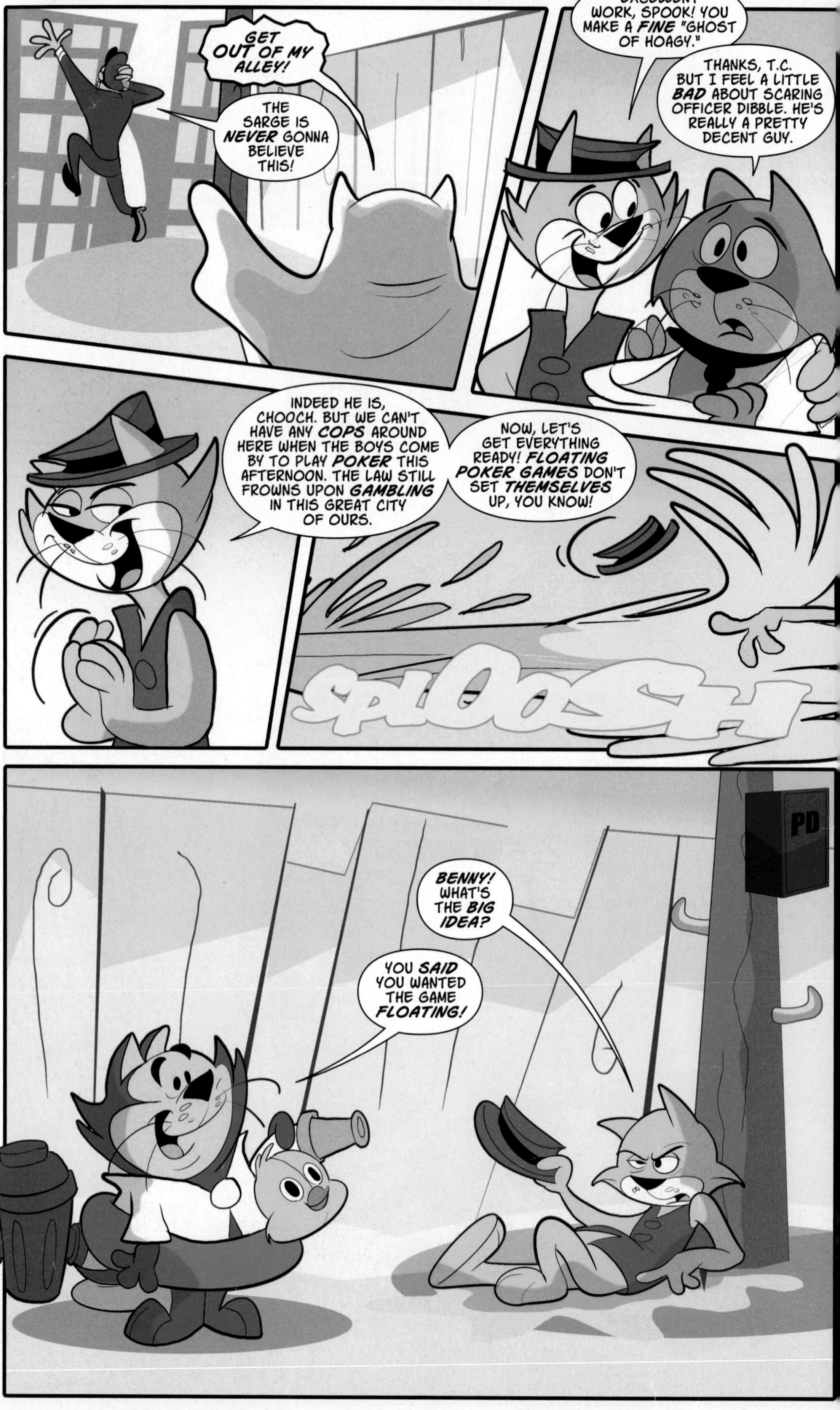
GET OUT OF MY ALLEY!
THE SARGE IS NEVER GONNA BELIEVE THIS!
EXCELLENT WORK, SPOOK! YOU MAKE A FINE "GHOST OF HOAGY."
THANKS, T.C. BUT I FEEL A LITTLE BAD ABOUT SCARING OFFICER DIBBLE. HE'S REALLY A PRETTY DECENT GUY.
INDEED HE IS, CHOOCH. BUT WE CAN'T HAVE ANY COPS AROUND HERE WHEN THE BOYS COME BY TO PLAY POKER THIS AFTERNOON. THE LAW STILL FROWNS UPON GAMBLING IN THIS GREAT CITY OF OURS.
NOW, LET'S GET EVERYTHING READY! FLOATING POKER GAMES DON'T SET THEMSELVES UP, YOU KNOW!
SPLOOSH
PD
BENNY! WHAT'S THE BIG IDEA?
YOU SAID YOU WANTED THE GAME FLOATING!

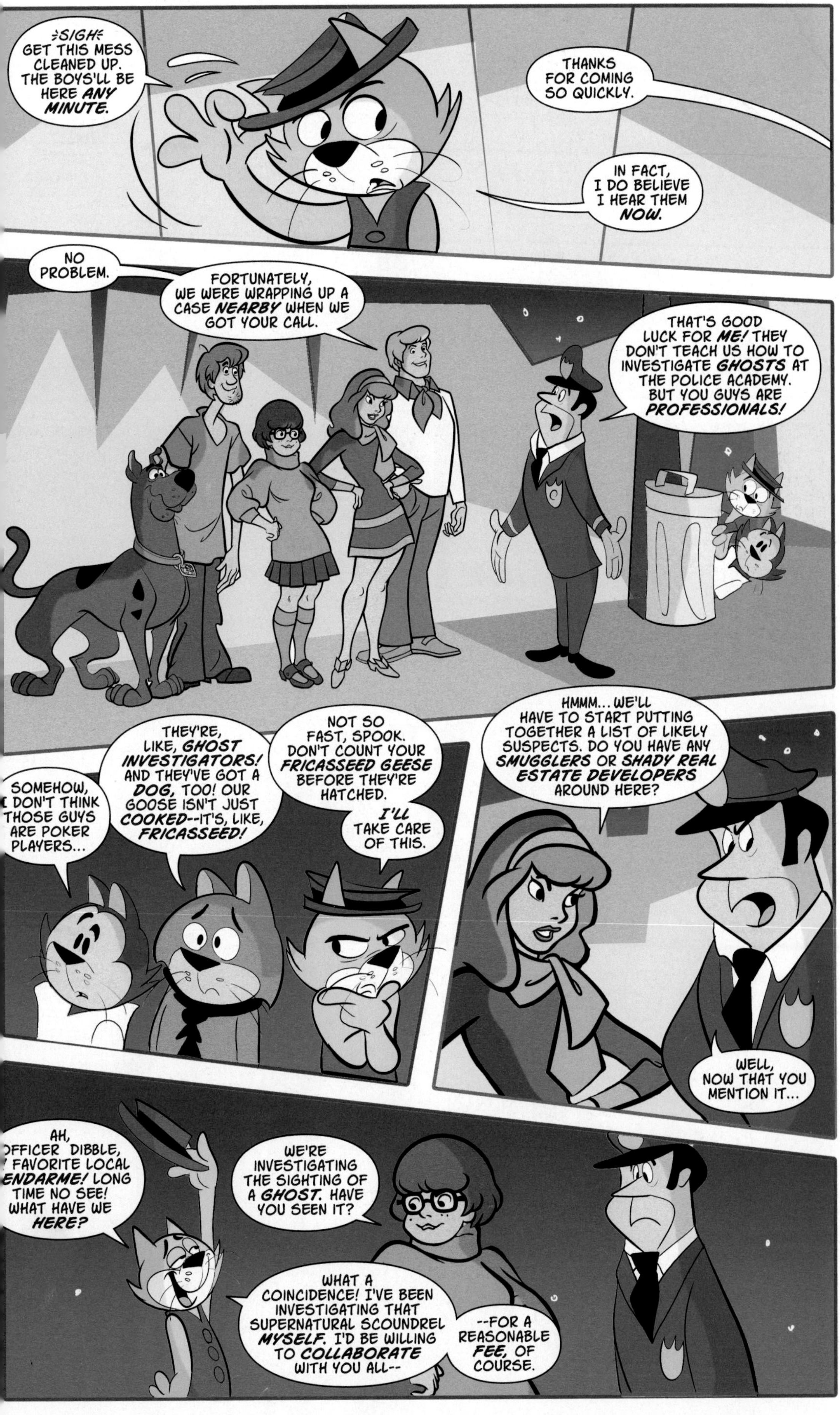

SIGH GET THIS MESS CLEANED UP. THE BOYS'LL BE HERE ANY MINUTE.
THANKS FOR COMING SO QUICKLY.
IN FACT, I DO BELIEVE I HEAR THEM NOW.
NO PROBLEM.
FORTUNATELY, WE WERE WRAPPING UP A CASE NEARBY WHEN WE GOT YOUR CALL.
THAT'S GOOD LUCK FOR ME! THEY DON'T TEACH US HOW TO INVESTIGATE GHOSTS AT THE POLICE ACADEMY. BUT YOU GUYS ARE PROFESSIONALS!
SOMEHOW, I DON'T THINK THOSE GUYS ARE POKER PLAYERS...
THEY'RE, LIKE, GHOST INVESTIGATORS! AND THEY'VE GOT A DOG, TOO! OUR GOOSE ISN'T JUST COOKED--IT'S, LIKE, FRICASSEED!
NOT SO FAST, SPOOK. DON'T COUNT YOUR FRICASSEED GEESE BEFORE THEY'RE HATCHED.
I'LL TAKE CARE OF THIS.
HMMM... WE'LL HAVE TO START PUTTING TOGETHER A LIST OF LIKELY SUSPECTS. DO YOU HAVE ANY SMUGGLERS OR SHADY REAL ESTATE DEVELOPERS AROUND HERE?
WELL, NOW THAT YOU MENTION IT...
AH, OFFICER DIBBLE, FAVORITE LOCAL ENDARME! LONG TIME NO SEE! WHAT HAVE WE HERE?
WE'RE INVESTIGATING THE SIGHTING OF A GHOST. HAVE YOU SEEN IT?
WHAT A COINCIDENCE! I'VE BEEN INVESTIGATING THAT SUPERNATURAL SCOUNDREL MYSELF. I'D BE WILLING TO COLLABORATE WITH YOU ALL--
--FOR A REASONABLE FEE, OF COURSE.

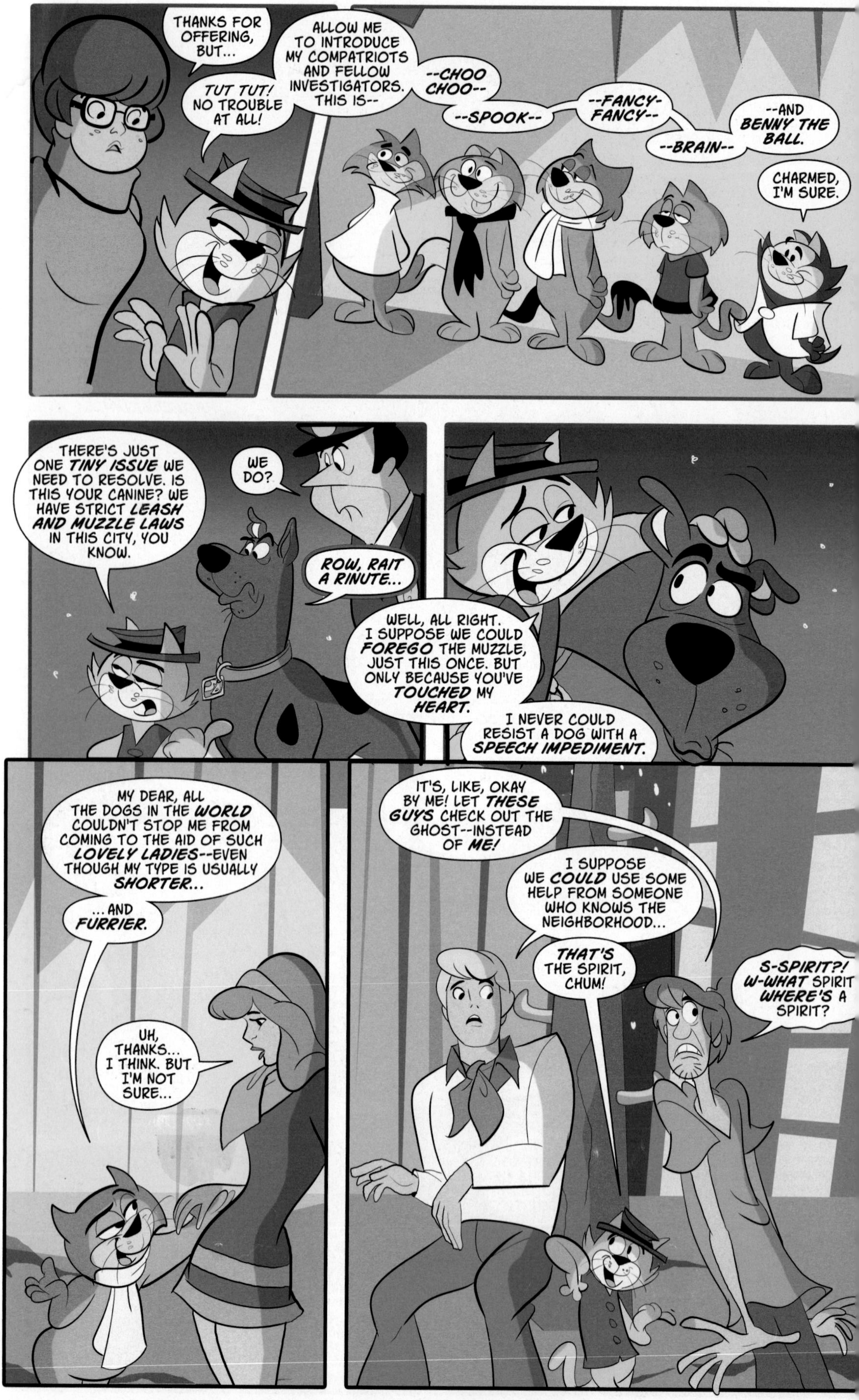
THANKS FOR OFFERING, BUT...
TUT TUT! NO TROUBLE AT ALL!
ALLOW ME TO INTRODUCE MY COMPATRIOTS AND FELLOW INVESTIGATORS. THIS IS--
--CHOO CHOO--
--SPOOK--
--FANCY-FANCY--
--BRAIN--
--AND BENNY THE BALL.
CHARMED, I'M SURE.
THERE'S JUST ONE TINY ISSUE WE NEED TO RESOLVE. IS THIS YOUR CANINE? WE HAVE STRICT LEASH AND MUZZLE LAWS IN THIS CITY, YOU KNOW.
WE DO?
ROW, RAIT A RINUTE...
WELL, ALL RIGHT. I SUPPOSE WE COULD FOREGO THE MUZZLE, JUST THIS ONCE. BUT ONLY BECAUSE YOU'VE TOUCHED MY HEART.
I NEVER COULD RESIST A DOG WITH A SPEECH IMPEDIMENT.
MY DEAR, ALL THE DOGS IN THE WORLD COULDN'T STOP ME FROM COMING TO THE AID OF SUCH LOVELY LADIES--EVEN THOUGH MY TYPE IS USUALLY SHORTER...
...AND FURRIER.
UH, THANKS... I THINK. BUT I'M NOT SURE...
IT'S, LIKE, OKAY BY ME! LET THESE GUYS CHECK OUT THE GHOST--INSTEAD OF ME!
I SUPPOSE WE COULD USE SOME HELP FROM SOMEONE WHO KNOWS THE NEIGHBORHOOD...
THAT'S THE SPIRIT, CHUM!
S-SPIRIT?! W-WHAT SPIRIT WHERE'S A SPIRIT?

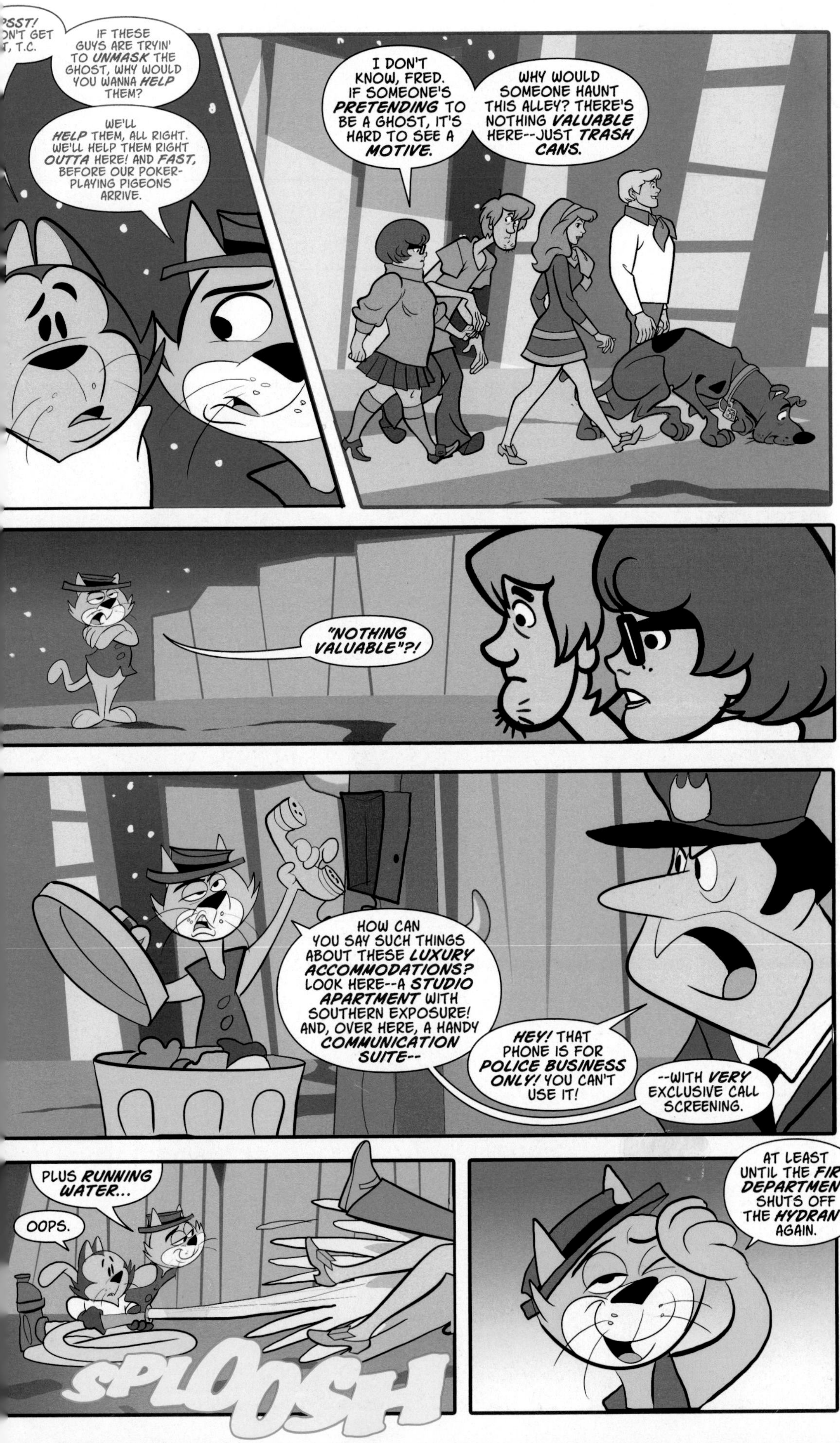
PSST! ...DON'T GET ...T, T.C.
IF THESE GUYS ARE TRYIN' TO UNMASK THE GHOST, WHY WOULD YOU WANNA HELP THEM?
WE'LL HELP THEM, ALL RIGHT. WE'LL HELP THEM RIGHT OUTTA HERE! AND FAST, BEFORE OUR POKER-PLAYING PIGEONS ARRIVE.
I DON'T KNOW, FRED. IF SOMEONE'S PRETENDING TO BE A GHOST, IT'S HARD TO SEE A MOTIVE.
WHY WOULD SOMEONE HAUNT THIS ALLEY? THERE'S NOTHING VALUABLE HERE--JUST TRASH CANS.
"NOTHING VALUABLE"?!
HOW CAN YOU SAY SUCH THINGS ABOUT THESE LUXURY ACCOMMODATIONS? LOOK HERE--A STUDIO APARTMENT WITH SOUTHERN EXPOSURE! AND, OVER HERE, A HANDY COMMUNICATION SUITE--
HEY! THAT PHONE IS FOR POLICE BUSINESS ONLY! YOU CAN'T USE IT!
--WITH VERY EXCLUSIVE CALL SCREENING.
PLUS RUNNING WATER...
OOPS.
SPLOOOSH
AT LEAST UNTIL THE FIRE DEPARTMENT SHUTS OFF THE HYDRANT AGAIN.

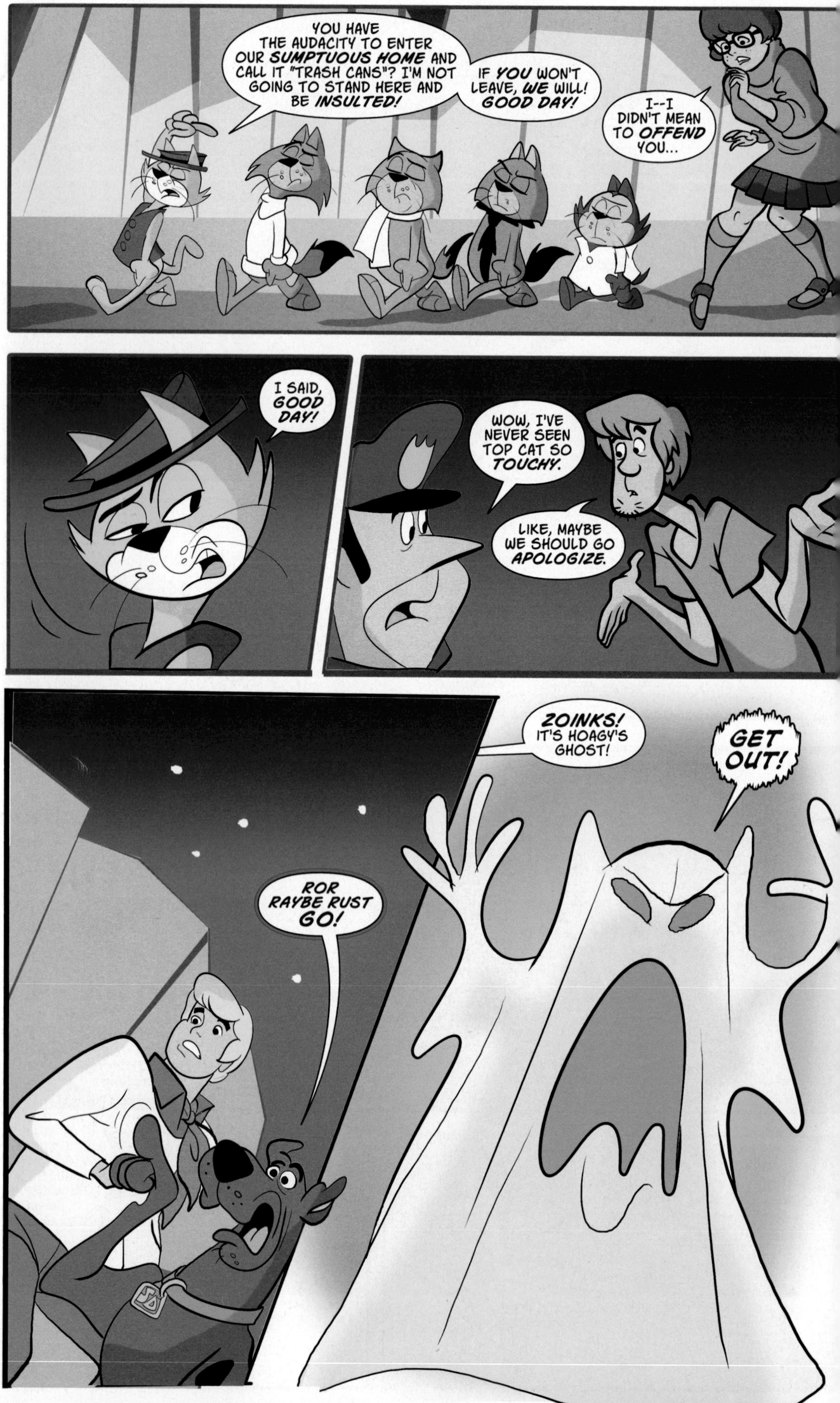
YOU HAVE THE AUDACITY TO ENTER OUR SUMPTUOUS HOME AND CALL IT "TRASH CANS"? I'M NOT GOING TO STAND HERE AND BE INSULTED!
IF YOU WON'T LEAVE, WE WILL! GOOD DAY!
I--I DIDN'T MEAN TO OFFEND YOU...
I SAID, GOOD DAY!
WOW, I'VE NEVER SEEN TOP CAT SO TOUCHY.
LIKE, MAYBE WE SHOULD GO APOLOGIZE.
ZOINKS! IT'S HOAGY'S GHOST!
GET OUT!
ROR RAYBE RUST GO!

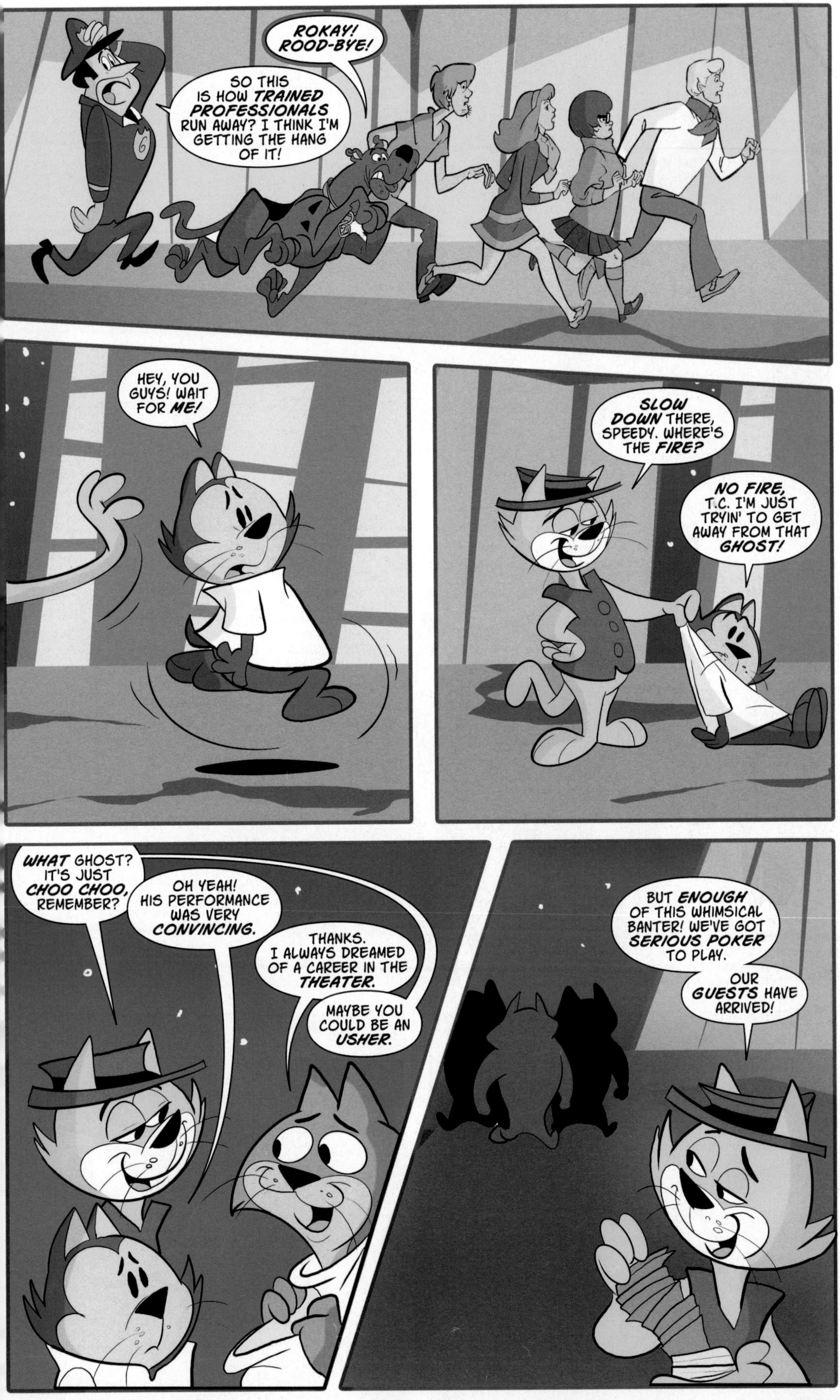
SO THIS IS HOW TRAINED PROFESSIONALS RUN AWAY? I THINK I'M GETTING THE HANG OF IT!
ROKAY! ROOD-BYE!
HEY, YOU GUYS! WAIT FOR ME!
SLOW DOWN THERE, SPEEDY. WHERE'S THE FIRE?
NO FIRE, T.C. I'M JUST TRYIN' TO GET AWAY FROM THAT GHOST!
WHAT GHOST? IT'S JUST CHOO CHOO, REMEMBER?
OH YEAH! HIS PERFORMANCE WAS VERY CONVINCING.
THANKS. I ALWAYS DREAMED OF A CAREER IN THE THEATER.
MAYBE YOU COULD BE AN USHER.
BUT ENOUGH OF THIS WHIMSICAL BANTER! WE'VE GOT SERIOUS POKER TO PLAY.
OUR GUESTS HAVE ARRIVED!

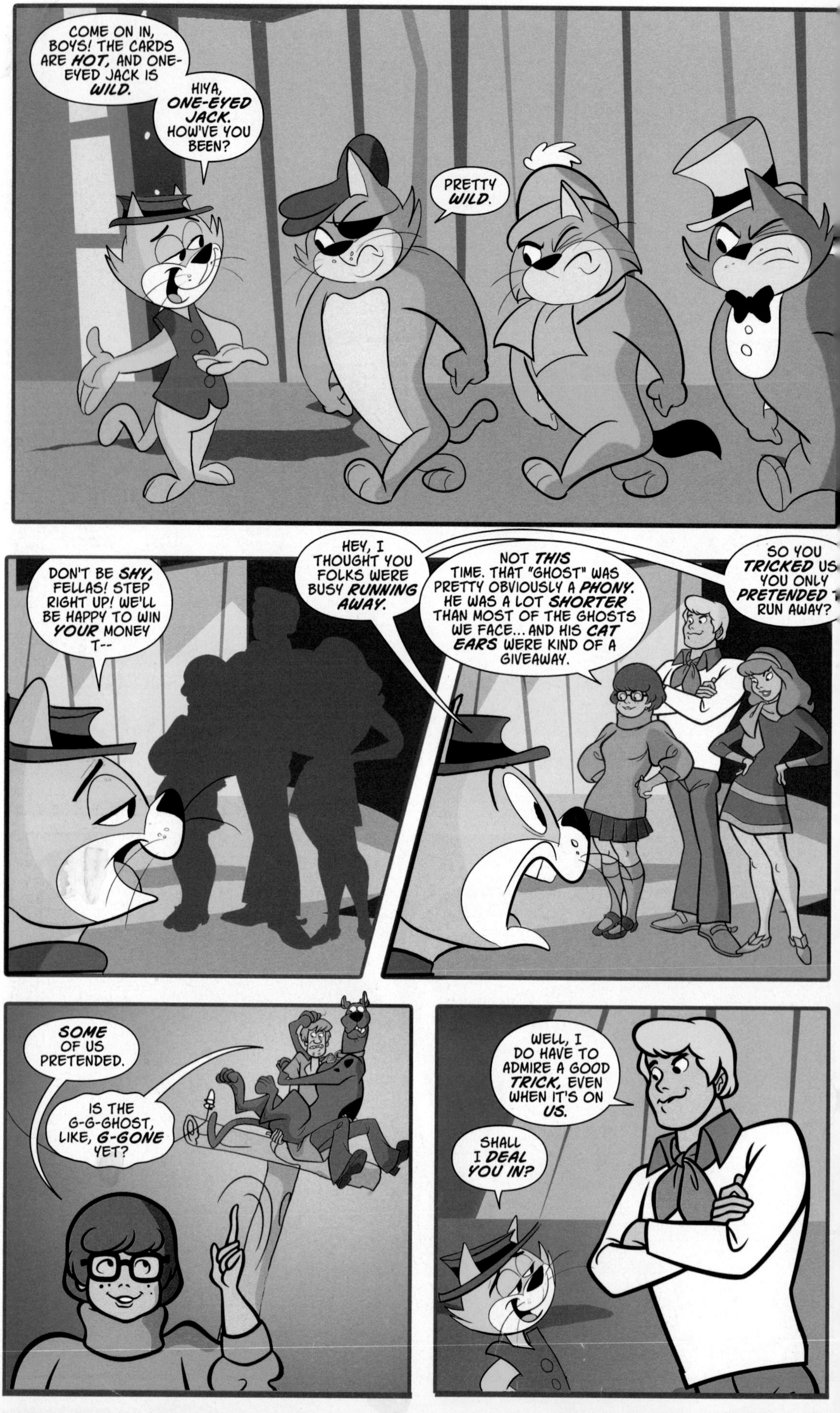

COME ON IN, BOYS! THE CARDS ARE *HOT*, AND ONE-EYED JACK IS *WILD*.
HIYA, *ONE-EYED JACK*. HOW'VE YOU BEEN?
PRETTY *WILD*.
DON'T BE *SHY*, FELLAS! STEP RIGHT UP! WE'LL BE HAPPY TO WIN *YOUR* MONEY T--
HEY, I THOUGHT YOU FOLKS WERE BUSY *RUNNING AWAY*.
NOT *THIS* TIME. THAT "GHOST" WAS PRETTY OBVIOUSLY A *PHONY*. HE WAS A LOT *SHORTER* THAN MOST OF THE GHOSTS WE FACE... AND HIS *CAT EARS* WERE KIND OF A GIVEAWAY.
SO YOU *TRICKED* US. YOU ONLY *PRETENDED* TO RUN AWAY?
SOME OF US PRETENDED.
IS THE G-G-GHOST, LIKE, *G-GONE* YET?
WELL, I DO HAVE TO ADMIRE A GOOD *TRICK*, EVEN WHEN IT'S ON *US*.
SHALL I *DEAL YOU IN*?

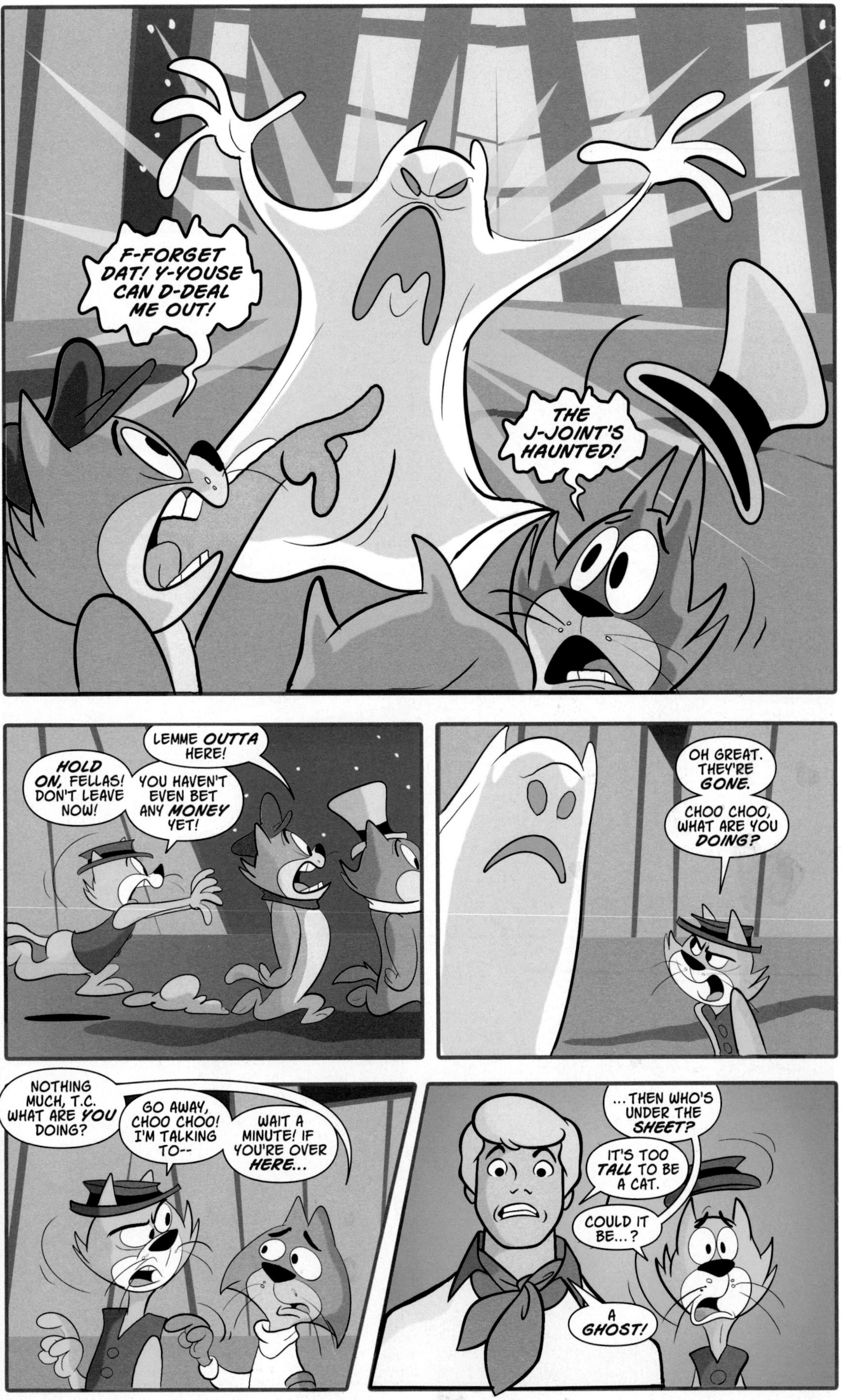
F-FORGET DAT! Y-YOUSE CAN D-DEAL ME OUT!
THE J-JOINT'S HAUNTED!
HOLD ON, FELLAS! DON'T LEAVE NOW!
LEMME OUTTA HERE!
YOU HAVEN'T EVEN BET ANY MONEY YET!
OH GREAT. THEY'RE GONE.
CHOO CHOO, WHAT ARE YOU DOING?
NOTHING MUCH, T.C. WHAT ARE YOU DOING?
GO AWAY, CHOO CHOO! I'M TALKING TO--
WAIT A MINUTE! IF YOU'RE OVER HERE...
...THEN WHO'S UNDER THE SHEET?
IT'S TOO TALL TO BE A CAT.
COULD IT BE...?
A GHOST!

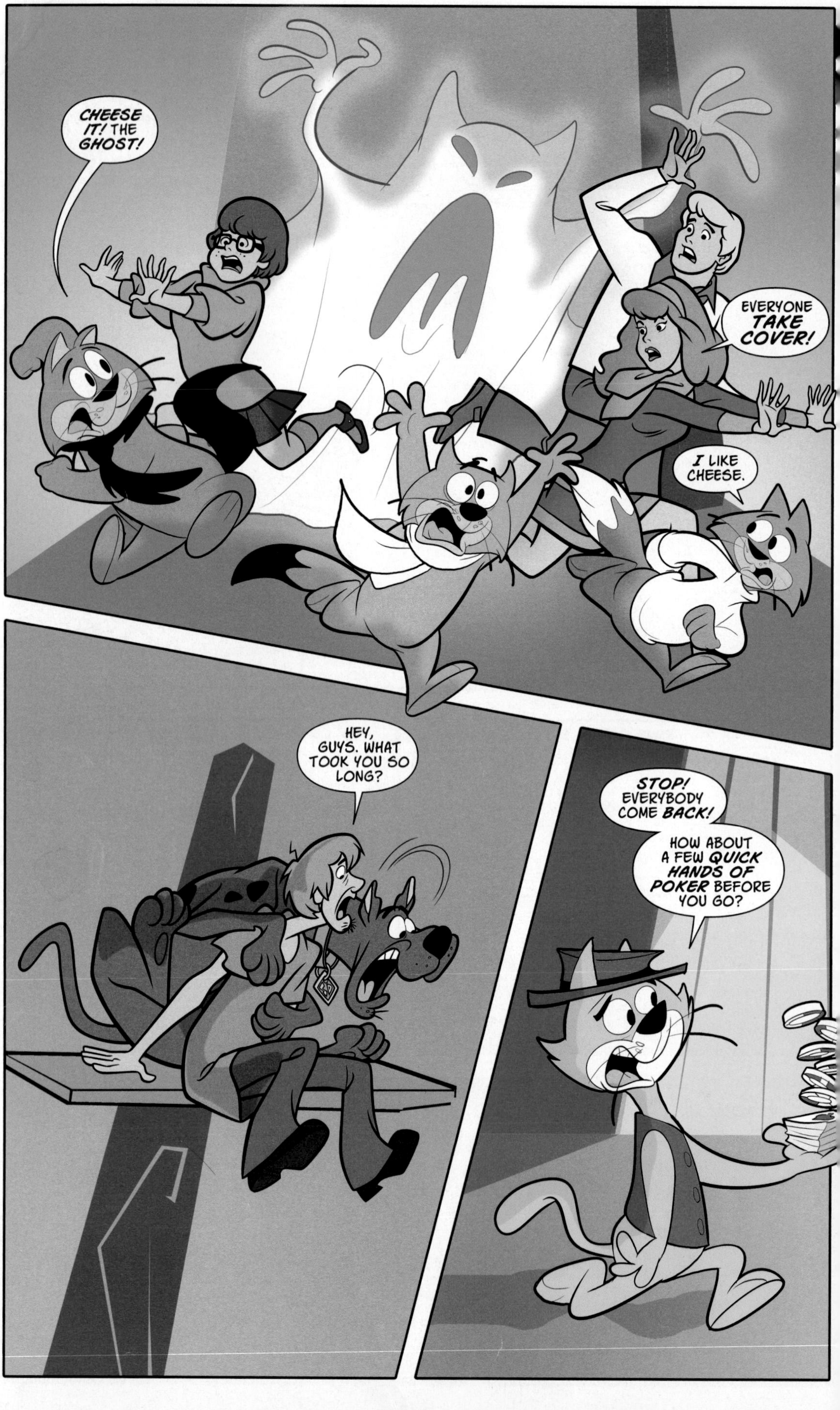
CHEESE IT! THE GHOST!
EVERYONE TAKE COVER!
I LIKE CHEESE.
HEY, GUYS. WHAT TOOK YOU SO LONG?
STOP! EVERYBODY COME BACK!
HOW ABOUT A FEW QUICK HANDS OF POKER BEFORE YOU GO?

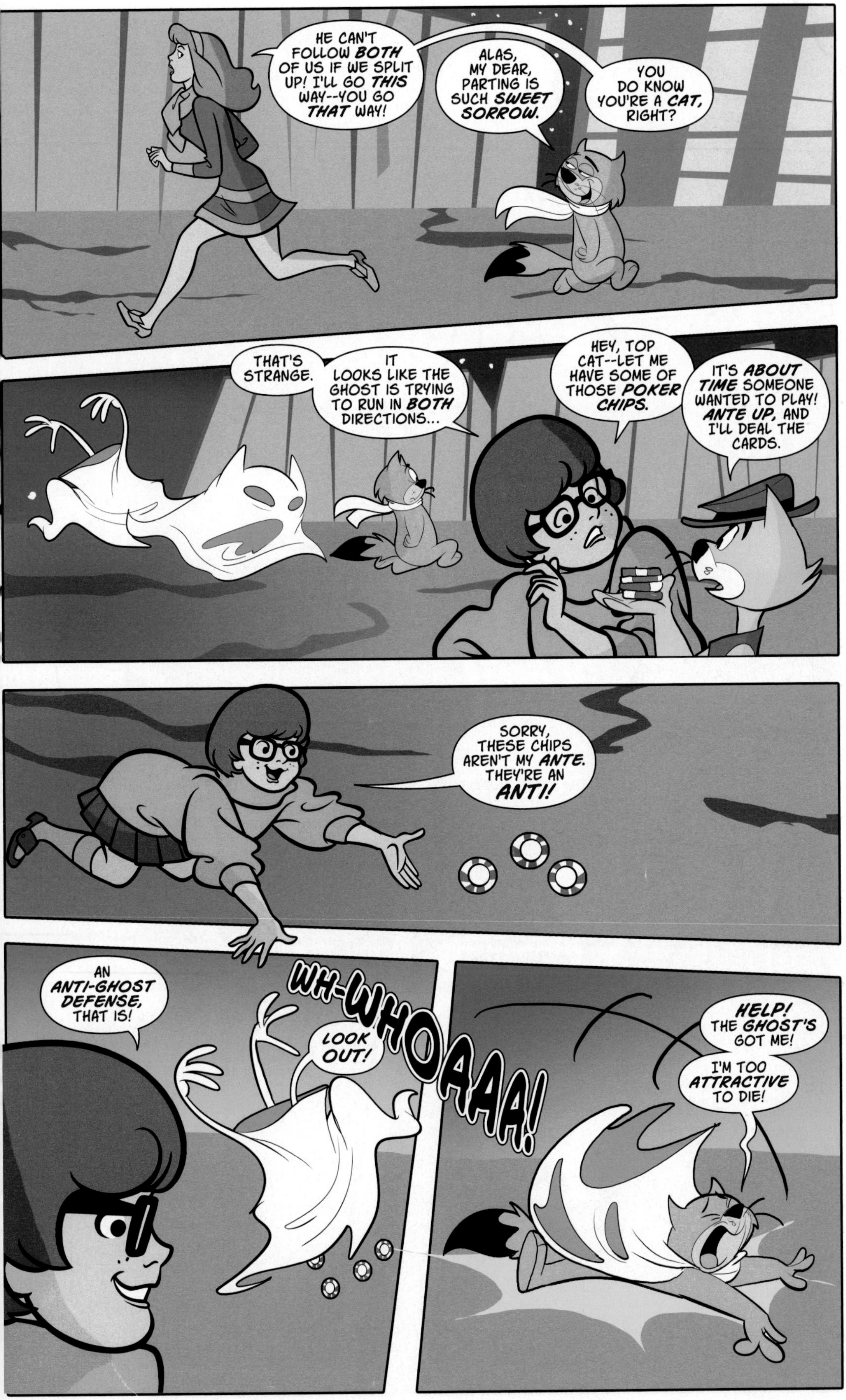
HE CAN'T FOLLOW BOTH OF US IF WE SPLIT UP! I'LL GO THIS WAY--YOU GO THAT WAY!
ALAS, MY DEAR, PARTING IS SUCH SWEET SORROW.
YOU DO KNOW YOU'RE A CAT, RIGHT?
THAT'S STRANGE.
IT LOOKS LIKE THE GHOST IS TRYING TO RUN IN BOTH DIRECTIONS...
HEY, TOP CAT--LET ME HAVE SOME OF THOSE POKER CHIPS.
IT'S ABOUT TIME SOMEONE WANTED TO PLAY! ANTE UP, AND I'LL DEAL THE CARDS.
SORRY, THESE CHIPS AREN'T MY ANTE. THEY'RE AN ANTI!
AN ANTI-GHOST DEFENSE, THAT IS!
WH-WHOAAAA!
LOOK OUT!
HELP! THE GHOST'S GOT ME!
I'M TOO ATTRACTIVE TO DIE!

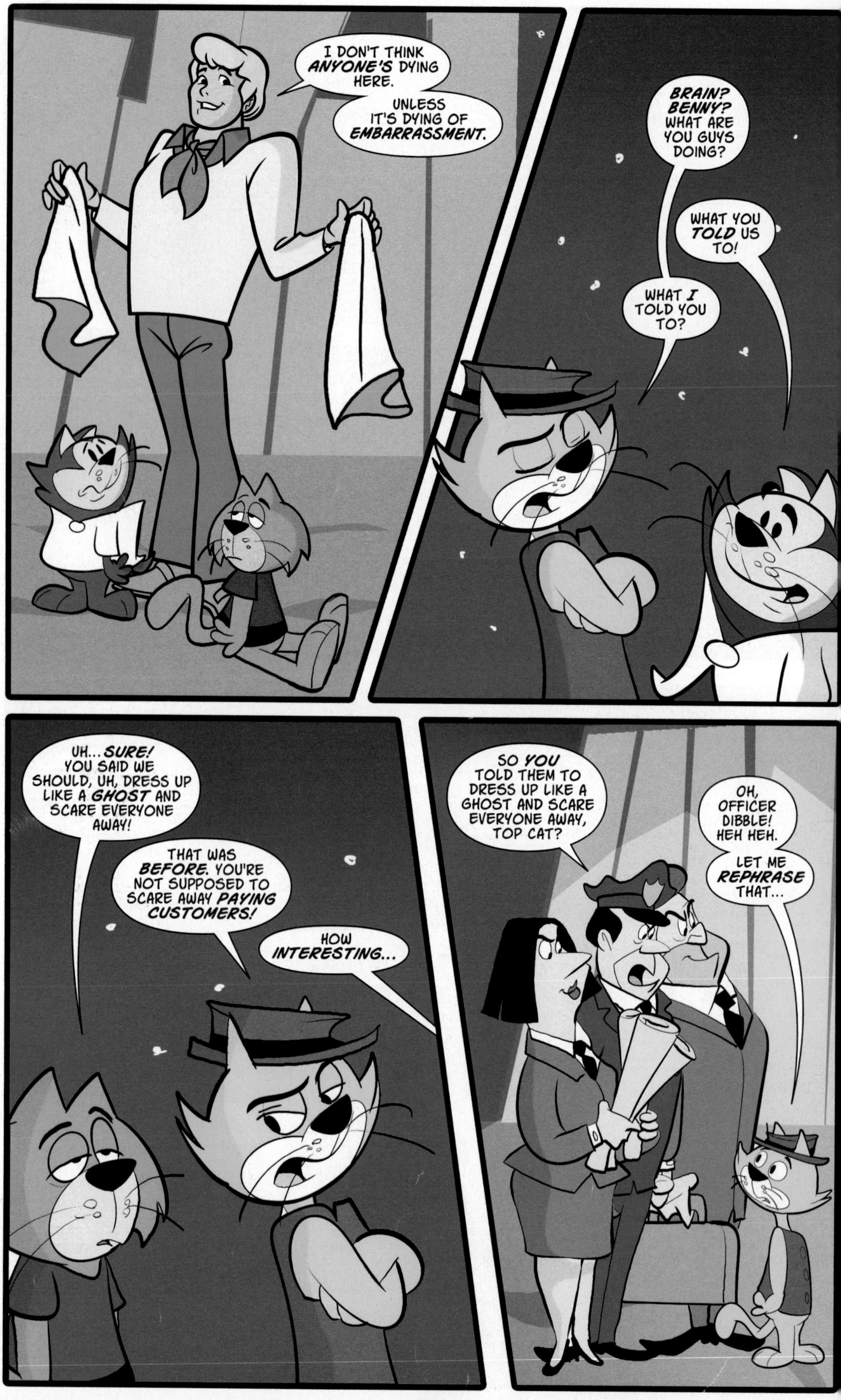

I DON'T THINK ANYONE'S DYING HERE.
UNLESS IT'S DYING OF EMBARRASSMENT.
BRAIN? BENNY? WHAT ARE YOU GUYS DOING?
WHAT YOU TOLD US TO!
WHAT I TOLD YOU TO?
UH... SURE! YOU SAID WE SHOULD, UH, DRESS UP LIKE A GHOST AND SCARE EVERYONE AWAY!
THAT WAS BEFORE. YOU'RE NOT SUPPOSED TO SCARE AWAY PAYING CUSTOMERS!
HOW INTERESTING...
SO YOU TOLD THEM TO DRESS UP LIKE A GHOST AND SCARE EVERYONE AWAY, TOP CAT?
OH, OFFICER DIBBLE! HEH HEH.
LET ME REPHRASE THAT...

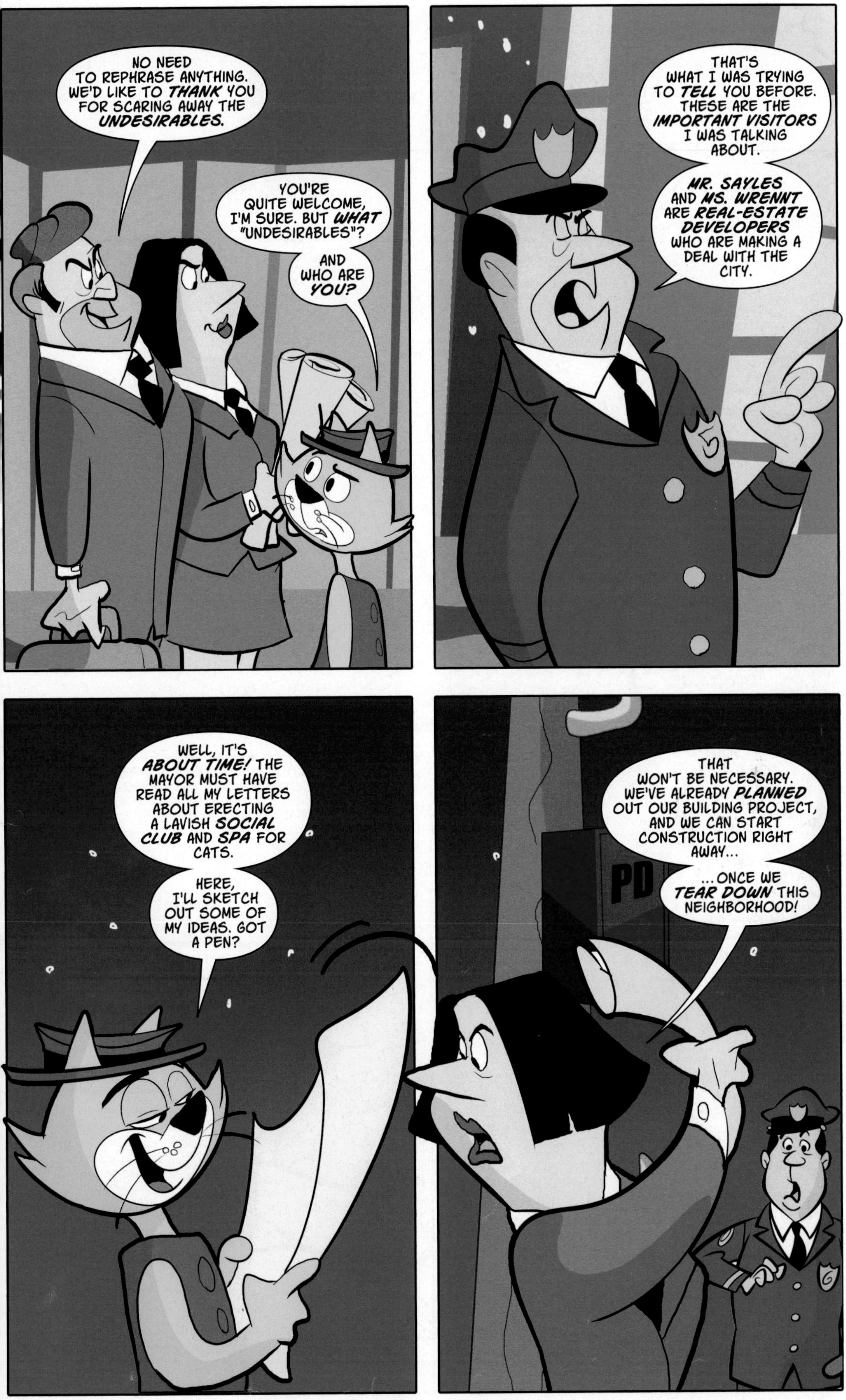
NO NEED TO REPHRASE ANYTHING. WE'D LIKE TO THANK YOU FOR SCARING AWAY THE UNDESIRABLES.
YOU'RE QUITE WELCOME, I'M SURE. BUT WHAT "UNDESIRABLES"?
AND WHO ARE YOU?
THAT'S WHAT I WAS TRYING TO TELL YOU BEFORE. THESE ARE THE IMPORTANT VISITORS I WAS TALKING ABOUT.
MR. SAYLES AND MS. WRENNT ARE REAL-ESTATE DEVELOPERS WHO ARE MAKING A DEAL WITH THE CITY.
WELL, IT'S ABOUT TIME! THE MAYOR MUST HAVE READ ALL MY LETTERS ABOUT ERECTING A LAVISH SOCIAL CLUB AND SPA FOR CATS.
HERE, I'LL SKETCH OUT SOME OF MY IDEAS. GOT A PEN?
THAT WON'T BE NECESSARY. WE'VE ALREADY PLANNED OUT OUR BUILDING PROJECT, AND WE CAN START CONSTRUCTION RIGHT AWAY...
...ONCE WE TEAR DOWN THIS NEIGHBORHOOD!
PD

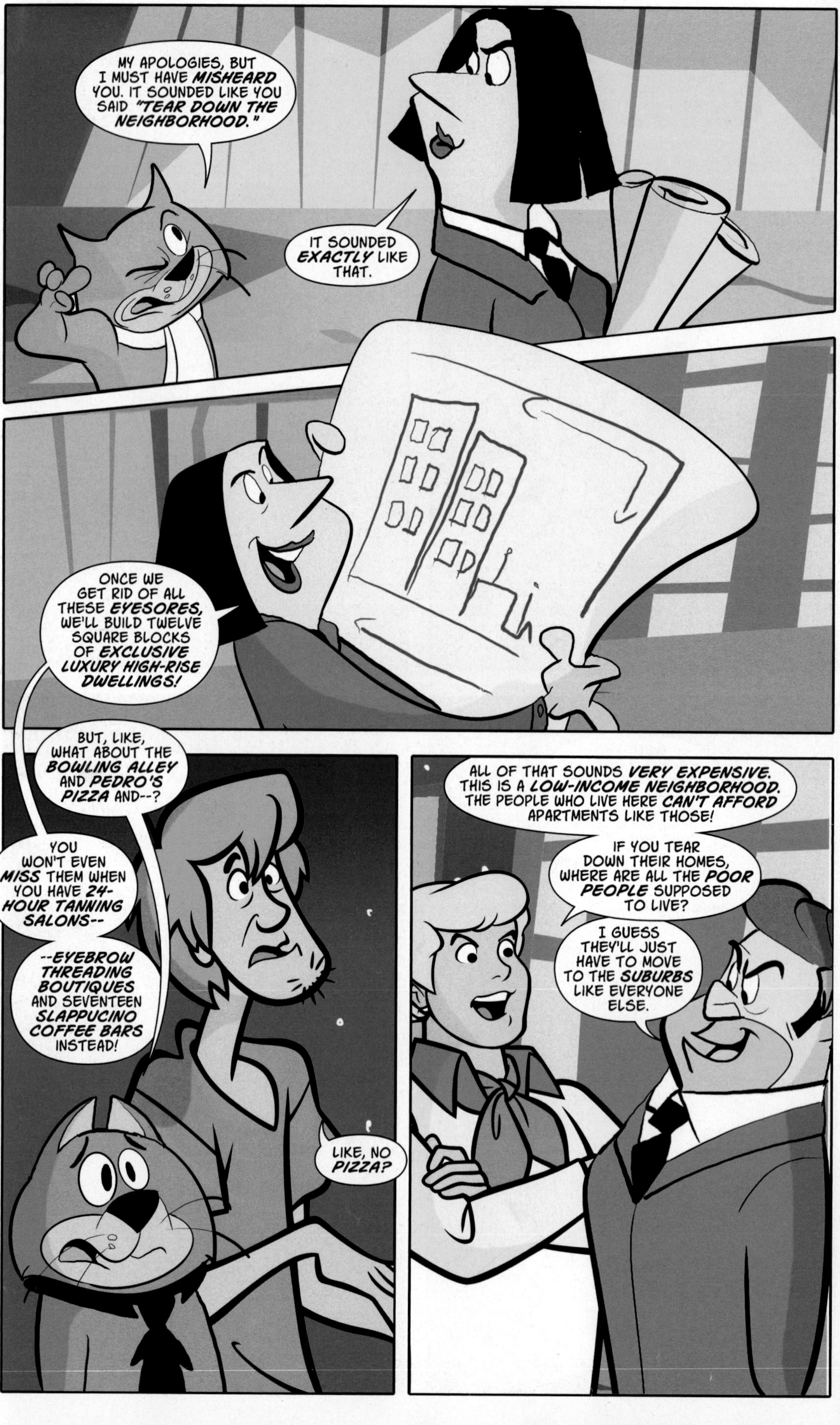
MY APOLOGIES, BUT I MUST HAVE MISHEARD YOU. IT SOUNDED LIKE YOU SAID "TEAR DOWN THE NEIGHBORHOOD."
IT SOUNDED EXACTLY LIKE THAT.
ONCE WE GET RID OF ALL THESE EYESORES, WE'LL BUILD TWELVE SQUARE BLOCKS OF EXCLUSIVE LUXURY HIGH-RISE DWELLINGS!
BUT, LIKE, WHAT ABOUT THE BOWLING ALLEY AND PEDRO'S PIZZA AND--?
YOU WON'T EVEN MISS THEM WHEN YOU HAVE 24-HOUR TANNING SALONS--
--EYEBROW THREADING BOUTIQUES AND SEVENTEEN SLAPPUCINO COFFEE BARS INSTEAD!
LIKE, NO PIZZA?
ALL OF THAT SOUNDS VERY EXPENSIVE. THIS IS A LOW-INCOME NEIGHBORHOOD. THE PEOPLE WHO LIVE HERE CAN'T AFFORD APARTMENTS LIKE THOSE!
IF YOU TEAR DOWN THEIR HOMES, WHERE ARE ALL THE POOR PEOPLE SUPPOSED TO LIVE?
I GUESS THEY'LL JUST HAVE TO MOVE TO THE SUBURBS LIKE EVERYONE ELSE.

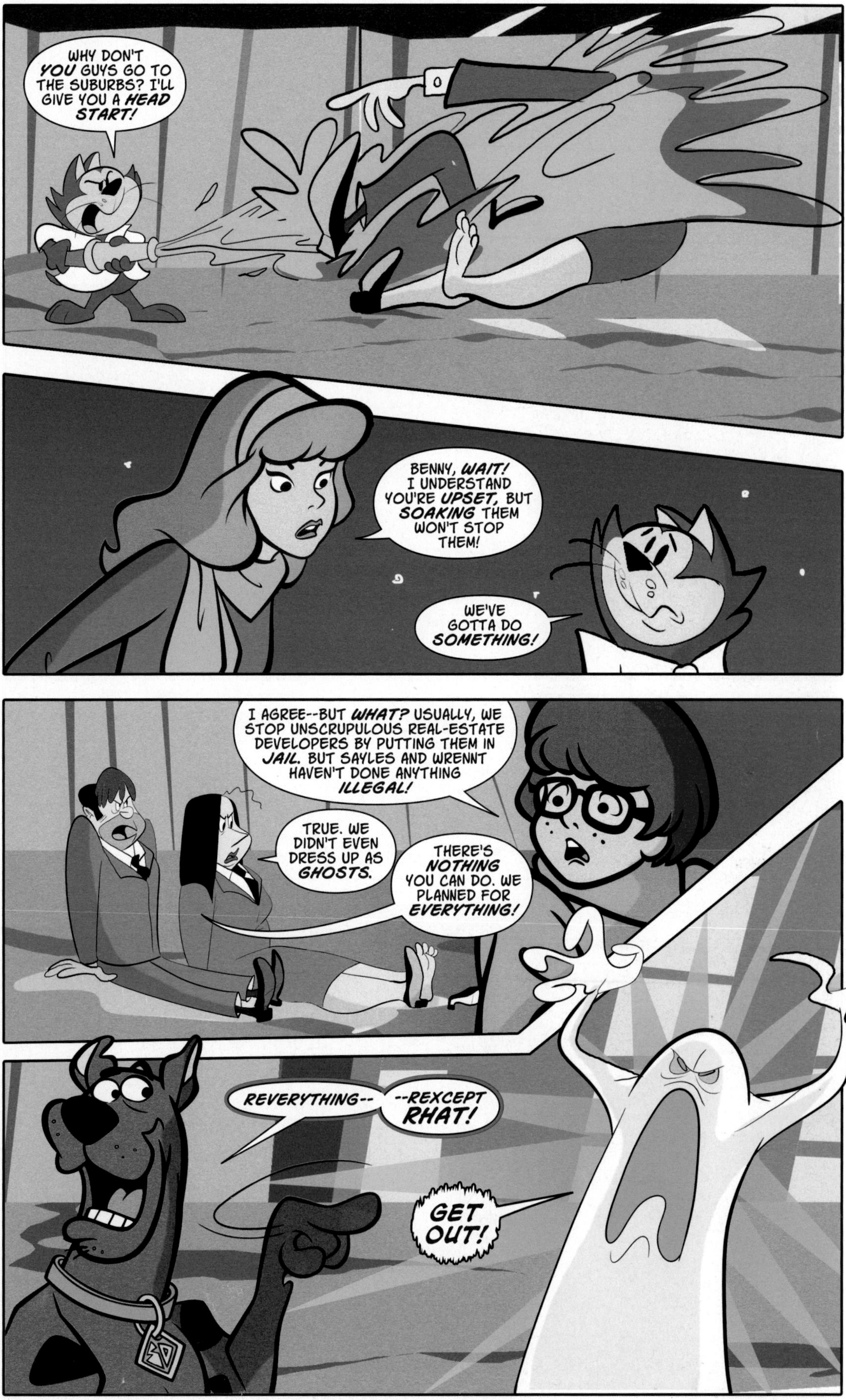
WHY DON'T YOU GUYS GO TO THE SUBURBS? I'LL GIVE YOU A HEAD START!
BENNY, WAIT! I UNDERSTAND YOU'RE UPSET, BUT SOAKING THEM WON'T STOP THEM!
WE'VE GOTTA DO SOMETHING!
I AGREE--BUT WHAT? USUALLY, WE STOP UNSCRUPULOUS REAL-ESTATE DEVELOPERS BY PUTTING THEM IN JAIL. BUT SAYLES AND WRENNT HAVEN'T DONE ANYTHING ILLEGAL!
TRUE. WE DIDN'T EVEN DRESS UP AS GHOSTS.
THERE'S NOTHING YOU CAN DO. WE PLANNED FOR EVERYTHING!
REVERYTHING--
--REXCEPT RHAT!
GET OUT!

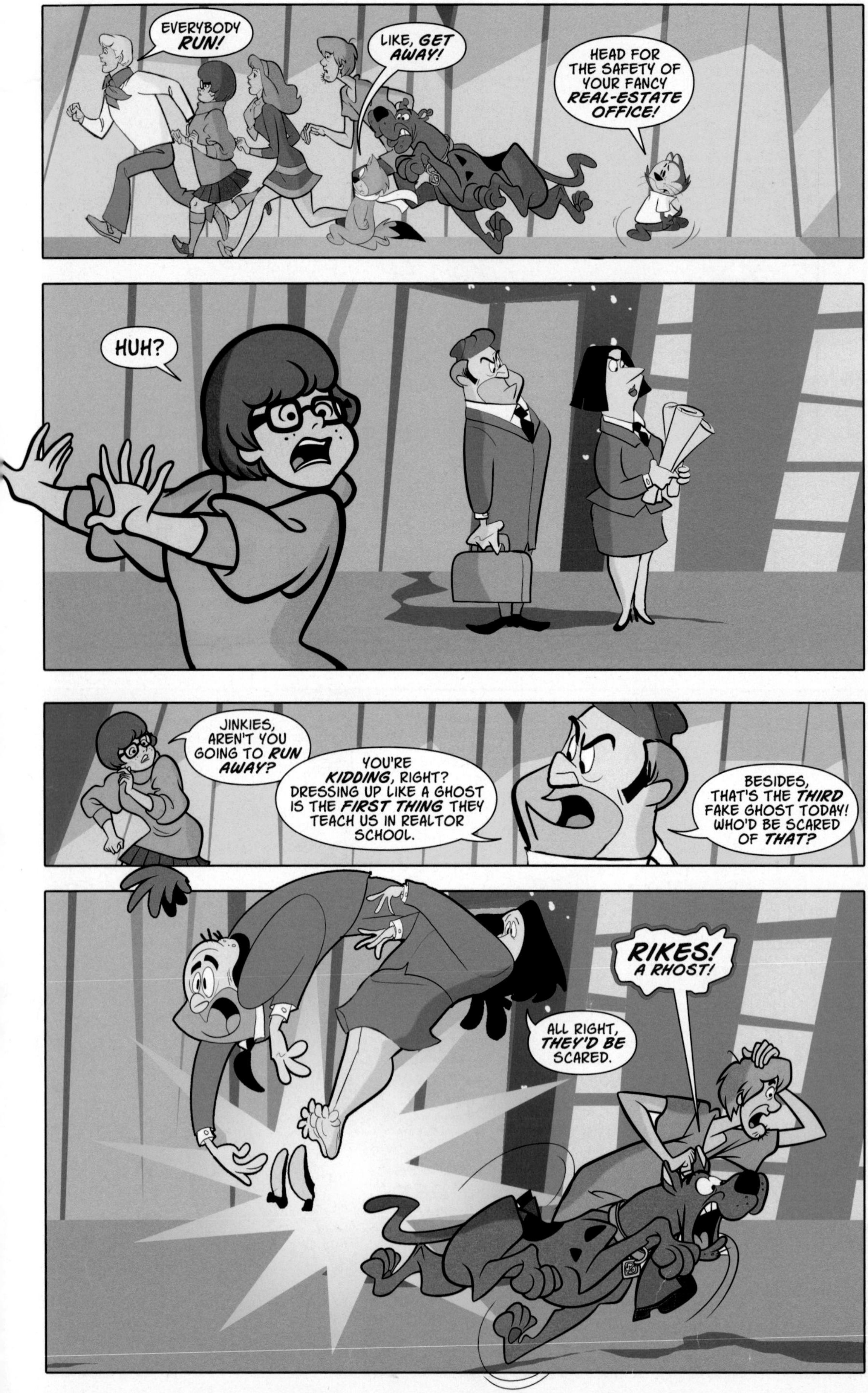
EVERYBODY RUN!
LIKE, GET AWAY!
HEAD FOR THE SAFETY OF YOUR FANCY REAL-ESTATE OFFICE!
HUH?
JINKIES, AREN'T YOU GOING TO RUN AWAY?
YOU'RE KIDDING, RIGHT? DRESSING UP LIKE A GHOST IS THE FIRST THING THEY TEACH US IN REALTOR SCHOOL.
BESIDES, THAT'S THE THIRD FAKE GHOST TODAY! WHO'D BE SCARED OF THAT?
ALL RIGHT, THEY'D BE SCARED.
RIKES! A RHOST!

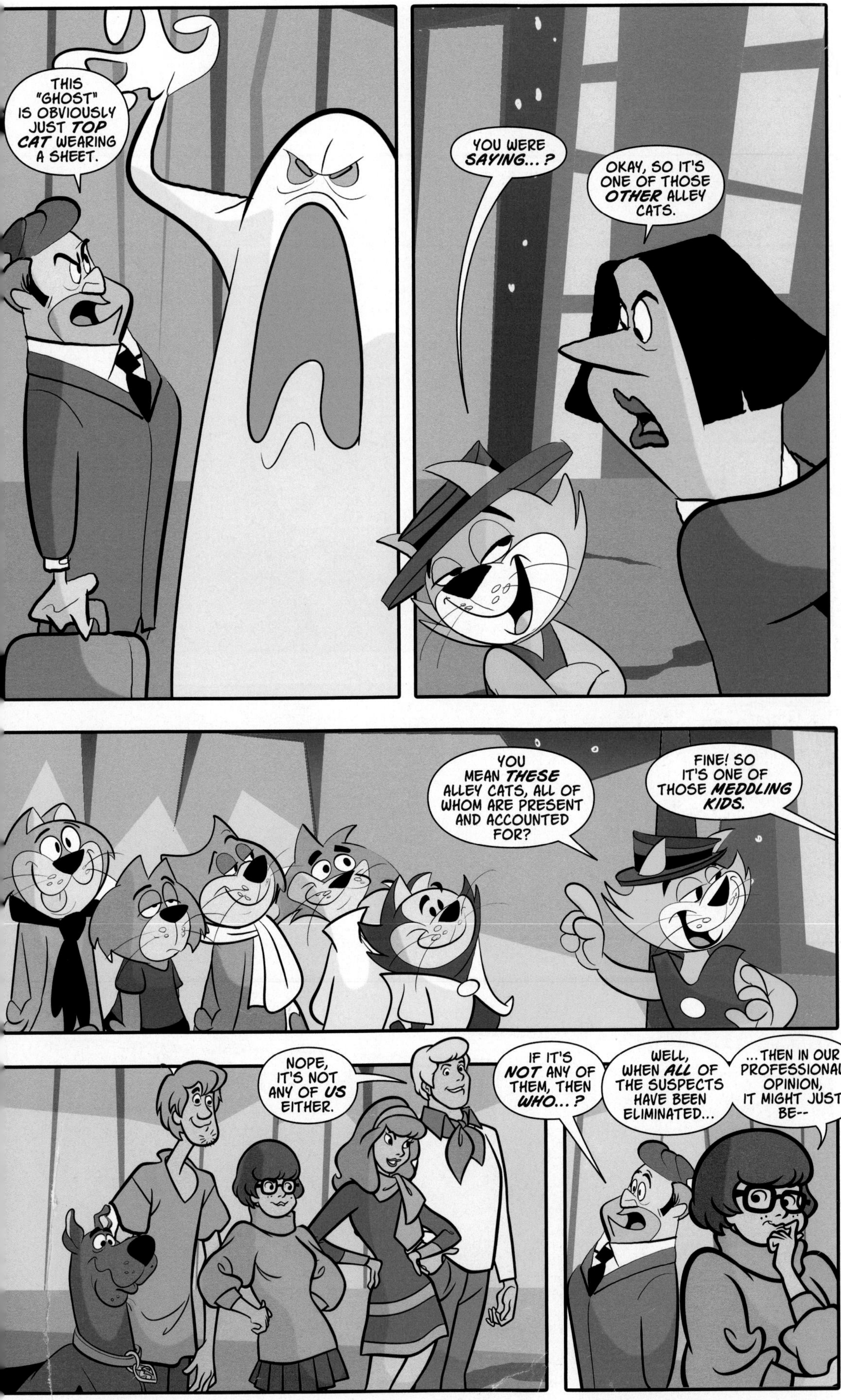

THIS "GHOST" IS OBVIOUSLY JUST TOP CAT WEARING A SHEET.
YOU WERE SAYING...?
OKAY, SO IT'S ONE OF THOSE OTHER ALLEY CATS.
YOU MEAN THESE ALLEY CATS, ALL OF WHOM ARE PRESENT AND ACCOUNTED FOR?
FINE! SO IT'S ONE OF THOSE MEDDLING KIDS.
NOPE, IT'S NOT ANY OF US EITHER.
IF IT'S NOT ANY OF THEM, THEN WHO...?
WELL, WHEN ALL OF THE SUSPECTS HAVE BEEN ELIMINATED...
...THEN IN OUR PROFESSIONAL OPINION, IT MIGHT JUST BE--

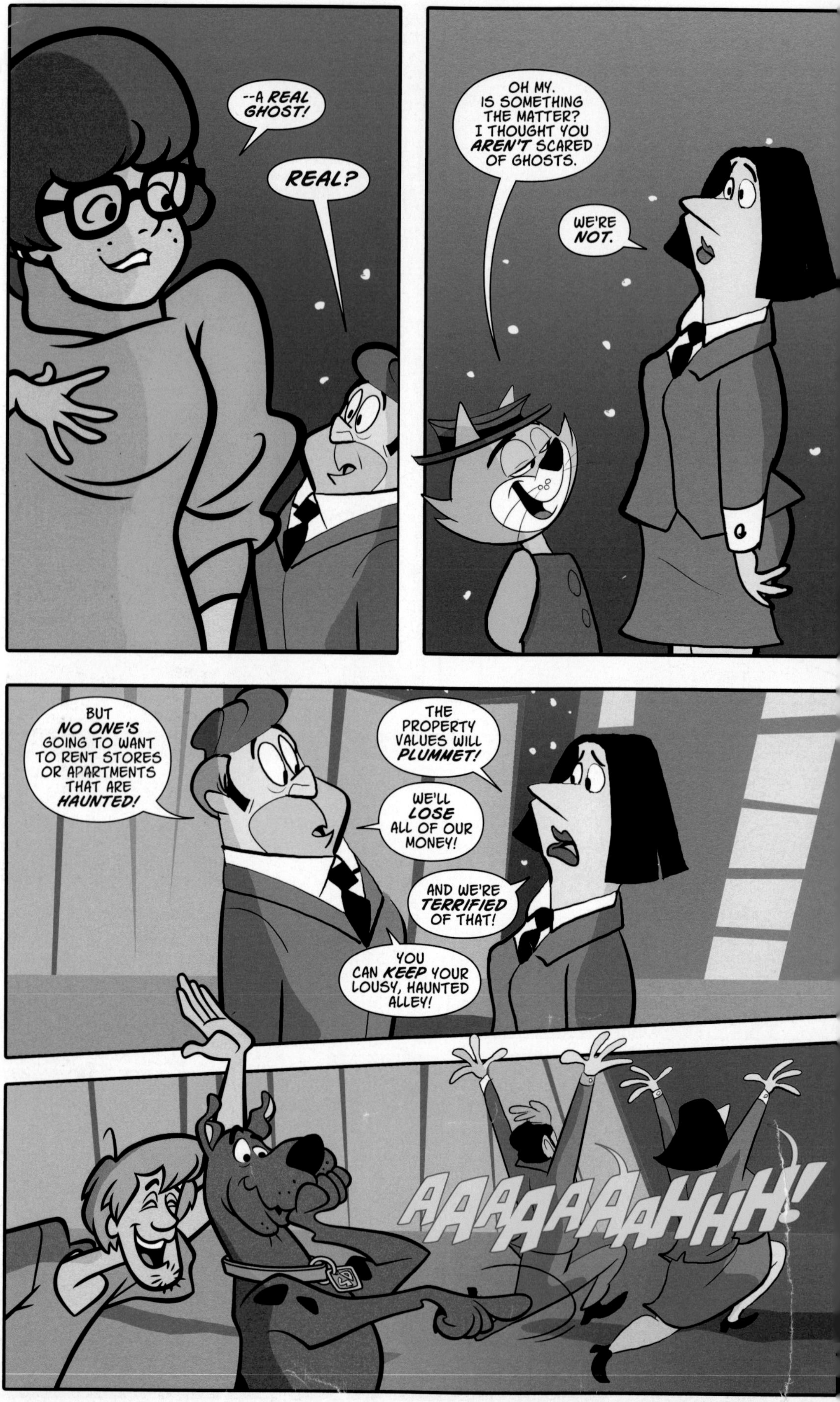
--A REAL GHOST!
REAL?
OH MY. IS SOMETHING THE MATTER? I THOUGHT YOU AREN'T SCARED OF GHOSTS.
WE'RE NOT.
BUT NO ONE'S GOING TO WANT TO RENT STORES OR APARTMENTS THAT ARE HAUNTED!
THE PROPERTY VALUES WILL PLUMMET!
WE'LL LOSE ALL OF OUR MONEY!
AND WE'RE TERRIFIED OF THAT!
YOU CAN KEEP YOUR LOUSY, HAUNTED ALLEY!
AAAAAAAAHHH!

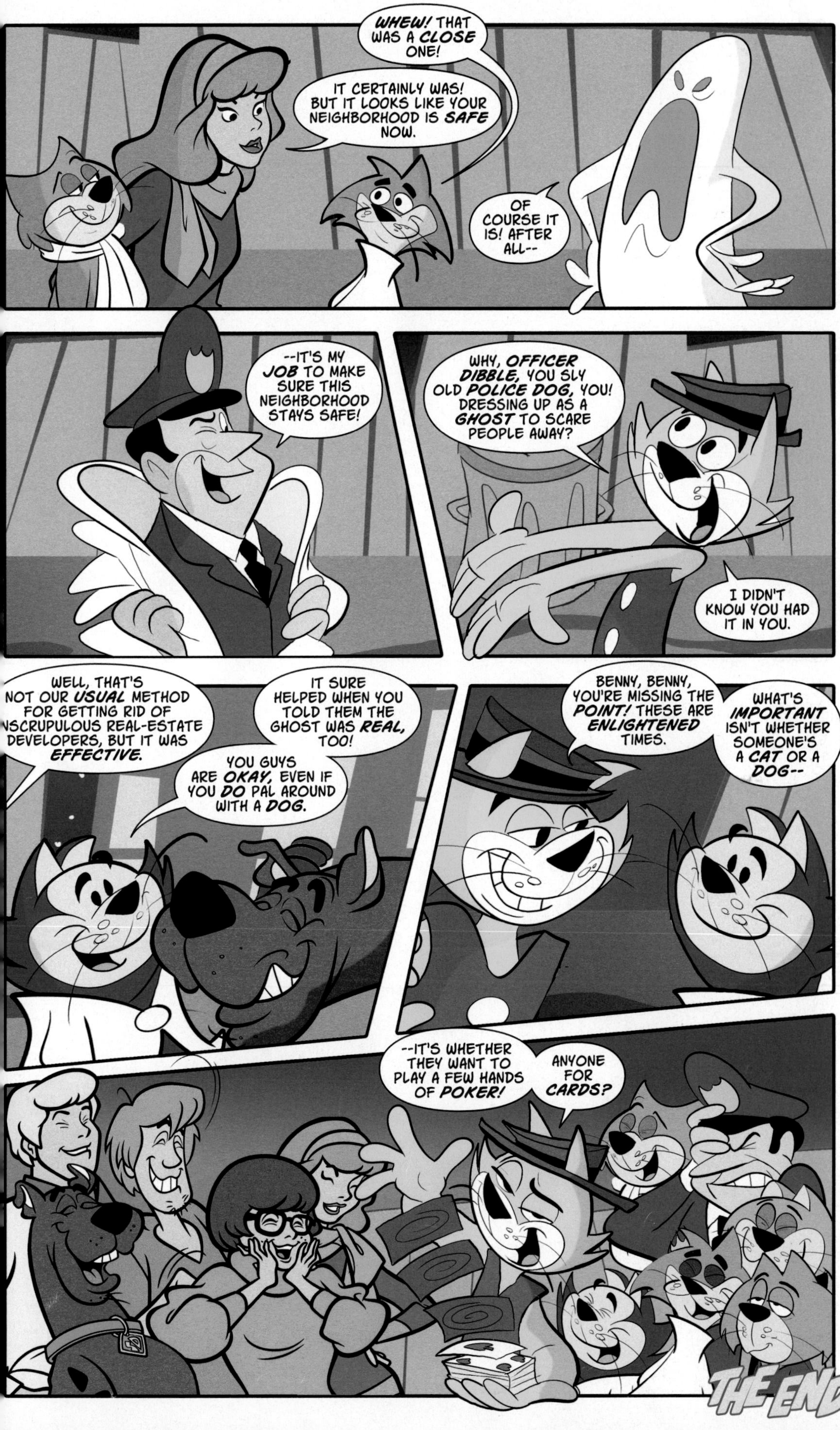
WHEW! THAT WAS A CLOSE ONE!
IT CERTAINLY WAS! BUT IT LOOKS LIKE YOUR NEIGHBORHOOD IS SAFE NOW.
OF COURSE IT IS! AFTER ALL--
--IT'S MY JOB TO MAKE SURE THIS NEIGHBORHOOD STAYS SAFE!
WHY, OFFICER DIBBLE, YOU SLY OLD POLICE DOG, YOU! DRESSING UP AS A GHOST TO SCARE PEOPLE AWAY?
I DIDN'T KNOW YOU HAD IT IN YOU.
WELL, THAT'S NOT OUR USUAL METHOD FOR GETTING RID OF UNSCRUPULOUS REAL-ESTATE DEVELOPERS, BUT IT WAS EFFECTIVE.
IT SURE HELPED WHEN YOU TOLD THEM THE GHOST WAS REAL, TOO!
YOU GUYS ARE OKAY, EVEN IF YOU DO PAL AROUND WITH A DOG.
BENNY, BENNY, YOU'RE MISSING THE POINT! THESE ARE ENLIGHTENED TIMES.
WHAT'S IMPORTANT ISN'T WHETHER SOMEONE'S A CAT OR A DOG--
--IT'S WHETHER THEY WANT TO PLAY A FEW HANDS OF POKER!
ANYONE FOR CARDS?
THE END

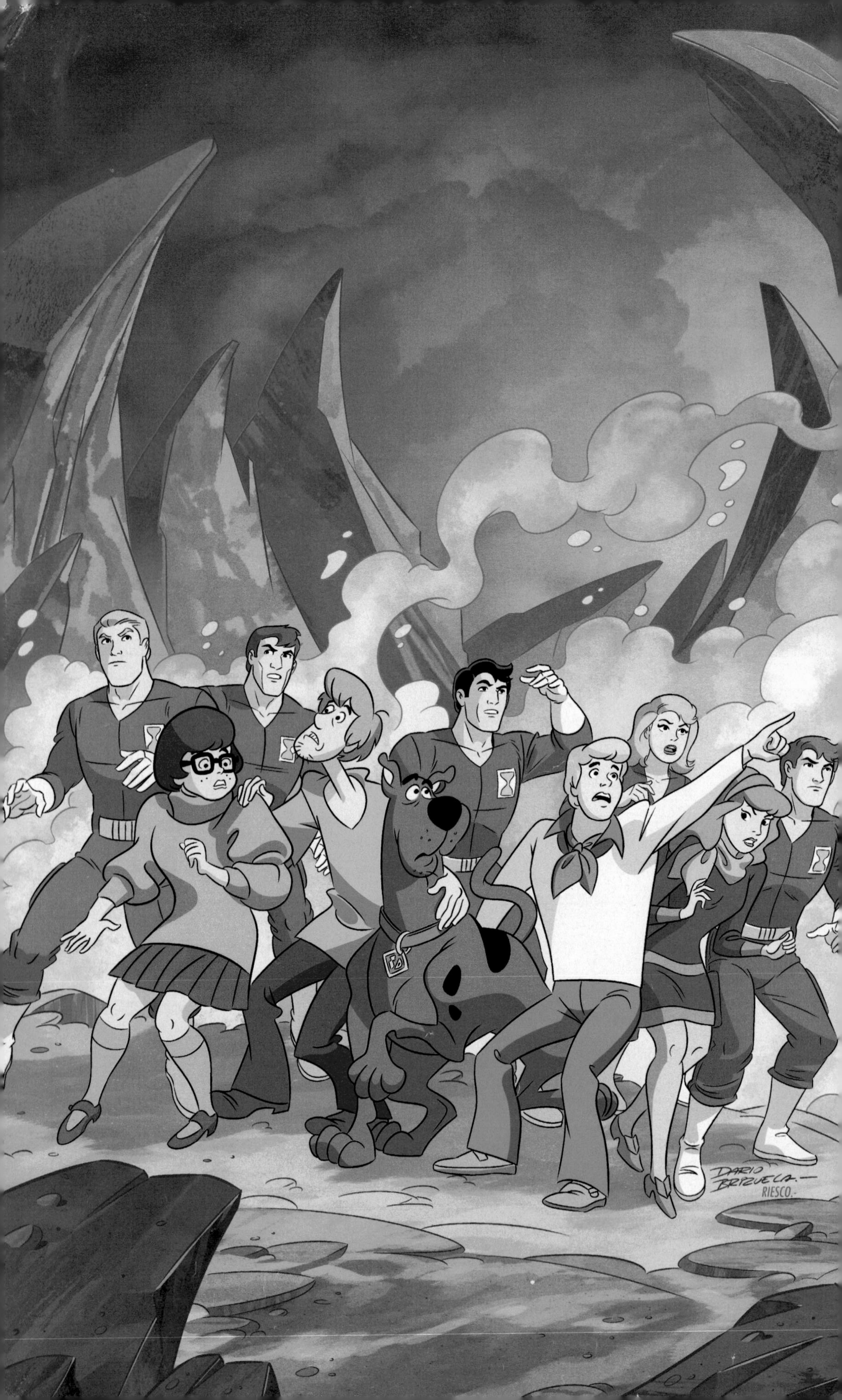
DARIO BRIZUELA
RIESCO.

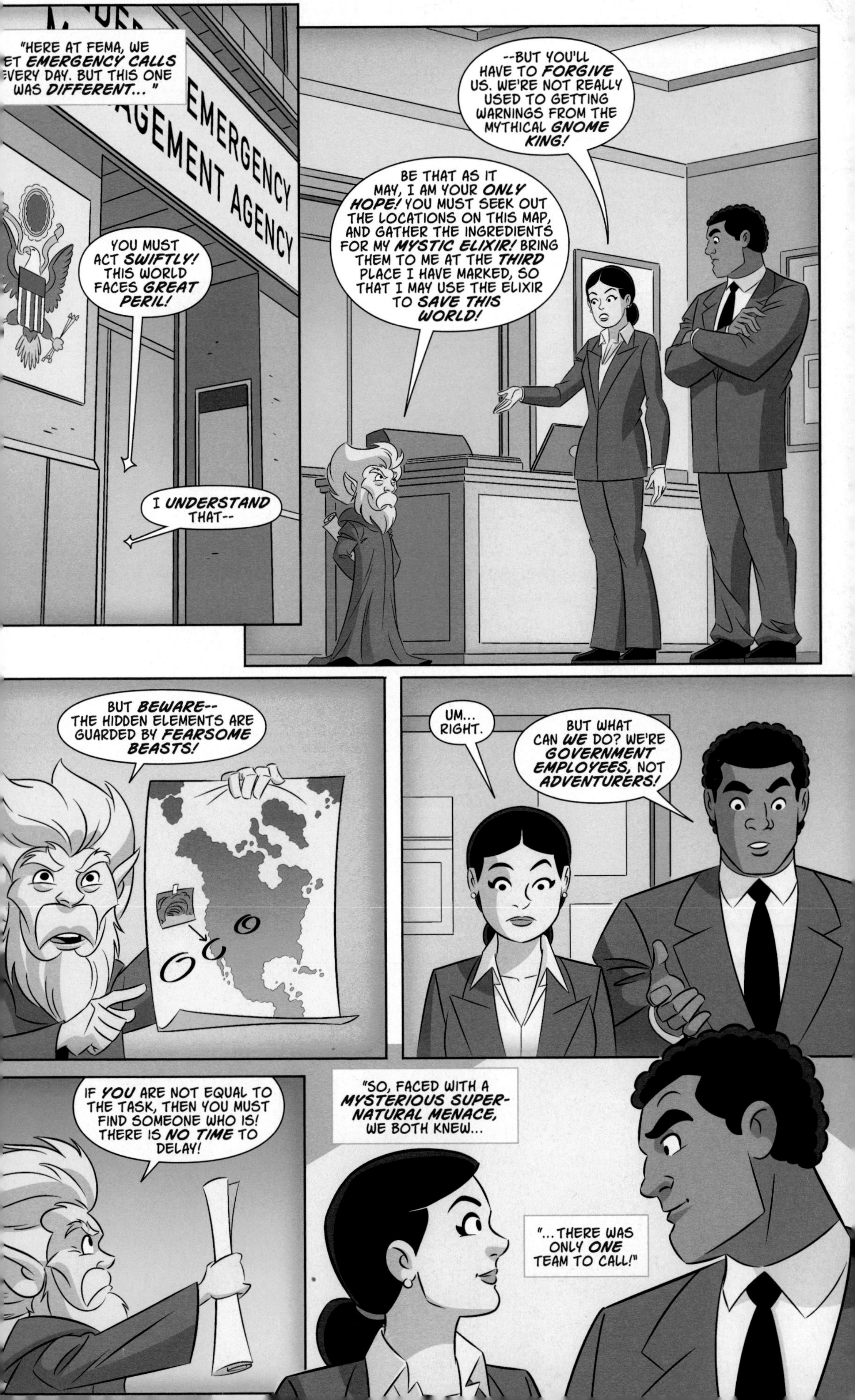
"HERE AT FEMA, WE GET EMERGENCY CALLS EVERY DAY. BUT THIS ONE WAS DIFFERENT..."
EMERGENCY MANAGEMENT AGENCY
YOU MUST ACT SWIFTLY! THIS WORLD FACES GREAT PERIL!
I UNDERSTAND THAT--
--BUT YOU'LL HAVE TO FORGIVE US. WE'RE NOT REALLY USED TO GETTING WARNINGS FROM THE MYTHICAL GNOME KING!
BE THAT AS IT MAY, I AM YOUR ONLY HOPE! YOU MUST SEEK OUT THE LOCATIONS ON THIS MAP, AND GATHER THE INGREDIENTS FOR MY MYSTIC ELIXIR! BRING THEM TO ME AT THE THIRD PLACE I HAVE MARKED, SO THAT I MAY USE THE ELIXIR TO SAVE THIS WORLD!
BUT BEWARE-- THE HIDDEN ELEMENTS ARE GUARDED BY FEARSOME BEASTS!
UM... RIGHT.
BUT WHAT CAN WE DO? WE'RE GOVERNMENT EMPLOYEES, NOT ADVENTURERS!
IF YOU ARE NOT EQUAL TO THE TASK, THEN YOU MUST FIND SOMEONE WHO IS! THERE IS NO TIME TO DELAY!
"SO, FACED WITH A MYSTERIOUS SUPER-NATURAL MENACE, WE BOTH KNEW...
"...THERE WAS ONLY ONE TEAM TO CALL!"

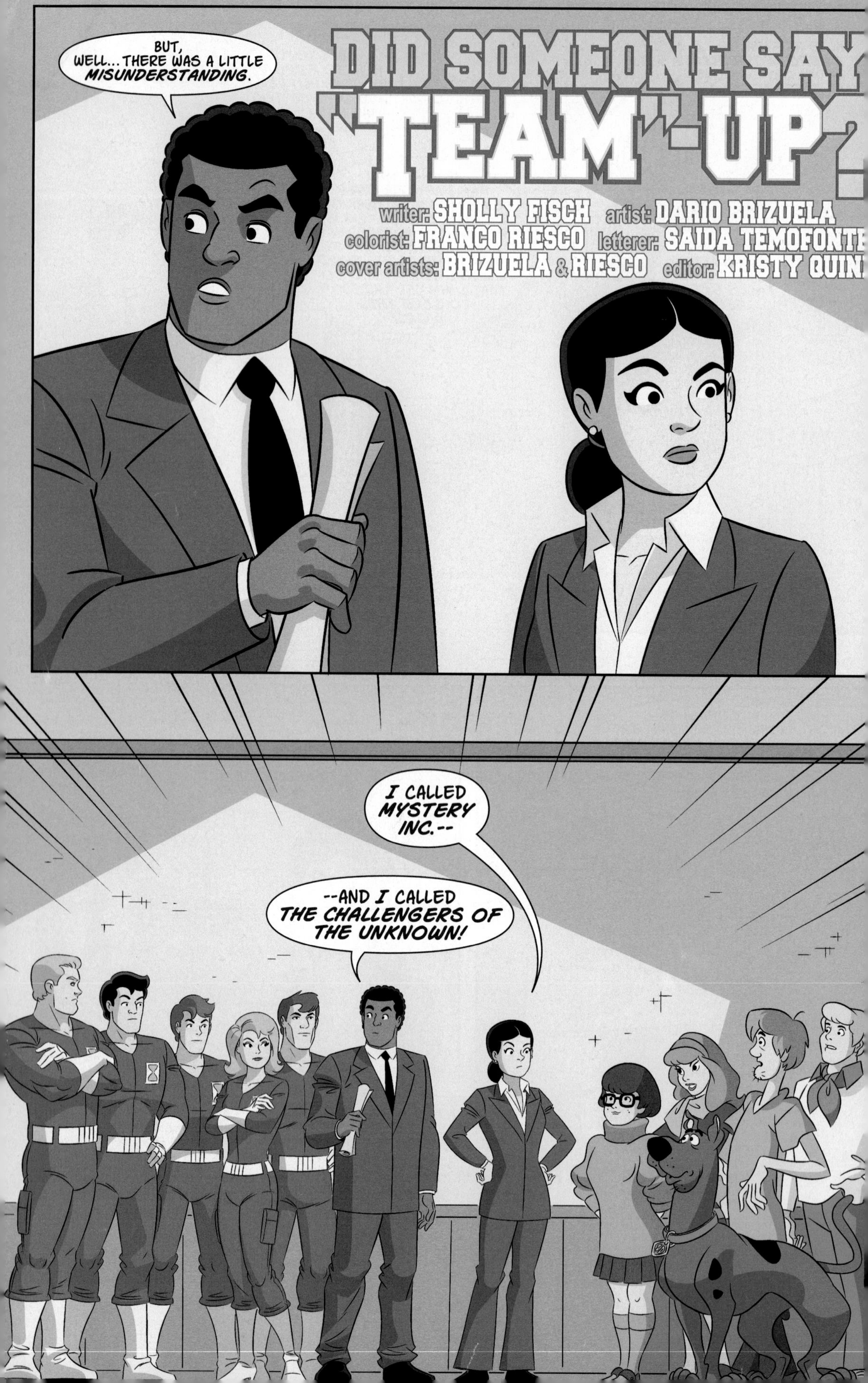
BUT, WELL... THERE WAS A LITTLE MISUNDERSTANDING.
DID SOMEONE SAY "TEAM"-UP?
writer: SHOLLY FISCH artist: DARIO BRIZUELA
colorist: FRANCO RIESCO letterer: SAIDA TEMOFONTE
cover artists: BRIZUELA & RIESCO editor: KRISTY QUIN
I CALLED MYSTERY INC.--
--AND I CALLED THE CHALLENGERS OF THE UNKNOWN!

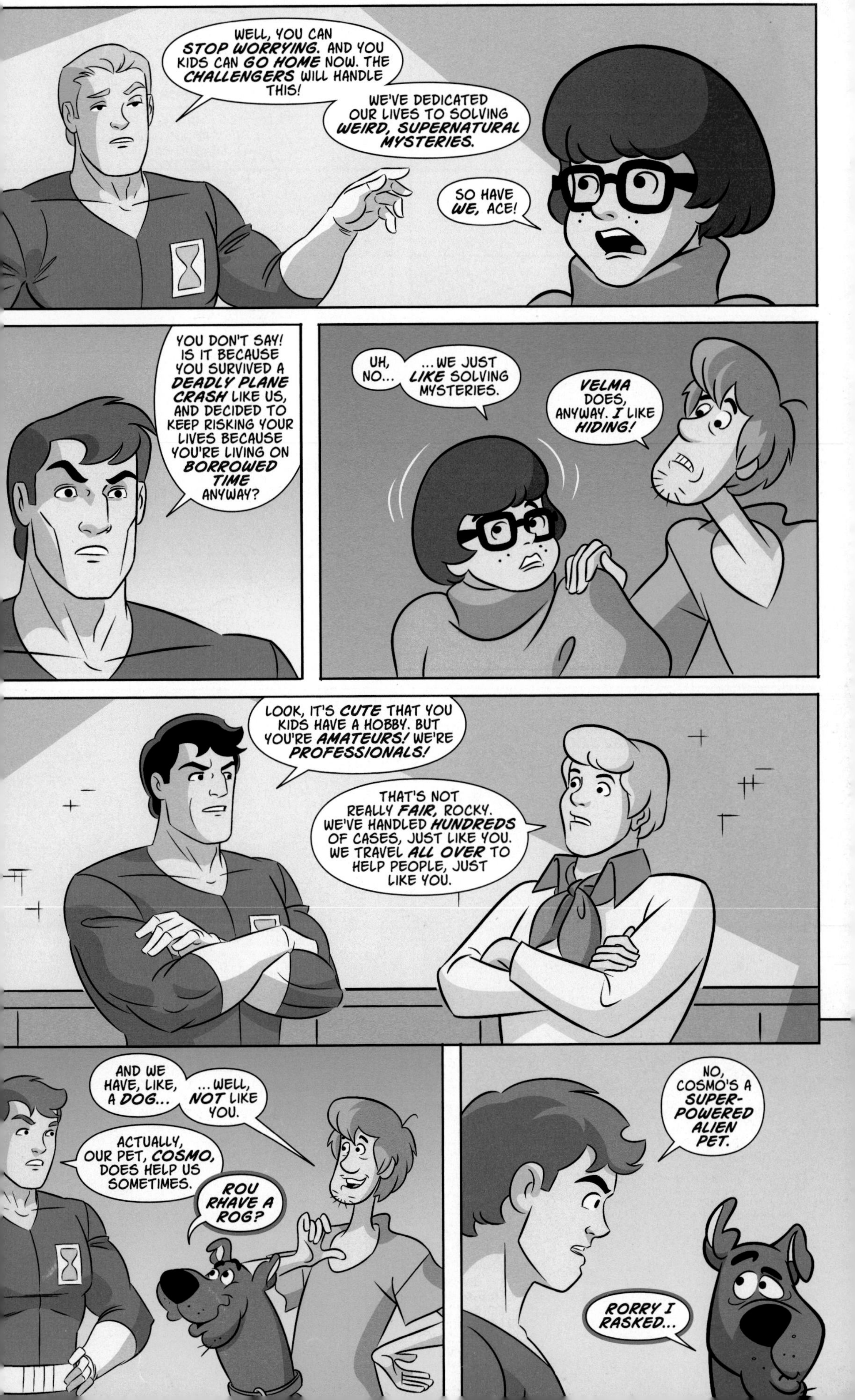
WELL, YOU CAN STOP WORRYING. AND YOU KIDS CAN GO HOME NOW. THE CHALLENGERS WILL HANDLE THIS!
WE'VE DEDICATED OUR LIVES TO SOLVING WEIRD, SUPERNATURAL MYSTERIES.
SO HAVE WE, ACE!
YOU DON'T SAY! IS IT BECAUSE YOU SURVIVED A DEADLY PLANE CRASH LIKE US, AND DECIDED TO KEEP RISKING YOUR LIVES BECAUSE YOU'RE LIVING ON BORROWED TIME ANYWAY?
UH, NO...
...WE JUST LIKE SOLVING MYSTERIES.
VELMA DOES, ANYWAY. I LIKE HIDING!
LOOK, IT'S CUTE THAT YOU KIDS HAVE A HOBBY. BUT YOU'RE AMATEURS! WE'RE PROFESSIONALS!
THAT'S NOT REALLY FAIR, ROCKY. WE'VE HANDLED HUNDREDS OF CASES, JUST LIKE YOU. WE TRAVEL ALL OVER TO HELP PEOPLE, JUST LIKE YOU.
AND WE HAVE, LIKE, A DOG...
...WELL, NOT LIKE YOU.
ACTUALLY, OUR PET, COSMO, DOES HELP US SOMETIMES.
ROU RHAVE A ROG?
NO, COSMO'S A SUPER-POWERED ALIEN PET.
RORRY I RASKED...

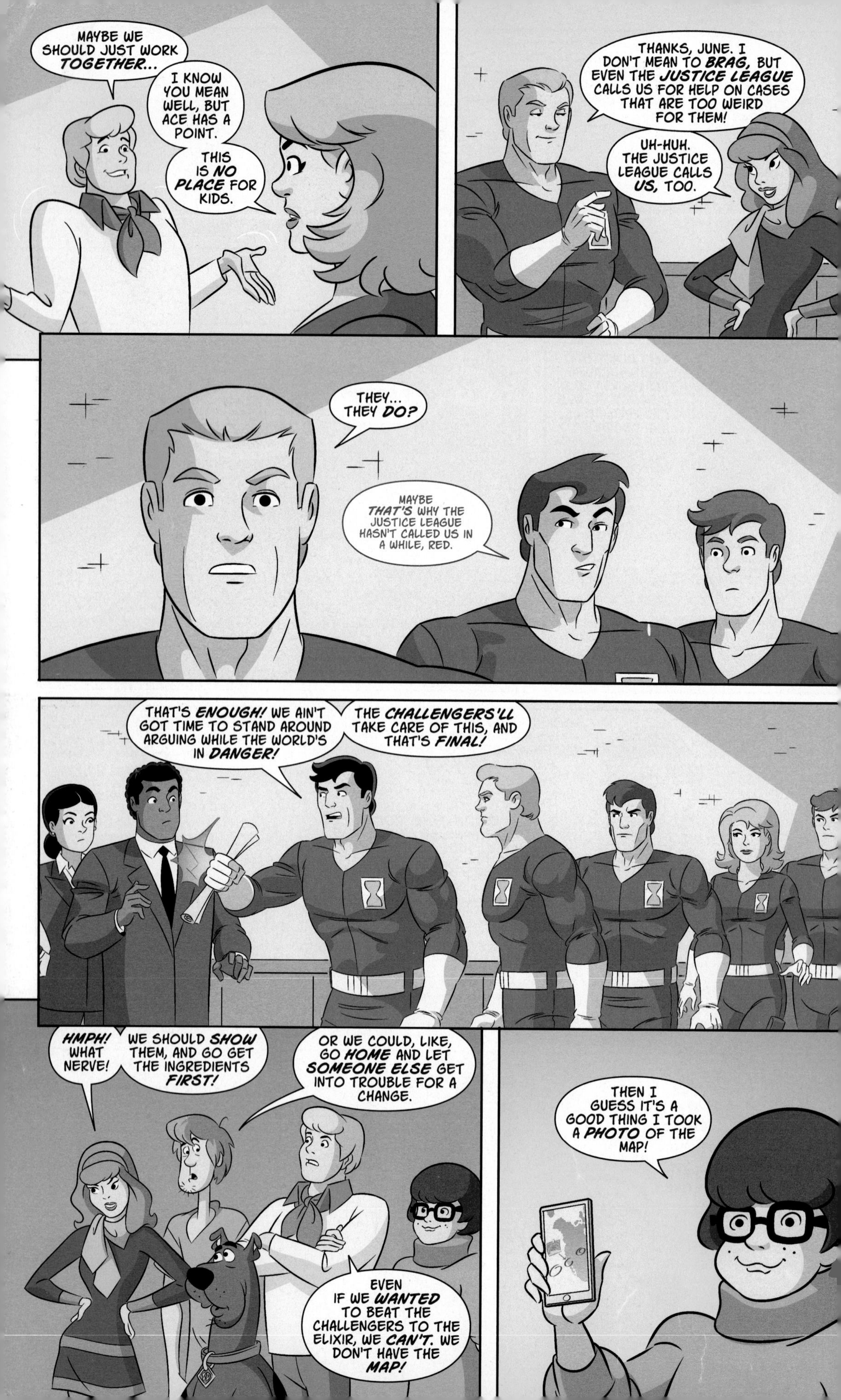
MAYBE WE SHOULD JUST WORK TOGETHER...
I KNOW YOU MEAN WELL, BUT ACE HAS A POINT.
THIS IS NO PLACE FOR KIDS.
THANKS, JUNE. I DON'T MEAN TO BRAG, BUT EVEN THE JUSTICE LEAGUE CALLS US FOR HELP ON CASES THAT ARE TOO WEIRD FOR THEM!
UH-HUH. THE JUSTICE LEAGUE CALLS US, TOO.
THEY... THEY DO?
MAYBE THAT'S WHY THE JUSTICE LEAGUE HASN'T CALLED US IN A WHILE, RED.
THAT'S ENOUGH! WE AIN'T GOT TIME TO STAND AROUND ARGUING WHILE THE WORLD'S IN DANGER!
THE CHALLENGERS'LL TAKE CARE OF THIS, AND THAT'S FINAL!
HMPH! WHAT NERVE!
WE SHOULD SHOW THEM, AND GO GET THE INGREDIENTS FIRST!
OR WE COULD, LIKE, GO HOME AND LET SOMEONE ELSE GET INTO TROUBLE FOR A CHANGE.
EVEN IF WE WANTED TO BEAT THE CHALLENGERS TO THE ELIXIR, WE CAN'T. WE DON'T HAVE THE MAP!
THEN I GUESS IT'S A GOOD THING I TOOK A PHOTO OF THE MAP!

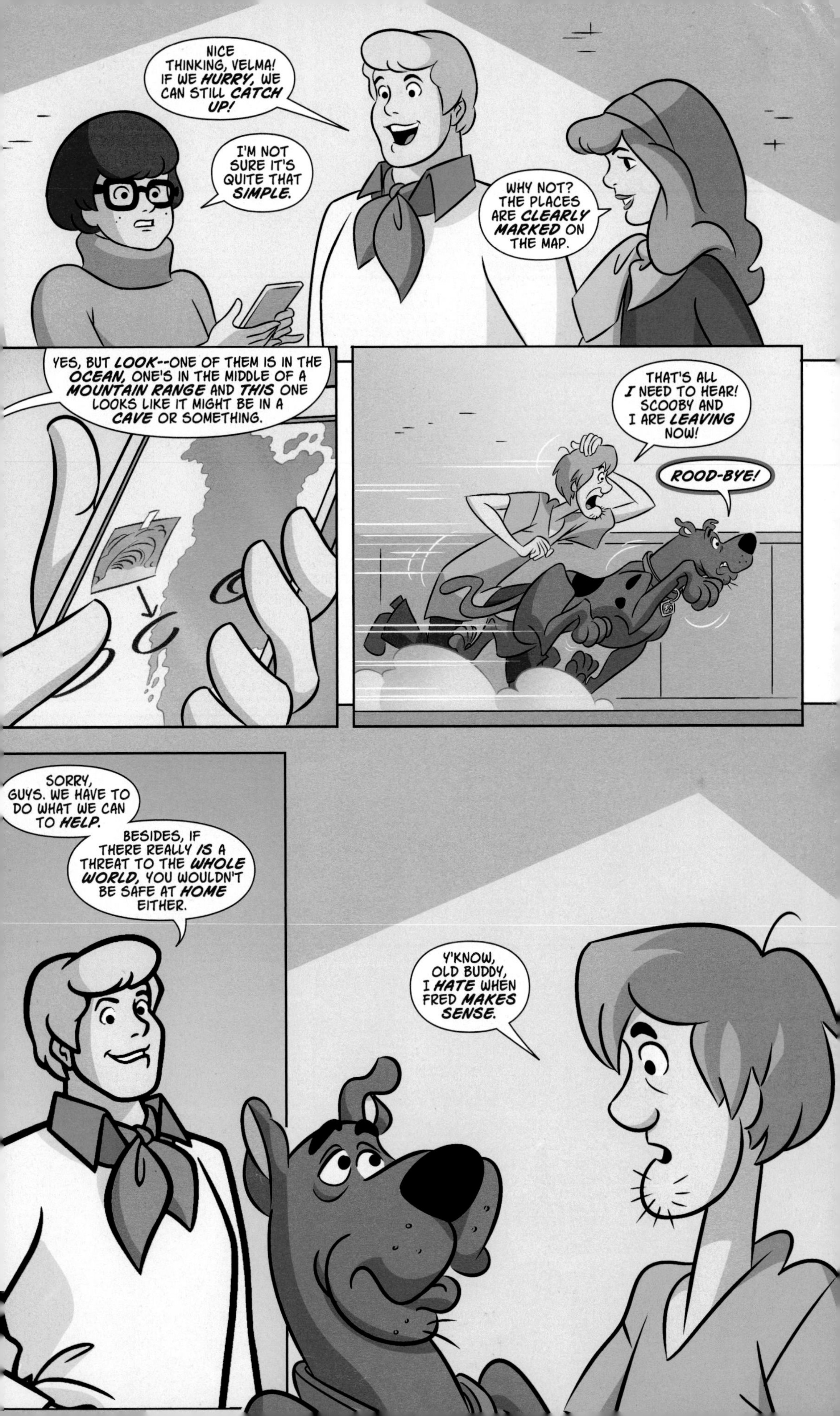
NICE THINKING, VELMA! IF WE *HURRY*, WE CAN STILL *CATCH UP!*
I'M NOT SURE IT'S QUITE THAT *SIMPLE*.
WHY NOT? THE PLACES ARE *CLEARLY MARKED* ON THE MAP.
YES, BUT *LOOK*--ONE OF THEM IS IN THE *OCEAN*, ONE'S IN THE MIDDLE OF A *MOUNTAIN RANGE* AND *THIS* ONE LOOKS LIKE IT MIGHT BE IN A *CAVE* OR SOMETHING.
THAT'S ALL *I* NEED TO HEAR! SCOOBY AND I ARE *LEAVING* NOW!
ROOD-BYE!
SORRY, GUYS. WE HAVE TO DO WHAT WE CAN TO *HELP*.
BESIDES, IF THERE REALLY *IS* A THREAT TO THE *WHOLE WORLD*, YOU WOULDN'T BE SAFE AT *HOME* EITHER.
Y'KNOW, OLD BUDDY, I *HATE* WHEN FRED *MAKES SENSE*.

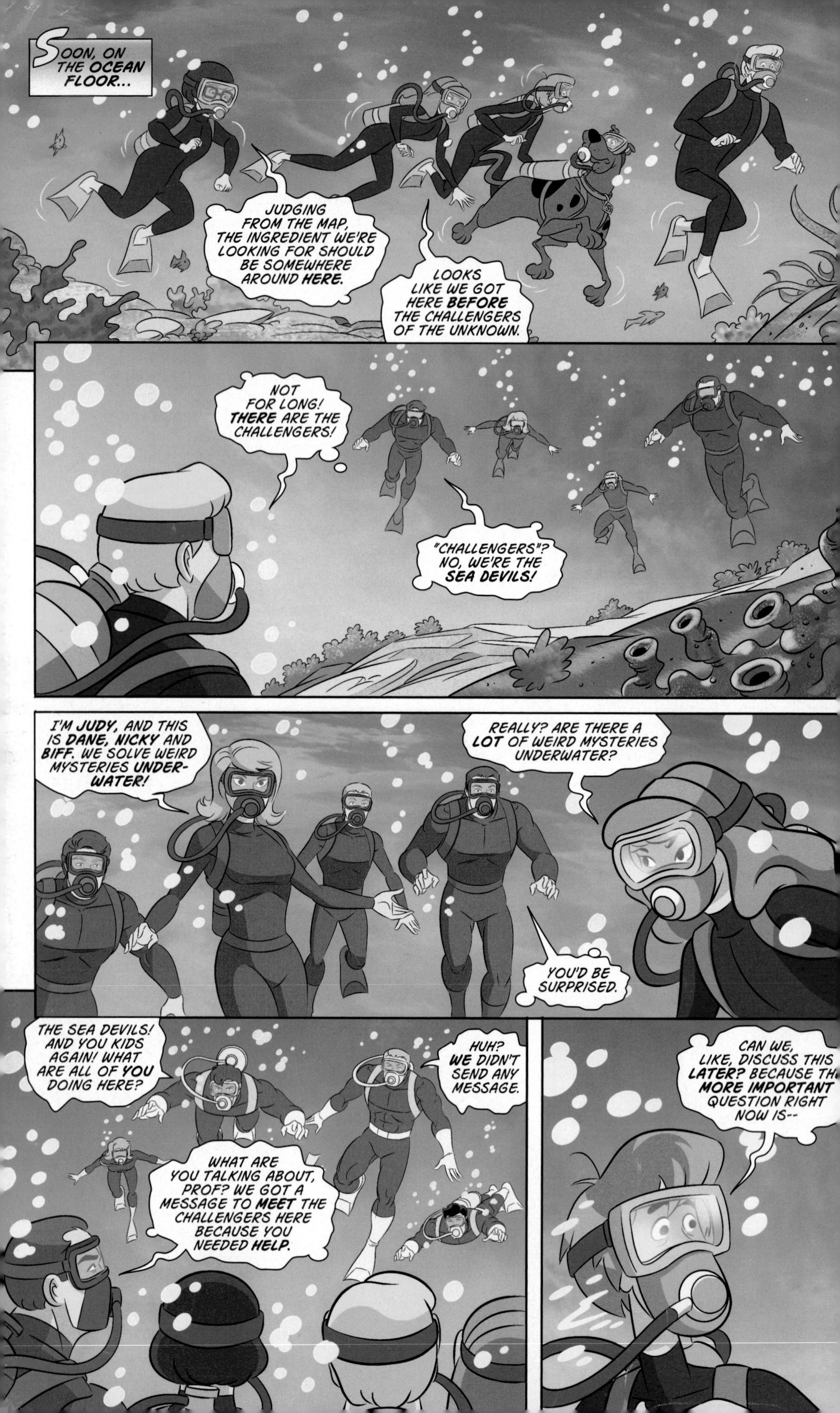
SOON, ON THE OCEAN FLOOR...
JUDGING FROM THE MAP, THE INGREDIENT WE'RE LOOKING FOR SHOULD BE SOMEWHERE AROUND HERE.
LOOKS LIKE WE GOT HERE BEFORE THE CHALLENGERS OF THE UNKNOWN.
NOT FOR LONG! THERE ARE THE CHALLENGERS!
"CHALLENGERS"? NO, WE'RE THE SEA DEVILS!
I'M JUDY, AND THIS IS DANE, NICKY AND BIFF. WE SOLVE WEIRD MYSTERIES UNDER-WATER!
REALLY? ARE THERE A LOT OF WEIRD MYSTERIES UNDERWATER?
YOU'D BE SURPRISED.
THE SEA DEVILS! AND YOU KIDS AGAIN! WHAT ARE ALL OF YOU DOING HERE?
HUH? WE DIDN'T SEND ANY MESSAGE.
WHAT ARE YOU TALKING ABOUT, PROF? WE GOT A MESSAGE TO MEET THE CHALLENGERS HERE BECAUSE YOU NEEDED HELP.
CAN WE, LIKE, DISCUSS THIS LATER? BECAUSE TH MORE IMPORTANT QUESTION RIGHT NOW IS--

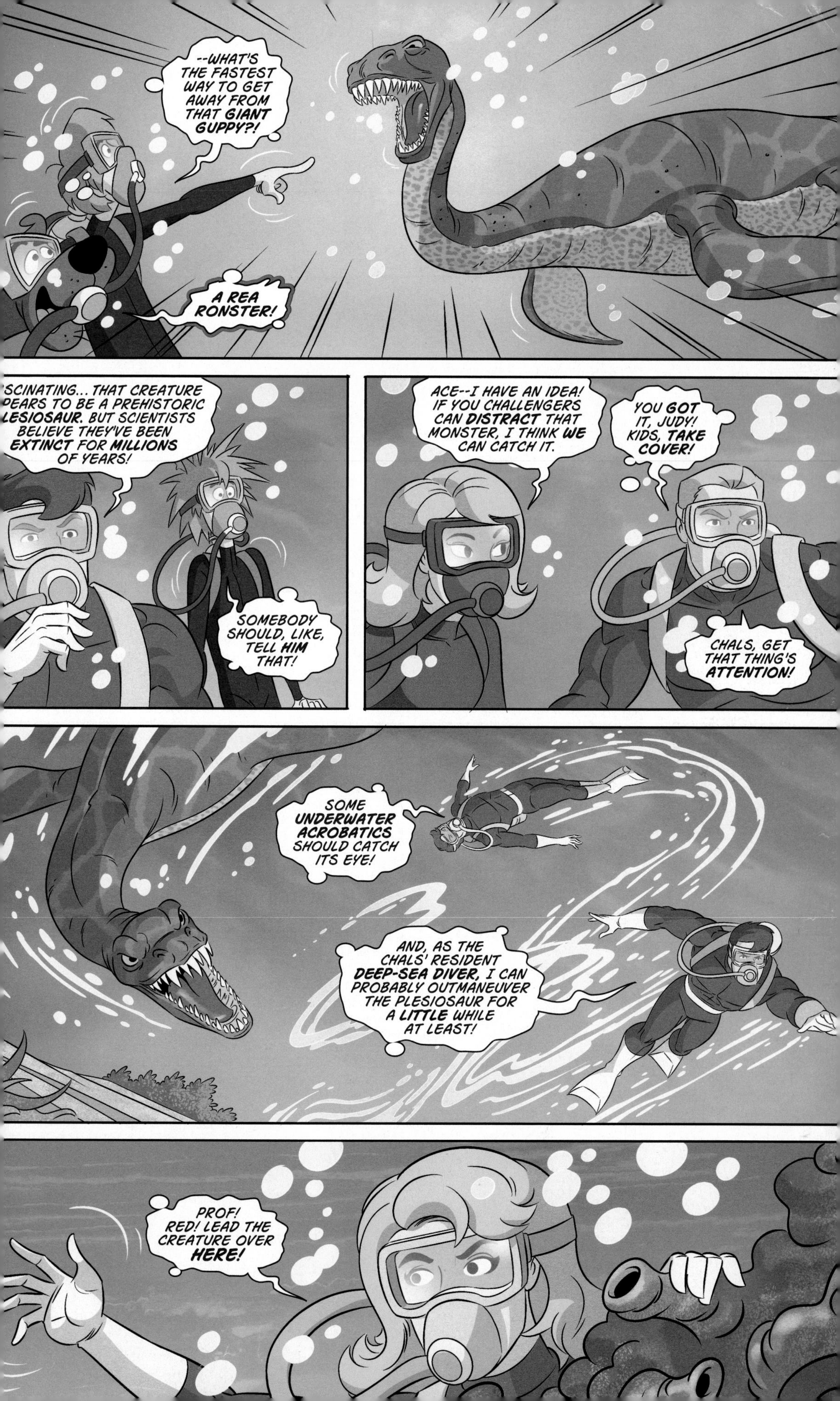
--WHAT'S THE FASTEST WAY TO GET AWAY FROM THAT **GIANT GUPPY?!**
A REA RONSTER!
SCINATING... THAT CREATURE PEARS TO BE A PREHISTORIC LESIOSAUR. BUT SCIENTISTS BELIEVE THEY'VE BEEN **EXTINCT** FOR **MILLIONS** OF YEARS!
SOMEBODY SHOULD, LIKE, TELL **HIM** THAT!
ACE--I HAVE AN IDEA! IF YOU CHALLENGERS CAN **DISTRACT** THAT MONSTER, I THINK **WE** CAN CATCH IT.
YOU **GOT** IT, JUDY! KIDS, **TAKE COVER!**
CHALS, GET THAT THING'S **ATTENTION!**
SOME **UNDERWATER ACROBATICS** SHOULD CATCH ITS EYE!
AND, AS THE CHALS' RESIDENT **DEEP-SEA DIVER,** I CAN PROBABLY OUTMANEUVER THE PLESIOSAUR FOR A **LITTLE** WHILE AT LEAST!
PROF! RED! LEAD THE CREATURE OVER **HERE!**

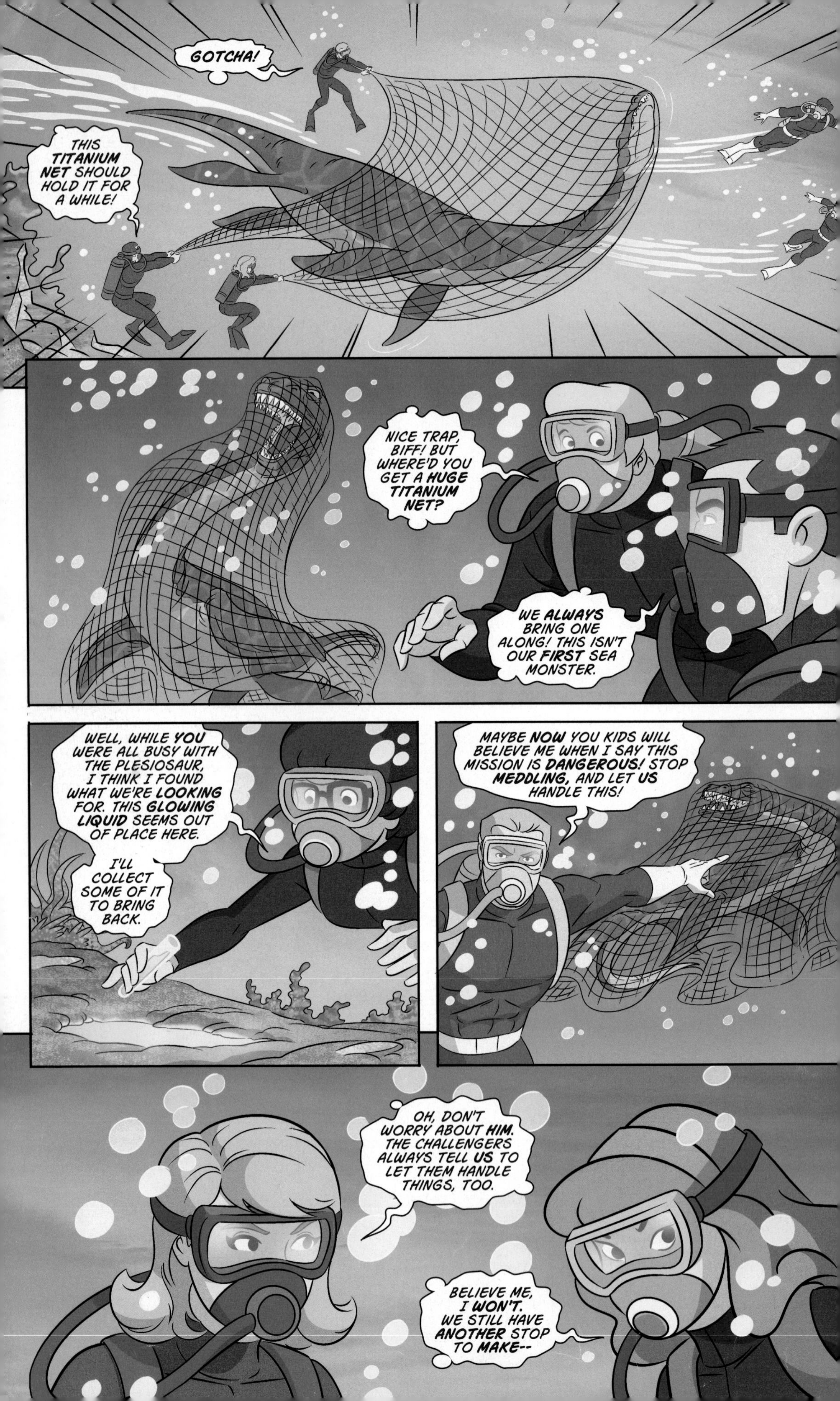
GOTCHA!
THIS TITANIUM NET SHOULD HOLD IT FOR A WHILE!
NICE TRAP, BIFF! BUT WHERE'D YOU GET A HUGE TITANIUM NET?
WE ALWAYS BRING ONE ALONG! THIS ISN'T OUR FIRST SEA MONSTER.
WELL, WHILE YOU WERE ALL BUSY WITH THE PLESIOSAUR, I THINK I FOUND WHAT WE'RE LOOKING FOR. THIS GLOWING LIQUID SEEMS OUT OF PLACE HERE.
I'LL COLLECT SOME OF IT TO BRING BACK.
MAYBE NOW YOU KIDS WILL BELIEVE ME WHEN I SAY THIS MISSION IS DANGEROUS! STOP MEDDLING, AND LET US HANDLE THIS!
OH, DON'T WORRY ABOUT HIM. THE CHALLENGERS ALWAYS TELL US TO LET THEM HANDLE THINGS, TOO.
BELIEVE ME, I WON'T. WE STILL HAVE ANOTHER STOP TO MAKE--

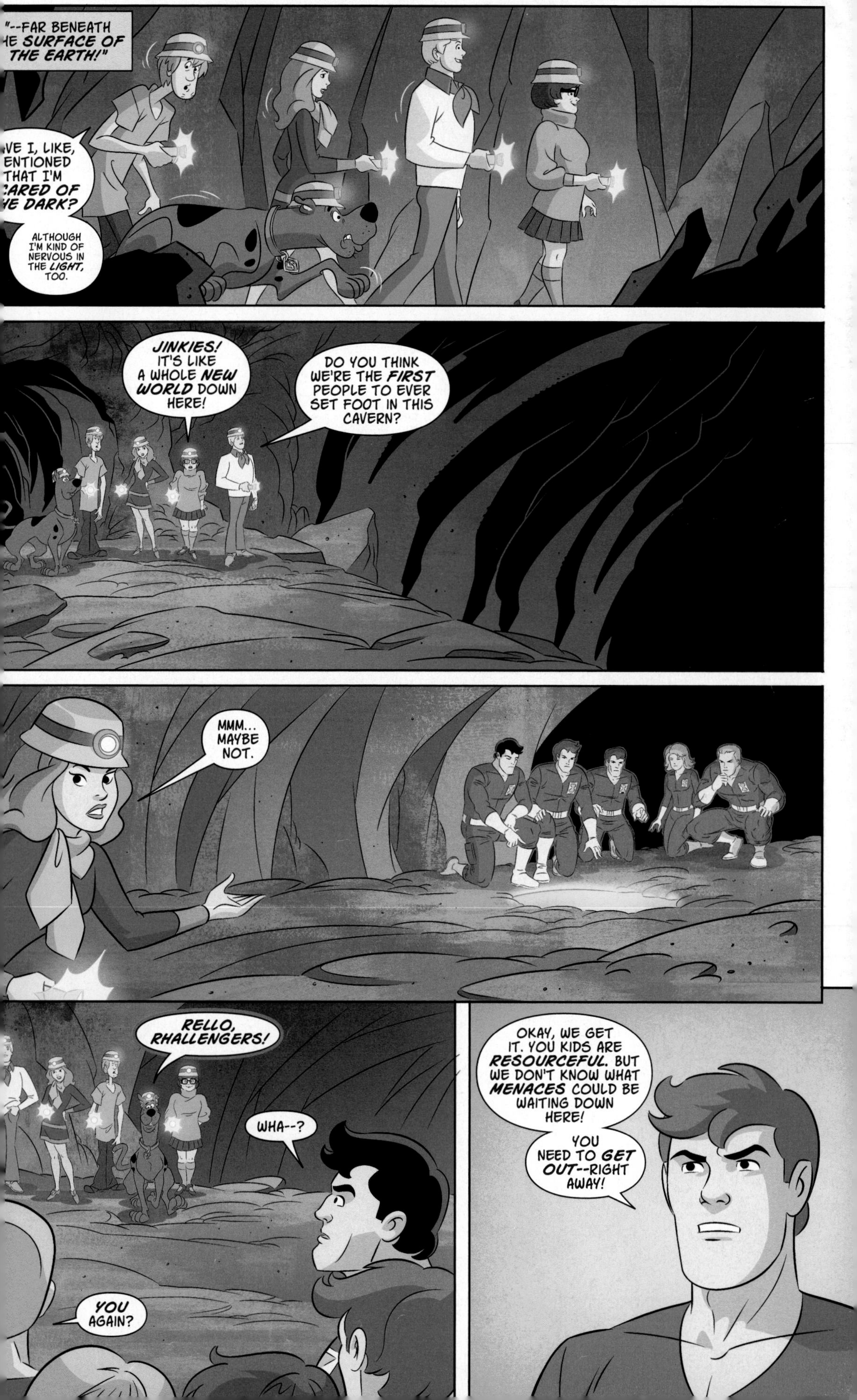
"--FAR BENEATH
HE SURFACE OF
THE EARTH!"
VE I, LIKE, ENTIONED THAT I'M CARED OF HE DARK?
ALTHOUGH I'M KIND OF NERVOUS IN THE LIGHT, TOO.
JINKIES! IT'S LIKE A WHOLE NEW WORLD DOWN HERE!
DO YOU THINK WE'RE THE FIRST PEOPLE TO EVER SET FOOT IN THIS CAVERN?
MMM... MAYBE NOT.
RELLO, RHALLENGERS!
WHA--?
YOU AGAIN?
OKAY, WE GET IT. YOU KIDS ARE RESOURCEFUL. BUT WE DON'T KNOW WHAT MENACES COULD BE WAITING DOWN HERE!
YOU NEED TO GET OUT--RIGHT AWAY!

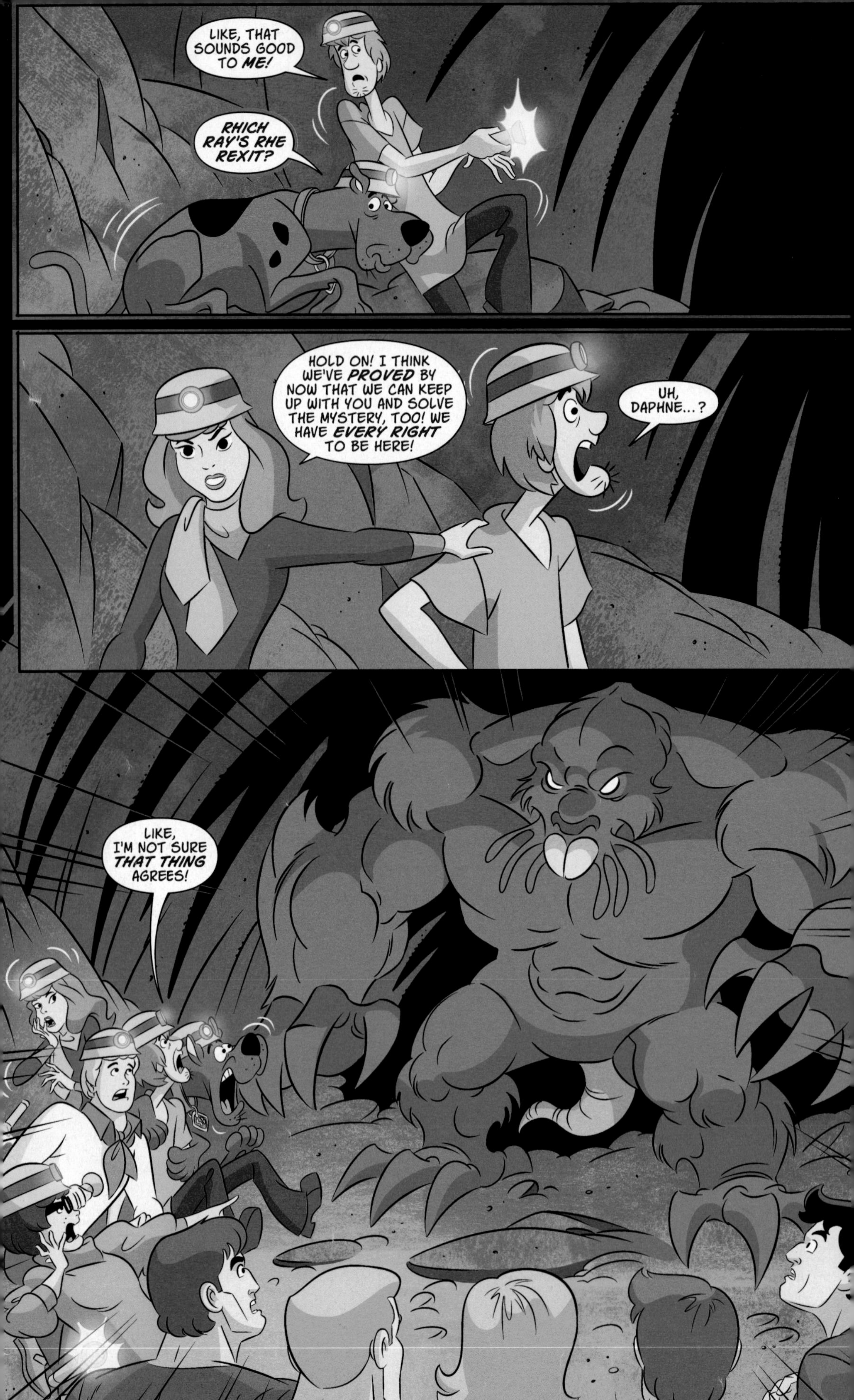
LIKE, THAT SOUNDS GOOD TO *ME!*
RHICH RAY'S RHE REXIT?
HOLD ON! I THINK WE'VE *PROVED* BY NOW THAT WE CAN KEEP UP WITH YOU AND SOLVE THE MYSTERY, TOO! WE HAVE *EVERY RIGHT* TO BE HERE!
UH, DAPHNE...?
LIKE, I'M NOT SURE *THAT THING* AGREES!

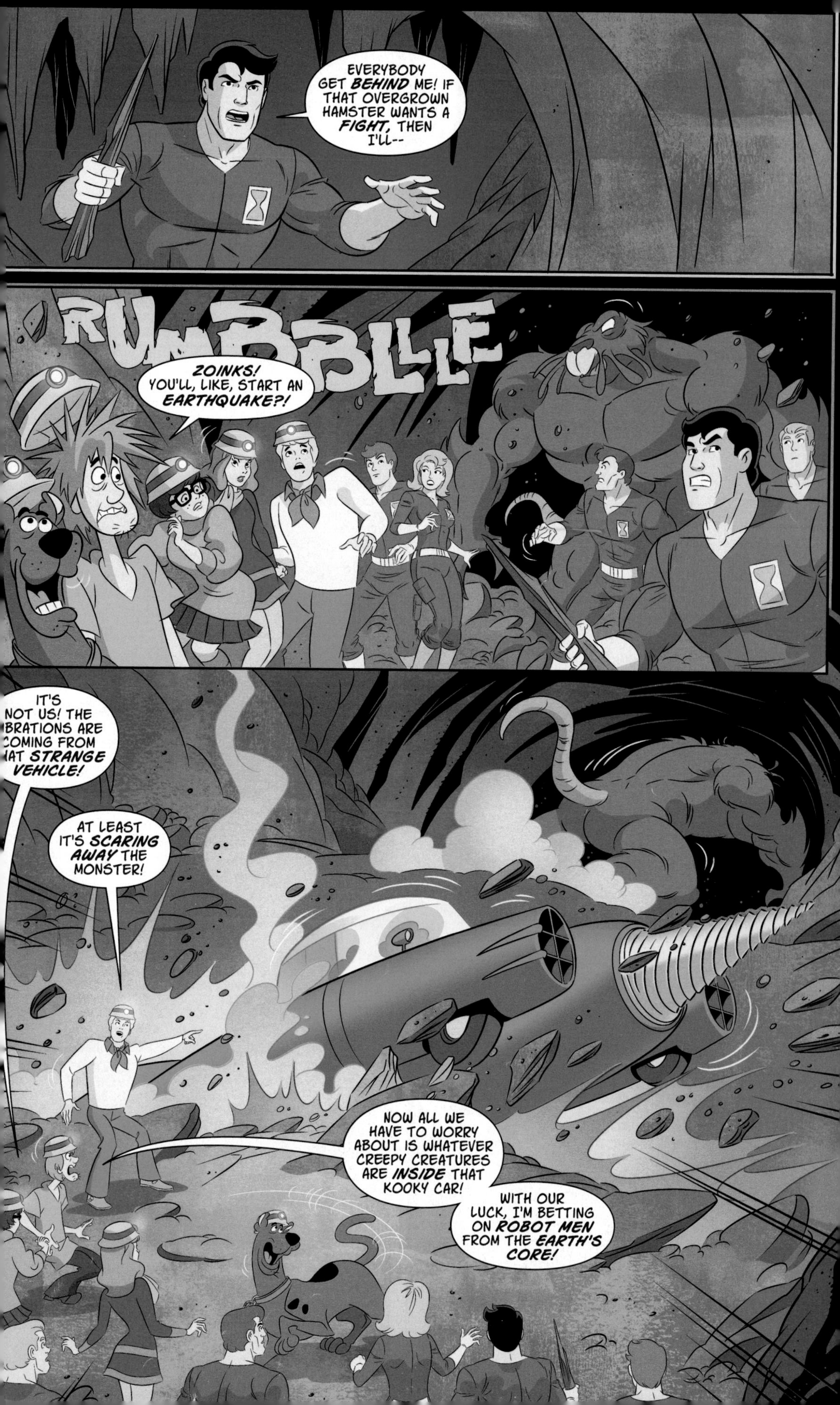

EVERYBODY GET BEHIND ME! IF THAT OVERGROWN HAMSTER WANTS A FIGHT, THEN I'LL--
RUMBBLLE
ZOINKS! YOU'LL, LIKE, START AN EARTHQUAKE?!
IT'S NOT US! THE BRATIONS ARE COMING FROM AT STRANGE VEHICLE!
AT LEAST IT'S SCARING AWAY THE MONSTER!
NOW ALL WE HAVE TO WORRY ABOUT IS WHATEVER CREEPY CREATURES ARE INSIDE THAT KOOKY CAR!
WITH OUR LUCK, I'M BETTING ON ROBOT MEN FROM THE EARTH'S CORE!

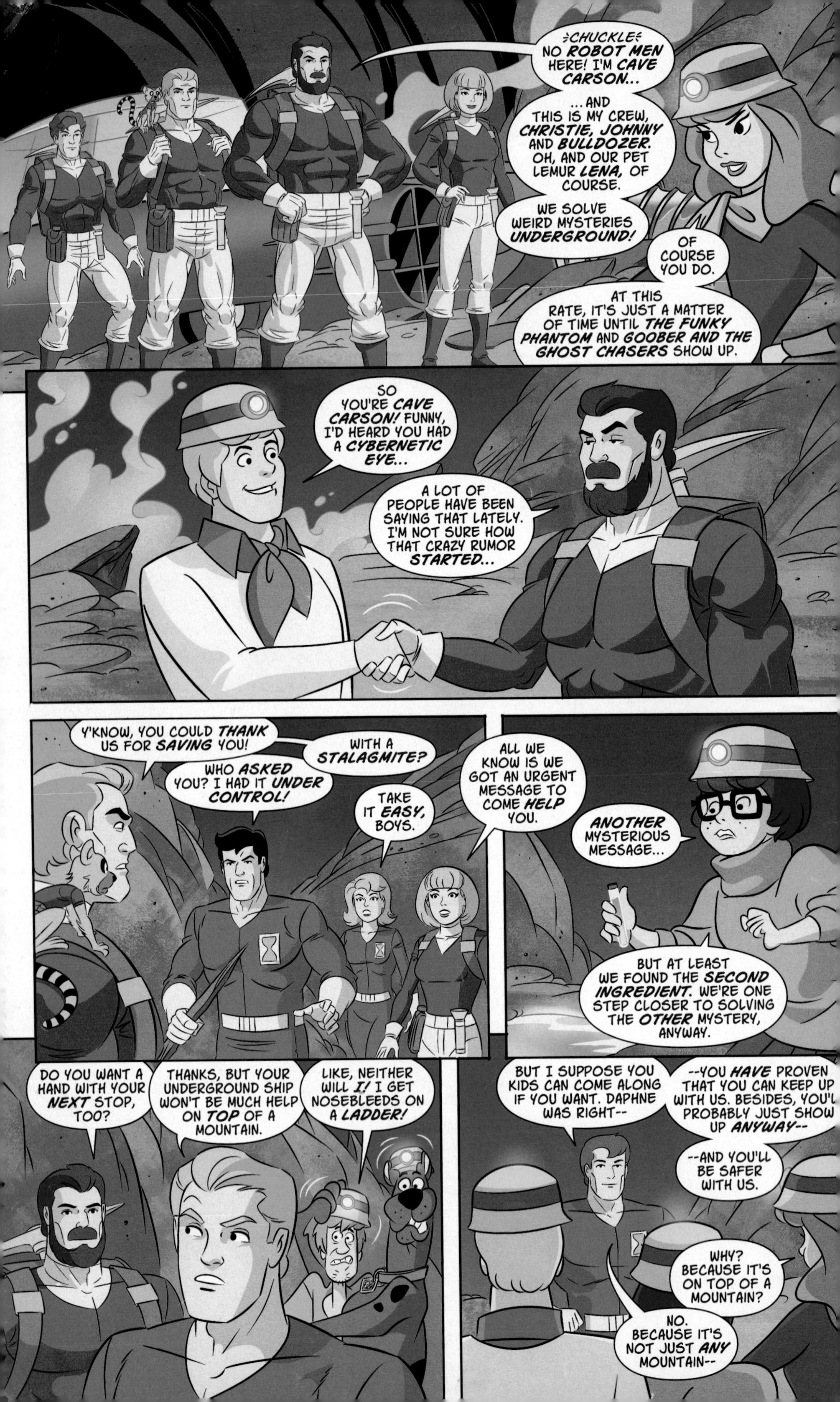

CHUCKLE NO ROBOT MEN HERE! I'M CAVE CARSON...
... AND THIS IS MY CREW, CHRISTIE, JOHNNY AND BULLDOZER. OH, AND OUR PET LEMUR LENA, OF COURSE.
WE SOLVE WEIRD MYSTERIES UNDERGROUND!
OF COURSE YOU DO.
AT THIS RATE, IT'S JUST A MATTER OF TIME UNTIL THE FUNKY PHANTOM AND GOOBER AND THE GHOST CHASERS SHOW UP.
SO YOU'RE CAVE CARSON! FUNNY, I'D HEARD YOU HAD A CYBERNETIC EYE...
A LOT OF PEOPLE HAVE BEEN SAYING THAT LATELY. I'M NOT SURE HOW THAT CRAZY RUMOR STARTED...
Y'KNOW, YOU COULD THANK US FOR SAVING YOU!
WITH A STALAGMITE?
WHO ASKED YOU? I HAD IT UNDER CONTROL!
TAKE IT EASY, BOYS.
ALL WE KNOW IS WE GOT AN URGENT MESSAGE TO COME HELP YOU.
ANOTHER MYSTERIOUS MESSAGE...
BUT AT LEAST WE FOUND THE SECOND INGREDIENT. WE'RE ONE STEP CLOSER TO SOLVING THE OTHER MYSTERY, ANYWAY.
DO YOU WANT A HAND WITH YOUR NEXT STOP, TOO?
THANKS, BUT YOUR UNDERGROUND SHIP WON'T BE MUCH HELP ON TOP OF A MOUNTAIN.
LIKE, NEITHER WILL I! I GET NOSEBLEEDS ON A LADDER!
BUT I SUPPOSE YOU KIDS CAN COME ALONG IF YOU WANT. DAPHNE WAS RIGHT--
--YOU HAVE PROVEN THAT YOU CAN KEEP UP WITH US. BESIDES, YOU'LL PROBABLY JUST SHOW UP ANYWAY--
--AND YOU'LL BE SAFER WITH US.
WHY? BECAUSE IT'S ON TOP OF A MOUNTAIN?
NO. BECAUSE IT'S NOT JUST ANY MOUNTAIN--

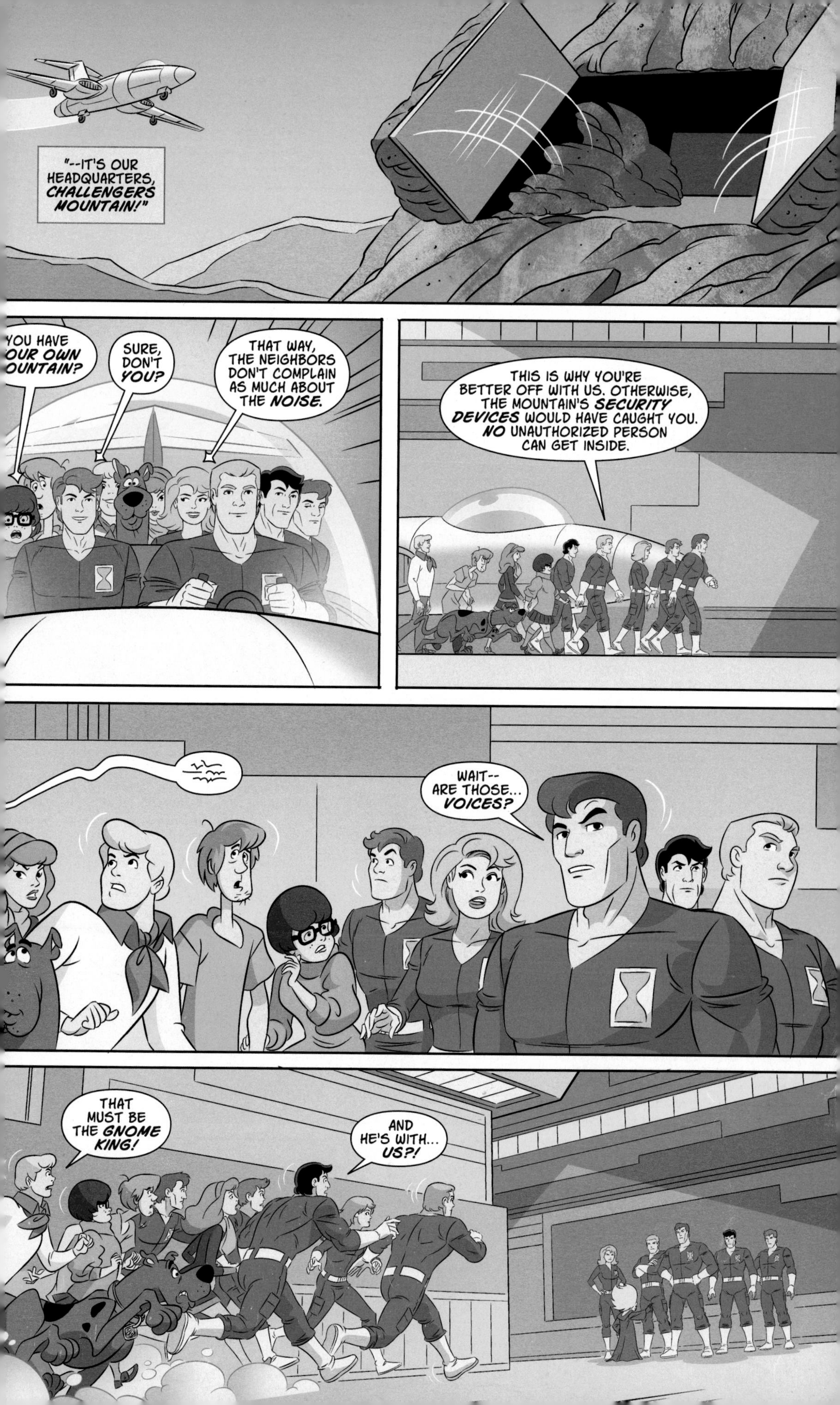
"--IT'S OUR HEADQUARTERS, CHALLENGERS MOUNTAIN!"
YOU HAVE OUR OWN OUNTAIN?
SURE, DON'T YOU?
THAT WAY, THE NEIGHBORS DON'T COMPLAIN AS MUCH ABOUT THE NOISE.
THIS IS WHY YOU'RE BETTER OFF WITH US. OTHERWISE, THE MOUNTAIN'S SECURITY DEVICES WOULD HAVE CAUGHT YOU. NO UNAUTHORIZED PERSON CAN GET INSIDE.
WAIT-- ARE THOSE... VOICES?
THAT MUST BE THE GNOME KING!
AND HE'S WITH... US?!

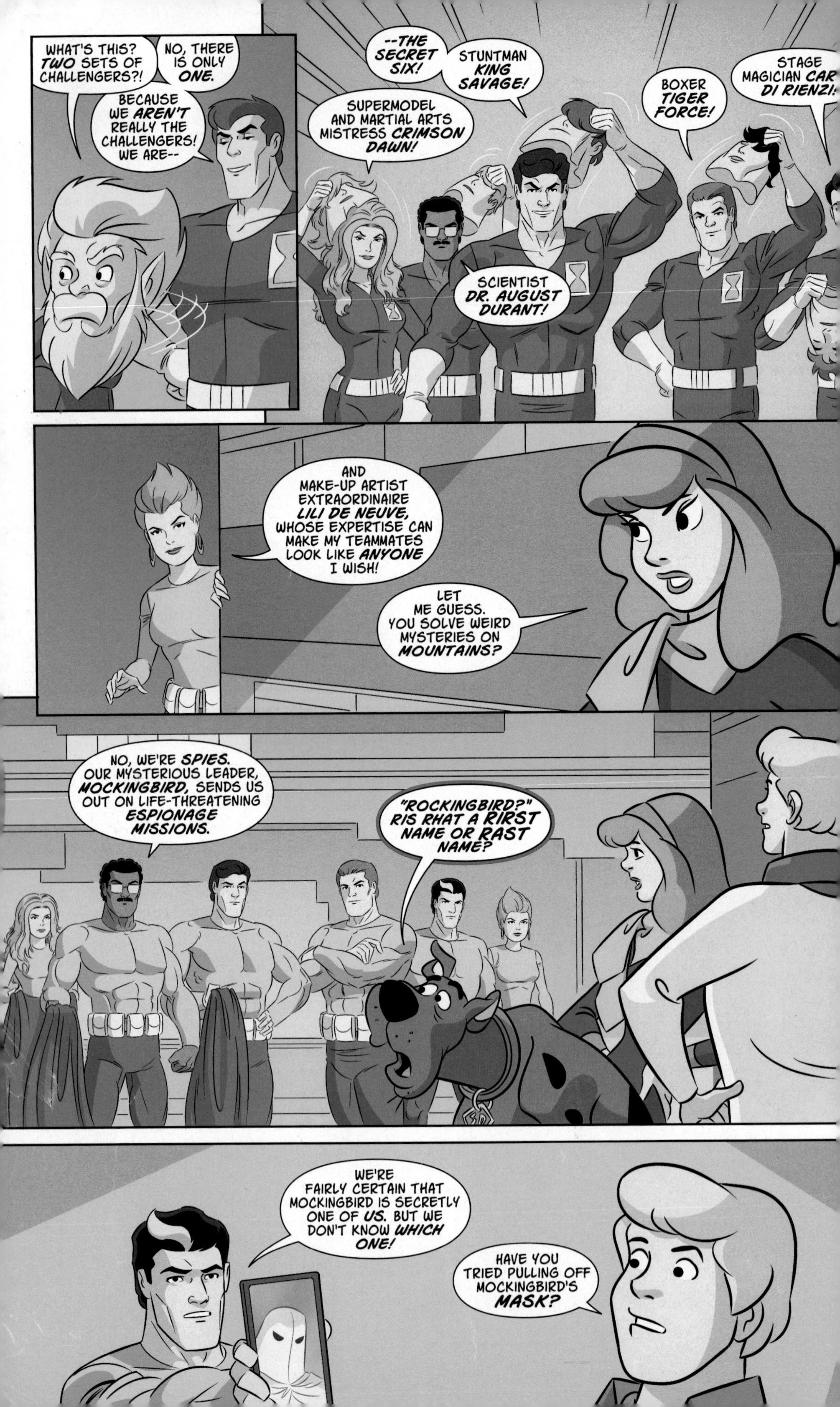

WHAT'S THIS? TWO SETS OF CHALLENGERS?!
NO, THERE IS ONLY ONE.
BECAUSE WE AREN'T REALLY THE CHALLENGERS! WE ARE--
--THE SECRET SIX!
STUNTMAN KING SAVAGE!
SUPERMODEL AND MARTIAL ARTS MISTRESS CRIMSON DAWN!
BOXER TIGER FORCE!
STAGE MAGICIAN CARL DI RIENZI!
SCIENTIST DR. AUGUST DURANT!
AND MAKE-UP ARTIST EXTRAORDINAIRE LILI DE NEUVE, WHOSE EXPERTISE CAN MAKE MY TEAMMATES LOOK LIKE ANYONE I WISH!
LET ME GUESS. YOU SOLVE WEIRD MYSTERIES ON MOUNTAINS?
NO, WE'RE SPIES. OUR MYSTERIOUS LEADER, MOCKINGBIRD, SENDS US OUT ON LIFE-THREATENING ESPIONAGE MISSIONS.
"ROCKINGBIRD?" RIS RHAT A RIRST NAME OR RAST NAME?
WE'RE FAIRLY CERTAIN THAT MOCKINGBIRD IS SECRETLY ONE OF US. BUT WE DON'T KNOW WHICH ONE!
HAVE YOU TRIED PULLING OFF MOCKINGBIRD'S MASK?

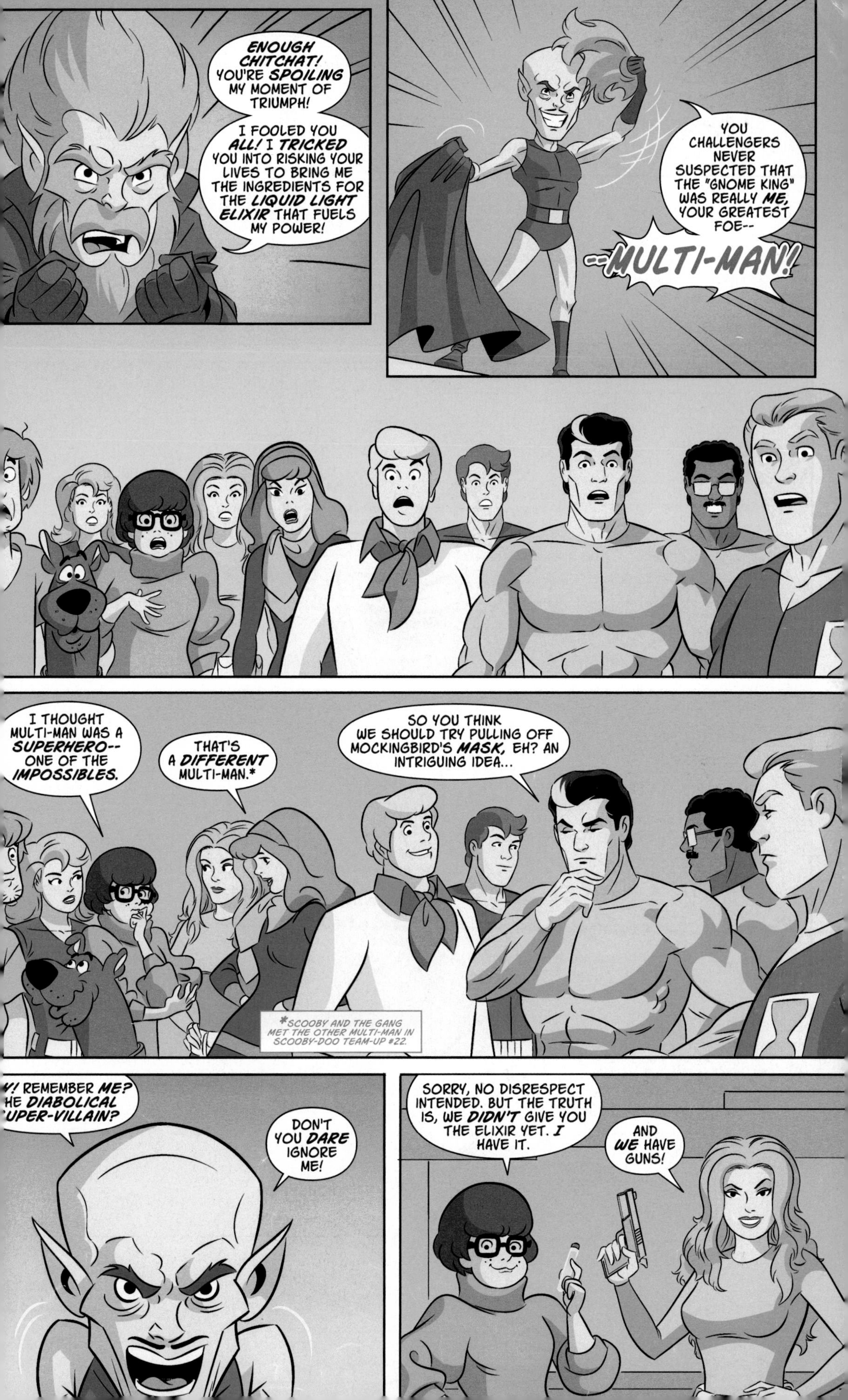

ENOUGH CHITCHAT! YOU'RE SPOILING MY MOMENT OF TRIUMPH!
I FOOLED YOU ALL! I TRICKED YOU INTO RISKING YOUR LIVES TO BRING ME THE INGREDIENTS FOR THE LIQUID LIGHT ELIXIR THAT FUELS MY POWER!
YOU CHALLENGERS NEVER SUSPECTED THAT THE "GNOME KING" WAS REALLY ME, YOUR GREATEST FOE--
--MULTI-MAN!
I THOUGHT MULTI-MAN WAS A SUPERHERO-- ONE OF THE IMPOSSIBLES.
THAT'S A DIFFERENT MULTI-MAN.*
SO YOU THINK WE SHOULD TRY PULLING OFF MOCKINGBIRD'S MASK, EH? AN INTRIGUING IDEA...
*SCOOBY AND THE GANG MET THE OTHER MULTI-MAN IN SCOOBY-DOO TEAM-UP #22.
REMEMBER ME? THE DIABOLICAL SUPER-VILLAIN?
DON'T YOU DARE IGNORE ME!
SORRY, NO DISRESPECT INTENDED. BUT THE TRUTH IS, WE DIDN'T GIVE YOU THE ELIXIR YET. I HAVE IT.
AND WE HAVE GUNS!

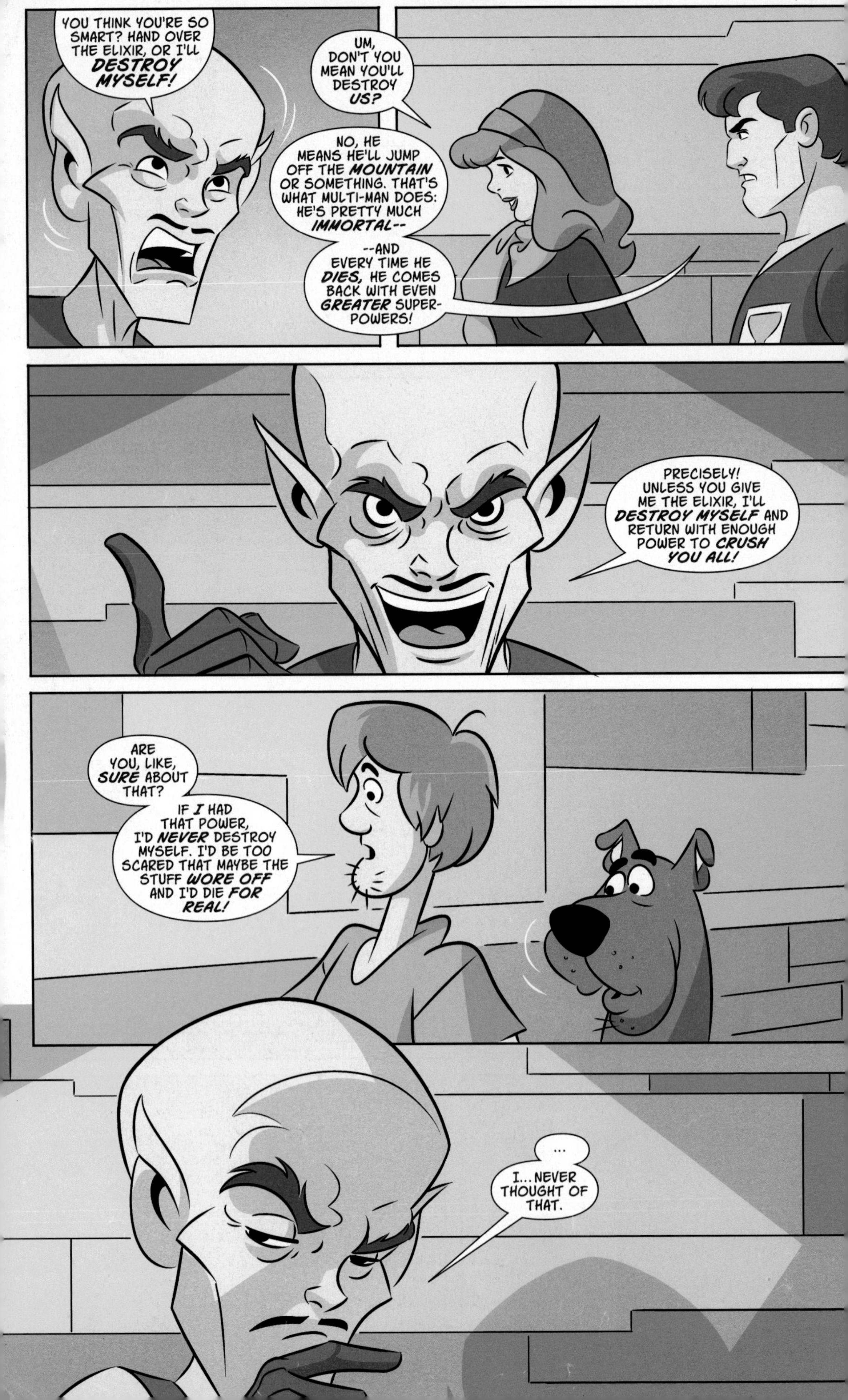
YOU THINK YOU'RE SO SMART? HAND OVER THE ELIXIR, OR I'LL DESTROY MYSELF!
UM, DON'T YOU MEAN YOU'LL DESTROY US?
NO, HE MEANS HE'LL JUMP OFF THE MOUNTAIN OR SOMETHING. THAT'S WHAT MULTI-MAN DOES: HE'S PRETTY MUCH IMMORTAL--
--AND EVERY TIME HE DIES, HE COMES BACK WITH EVEN GREATER SUPER-POWERS!
PRECISELY! UNLESS YOU GIVE ME THE ELIXIR, I'LL DESTROY MYSELF AND RETURN WITH ENOUGH POWER TO CRUSH YOU ALL!
ARE YOU, LIKE, SURE ABOUT THAT?
IF I HAD THAT POWER, I'D NEVER DESTROY MYSELF. I'D BE TOO SCARED THAT MAYBE THE STUFF WORE OFF AND I'D DIE FOR REAL!
...
I... NEVER THOUGHT OF THAT.

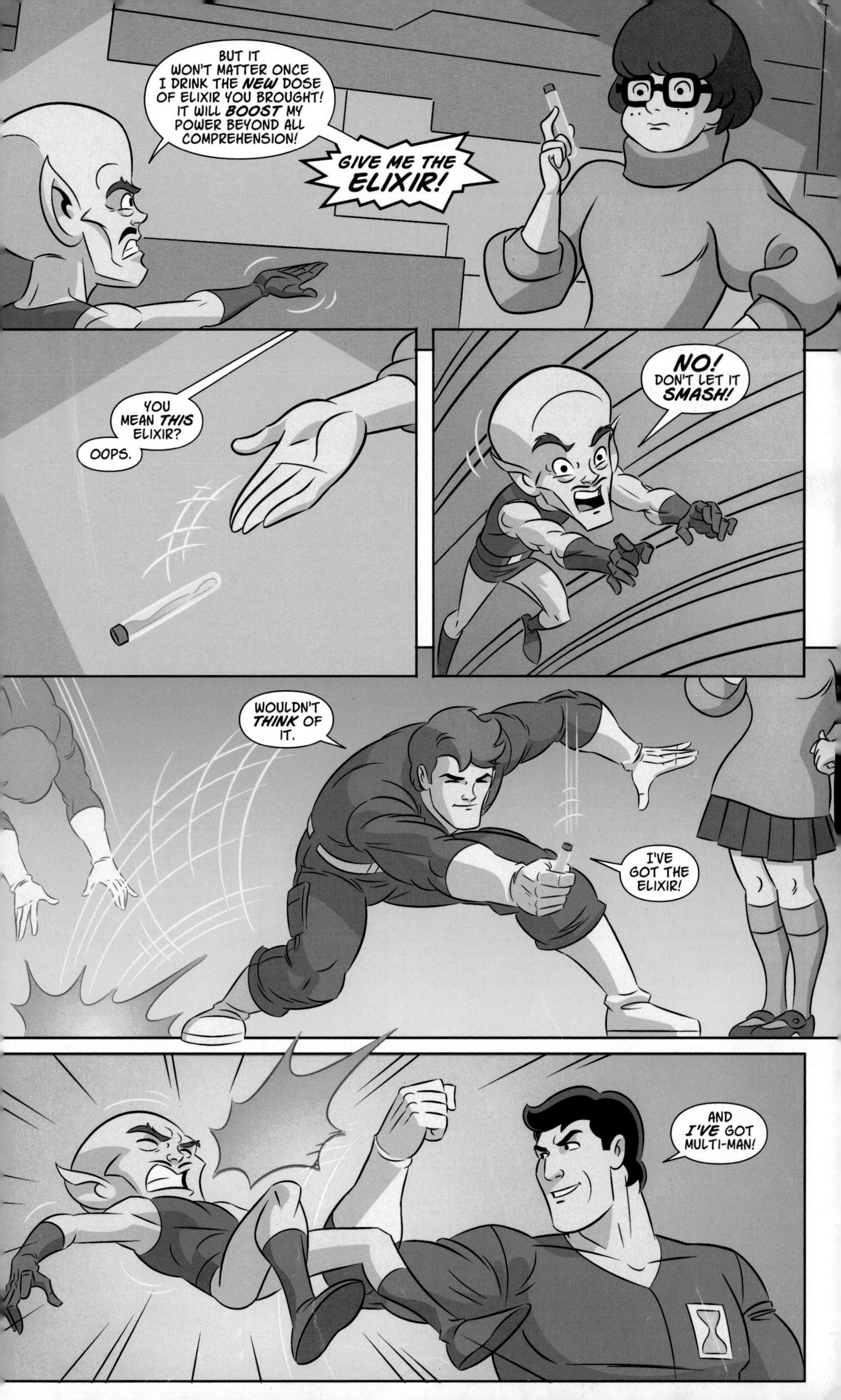

BUT IT WON'T MATTER ONCE I DRINK THE *NEW* DOSE OF ELIXIR YOU BROUGHT! IT WILL *BOOST* MY POWER BEYOND ALL COMPREHENSION!
GIVE ME THE ELIXIR!
YOU MEAN *THIS* ELIXIR?
OOPS.
NO! DON'T LET IT *SMASH!*
WOULDN'T *THINK* OF IT.
I'VE GOT THE ELIXIR!
AND *I'VE* GOT MULTI-MAN!

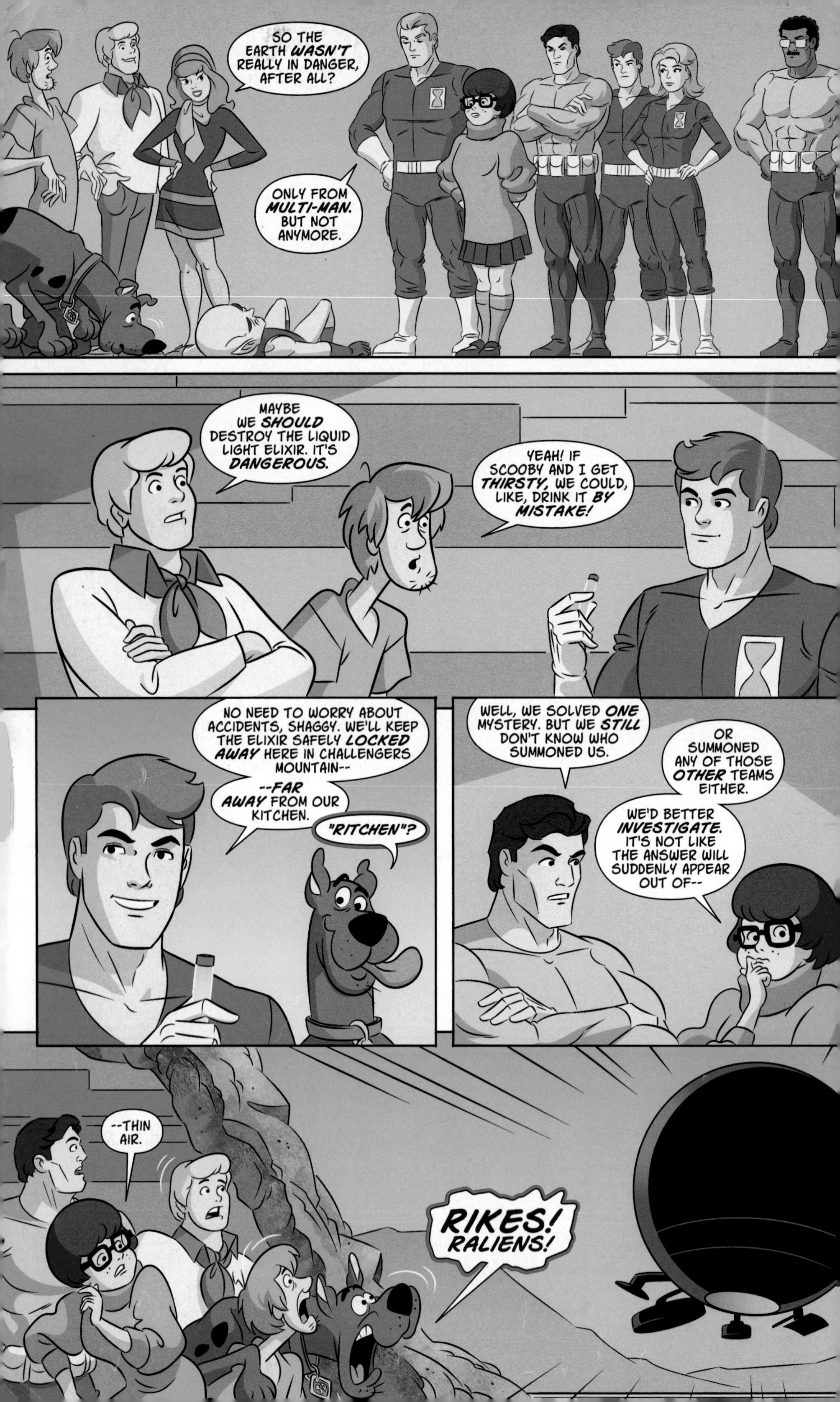
SO THE EARTH WASN'T REALLY IN DANGER, AFTER ALL?
ONLY FROM MULTI-MAN. BUT NOT ANYMORE.
MAYBE WE SHOULD DESTROY THE LIQUID LIGHT ELIXIR. IT'S DANGEROUS.
YEAH! IF SCOOBY AND I GET THIRSTY, WE COULD, LIKE, DRINK IT BY MISTAKE!
NO NEED TO WORRY ABOUT ACCIDENTS, SHAGGY. WE'LL KEEP THE ELIXIR SAFELY LOCKED AWAY HERE IN CHALLENGERS MOUNTAIN--
--FAR AWAY FROM OUR KITCHEN.
"RITCHEN"?
WELL, WE SOLVED ONE MYSTERY. BUT WE STILL DON'T KNOW WHO SUMMONED US.
OR SUMMONED ANY OF THOSE OTHER TEAMS EITHER.
WE'D BETTER INVESTIGATE. IT'S NOT LIKE THE ANSWER WILL SUDDENLY APPEAR OUT OF--
--THIN AIR.
RIKES! RALIENS!

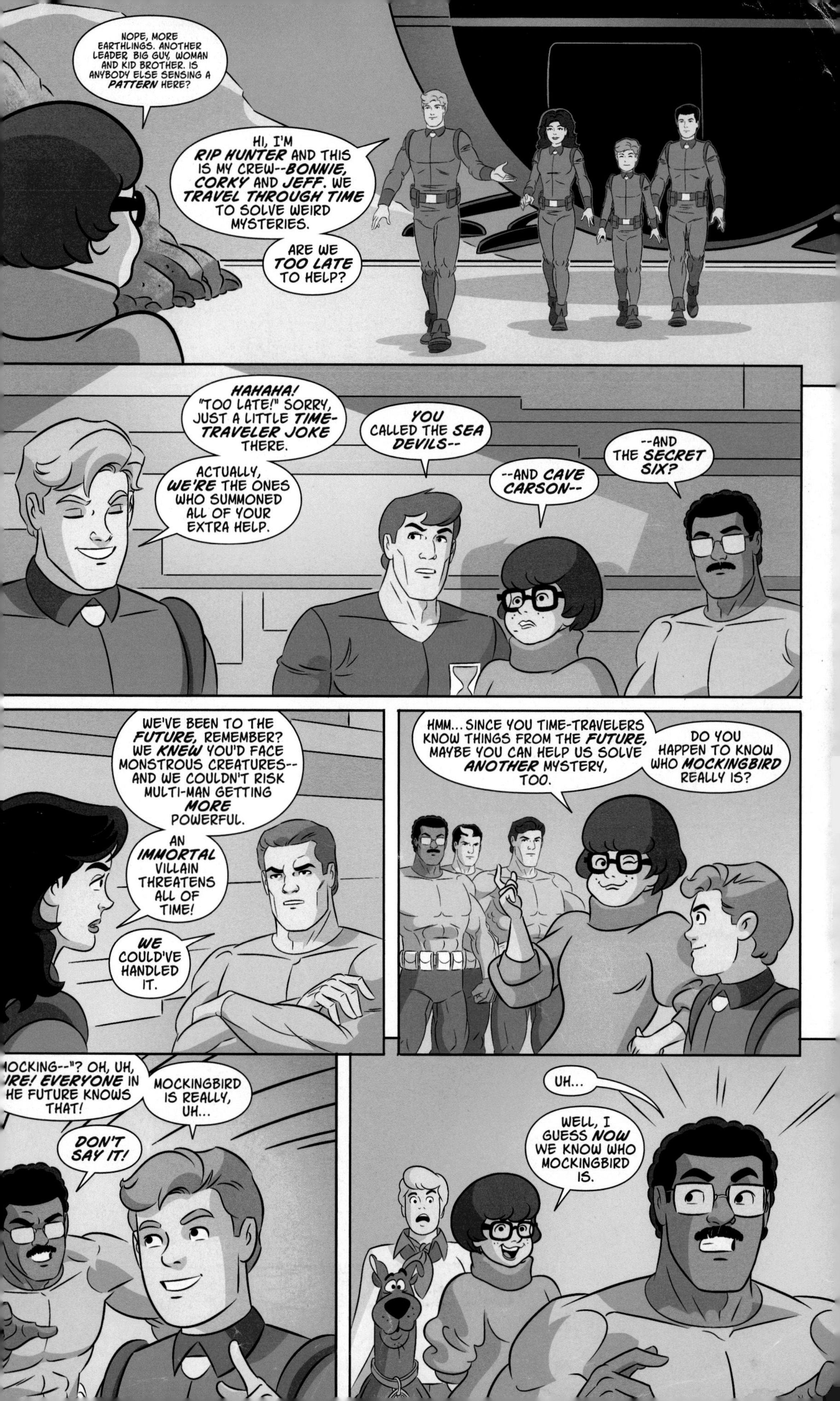
NOPE, MORE EARTHLINGS. ANOTHER LEADER, BIG GUY, WOMAN AND KID BROTHER. IS ANYBODY ELSE SENSING A PATTERN HERE?
HI, I'M RIP HUNTER AND THIS IS MY CREW--BONNIE, CORKY AND JEFF. WE TRAVEL THROUGH TIME TO SOLVE WEIRD MYSTERIES.
ARE WE TOO LATE TO HELP?
HAHAHA! "TOO LATE!" SORRY, JUST A LITTLE TIME-TRAVELER JOKE THERE.
ACTUALLY, WE'RE THE ONES WHO SUMMONED ALL OF YOUR EXTRA HELP.
YOU CALLED THE SEA DEVILS--
--AND CAVE CARSON--
--AND THE SECRET SIX?
WE'VE BEEN TO THE FUTURE, REMEMBER? WE KNEW YOU'D FACE MONSTROUS CREATURES--AND WE COULDN'T RISK MULTI-MAN GETTING MORE POWERFUL.
AN IMMORTAL VILLAIN THREATENS ALL OF TIME!
WE COULD'VE HANDLED IT.
HMM... SINCE YOU TIME-TRAVELERS KNOW THINGS FROM THE FUTURE, MAYBE YOU CAN HELP US SOLVE ANOTHER MYSTERY, TOO.
DO YOU HAPPEN TO KNOW WHO MOCKINGBIRD REALLY IS?
MOCKING--"? OH, UH, URE! EVERYONE IN HE FUTURE KNOWS THAT!
MOCKINGBIRD IS REALLY, UH...
DON'T SAY IT!
UH...
WELL, I GUESS NOW WE KNOW WHO MOCKINGBIRD IS.

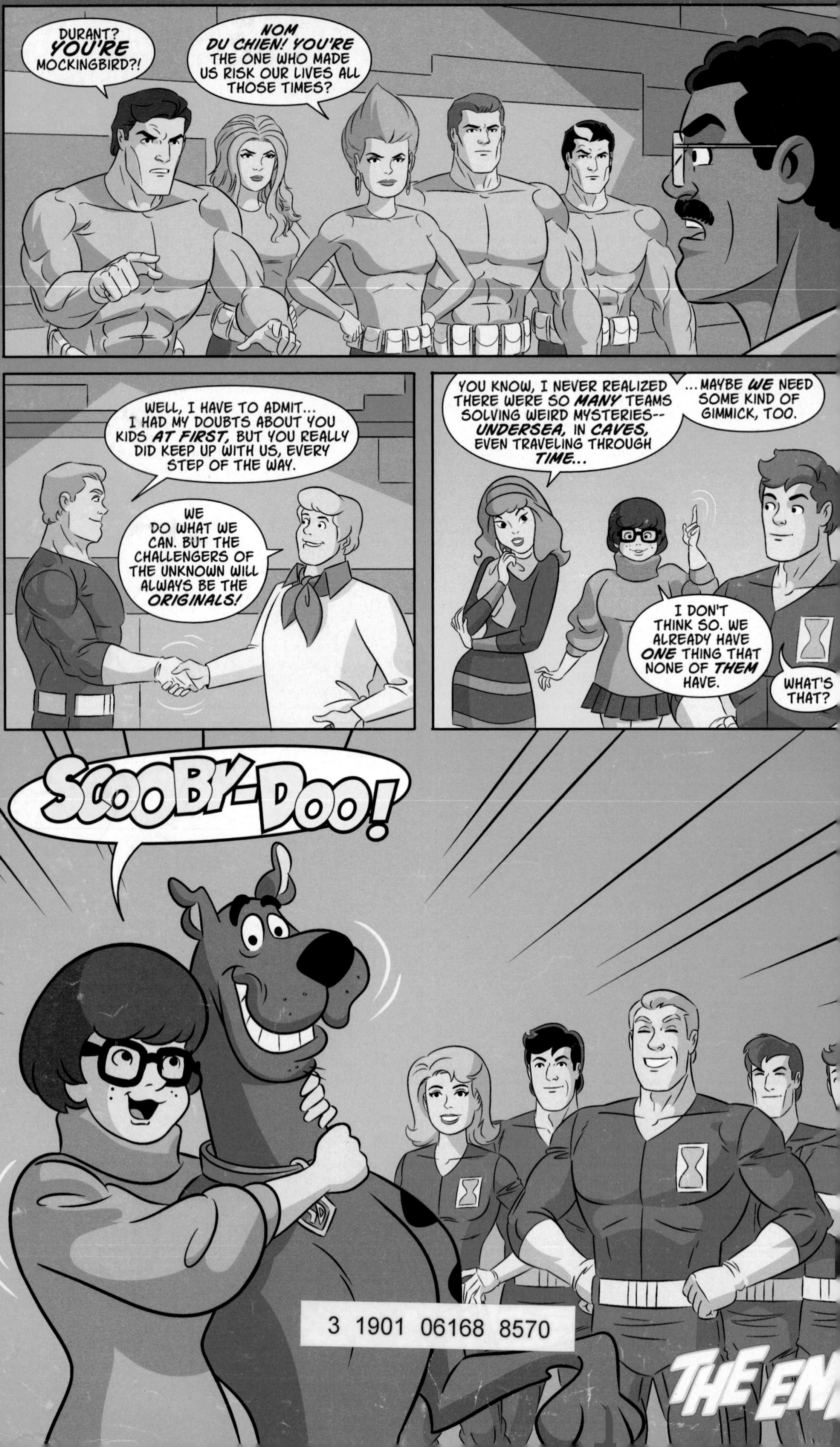
DURANT? YOU'RE MOCKINGBIRD?!
NOM DU CHIEN! YOU'RE THE ONE WHO MADE US RISK OUR LIVES ALL THOSE TIMES?
WELL, I HAVE TO ADMIT... I HAD MY DOUBTS ABOUT YOU KIDS AT FIRST, BUT YOU REALLY DID KEEP UP WITH US, EVERY STEP OF THE WAY.
WE DO WHAT WE CAN. BUT THE CHALLENGERS OF THE UNKNOWN WILL ALWAYS BE THE ORIGINALS!
YOU KNOW, I NEVER REALIZED THERE WERE SO MANY TEAMS SOLVING WEIRD MYSTERIES-- UNDERSEA, IN CAVES, EVEN TRAVELING THROUGH TIME...
...MAYBE WE NEED SOME KIND OF GIMMICK, TOO.
I DON'T THINK SO. WE ALREADY HAVE ONE THING THAT NONE OF THEM HAVE.
WHAT'S THAT?
SCOOBY-DOO!